More THAN
WORDS CAN Say

More THAN WORDS CAN Say

KAREN WITEMEYER

BETHANYHOUSE

a division of Baker Publishing Group
Minneapolis, Minnesota

Published by Bethany House Publishers
11400 Hampshire Avenue South
Bloomington, Minnesota 55438
www.bethanyhouse.com

Bethany House Publishers is a division of
Baker Publishing Group, Grand Rapids, Michigan

Printed in the United States of America

Library of Congress Cataloging-in-Publication Data
Names: Witemeyer, Karen, author.
Title: More than words can say / Karen Witemeyer.
Description: Bloomington, Minnesota : Bethany House Publishers, [2019]
Identifiers: LCCN 2018058133| ISBN 9780764232190 (trade paper) | ISBN
    9780764234118 (hardcover) | ISBN 9781493418602 (ebook)
Subjects: | GSAFD: Love stories.
Classification: LCC PS3623.I864 M68 2019 | DDC 813/.6—dc23
LC record available at https://lccn.loc.gov/2018058133

Scripture quotations are from the King James Version of the Bible.

This is a work of fiction. Names, characters, incidents, and dialogues are products of the author's imagination and are not to be construed as real. Any resemblance to actual events or persons, living or dead, is entirely coincidental.

Cover design by Dan Thornberg, Design Source Creative Services

Author is represented by the Books & Such Literary Agency.

19 20 21 22 23 24 25   7 6 5 4 3 2 1

To Peter.

You're the quiet one of the family, but you have a huge heart when it comes to connecting with others. I admire the young man you already are, and I am enjoying the journey of watching God transform you into the mature man of faith He's designed you to be. You make your mama proud!

But as for you, ye thought evil against me;
but God meant it unto good.

—Genesis 50:20

CHAPTER

1

MAY 1896—HONEY GROVE, TX

"The council has denied your appeal, Miss Kemp." Mayor Longfellow delivered the blow with a finality that threatened to buckle Abigail's knees.

His aldermen, who had risen to their feet when she entered the City Hall meeting room, shifted around the large table until they all stood on one side, leaving her alone on the other. Some of the more pompous officials nodded in solemn agreement with the mayor's pronouncement. Others wore more sympathetic expressions. One or two even cast her apologetic glances. A timid fellow in the back avoided her gaze entirely.

Despite the displays of regret, however, *none* of them spoke up against the injustice being done.

"This isn't right." Abigail Kemp, her legs wobbling, strode up to the table and pressed her hands into the polished oak surface next to the stack of ledgers she'd left them to review and the business plan she'd written to demonstrate her capability. "I've been running the Taste of Heaven Bakery on my own for more than a year, ever since my father took ill. In that time, the bakery has earned a profit every quarter." She grabbed the top ledger and opened it to a middle page, jabbing her finger at the numbers that proved her words true. "We pay our taxes on time and support all civic activities on the town square. You have no right to take away my bakery."

"No one is doubting your abilities, Miss Kemp," the mayor said as he rounded the table. His voice was calm, his smile friendly, if a tad condescending.

Feeling like a wounded deer facing down a pack of wolves, Abigail straightened and threw her shoulders back to regain every inch of her five foot, six-inch stature.

Chester Longfellow bared no fangs, however. Neither did he lunge for her jugular. He simply closed the cover of her ledger and stacked it neatly atop the other evidence she'd provided in support of her appeal. "I'm afraid the law is the law, Miss Kemp." He picked up her papers and held them out to her. "We consulted Judge Hardcastle for his recommendation, and the judge concurred. The ordinance must be upheld."

Abigail made no move to take her ledgers. To do so would be to concede defeat, and she wasn't done fighting. Not when her livelihood was at stake. If she lost the bakery, she'd have no means of providing for her sister. Besides, the Taste of Heaven was her family's legacy. *Her* legacy now.

"That ordinance is completely outdated and should have been repealed years—*decades*—ago. The idea that women be forbidden from owning business property within the city limits is ridiculous. There are dozens of women successfully running their own enterprises in town. Dora Patteson's millinery shop. Judith Kell's laundry. Norma Wilson's dressmaking—"

"Yes, we are aware," Mayor Longfellow interrupted. "You've already argued this point, Miss Kemp, and rehashing it now will not gain you any benefit. The ladies you mention all rent their space from male property owners. They don't own their businesses outright. When you inherited the Taste of Heaven following your father's death, you became a business owner and therefore have been operating these last several months in violation of the laws of this city. We extended grace in giving you time to grieve your father before confronting you on this issue, but I'm afraid we can postpone no longer." He extended the ledgers again, nearly prodding her midsection with them.

With no choice but to accept them, she folded the books against her chest but lifted her chin in silent defiance. She would not bow her head in defeat. Not today. Not ever.

Mayor Longfellow showed no sign of being impressed by her fighting spirit. His bland expression assured that no matter her opinion, the matter was settled. "You have until the end of the month to either put your property up for sale or find a financial backer to serve as a silent partner."

Abigail set her jaw. No, she had until the end of the month to construct and execute a third option, because neither of the ones he'd presented were acceptable.

Two weeks didn't give her much time, but she was no stranger to working under pressure. She'd find a way around this discriminatory ordinance. These stuffy male councilmen might want to hold her down, but like a well-made bread dough, she planned to rise to the occasion.

⋈———⋈

Abigail strode away from City Hall on a full head of steam. Her face must have given away her mood, for any pedestrians she encountered along her path gave her a wide berth. None made an effort to approach or even wave at her. None, save the person she least wanted to see.

"Afternoon, Miss Kemp." A thin man approached from the

opposite direction, his gaze fixed on her as if she were his destination and not simply an acquaintance met along the way.

Abigail gritted her teeth. A smile was out of the question, but she managed a slight dip of her head to the drugstore owner who had been trying to convince the Kemps to sell him their property ever since her father took ill.

"Mr. Gerard." Her steps did not slow. In fact, she picked up her pace as she brushed past him. It might not be precisely polite, but she'd been dictated to enough for one day and feared what might happen if Samson Gerard chose this moment to proposition her again.

He proved dauntless in his pursuit, however, for after tipping his bowler hat, he immediately pivoted and matched his stride to hers. His infuriatingly long-legged gait made it impossible for her to outdistance him without running.

"I wondered if I might have a word," he said.

Abigail kept her gaze focused on the street in front of her, doing everything in her power to discourage this conversation. "I'm afraid this is not a good time, sir. As you can see, I'm in a bit of a hurry."

"Yes, your pace is rather, um, brisk, but I believe I can keep up. No need to slow on my account."

Breaking into a run was growing more tempting by the moment. Yes, she'd make a spectacle of herself, but the chances of Mr. Gerard joining her in such a display were exceedingly slim. Unfortunately, while working in a bakery all day gave one prodigiously strong fingers, wrists, and forearms, it did little for the legs or lungs. She could already feel perspiration gathering on her upper lip, and her chest had begun to heave ever so slightly.

Yet the sooner she reached the bakery, the sooner she could be rid of this man. So she pressed on, doing her best not to huff when she asked, "What do you want, Mr. Gerard?"

"Your building, of course."

That brought her up short.

Abigail halted and spun to face him. His smug smile rankled, but it was the calculating gleam in his eye that put her on her guard. "What did you say?"

He shrugged and kept on smiling, as if unaware of the daggers he tossed at her heart. "I want your building. That can't be a surprise to you. Perhaps I stated my intention a tad bluntly, but in deference to your apparently tight schedule, I decided to omit the standard niceties and cut to the chase. My offer to buy still stands. My price is fair and will allow you to set up shop in another town that doesn't have such strict ordinance codes."

Ordinance codes? He knew about the appeal. About the decision. But how?

Abigail narrowed her eyes and lowered her voice to keep any passersby from overhearing. "You put the council up to this, didn't you? Dug up this obsolete ordinance about women not owning businesses and somehow persuaded them to enforce it. Just so you can get your hands on my shop. Well, I promise you, Mr. Gerard, that if I sell, it won't be to you."

"Careful where you fling those unfounded accusations, Miss Kemp." He chuckled, though no levity softened his gaze. He placed his hand over his heart and sketched a slight bow. "I assure you that I had nothing to do with uncovering that ordinance. In truth, I didn't even know it existed. Not that I'm sorry it came up, of course. Whoever dug up that old law did me a great service."

Samson Gerard was a slug, but Abigail had to admit that he'd always been aboveboard in dealing with both her and her father. Yes, he coveted their prime real estate on the town square and made no secret of that fact. Yet theirs wasn't the only business he'd sought to buy out. Many of her neighbors had received similar offers.

But if *he* hadn't targeted her with this obscure law, who had? The mayor might have made it sound like they had given her time to grieve before bringing the issue forward, but the more likely scenario was that no one recalled the ordinance's existence until someone brought it to the council's attention. That someone could have been Mr. Gerard, but that idea didn't sit as well with her now as it had a moment ago.

"How did you know about the council's decision?" she challenged, not quite ready to deem him innocent. "I just came from meeting with them. The rumor mill works fast in Honey Grove, but not *that* fast."

"You forget that my wife's father is an alderman. He knows of my interest in your property and informed me of the council's decision ahead of time. He knew your appeal would be denied. The law was too clear to argue. So he told me the date and time of your hearing so I might be the first to offer a solution to your problem."

"You are not the solution to my problem, because I won't be selling."

"You will if you don't find a financial backer." Did he really have to look so sure of her demise? It was hard enough to hold on to hope amid her own doubts without someone else shoveling skepticism on her head. "And no man in town will invest in a business without being given a say in how to run it. I may not know you well, Miss Kemp, but you've proven to have a stubborn streak—one that would surely irritate any business partner you might acquire. Knock heads on too many issues, and you'll find yourself on the losing end of a dissolved partnership, which would leave you without a building altogether. Once you're out of the way, your partner—whose name will be on the deed to your property—will be clear to sell. I'll make him the same offer I've made to you, and my guess is he'll accept. So your choice is to take my money now, or watch me give it to someone else in a few months. Either way, you end up without a storefront. You can ensure you have the funds necessary to start over elsewhere if you deal with me, or roll the dice on a financial backer and risk losing everything your father built. The wise choice is clear."

Clear to him, maybe, but she wasn't ready to concede. Not yet.

"You are entitled to your opinion, sir. Now, if you'll excuse me." Abigail turned away from the irritating man and resumed her trek to the bakery, wishing she could leave all her problems behind so easily.

Mr. Gerard didn't follow, but he did call after her. "Unless you have a secret male relative lying around who will stand up for you, Miss Kemp, my offer is the best you're going to get."

Abigail stiffened but kept walking. If she had a male relative, she wouldn't be in this predicament in the first place, because her father would have willed the bakery to him. He'd never thought a daughter good enough to carry on the family business.

She stewed over that regret for a moment or two, but as she let go of the old hurt, it fell into fertile soil and germinated an idea. An idea so crazy it just might work.

A smile creased her face. Only God could bring good out of a meeting with Samson Gerard. He might be a slug, but he'd given her a strategy. One that, if it worked, would give her father the male heir he'd always wanted.

CHAPTER

2

Choosing a husband was much like choosing a good baguette. One looked for a strong outer shell, a tender interior, and most importantly, a tractability of dough to hold whatever shape the baker deemed appropriate.

Abigail needed a good baguette by the end of the week.

The crust could be a little stale. The crumb could be chewy and tough. Beggars couldn't be choosers, after all. But she refused to scrimp on malleable dough. Too much depended on the outcome.

From her place behind the Taste of Heaven Bakery's counter, Abigail eyed the three matrimonial candidates breakfasting in her small eating area. None of them *knew* they were matrimonial candidates, of course. If they did, they'd probably knock one another over in a race for the exit. Thankfully, their ignorance was to her advantage.

Bachelor Number One sat by the window. Bran muffin and tea with sugar. Man and muffin shared a remarkable resemblance—both a bit squatty and thick around the middle with smooth, round tops. Abigail forced her quirking smile back into a straight line. *Be kind, Abby. You might end up married to that muffin man.*

Elmer Beekman was a sweet man. A deacon at their church, soft-spoken and mild-mannered. She'd never witnessed him lose his temper or even raise his voice. She couldn't imagine him as a dictatorial husband. If his wife insisted on continuing to run her family's bakery, he might make a cursory objection, but if said wife held firm to her intentions, he'd capitulate in order to keep the peace. A quiet man who valued a quiet life. She could work with that. Unfortunately, Mr. Beekman was nearing fifty and had breath that could kill a bread dough's rise at twenty paces. A plain woman herself, Abigail didn't put much value in physical appearance, but odors lingered even when eyes were closed and lights were doused.

Bachelor Number Two sat near the entrance, chatting amiably with a striking older woman. He was a well-dressed fellow with a full head of hair and a slender build, similar in age to Abigail and possessing non-lethal breath. He exhibited impressive solicitousness toward his companion as well, a trait that marked him as biddable—the attribute at the top of her husbandly qualities list. Yet the very feature that made him an ideal candidate for her purposes was also his greatest liability, for he was already firmly entrenched beneath the thumb of another woman—his mother.

As if sensing Abigail's regard, the austere woman sitting across from Clarence Ormandy *accidentally* dropped her teaspoon. The utensil clattered to the floor. "Clarence, be a dear, would you?"

Her son leapt from his chair and retrieved the fallen spoon. When he handed it back to her, however, his mother arched a brow in disapproval. Clarence circled back to his seat, his face red. But then he brightened. He passed his unused teaspoon across the table to her and claimed the fallen spoon for himself, taking a moment to wipe invisible dust off it with his napkin before searching his matriarch's face for approval.

This time it came. A hint of a smile and a nod, much like a pat on the head for a well-trained pup. Abigail half-expected to hear the thump of a wagging tail against her floorboards.

With a barely perceptible twist of her chin, Madeline Ormandy arrowed a barbed glance at Abigail. With nothing more than a lift of her brow, she made her position clear. Clarence might enjoy Abigail's croissants, but he wouldn't be turning his attentions in a direction Madeline did not approve. And a baker's daughter did *not* qualify for Madeline's approval. Abigail doubted any woman did.

Pretending to be oblivious of the meaning behind the motherly glare, Abigail smiled sweetly before turning her attention to straightening a tray of cheese scones in her display case. Perhaps she should remove Clarence from her list of potential grooms. In his mother's absence, he had actually flirted with Abigail a time or two over the bakery counter, so she'd initially thought him the most likely to say yes to her unconventional proposal, but now she felt it prudent to recalculate. Even if she could convince Clarence to marry her against his mother's wishes, Abigail doubted she could shift his loyalties enough to be effective. More than likely she'd inherit a mother-in-law who would not only try to run her son's life but her daughter-in-law's as well. That would never do. The whole reason Abigail was seeking a husband in the first place was to retain control of her family's bakery. Autonomy and authority were key, and with Madeline Ormandy in the picture, Abigail's sovereignty would be constantly threatened.

Which left Bachelor Number Three. Zacharias Hamilton. A man who met none of her qualifications save one—he was single.

Abigail finished straightening the scone tray and angled her attention discreetly toward the dark-haired man in the far corner. He always sat there, in the shadows, back against the wall, as far from the other patrons as he could get. He ordered the same thing every day: two sticky buns and black coffee. She'd taken to having it waiting for him at seven thirty each weekday before his shift started at Sinclair's Lumberyard at eight. He'd come in, take off his hat, and look her way. She'd smile, walk the plate over to his corner table, and pour his coffee. He'd nod and take his seat. When finished, he'd leave the payment on the table along with a tip, stand, catch her eye, and nod his thanks as he fit his hat back onto his head and ambled out the door. No words required.

After attempting to make polite conversation with him and receiving little to no response when he first started coming in, like any savvy businesswoman, she'd noted her customer's preference and made adjustments. They might not speak, but they were at ease in each other's company, like old friends who knew what the other was thinking. At least when it came to breakfast. He was a complete mystery to her in every other regard. Yet when his gaze sought hers, either when arriving or departing, little flutters danced in her chest.

It was silly, she knew. Mr. Hamilton appreciated her sticky buns, not her person. Ruggedly handsome men didn't seek out plain, plump dough slingers for anything other than baked goods. Nevertheless, those silly flutters had her adding the completely unbiddable, and therefore unsuitable, man to her list of matrimonial candidates.

Abigail's younger sister materialized at her side. "Have you made your decision yet?" Coffeepot in one hand, teapot in the other, Rosalind Kemp paused behind the counter before heading out to refill their customers' cups. "We're running out of time."

"I know." Abigail rubbed an itchy spot on her nose before recalling the flour still on her hands. She'd been kneading the yeast dough that had risen overnight so she could separate it out into loaf pans for a second rise when she'd heard the Ormandys come in. Mrs. Ormandy's demanding tones were impossible to mistake. Realizing all three of her bachelors had converged on her shop at once, she'd abandoned her loaves to take stock of the potential grooms on the other side of the counter.

"Here." Rosalind set down the teapot and retrieved a lacy handkerchief from her skirt pocket. She made short work of wiping the flour from Abigail's face, then, with a considering look, tugged a few wisps of hair free of Abigail's bun and twisted each tendril around her finger—as if that would do any good. Abigail's hair was as straight as a stick. Rosalind gave Abby's cheeks a pinch before stepping back. "That's better." She smiled, true affection shining through. "Just flash those dimples, and whichever one you choose will be helpless to resist."

"Right." Abigail snorted softly.

Rosalind was the pretty one of the family. Curves in all the right places, thick golden waves of hair that looked gorgeous even when falling out of their pins, wide blue eyes framed by dark lashes, and delicate facial features that were purely angelic, much like the heart that beat beneath her beautiful exterior.

Abby also possessed her fair share of curves, only they centered around her belly and caboose instead of the areas known to draw a man's eye. Her sturdy frame and independent spirit offered little enticement to the male population of Honey Grove, but that failed to signify. She didn't plan on offering her meager charms as bait for the marriage hook. In fact, she much preferred a business arrangement that circumvented physical appetites altogether. Well, non-stomach-related appetites, anyway. She'd gladly use her baked goods as bribery.

"Don't scoff," Rosalind said, her brows dipping down to scrunch the skin above the bridge of her nose. Even her scowls were adorable. "You know I've always envied your dimples. When you smile, the entire room lights up. Any man who fails to see that beauty is a dolt. And really, you don't want to saddle yourself with a dolt."

Abigail chuckled. "I love you, Rosie."

Her sister grinned. "I love you too." She stepped back to Abigail's side and scanned the handful of tables. "Now, who's it going to be?"

"I don't know." Abigail sighed. "Who would *you* pick?"

"Mr. Hamilton, no question."

Abigail's gaze swung to the dark-haired man in black. "Because he's the best-looking?"

"No." Rosalind shook her head emphatically. "Because he's the scariest."

Abigail's attention jerked to her sister. "Why would you want to marry someone who scares you?"

An odd look crossed Rosalind's face, but it vanished before Abigail could interpret it. Then Rosie's charm took over, and Abigail decided she must have imagined the tension.

"Oh, not scary to me." Rosalind met her sister's gaze. "Scary to the town council. If you're going to win the fight to save our bakery, you need a warrior on your side. Elmer's a cream puff—sweet and all, but hardly one to stand up to a challenge. And Clarence? Well, his mama could scare the starch out of the city council's collars, but Clarence himself would fold at the first nudge. Mr. Hamilton might be a lone wolf, but he strikes me as the type who would defend his territory vigorously. Get him on your side, and the city council won't stand a chance."

The man in question scooted back his chair and stood, his

height impressive, his shoulders broad, his movements panther-like in their grace as he collected his hat and slid his chair back under the small round table. Her sister might have a point. This wasn't a man others dismissed. If he were her champion . . .

His gaze met hers, and those annoying flutters immediately lurched into chaotic flight, ricocheting off her ribs and ratcheting up her pulse. Zacharias Hamilton fit his hat to his head, then tipped the brim in her direction. Hers. Not Rosalind's. How had she never noticed that before? He nodded politely to Rosie, of course—no gentleman would offend a lady by ignoring her completely—but his gaze had sought Abigail's first.

If he had more appreciation for a well-made sticky bun than youthful beauty, Abigail's prospects might not be quite as dire as she feared.

CHAPTER

3

Zach Hamilton strolled the two blocks between the bakery and Sinclair's Lumberyard with a heavier step than usual. Something had been off with Miss Kemp today. Nothing he could put a finger on—the buns had melted in his mouth as always, the coffee scalded his gullet just the way he liked, she'd smiled at him as she did every day—but the atmosphere had felt . . . weighted.

He shook his head as he crossed Market Street, sidestepping a man on horseback and waving absently to Mr. Gordon, who was unlocking the corner hardware shop.

Miss Kemp and her weighted atmosphere were none of his concern. Zach's days of getting involved in other people's troubles were past. He'd done his duty. More than his duty. Now that he'd started carving out the freedom he'd craved his entire life, nothing would lure him off his path. Not even a pair of dimples and golden-brown eyes that matched his favorite breakfast food.

After thirty years of life, he was finally his own man, free to pursue *his* dreams, *his* goals. No harsh taskmaster of a grandfather working him into the ground, no orphanage matron dictating his every waking moment, no younger siblings depending on him for their survival. Not that he begrudged Evie or Seth the years he'd spent looking out for them. As families went, they were better than most. A little naggy from time to time, but they always had his back.

Even when he didn't deserve it.

Zach slammed the door on that bit of discomfort from the past and concentrated instead on the future he'd plotted for himself. One that entailed freedom, financial security, and absolutely *no* farming. He'd choose sawdust over dirt clods every day of the week.

Perhaps living unencumbered wasn't the grandest of aspirations, but for a fellow who'd spent his entire life gritting his teeth as circumstances dictated his path, having the freedom to make decisions as they came without worrying about how his choices might impact anyone other than himself was a luxury that would never grow tiresome. If he wanted to leave the lumberyard and take a job laying track for the railroad, he could. If he decided to ride down to Galveston and catch a ship bound for England in order to see the queen, no one would stop him. Not that he had any desire to do either of those things, but simply knowing that he *could* gave him a level of contentment he'd never enjoyed before. Strange how light a man could feel without the weight of obligation pressing down on him.

As Sixth Street dead-ended at the T&P Depot, Zach pivoted left into Sinclair's Lumberyard, opened the office door, and stepped into chaos.

Ah, yes. Last Tuesday of the month. The day Mrs. Audrey Sinclair had breakfast with her sister and saddled her husband with their zoo of children. Monkeys hung from the rafters, a dancing bear twirled amid chairs and cabinets, and a lady riding an elephant paraded past.

The oldest two children were in school, thank the Lord, but the remaining four ran amok in the office. Not that Zach's business partner seemed to care. He tromped around on all fours, giving two-year-old Tali an elephant ride across the carpet. The little girl grabbed his neck and giggled in glee as Reuben Sinclair reared up on his hind legs to see who had entered.

"Zach! Just in time. Peel Ash and Zeb off the ladder, will you? Their mother will have my hide if they fall."

Zach had been giving the office a fresh coat of paint yesterday and had left the ladder out in order to touch up any missed spots. Thank heaven the paint remained sealed up tight in its canister in the corner. He didn't want to think about what mischief the twins could manage with half a can of paint.

Zach carefully sidestepped three-year-old Ephraim, who'd decided that spinning in circles until he got dizzy enough to fall over was the best game ever invented, and made a grab for the boys whose competitive quest for the top step had set the ladder to wobbling enough to give even Zach's heart palpitations. Fastening a fist onto each boy's suspenders, Zach swung the twins off of the ladder and let them dangle a couple feet off the ground on either side of him.

"Where do you want 'em?"

Reuben reached behind his back to hold his daughter in place as he rose to his feet. He shifted the little girl to his front and reached out to halt the whirling dervish that was Ephraim. Reuben was only a couple years older than Zach, but he'd married early and obviously taken the charge about being fruitful and multiplying to heart.

"I thought to let them climb on the wood piles until Audrey gets back, but I didn't want to unleash them without reinforcements."

"Shoulders, Mr. Zach. Shoulders!" Ash demanded, his little body growing heavy at the end of Zach's arm.

"Yeah! Shoulders!" Zeb was never one to let his twin outdo him. They might not be identical in appearance, but they possessed the same adventurous spirit and rivalrous nature.

With a grunt, Zach complied and hefted up both boys, setting one on each shoulder. He moved his hands to their waists to secure their seats even as they tucked their heels into his armpits.

Reuben chuckled. "You're a big pushover. You know that, right?"

Zach shrugged, or would have if his shoulders hadn't been held down by two crowing boys. "I figure they can clean out the cobwebs while they're up there. Hand me a rag."

Reuben made a show of looking around. "Don't see one handy. Just use their hair. Those mops ought to be good for something."

"No, Papa." Zeb squirmed, his fear of spiders a well-documented family fact.

Zach lowered him to the ground while his sibling, the cleverer of the two, grabbed Zach's hat and crammed it on his own head. It probably fell down to his nose, but Zach had to give the kid credit. He'd outsmarted the two adults at their own game.

Zach shared a wink with Reuben, who seemed equal parts exasperated and proud of his son's antics.

As Zach straightened, Ash hooked a leg around his neck to situate himself more securely. "Giddyup, Mr. Zach!" He grabbed Zach's ears as if they were reins.

How much longer until Mrs. Sinclair returned? Zach rolled his eyes and grabbed the boy's ankles. Didn't matter. It was already too long.

Reuben held the door open and shooed Ephraim and Zeb through it while Zach ducked to ensure Ash didn't hit his head on the jamb.

Steering the kids past the dressed lumber shed, Reuben let

them loose in the raw lumber section. There were more planks and posts to climb on, and since none of the wood had been planed, the kids couldn't do much to hurt its value.

Zach crouched to let Ash scramble down. The lad shot off to join his brother, who now had a head start climbing the stairsteps of wood planks.

A grin tugged at Zach's mouth. Kids might be a hassle and crimp a man's freedom, but seeing them laugh and play without a single care stirred satisfaction in his crusty soul. This was what childhood was supposed to be like. Not the mishmash of tragedy and hardship he'd been forced to endure.

"You're good with them," Reuben said without turning to look at Zach. He knew better than to take his eyes off his energetic brood. "It's the reason I chose you from the other applicants I had last year."

Shock vibrated through Zach. Him? Good with kids? Ha! He did all he could to avoid the little monsters.

Reuben chuckled softly. "You might grumble and grouse about them, but you let them climb all over you. You even took little Tali when Audrey shoved her at you that first day. Remember?"

How could Zach forget? Tali hadn't even been a year old. He and Reuben had been in the midst of a discussion about buying into the business when Mrs. Sinclair had thrown open the office door, letting a flood of miniature invaders inside. The twins had rushed their father, immediately monopolizing his lap, so she had thrust baby Tali at Zach with some excuse about Simeon, the oldest Sinclair boy, having bloodied his nose and her needing to tend to him while Dinah, the eldest girl, minded the stove. In a blink, Audrey disappeared, leaving a fussy babe in a stranger's arms and a toddler roaming the floor where he could get into all sorts of mischief.

Zach had zero experience with babies, but he'd raised a little sister from the time she was four, so he figured as long as he didn't have to change any diapers, he should be all right. A few bounces on his knee had settled Tali, and a quick snatch of Ephraim as he rolled toward the corner edge of the desk had averted disaster until the missus blew back in five minutes later and shuffled the children out with a half-hearted apology for the interruption.

"Audrey wanted me to partner with a family man," Reuben explained. "Someone established, with a wife and children of his own. She worried a bachelor wouldn't be dependable in the long run without a family to anchor him to the community. But I couldn't escape the feeling that you were the one God meant for me to bring into the business. So we arranged a test."

"That whole bloody nose fiasco was a *test*?" Zach shook his head.

Reuben slapped him on the back, finally meeting his gaze. "One you passed with flying colors, my friend. Audrey gave your selection her full endorsement after she saw the way the children took to you. She assures me kids have a sense about people."

Reuben quickstepped to the side to take a dead beetle out of Tali's little fist before she could get it into her mouth. After tossing the bug into a far corner of the lumber shed, Reuben turned a teasing glance back on Zach.

"Now she wants me to find you a wife so you can start becoming the family man she intended you to be in the first place."

"Not gonna happen," Zach grumbled. Family didn't fit into his plans. Freedom did. A married man wasn't free. He was tied to responsibilities, demands, expectations. Expectations that could ruin a man when he failed to live up to them. He'd tried the family thing once, only to hurt those he cared about most. He wouldn't fall into that trap again.

"Here you are." A feminine voice echoed from the shed entrance.

Reuben's face lit up, and he turned faster than a spindle on a lathe to greet his wife. She was a tiny thing. Her head barely reached Reuben's shoulder, and her thin frame gave her a delicate appearance that was pure bunk. She might look like a bird, but she had birthed six healthy babes, and even more impressive, she actually managed to control them. Even now, the menagerie clomped down the stairstep planks with exclamations of "Mama!"

She ignored the calls momentarily, her attention focused solely on her husband as he strode across the expansive lumber shed to meet her. He wrapped her in an enthusiastic embrace, as if they hadn't seen each other a scant hour earlier, and she gazed up at him with an adoration that pained Zach to watch.

He turned away from the tender display, a far too common occurrence where the Sinclairs were concerned. It was the only downside to this partnership. Reuben was disgustingly in love with his wife and didn't care who knew it.

An ache radiated through Zach's chest, but he ignored it. Sure, having a woman who looked at you as if you were the hero of her dreams would have its merits, but since Zach was the furthest thing from hero material, envy served no purpose. No female would ever look at him that way, and it was just as well, since the only thing worse than not having a woman look at you that way was to disappoint one who did and having to watch the admiration seep from her gaze. He knew that pain.

Sweet, cheerful, loyal-to-the-death Evie. The little sister who had adored him, called him her hero, and placed him on a pedestal he had no right to occupy. Yet her adoration made him believe he was better than he was, that he might actually deserve her high opinion. He hid the uglier parts of his nature from her, and for several years had even managed to hide them from himself. But nothing stayed hidden forever, and when the truth of his darkest deed came to light, her adoring gaze had faltered and fizzled into disappointment and shame.

Every time she looked at him after that, he felt the change. A carpenter shaving away at his heart with a chisel couldn't have hurt more. She might still love him and proclaim him family, but things had changed between them and would never go back to the way they had been before. It was why he'd left.

Part of why he'd left, Zach corrected, as he pasted what he hoped was a passably pleasant expression on his face. The Sinclairs were headed his way, their brood swarming around their feet.

He'd *mainly* wanted to escape the sorghum farm and cut the familial tether that kept him from the freedom he craved. A freedom he now enjoyed. Audrey Sinclair could scheme all she liked. Zach wouldn't be shackling himself to any female. Ever.

CHAPTER

4

I can't believe I'm doing this. Abigail smoothed the skirt of her second-best ensemble, wishing she could eradicate her nerves as easily as smoothing a few wayward wrinkles from the russet fabric of her skirt. The high collar of her ivory shirtwaist didn't help matters, strangling her with the jet brooch she wore at her neck in honor of her father's passing.

With trembling fingers, she retrieved the business proposal sitting on the hall table in her rooms above the bakery. She'd spent the better half of the last week crafting and reconfiguring the document until she had the recipe just right. Her family's future depended on her ability to bribe a man into marriage without forfeiting her control of the bakery. No easy task.

Then again, running a bakery on her own for the last year while her father lay ill had been no easy task, either, and she'd accomplished that feat. She'd manage this one as well.

Lifting her chin, Abigail slid the document into the small satchel already hanging from her right shoulder and marched down the stairs into the darkened bakery.

They closed at three in the afternoon, since most of her breads sold out by midday, which gave her a few precious hours to conduct business of her own before everyone scattered to their homes for the evening. She'd spent one of those hours bathing and debating with her sister over which outfit to wear. Rosalind had wanted her to wear something bright and cheerful. Abigail preferred a more sober, businesslike ensemble. This wasn't a romantic rendezvous, after all. It was a negotiation. Besides, they were still mourning Papa. Standards might be more lax in the west than back east, but even here, pinks and yellows would be frowned upon by the townsfolk. So they'd compromised on the ivory blouse with the mourning brooch. The touch of lace on the bodice along with the gently puffed sleeves would have to suffice for displaying her femininity.

Exiting from the kitchen into the alley, Abigail locked the door behind her, then turned her feet toward Sinclair's Lumberyard. She might as well try for the top prize first. If he didn't pan out, she'd approach the next bachelor on her list.

Unfortunately, she only made it halfway to her destination before being waylaid by a man who was neither a bachelor nor on any type of desirable list in her estimation.

"Miss Kemp." Samson Gerard waved and crossed the street, neatly blocking her path along the boardwalk and making it impossible for her to pretend that she hadn't seen or heard him.

Abigail halted and nodded, not trying terribly hard to hide her impatience. "Mr. Gerard." The spindly man looked even less Samson-like than usual today, dressed in a brown checkered suit with trousers so tapered that his legs resembled sticks. Perhaps if Mrs. Gerard frequented the bakery more regularly than the milliner's, her husband would have a little more flesh on his bones.

"Are you ready to accept my offer?" His unctuous smile settled on her like a family of bugs crawling over her skin. "I've asked around town, and it doesn't seem that you've sought a partnership with any of our local businessmen. I applaud your intelligence in forgoing that route."

Abigail bristled at his condescending tone. She hadn't needed Samson Gerard to point out the perils of partnering with a third party who didn't share her passion for the bakery. Handing over the reins to a man who deemed himself better equipped to make financial decisions than his female partner simply because he had the ability to grow chin whiskers grated on her every nerve and would surely cause dissention. Not to mention the fact that an outsider helping himself to a hefty chunk of her profits every month would leave her and Rosalind with a pathetically small income.

Abigail longed to tell Gerard to stuff his offer in his hat and leave her be, but a wise woman never burned a bridge she might need to cross at a future date. If her marriage scheme didn't pan out, she might find herself at Gerard's door.

She smiled around her grinding teeth. "I have a few more avenues to explore first, but I'll let you know if I change my mind."

His composure slipped a notch. "What other avenues?" he pressed, as if he had the right to know.

"I'm not at liberty to say."

Tired of playing mouse to Gerard's cat, Abigail strode forward, hoping he'd take the hint and get out of her way. Even if he didn't, she figured her greater heft would prevail. Sometimes being a *woman of substance* paid dividends.

"I'm sorry to dash off," she said as she bowled forward, sending Gerard skittering toward the storefront to avoid the collision course she'd set, "but I have a pressing matter to attend to. I'm sure you understand." She threw a consolation smile in his direction as she swept past. "Have a pleasant evening."

"You . . . too." He tugged the brim of his hat, but the move seemed more automatic than deferential.

Abigail sighed as she continued her march. Samson Gerard might be rooting for her demise, but he didn't deserve to be treated shabbily. She could have been more patient with him. It was just that she was already wound so tight. She pressed her lips together as she stepped down from the boardwalk into the street. Proposing to a man completely out of the blue wasn't exactly an everyday occurrence. She'd been storing up courage for this since that awful ruling last week, and now that she'd begun, she wanted to get it over with before she lost her gumption.

She still couldn't believe Judge Hardcastle hadn't overturned that ridiculous ordinance in her favor. From what she'd been able to uncover, that antiquated law had been added to the books half a century ago in order to rid the town of a female brothel owner. Clearly the spirit of the law had been to protect the citizens of Honey Grove from a den of iniquity. What were they trying to protect Honey Grove from in her case? Promiscuous popovers? A new century loomed on the horizon, yet these curmudgeons had the gall to assert that the spirit of the law meant nothing. It was the letter of the law that must be upheld at all cost.

Or at least at *her* cost.

Why she had expected anything different, she couldn't fathom. Her own father would have voted right along with the rest of them.

Edward Kemp had owned the Taste of Heaven storefront outright, had been inordinately proud of that fact, and had dreamed of passing it down to his son one day. Only he'd had no sons, despite driving Mama to an early grave trying to produce one. His only surviving progeny had been female. His greatest disappointment.

When Abigail showed an aptitude in the kitchen, he'd grudgingly agreed to train her, and when she proved her mettle, he put her to work. They'd punched dough side by side for years, until his bad heart slowed him down. Gradually, she took over. The baking, the books—everything but the name on the deed. In the meantime, Papa schemed to use his younger daughter's beauty to land a son-in-law he could train to take over the business that Abigail had earned. Thankfully, his illness delayed his plans for the youngest Kemp sister. Rosalind deserved to marry a man of her own choosing instead of being bartered away like a horse at auction.

Abigail might be bartering herself, but it was her choice to do so, and she fully intended to maintain control over the negotiations. The man she chose would agree to her terms or have his candidacy rescinded.

Fueled by indignation and desperation, her steps quickened, and before she knew it, Abigail stood in front of Sinclair's Lumberyard. Like a kettle that had run out of steam, her footsteps faltered. She stared at the door looming before her, apprehension billowing.

You've come too far to turn back now.

Setting her chin, she grasped the handle and strode inside. Only to find the small office empty save for a young boy around eight or nine years of age seated behind a desk that dwarfed his small frame. The lad looked up from the schoolbook he'd been reading, then shot to his feet.

"Afternoon, ma'am." He darted around the desk and stood at attention before her. "How can Sinclair's Lumberyard serve you today?"

Abigail couldn't help but be impressed by the young man's professionalism. His parents had trained him well. She could remember her own parents instructing her on how to interact with customers. She'd always been more comfortable in the kitchen than in the front of the shop, but her father had made sure she could handle both duties from an early age. Good posture, eye contact, a deferential tone, and most important, a smile. Young Simeon Sinclair exhibited all four hallmarks.

Abigail returned his smile. "I'm looking for Mr. Hamilton. Do you know where I might find him?"

Simeon nodded. "Yes, ma'am. He and my pa are planing in the dressing yard. I can take you there, if you like."

"Yes, thank you." She'd hoped to find Mr. Hamilton alone, but this was not a day to let embarrassment keep her from her objective. A woman on the verge of losing her business couldn't afford the luxury of pride. The whole town would learn of her scheme eventually, anyway.

She followed the sandy-haired boy out the office's rear door and through the main yard to a covered area that housed the dressed wood. Inside, a pair of men worked at matching benches, scraping long planks with a rectangular box that must contain a blade of some sort, for a curl of shaved wood pushed out the top as they moved. Well, she assumed both men produced shavings. In truth, she had no idea what Reuben Sinclair did or did not produce. Her gaze had focused solely upon Zacharias Hamilton the instant she'd spotted his dark head bent over his work.

A craftsman, like herself, he moved methodically, his strokes rhythmic. The scrape of the plane ebbed and waned in perfect symmetry as he scraped, stepped forward with arms still in place, then scraped again, along the entire length of the board pinned to the workbench with a set of vises.

"Miss Kemp?"

The voice did not belong to Mr. Hamilton, but at the sound of her name, his head lifted, and for a heartbeat, their gazes held. Feeling a blush warm her cheeks, Abigail looked away and focused instead on Mr. Sinclair as he set aside his tools and strode forward to greet her.

"How can I be of assistance?"

Simeon, bless his enthusiastic heart, blurted out her business before she could find the wherewithal to answer. "She's here to see Mr. Zach, Pa."

"I see." Mr. Sinclair turned a teasing grin toward his partner. "I suppose I could spare him for a few minutes." He crooked an arm around his son's neck. "Simeon and I will start inventorying that shipment of pine that just came in."

Abigail peeked back at Mr. Hamilton. He stood beside his bench, one brow quirked slightly higher than the other. Yet he said nothing. Just waited for her to get on with whatever had brought her here.

The Sinclairs' footsteps faded. Abigail shot a glance at the departing father and son to make sure they were out of earshot, then gripped the satchel slung over her shoulder and marched forward.

Mr. Hamilton stood in place, his legs braced slightly apart as if prepared for any eventuality. This was not a man who would be easily bowled over. The observation should have given her pause, seeing as how she aimed to be in charge of this arrangement, yet she found it oddly comforting instead. He wouldn't be blown off course when life's storms battered his hull. He'd hold fast, a shelter for those under his protection.

Now all she had to do was convince him to take on a passenger with sizeable baggage and a penchant for steering the ship.

Before she could lose her courage, Abigail unstrapped her satchel and retrieved the marriage contract she'd constructed.

"Mr. Hamilton," she said, thankful that her voice trembled only slightly, since her insides were quaking like the ground beneath a racing locomotive, "I have a proposition for you."

CHAPTER

5

Zach picked up the steel square edge from his workbench, but instead of testing the board he'd been planing for perpendicularity like he normally would, he fiddled with the L-shaped tool while he stared at the woman before him.

She'd changed her clothes since that morning. Why he should notice that insignificant detail, he couldn't imagine, but he had. She looked different without her apron. And without the flour that more often than not dusted some part of her face. Looking for the telltale streak each morning proved entertaining, not that he'd ever admit that he enjoyed examining her face. Someone might get the wrong idea.

But her countenance at the moment provoked no entertainment whatsoever. Her brown eyes glowed with purpose, and her chin angled upward in a manner that reminded Zach of his little sister when she was in the mood to lecture him.

What kind of proposal could Miss Kemp possibly have for him? If she needed shelves for the bakery, surely she would have included Reuben in the discussion, yet she'd looked relieved when he and Simeon had left.

And now her cheeks were growing pink. Probably because he was just standing here staring at her like an idiot instead of saying something.

Tightening his grip on the square, he cleared his throat. "What kind of proposition?"

She thrust a set of papers at him, the sheets crinkling as the corners bent against his chest. "A business proposition. A rather, um, unconventional one, but one I believe will prove beneficial to both of us if you'll look past the first hurdle."

He reached for the papers. "That hurdle being?"

She straightened her posture, which was an impressive trick of engineering, since she was already standing as stiff as the board he'd been working on moments ago. Then she met his gaze, and something grabbed at his gut. "Marriage," she said. "To me."

A cough exploded in his throat. He ducked his chin and turned aside, the choking sensation worsening to the point that he had to brace his arms against the workbench as he struggled to control the spasms. He'd always wondered how his brother Seth felt when an asthma attack hit. Now he knew.

"It might appear to be a beggar's bargain on the surface," she said from behind him, "but I promise there are benefits."

At the word *benefits*, images jumped immediately to Zach's mind. Vivid images. Of bedsheets and unpinned hair. Of luscious curves, dimpled smiles, and welcoming glances.

His throat constricted further. Not even a cough could escape now.

"To start with, you can have all the sticky buns you like free of charge. For life."

Breakfast. She was talking about breakfast.

A bit of air seeped into his lungs, allowing him to wrestle his unruly thoughts into submission as he turned to face Miss

Kemp. He leaned back against the workbench, not yet trusting his knees to hold him up on their own, and forced himself to meet her gaze.

He thrust the crumpled papers back at her. "I ain't lookin' for a wife."

She made no move to take the documents. "Well, I wasn't looking for a husband either, until Judge Hardcastle backed me into a corner."

Zach jerked upright. That randy old goat had assaulted her? Was she pregnant? What else could have set her on this desperate course? "Did he hurt you?" he growled through clenched teeth.

Her brow scrunched. "Who? Judge Hardcastle? No. Why would you . . . ?" Her face cleared as comprehension dawned. "Oh. No. Sorry." Flustered, she stumbled over her words, making it even more difficult for him to follow. "I can see how you might have thought—with the whole marriage thing . . . it was a proverbial corner he backed me into, not a literal . . ." The explanation died beneath a heavy sigh. "Heavens, but I'm making a mess of this."

Zach relaxed. The judge hadn't accosted her. Thank God. The thought of someone as sweet as Abigail Kemp being ill-treated in such a despicable fashion made him want to tear whoever dared touch her limb from limb. But if she wasn't with child, why was she proposing marriage? And why to him? Surely there were other men in town more suitable, more . . . worthy.

"There's a law," she blurted. "A ridiculously archaic city ordinance that precludes women from owning businesses in Honey Grove. So after my father died, the city council gave me three months to grieve, then approached me with an ultimatum. If I don't sell the business, I can either partner with a male financial backer by the end of the month or have the marshal close the bakery doors for me. Permanently."

Zach frowned. That seemed a bit extreme, but he didn't doubt her word. Plenty of men believed that women belonged in the home and nowhere else. And he wouldn't put it past them to enforce their will by dusting off some outdated legislation.

"That's unfortunate, but I still don't see what this has to do with me."

Her dimples appeared for the first time that afternoon as her lips curved in a triumphant grin. "You, my dear sir, are option number three."

He raised a brow.

"I can't sell Taste of Heaven. Even if I accepted Samson Gerard's adequate offer for the bakery, it would take years to build up a clientele in another town. Starting from scratch would mean leaving our home and friends, all with no guarantee of success. And taking on a partner opens me up to all kinds of potential problems. First and foremost being that I'd have to share the profits. Just because someone in trousers was named on the deed." She sliced her hand through the air. "Not a chance. I plan to keep all the Kemp profits within the Kemp family."

Zach shifted his weight and leaned a hip against the workbench, interested in hearing how she planned to do that.

"Option three entails expanding my family. A husband will give me a male name to put on the deed while keeping all the profits within the family unit." Something in her eyes changed as she looked at him. They softened a bit, her attention becoming more personal, less theoretical. "I know I'm not the grand beauty men typically favor, but if you were to marry me, Mr. Hamilton, you'd receive many other benefits."

Great. Now she had him thinking about *benefits* again. This woman was going to be the death of him.

"First, I can offer financial benefits. You can move into our rooms above the bakery, thus no longer paying rent for your

40

living quarters. Meals would be provided. Laundry and mending services, as well. In addition, I would not expect you to pay any of the bakery's expenses with your earnings from the lumberyard. Our accounts and books would be kept separate. I've stipulated that in the contract." She nodded to the forgotten papers in his right hand. "You would not be held liable for any financial difficulty the bakery might face—not that I anticipate any, but I wanted to make sure you were protected."

Thoughtful. Smart, too. Showed foresight.

Also showed a bit of canniness. She might be talking about protecting his assets, but judging by the angle of her jaw, what she was really after was keeping her potential husband out of the workings of her bakery. Having his name on the deed might give him rights over the property itself, but Miss Kemp was obviously taking steps to ensure he had no control over the business. She had a brain behind those dimples. And the guts to forge her own path when the world tried to confine her to established roads.

He'd liked her well enough before as a talented baker who knew when to leave a man alone instead of yapping his ear off when he was trying to eat, but now true admiration stirred.

"With your living expenses reduced," she continued, "you would enjoy increased profits from your own work. Plus, you'd have access to all the baked goods you could ever want, at no cost."

She smiled again, and his gut clenched. It wasn't fair for her to be all soft and sweet and tempting like that. It made a man forget all the reasons marriage was a bad idea.

Freedom. That was what he craved. More than baked goods. More than increased profits from his work. More even than the *benefits* he'd been picturing earlier. Benefits that, come to think of it, she'd made no reference to. She probably wanted one of them marriages of convenience with separate sleeping quarters. As if any red-blooded man could live in the same house with all those curves, knowing they were legally his to enjoy, and not go insane from the wanting.

No, thanks. He preferred to be of sound mind.

"Then there's the intangibles," she continued. "The marriage-minded mamas of the town will cease throwing their daughters in your path. I've, um, noticed how quickly you escape the churchyard when the females start flocking in your direction after services, and how you avoid most social events. Once you are off the market, the flocks will focus their attention elsewhere."

That was the most compelling argument she'd made yet. Nothing wore down his patience faster than a gaggle of geese honking and cutting him off at every turn. He'd thought the attention would stop when the novelty of his being the new man in town wore off, but he'd been here over a year, and the problem had only grown worse. A few had given up or married elsewhere, but there always seemed to be a fresh batch waiting to whittle on him. Pretty soon he'd be worn so thin he'd snap. No telling what damage he'd cause then. Those same mamas who'd been so eager for him to tie the knot with their daughters would probably lead a campaign to run him out of town.

Wait. What was he thinking? He couldn't protect his bachelorhood by getting married. That was about as oxymoronic as one could get.

No. His answer was still no.

Figuring she wouldn't accept the papers from him since he'd made zero effort to read them, he reached for the strap on her satchel, tugged the bag toward him, and stuffed the contract inside.

"I'm sorry for the predicament you're in, Miss Kemp. The

council's wrong for railroading you, for sure. But I'm not your man."

Her face fell, though she firmed up her mouth in a quick attempt to hide it. Did she actually *want* to marry him? Surely not. He was just expedient, that was all. And really, he was doing her a favor. No woman as pleasant as Abigail Kemp deserved to be saddled with a grouchy bachelor with a shady past. All she knew of him was that he was punctual and liked sticky buns. If she knew the truth, she'd thank her lucky stars he'd turned her down.

He was doing her a favor.

"You should ride over to Bonham and appeal to a judge there," he suggested, hating to leave her with no help whatsoever. "Maybe a ruling from the county seat would carry more weight with our local council."

She shook her head. "Judge Hardcastle made it clear that I had no grounds for further appeal unless the ordinance was rescinded. Mayor Longfellow assured me the council had no intention of removing the law from the books at this time. Perhaps at some ambiguous future date . . ." She waved her hand dismissively. "But that would be too late to do me any good. I have to have a man in place in some capacity by the end of the month, or I lose my bakery."

Five days. Actually, only three, as the month ended on a Sunday. Bankers and lawyers didn't work on the weekend, and both would be needed to draw up whatever paperwork would be required to transfer ownership. She didn't have many options.

But that wasn't his problem.

Zach clenched his jaw and steeled his heart against any sympathy trying to worm its way inside. He was no one's hero. Not anymore. Never should have been in the first place. As soon as a fellow like him tried to be a hero, he doomed himself, along with those he cared about.

Freedom. That was what he needed.

Unencumbered freedom.

"Well, I won't waste any more of your time, Mr. Hamilton." Her gaze dropped as she straightened the papers he'd rammed inside her satchel with his big oaf fingers. Her cheeks glowed pink, and she started backing away. Then her chin lifted, and a determined light sparked in the gold of her eyes. "I'll be on my way. I have two more candidates to interview before nightfall. Good day."

With that, she pivoted smartly and marched out of the shed. He watched her go, admiring her spirit as well as the sway of her walk. Regret tugged softly at him—not hard enough to make him modify his decision, but enough to make him wonder what he was missing out on by refusing her offer.

Once she disappeared through the shed door, the fog in his brain cleared, and he turned back to the workbench and picked up his plane.

As his fingers connected with the wood, her parting words connected with his brain. Zach jerked his head up and took three long strides toward the doorway, the plane gripped so tightly in his right hand that his muscles began to cramp.

She was planning to proposition *other* men? What if they were cads or cruel or planned to take advantage of her business despite her documents? She'd be at their mercy.

Zach forced himself to stop, but his nostrils flared in protest. *Not my problem.*

He repeated the words in his head five times before he managed to retreat to his workbench.

CHAPTER

6

She was not going to cry. Abigail held her head high as she strode away from the lumberyard. She might have to blink more than usual and press her lips together to keep them from trembling, but she was *not* going to cry.

She'd expected Mr. Hamilton to turn her down. Getting upset over the fact that he'd done precisely as she'd predicted was ridiculous. A man needed more than the promise of a few extra coins in the bank and free breakfast sweets to bribe him to the altar. Yet all the logic in the world couldn't stop rejection's sting. A small part of her had foolishly hoped for a storybook ending despite the warnings of her pragmatic nature, and the disappointment left her spirit bruised. She'd need to compose herself before she approached Mr. Beekman. It wouldn't do to extend her proposal to her next potential groom with any less enthusiasm than she'd extended to her first.

Elmer Beekman was a good man. So what if flutters failed to dance in her midsection when she encountered him? Infatuation and physical attraction faded over time. Mutual respect and kindness made a much stronger foundation for a lifelong commitment. Besides, he'd be easier to bend to her will than Zacharias Hamilton. Rosalind had a valid point about Hamilton being more likely to stand up to the council, but if Abigail gave the council what they wanted—a man at the helm of her business, at least on paper—she shouldn't have any need of a warrior to fight battles on her behalf.

Unless a new obstacle cropped up.

Like a peacock thrusting itself into her path.

"Abigail!" A stylish brunette in a vibrant blue walking dress and a hat sporting not only a peacock feather but a pair of dyed ostrich plumes swept out of the milliner's shop and linked her arm through Abigail's as if the two of them were fast friends.

They had been once, but that was a long time ago.

Abigail forced her teeth to unclench. "Sophia."

She tried to extricate her arm, but Mrs. Chester Longfellow wasn't ready to let go. And no one gainsaid the mayor's wife when she was on a mission. Abigail just wished *she* wasn't the mission.

First Samson Gerard had accosted her with his bid for her storefront, and now Sophia had cornered her with who knew what agenda. The streets of Honey Grove were becoming downright treacherous to traverse these days.

Sophia smiled that diplomatic smile of hers that had gotten her husband elected to office—everyone knew who the true political animal of the Longfellow family was—but when her gaze met Abigail's, her brow crinkled slightly.

"Whatever is the matter, dear?" She dragged Abigail to a halt in the middle of the boardwalk. "You look on the verge of tears."

It was really quite impressive how Sophia could jab at one's weakness while disguising her barb as friendly concern.

Abigail lifted her chin. The little girl inside her might mourn the best friend who'd once shared all her secrets, but the independent woman she'd become wouldn't allow old sentiment to soften her resilience. "It's nothing."

Sophia clucked her tongue. "It's this terrible business with the bakery, isn't it? Such a shame."

Of course Sophia knew about the city council's ruling. Sophia knew everything that happened in town.

"Things will work out," Abigail assured her with more confidence than she actually felt. "They always do."

Sophia's mask of amiability vanished at the flippant statement, and her gaze stabbed into Abigail. "Not always."

Abigail ducked her head. "No. Not always." And apparently she'd never stop paying for the time they hadn't.

In a blink, Sophia's political charisma reappeared. She patted Abigail's arm. "In this case, I'm sure you're right, though. Just think how much leisure time you'll have once you sell the bakery. No more getting up before the sun to slave away in that dreadful kitchen. You'll have enough ready money to tide you over until Rosalind can make a match. She's such a beauty, I'm sure she'll snag a man who can keep the both of you in style." Another pat.

Abigail bristled at the implication that her own snagging of a husband was so unlikely a prospect as not to factor into the equation at all. A particularly painful gibe on the heels of Mr. Hamilton's rejection.

Thankfully, there was no way Sophia could know about that particular humiliation. She simply spoke in generalizations. Unflattering ones. As if Abigail would ever insinuate herself into her sister's marriage like an awkward third wheel. She was the eldest. It was *her* responsibility to provide for Rosie, not the other way around.

And if Sophia patted her arm one more time . . .

Abigail smiled through gritted teeth. "I'm not selling the bakery."

"Oh, then you've found a partner? Good for you." Pat, pat, pat.

Abigail snatched her arm out of Sophia's grip with enough force to cause the other woman's eyes to widen in surprise. Then a sparkle of triumph flashed. Abigail bit the inside of her cheek. Drat it all. She'd let Sophia goad her into losing her temper. She knew better.

"Mercy, Abigail. Are you quite all right? Perhaps you should schedule a visit with Dr. Sellers to see about that twitch. That can't be healthy."

How could Sophia sound so genuinely solicitous while throwing verbal daggers? She was an artist. Too bad Abigail's hide was her favorite canvas.

"Thank you for your concern." Abigail took full advantage of her freedom and stepped off the boardwalk into the street. Sophia hated to soil her hems, so she'd be unlikely to follow. The mayor's wife might know Abigail's insecurities, but Abby knew Sophia's foibles too and wasn't afraid to use them to her advantage when necessary.

"Sorry I can't stay and chat," Abigail said as she gauged the distance between herself and the plodding farm wagon making its way toward her, "but I have an appointment. I'm sure you understand."

"Of course." Sophia's condescending expression clearly communicated her *understanding*. She had Abigail on the run. And while she might be disappointed at having her fun in jabbing needles into her favorite pincushion cut short, she still derived satisfaction from displaying her dominance in a game Abigail had never been interested in playing.

Mostly because she tended to come out on the losing end.

As she crossed in front of the farm wagon and mounted the boardwalk on the opposite side of the street, Abigail fought for composure. She couldn't afford to doubt herself. Too much depended on her success. Yet as she made her way to the Taste of Heaven Bakery, she couldn't seem to focus on anything *but* doubts.

Why would any man willingly chain himself to her? Too fat, too bossy, too busy with the bakery to feather a nest. She had nothing to offer. Zacharias Hamilton had recognized the truth and all but run in the opposite direction. Could she blame him?

Abigail pushed open the back door to the bakery and nearly stumbled over her sister, who had apparently been lying in wait.

Rosalind jumped up from the chair by the kitchen workbench and set aside the issue of *The Delineator* she'd been perusing. She took one look at Abigail, and the hopeful smile that had started to bloom across her face withered. "He said no?"

Abigail nodded, unable to voice her failure. Then she met her sister's gaze, and the tears she'd valiantly held at bay leaked past her defenses.

"Oh, Abby." Rosalind was at her side in an instant, wrapping her arms around her. "Men can be such dunderheads."

A giggle broke through Abigail's tears. Leave it to Rosie to find the right thing to say.

Abigail sniffed and wiped her cheeks even as a grin tugged at the corner of her mouth. "It wasn't as bad as all that," she insisted as she pulled back from her sister's embrace.

She did take Rosie's hand, though, and held it tight. She might be the eldest, but Rosie was the strongest. No inner demons to weaken her spirit. Just an anchor of loyalty and support.

"Mr. Hamilton was kind. He didn't laugh or anything." Abigail took some measure of comfort in the fact that she'd managed to hold on to her dignity throughout the entire ordeal. It could have gone much worse. "I'm sure my pulling a proposal out of thin air stunned him. I'll try to refine my presentation before I visit Mr. Beekman. Of course, running into Sophia afterward didn't help matters."

Rosalind squeezed Abigail's hand, a fierce light in her eyes. "What did that shrew say to you? No. Don't tell me. I'm sure it's not worth repeating. Whatever she said was nonsense. You will ignore it."

Abigail grinned. "I love you, Rosie."

"I love you too, and whichever man is lucky enough to marry you will love you as well. He won't be able to help himself."

Well, that was probably taking things a bit too far, but Abigail appreciated the sentiment. Heaven knew her fragile ego could use a bit of shoring up before she tried to barter herself to the next man on her list.

"Now, I want you to go upstairs," Rosalind ordered, "fix yourself a cup of tea, and pamper yourself for at least thirty minutes. Read over that contract again. Remind yourself of all you have to offer. Then list at least ten things you offer that are not in that document. I'll even give you three to start with: you're smart, hard-working, and sweeter than the day is long. You're a catch, Abigail Kemp. But you have to believe it yourself before anyone else will. So take some time to get in the proper frame of mind."

Rosalind was the true catch, as beautiful on the inside as she was on the outside. If only Abby could mimic her confidence and self-assurance. But outside the kitchen, those commodities proved incredibly slippery. Even now, she found herself shaking her head and taking refuge in what she knew she was good at—work.

"As lovely as your advice is, Rosie, I don't have time to sip tea and make lists. I need to deliver the widow bread, then pay my call on Mr. Beekman. If I delay, he might be sitting down to supper when I arrive, and no man appreciates having his supper interrupted."

Rosalind didn't usually demand her way, but her expression took on a decidedly mulish cast as she strode to the basket that held the day-old loaves they donated each evening to a family in need. "I'll take the bread," she insisted, fitting the basket handle to the crook of her elbow. "You"—she pointed to the stairs—"sip tea and clean the mental slate. Mr. Beekman's boardinghouse doesn't serve supper until six. You've got time."

Abigail surrendered with a shake of her head. "All right, all right. I'll take a few minutes to regroup." It wouldn't hurt to go over her persuasive tactics again anyway, seeing as how she'd fumbled the delivery with Mr. Hamilton. Although the distracting flutters that beset her whenever she was in his presence were probably more to blame than her arguments. Since Mr. Beekman's presence was blessedly flutter-free, conversing with him should be less prone to disaster.

"More than a few minutes, Abby," Rosalind hounded. "Promise me."

Why was this so important to her? Why not just get it over with? Yet something in her sister's eyes compelled Abigail to agree. "Fine. I'll stay long enough to brew a cup of tea and read over the contract. Happy?"

Rosalind strode to the door, triumph in every step. "Yes." She gave a wink, then shuffled out the door.

Forgetting to close it behind her. That girl.

Abigail stuck her head out into the alley, intending to tease her sister with a scold about living in a barn, but changed her mind when she noticed Rosie heading south down the alley instead of north.

"You're going the wrong way," Abigail called. "The Prescotts live on Elm."

Rosalind pivoted to face her sister but kept moving down the alley, walking backward. "I know. I have a quick errand to run first." Then she spun around and scurried around the corner leading to Sixth Street.

Abigail shrugged and pulled the door closed. Where on earth Rosalind thought to go with a basket of day-old bread getting in the way, Abby couldn't imagine. But wherever it was, she sure seemed keen to get there.

CHAPTER

7

Zach had just stored his plane in the large tool chest beneath his workbench when young Simeon arrived with a second female in tow. The lad's face glowed beet red as he escorted the girl in, his gaze veering to her so frequently that it was amazing he didn't trip over his feet.

"Mr. Zach. A, uh, 'nother Miss Kemp to see ya."

Zach sighed. He hadn't thought Abigail the type to gang up on a fella. Sending the sister to plead on her behalf was beneath them both. Unless . . .

He narrowed his gaze at the blond woman with too much hair and a deficit of dimples. "You're not here to make the same offer, are you? 'Cause my answer won't be changin'."

Instead of taking offense, she smiled at him. Then she turned to the boy at her side. "Thank you for showing me the way, Simeon." Her smile beamed, and the lad nearly face-planted, so steep was his lean toward her. Rosalind reached into the oversized basket dangling from her left arm and pulled out a pair of dinner rolls. "Why don't you share these with your pa while I have a few words with Mr. Hamilton."

Simeon just stared at her without making a move for the bread.

Zach rolled his eyes. At this rate, he'd never get out of here. He yanked the bread out of Rosalind Kemp's hand, shoved it at Simeon, then gave the kid a push in the right direction. "Tell Reuben I'll close up the shed," he said, wanting to make sure the besotted boy didn't make up some excuse to come back and gawk at the Kemp girl.

Simeon nodded, his feet moving automatically in the direction Zach had started him. He dawdled but kept moving and eventually disappeared into the main lumberyard.

"Look," Zach grumbled, "I don't know why your sister sent you, but—"

"Oh, Abigail doesn't know I'm here," Rosalind said as she spun to face him. All residual pleasantness faded from her features, leaving a slightly panicked look in her eyes that snagged Zach's attention. "I don't have much time."

He crossed his arms over his chest, not wanting to look too interested. Pretty girls had ways of getting their hooks into fellas before they knew what was happening, and while Abigail's sister had never flirted or pestered him, she might not be above using wiles to try to manipulate him. Not that he'd let her, of course. He could read truth on a person's face the way a preacher read it from the Bible. Learning at the knee of the most renowned riverboat gambler on the Mississippi had given him a distinct advantage: he could spot a bluff a mile away.

"I'm listening."

She set the bread basket on the ground, then stepped close and laid a hand on his arm. "You need to marry my sister."

Well, she could get to the point. That was a mark in her favor.

"To save your bakery, I know. But there are other ways to

save it that don't require a leg-shacklin' on my part. She might not like the idea of joinin' up with a partner, but—"

"It's more than the bakery." Rosalind bit her lower lip and cast a quick glance around before turning back to him. The fear in her eyes was real. He'd stake a year's wages on it. "I did . . . something a while back. Something Abigail knows nothing about. Something that started a chain of events I can't seem to undo. No danger has touched Abigail yet, but there's a chance . . ." She bit her lip again.

Zach heard the unspoken words. The danger might not have touched Abigail yet, but it had touched Rosalind. Enough to put that panic in her eyes.

"If you don't marry her, she's going to propose to Elmer Beekman, and I'm pretty sure he'll say yes. He's about as tepid as they come, and at his age, he's sure to jump at the chance to gain a young wife with nothing beyond agreement required on his end. But he won't be able to protect her, Mr. Hamilton." Her grip on his arm tightened. "Not from the council. Nor from . . . other trouble."

Elmer Beekman? *That* was who she planned to replace him with? The man was a mouse. Timid, bland, and old enough to be her father, for Pete's sake. She could do better. *Much* better. And her sister was right. Beekman would be about as useful in a fight as wet newsprint.

Tension radiated up Zach's spine, crimping his neck. He rolled his head back and forth on his shoulders to loosen the muscles, then looked down at the girl before him. "What kind of trouble we talkin' about?"

Rosalind couldn't quite meet his gaze. "The pushy, male, won't-take-no-for-an-answer kind." Slowly she lifted her chin and forced her blue eyes to meet his, impressing him with her fortitude. "I won't go into the details with someone who's not family, but I swear that if you marry Abigail, I'll tell you everything. She doesn't deserve to pay for my mistake, but I fear that's exactly what will happen if things continue unchecked."

Miss Kemp released her hold on him, paced a few steps away, then pivoted to face him again. "I don't trust Elmer Beekman or Clarence Ormandy to be of much use. Elmer would say a prayer, then hide his head in the sand, and Clarence would run to his mother. Mrs. Ormandy would never risk her position in Honey Grove society by taking up for a pair of girls touched by scandal, even if one of them happened to be married to her beloved Clarence. She'd more likely use her influence to have the marriage annulled. And while I believe in prayer and utilize that weapon every day, when one faces Goliath, it's best to have a rock in the sling."

And he was the rock she planned to have on hand.

Zach frowned. Elmer and Clarence had to be the two biggest milksops in Fannin County. What was Abigail thinking? They'd be of no help whatsoever.

Which was why she came to you first, knucklehead.

Zach turned his back on Rosalind Kemp, unfolded his arms, and braced his palms against the surface of his workbench. His fingers gripped the wood tighter than the vise jutting out from the side.

This wasn't his problem. His knuckles whitened. It wasn't. His shoulders hunched. His head dropped. It *wasn't*. His eyes closed.

Mistake.

Images popped up behind his lids. Evie. A distraught four-year-old girl with mismatched eyes, unwanted by adoptive families and in need of a big brother's protection and guidance. Then there was Seth. Asthmatic, weak, wouldn't last through the year without someone looking out for him. They hadn't been

Zach's problem either. Not until Evie's brother saved Zach's life, losing his own in the process. A promise to a dying kid had changed the course of Zach's future. Changed him from loner to head of a family at age thirteen. He'd been too young to understand the ramifications of having others depend on him. At thirty, he understood plenty. Especially his own inadequacies and his likelihood of disappointing those who relied on him. But would he disappoint Abigail any more than Elmer Beekman or Clarence Ormandy would?

He snorted in disdain. Not if she was looking for a rock, as her sister suggested. His competition offered nothing but down fluff—a worthless commodity if trouble came knockin'.

Zach had lived through trouble those milksops couldn't even imagine. Orphaned, worked nearly to death by a bitter grandfather, train-wrecked, and left on his own with two scrawny kids to provide for when he was still a kid himself. Yet his adopted siblings had never gone hungry. They'd never suffered physical harm. They'd grown into remarkably normal people despite his rough ways and less-than-conventional methods, because they'd known he always had their backs. *Always.* They'd even found love. Surely that counted for something.

What did Beekman or Ormandy have on their résumés?

Nothing that amounted to a hill of beans. That was what.

Yet this wasn't his problem. As much as he liked the Kemp sisters, Abigail in particular, this still wasn't his problem. On the other hand, what would happen if he left them to fend for themselves, two lambs in a world of wolves?

He'd done things in his life he wasn't proud of—*lots* of things, things that made him a poor match for a woman like Abigail Kemp—but he'd never deliberately allowed harm to come to an innocent person when he had the power to stop it. And while Abigail deserved better than the likes of him, Beekman and

Ormandy didn't measure up either. At least he could offer protection from whatever trouble knocked on the Kemps' door. All Beekman could do was be a name on a piece of paper. He'd be worthless if any real danger came calling.

And the idea of Abigail sharing a marriage bed with that paunchy, middle-aged softy left Zach queasy.

Slowly he straightened and turned. Rosalind stood quietly, hope glittering in her blue eyes. Yep, the kid needed a big brother, all right. Vulnerable, young, and pretty enough to cause a stir. She reminded him of Evie.

But her sister? The last thing he felt for Abigail Kemp was brotherly concern. If he was going to marry her, they were definitely having a discussion about benefits. 'Cause not even a saint could manage a marriage of convenience with that combination of spunk and curves. And Zach was no saint.

"So?" Rosalind prompted. "Will you do it? Will you marry my sister?"

"I ain't ready to say yes just yet. I'll need to look over those papers she kept trying to pawn off on me, and possibly renegotiate a few—*oomph*."

The fool kid smacked into his chest and wrapped her arms around his waist before he had the wherewithal to fend her off. She reminded him more of Evie by the minute.

"Oh, thank you!" She kissed his cheek then jumped back. "You won't regret this. I know it! Abigail is the dearest soul in the world. The two of you will be a splendid pair. You'll see."

Zach backed up a step, then another, his gaze going a bit black around the edges. "Hold up, now. I ain't made any promises. Just said I'd read her papers and consider things."

Her smile didn't dim one iota. "You'll marry her. You've already decided. I can see it in your eyes. You're just dragging your feet now at the prospect of abandoning your bachelorhood, but believe me, you'll be gaining far more than you'll be giving up."

His bachelorhood. His freedom. The freedom he'd waited thirty years to claim. The thought of sacrificing it again made his knees weak. He reached for the worktable behind him. "I'm gonna need a few days to think things through."

She shook her head. "Sorry. I've already given you more time than we can afford. When Abigail gets her mind set on something, she doesn't rest until the job's done. I made her promise not to leave the bakery until she brewed herself a cup of tea, but she's probably already swigged that down and is making for Mr. Beekman's boardinghouse even now. If you don't stop her before she gets there, this whole conversation will be moot." Rosalind grabbed his hand and tugged. "Go after her, Mr. Hamilton. Now. Before you and I both are stuck with regrets we can't undo."

Zach ignored her pulling, not swaying an inch. He wouldn't be bullied into marriage, not even by a sweet girl who reminded him of his sister.

But those regrets . . . he already had a sizeable collection. He didn't care for more. But what of his freedom?

A picture of Elmer Beekman standing before a preacher with Abigail Kemp rose in his mind. The bald pudding of a fellow putting his hands on her and leaning in for a kiss . . .

Zach clenched his fists and marched toward the door of the shed.

Some crimes were just too great for a man to stand by and take no action.

CHAPTER

8

Providence must have taken pity on Abigail, for she ran across Elmer Beekman in the lane outside his boardinghouse, giving her the chance to conduct her awkward interview in the relative privacy of the outdoors instead of the overheated parlor where any of the other residents might overhear.

"Mr. Beekman," she called, lengthening her stride as she came up behind him. When he turned, she plastered a smile to her face and waved. "Just the man I wanted to see. Might I have a word?"

He dipped his chin as she closed the remaining distance. "Of course, Miss Kemp. How can I be of service?"

The potency of his breath apparently didn't wane during the course of the day. Unfortunate. She'd hoped . . . never mind what she'd hoped. She'd just invest in mint tooth powder or something. She would not be deterred from her course. Though it might be prudent to put a bit more distance between herself and her intended.

Abigail leaned back slightly, careful to keep her smile in place.

"I find myself in a rather difficult predicament," she confided, "but you have the power to set it all to rights, Mr. Beekman."

His eyes widened. "Me?" He looked bewildered and not a little alarmed.

Botheration. She'd been hoping to inspire heroism, not terror.

Abigail took hold of his arm. "Don't worry. There are no actual dragons to slay, but I do find myself in need of your assistance." She tried to look as helpless as possible and even batted her lashes once. Desperate times called for desperate measures, after all. "Is there someplace we can speak? Privately?"

He blinked as if he couldn't quite make sense of the woman before him, but his kind heart took over. He patted her hand, then offered his arm for her to take in a more conventional manner. "Of course. There's a bench here, around the oak. Why don't we sit?"

"Perfect!" Abigail allowed him to lead her toward the slender oak that shaded the side of the boardinghouse. Someone had built a circular bench around the base of the trunk, creating a quiet place for reading or conversing.

She swept her skirts beneath her and took a seat, trying not to notice the way the buttons on her companion's vest strained as he sat. She could make him new ones that fit better, emphasizing his stature instead of his girth. Well, maybe not his stature. He was actually an inch or two shorter than her. Maybe she could simply let out the side seams. She knew firsthand how uncomfortable clothes that were made with average measurements in mind could be. They pinched in all the worst places and pooched in others. Thankfully, she had a sister who was a whiz with a needle and who had taught her the art of fitting clothes to the body she had instead of trying to stuff her body into patterns made for someone else's shape. Abigail could do the same for Mr. Beekman.

Feeling a renewed comradery with the man at her side, Abigail smiled with genuine warmth.

"How can I be of help to you, Miss Kemp?" His brown eyes had a lovely softness to them. Perhaps if she focused on his eyes, hers would be less likely to water when he spoke.

She pulled her satchel across her lap to retrieve her papers. Hoping he wouldn't notice their slightly crinkled state and realize he wasn't the first would-be rescuer she'd approached, she slid them out of the bag.

"You might not be aware," she began, "but the city council has chosen to enforce an outdated law prohibiting women from—"

"There you are, Miss Kemp." A shadow fell over her. A large shadow with considerable stature and a broadness to its outline that made her words stick to the roof of her mouth. "Not trying to give my contract to another fellow before I have the chance to read all the details, are you? That's not very sporting."

"Mr. H-Hamilton!" Elmer Beekman lurched to his feet and backpedaled as if the papers the lumberman reached for were a pair of loaded six-guns.

Abigail bristled, snatching the contract out of Zacharias Hamilton's grasp. "You already made your position on this matter quite clear, Mr. Hamilton." Did he have to look so handsome and heroic standing there? He made poor Mr. Beekman look like a mouse in comparison.

A mouse with kind brown eyes, Abigail reminded herself firmly as she gained her feet and pushed her way past the boulder in her path. Not that the boulder moved so much as an inch. She had to contort herself around the bench to squeeze by and chase down her prospective groom. Because a mouse with kind brown eyes was infinitely better than a kitten with a bobcat for a mother. She'd rather not spend her days dodging

Mrs. Ormandy's swiping claws and sharpened teeth. Holding one's breath to avoid halitosis was definitely the lesser of two evils. And her lesser evil was getting away.

"Please, Mr. Beekman, ignore him. I just need a few minutes of your time to explain my predicament."

But he was already shaking his head and backing toward the boardinghouse. "I'm sorry, Miss Kemp, but I really don't think I'm the one to assist you. Mr. Hamilton seems better suited to your needs." He tripped over an empty milk bucket that had been standing by the back door. The clanking of tin echoed loudly in the charged atmosphere. Elmer reddened but didn't slow his retreat. He latched on to the door handle and, without much more than a hasty dip of his chin, disappeared into the boardinghouse.

Abigail's shoulders drooped as the door closed on her best hope for a peaceful marriage.

"So, can I look at those papers now?"

The deep, masculine voice stiffened her spine faster than ice hardened butter.

She spun to face him, snapping the contract behind her back. "What are you doing here? Was rejecting my offer not enough humiliation for one day? Did you decide to heap on a second helping by chasing off my best chance at an actual acceptance? I know I'm not the kind of woman men like you want, but I might have convinced Mr. Beekman that a wife with extra padding and a business to keep her out of his hair wasn't such a bad deal. Just because I couldn't tempt you with the offer doesn't mean *no* man would be interested."

He stood there like the boulder he was, stony-faced, hard, and implacable. Then he raised a single brow. "You finished?"

Abigail scowled, wishing she had more charges to harangue him with, but she couldn't come up with anything at the moment. She lifted her chin. "For now."

"Good." He advanced a step, bringing him nearly toe-to-toe with her.

She had to crane her neck back to see his face, then regretted it, as his dark blue eyes sparked with an indignation that made her rethink the wisdom of challenging him.

"First off," he said, "I've never intentionally humiliated a woman in my life. Scared more than a few and riled more than my share over the years, but never humiliated them."

Abigail's forehead scrunched. Was he admitting to purposely frightening females? That didn't fit what she knew of him at all. Of course, neither did her charge of humiliation. Just because she'd felt humiliated didn't mean he'd set out to embarrass her.

"Second, what's this nonsense about you not being the type of woman men like me want? What do you know about what I want, anyway? You talk about yourself as if you're some kind of penalty or consolation prize. Any man who has to be *convinced* of your value is an imbecile and not worth your time."

Abigail blinked. Had that been a compliment? It was hard to tell amid all the grouching and lecturing, but the way her heart fluttered made her suspect there might have been one tucked in there. Her pulse gave a little leap.

"And speaking of fellas not worth your time, if Elmer Beekman can't even stand up for you during a friendly discussion, how in the world do you expect him to stand up for you with the city council? He's not the man for you."

"Neither are you," she murmured, "according to your response earlier today. I believe your exact words were, *I'm not your man.*"

The intensity of his features softened slightly, and for a moment she swore she saw a touch of red beneath his swarthy skin. "Yeah, well, I might have misspoken."

Might have . . . ? "What exactly are you implying, Mr. Hamilton?"

"The name's Zach." He grabbed the back of his neck and shifted his weight. Then he blew out a breath—one that did not smell of garlic and onions, she was happy to note—and met her gaze. "Can I look at that contract you got hiding behind your back or not?"

Hands trembling, Abigail handed over the papers. He took them from her and started reading. His lips moved slightly as he read, like a young boy not terribly confident in his ability. The unexpected vulnerability in one so fierce utterly enchanted Abigail, leaving her more bemused than bewildered.

She had no idea why Zacharias Hamilton had changed his mind or how he happened to find her outside Mr. Beekman's boardinghouse, but she wasn't so foolish as to look a gift horse in the mouth. He was here. Reading her contract. And scaring off the competition. If God could part the Red Sea and lead his people across, she supposed he could send a reluctant bachelor across town. She wouldn't question the how or why. She'd just pray that the miracle continued.

After he'd finished the second page, Zach sought her gaze. "I don't see anything in here about relations."

Relations? "You mean my sister?" Rosie was her only living relation and not yet at the age of her majority. "She'd live with us, of course. Continue working in the bakery."

He shook his head. "Not those relations." He cleared his throat. "Marital ones."

Marital . . . ?

Oh.

Fire lit Abigail's cheeks. She'd been so concerned about preserving her business, she hadn't stopped to consider the more *personal* aspects entailed in marriage. "I, ah, hadn't given it much thought."

"Well, it's a pretty big piece of this whole arrangement, so I need to know what I'm getting myself into."

Good grief. What had she gotten *herself* into? Discussing marital relations in the middle of a public thoroughfare? All right, in a private yard several feet away from the public road, but still. Not exactly a topic of conversation young ladies received training in.

Yet she couldn't dismiss his concerns. Uncomfortable they might be, but they were also legitimate. And really, his desire to get things out in the open at the start boded well for how the two of them would get along. No guessing and tiptoeing around. Just a practical, straightforward addressing of pertinent issues. She could do this.

Abigail stiffened her posture. This was her chance to set ground rules, boundaries her mother never had the chance to establish. "I'm a businesswoman first and foremost, Mr. Hamilton, and this arrangement is of a practical nature."

"Speaking from a purely *practical* perspective, Miss Kemp," he interrupted, "a man can't be expected to live like a eunuch when the woman he's married to looks like you." His gaze scanned her from head to toe, lingering ever so briefly on the places where her curves were most prominent. Curves she'd always believed defined her as *fat*. Yet under his regard, she suddenly wondered if *voluptuous* might be an adjective that could apply. "Too tempting by half."

He actually found her attractive? The ground beneath Abigail's feet must have shifted, for all sense of balance abandoned her.

"I'm willing to sign your contract, but only if you agree to include marital relations in the bargain." His face looked as soft as granite at that pronouncement. Not a touch of romance or sentimentality to be seen. But then, she was the one who had emphasized the practical nature of their arrangement. And it wasn't as if they were truly courting.

Nevertheless, she couldn't agree to his demands with nothing but cold practicality between them. To do so just felt . . . wrong.

Besides, she'd sworn not to repeat her mother's mistakes, and this might be her only chance to negotiate terms that would allow her to uphold that vow.

Abigail nibbled on her lower lip. The bakery had to come first. Her livelihood. Her passion. The key to Rosie's future. Perhaps it would be better to give him the agreement he wanted. They could work out the details later.

Abigail discarded that idea as quickly as it had formed in her mind. She respected Zach too much to trap him into a life-long commitment without full honesty between them. If he'd been content with a marriage of convenience, things would be different. They could simply go on as friends, their separate lives only intersecting at meals and social occasions. No need to go into more personal matters. But such an idealized plan had been woefully naïve.

Zach seemed willing to sign the contract—to relinquish his freedom and save her bakery. All he asked for in return was a real marriage. The one thing she wasn't sure she could give. As much as she loved the bakery, she couldn't forget what had happened to her mother. Either she would forfeit her vow and come to resent her husband, or she would hold firm and earn his resentment instead. Neither boded well for a lifetime of cohabitation.

She needed to tell him, to explain. If they could somehow find a middle ground, maybe they could both get what they wanted.

Glancing at the bench, Abigail dredged up her courage, then forced herself to meet Zach's gaze. "Can we sit for a minute?"

CHAPTER

9

Zach nodded and lowered himself to the bench. If he'd learned one thing from raising Evie, it was that females felt better when they talked a problem to death. They didn't necessarily have to solve it; they just wanted to spill out their worries and hopes and have someone listen. Seemed like a waste of time to him. Better to slap on an answer and get busy fixing it than chewing it to a pulp, but he wasn't the one in charge of this particular predicament. Abigail was calling the shots. So he'd play by her rules.

'Cause the other lesson his baby sister had taught him was that his chances of getting the response he wanted exponentially increased if he let her yak a spell. Shortcutting the process and demanding an answer up front had a tendency to inspire obstinacy and flare tempers. Since he actually wanted Abigail to like him at the end of this discussion *and* come around to his way of thinking, it seemed prudent to keep his trap shut and his ears open.

Besides, when she sat down next to him, her knee rubbed against his in a way that made him want to grab her waist and scoot her closer so he could feel the entire length of her against him.

Yep. Relations were a must.

Then she turned those golden-brown eyes on him, and the vulnerability in her gaze sucker-punched him in the gut. Pain— old, deep, and tender when prodded. He knew the type. Something besides maidenly modesty lurked behind her hesitancy, and that realization made him feel like a heel for pressing the issue.

"My father always wanted a son," she began. "He ignored Rosie and me for the most part when we were small, then tolerated us when we were old enough to be useful."

The man sounded like a fool.

"My mother died when I was fourteen." Abigail glanced down at her lap, then slowly raised her face and pinned him with her gaze. "After her seventh miscarriage."

Zach winced at the number.

"After the fifth loss, the doctor warned her that another pregnancy could kill her. That her body was just too worn out to carry a babe. Yet my father craved a son, so they kept trying. And failing. The first was a stillborn boy who came two years after me. Then Rosie. Then a series of seven pregnancies over the next decade that never lasted past the fifth month." Abigail set her chin and fisted her hands in her lap. "He killed her, and she let him."

Zach stared at his knees. What was he supposed to say to that? Reassure her that he wasn't the callous beast her father had been? Tell her that she was made of sterner stuff than her mother? Yeah, 'cause putting down her dead mother would win him points. And with his luck, she'd probably take his comment as an insult, with all her skewed ideology about men wanting delicate filigree instead of solid mahogany.

Wasn't there some proverb about how even a fool looked wise if he kept his mouth shut? Zach locked his jaw in the upright position and left Abigail at the reins.

"If we are to include *relations* in this agreement," she said, impressively looking him in the eyes despite her obvious discomfort with the topic, "I'll want to set some ground rules."

Well, she hadn't completely closed the door. That was something.

"What kind of rules are you proposing?" He kept his voice as nonchalant as possible. He didn't want to give away too much bargaining power by letting her sense his level of investment.

"Well, for starters, I'd like time to get to know you better on a personal level before we broach certain . . . intimacies." Her courage finally gave out, and her gaze dropped. "Due to my business circumstances, we are jumping straight into marriage without the usual courtship period. But I don't want to be made to feel like a . . . a woman who . . . sold her virtue for the price of a bakery." Her voice dropped to a whisper. "Or treated like a . . . a . . . ."

Prostitute. She didn't have to say it. Zach knew exactly what she meant. And if he'd been alone, he would've slammed his fist into the back wall of the boardinghouse for making her feel that way for even a moment.

"Abigail," he demanded, his voice gruffer than it should have been, "look at me."

She lifted her face, the shame in her light brown eyes hurting him worse than that wall would have.

"I'd *never* want you to feel like you were being used. And if you ever did, that would be my dishonor, not yours." He shook his head and searched for some pretty words to make her feel better, but none came to him. So he opted for plain speaking. "I'm a man," he stated baldly, "and men tend to focus on the physical side of relationships. But if we do this, we're equal partners. In all matters. You'd have the right to say no whenever you wished, and I would respect that. And if you want to postpone relations until after you get to know me better, fine. Though I have to warn you that you might not like all of what you learn."

That brought a hint of a dimple out of hiding. "Well, I have a few warts myself."

"Really? Where?"

Her eyes widened. "Oh, not actual warts . . . I . . ."

He grinned to let her know he was teasing, and the shy smile he received in return zinged straight to his heart. He could think of worse ways to spend a lifetime than making this woman smile.

Growing serious again, he returned to the topic at hand. "As long as I have your promise that you will keep an open mind about the physical side of our union, I'm willing to consider this marriage scheme of yours."

He might need to have a few private conversations with Reuben about the best way to seduce one's wife. The man had six kids. He had to know a trick or two. But Zach would work out those details later. Right now he just had to convince this sweet innocent that if he met her at the altar, he wouldn't pounce on her the moment they swapped *I do*'s.

Her chin went all pointy again as she set her jaw. "And what if I don't want children—at least not right away? If I want to focus on the bakery?"

He wasn't exactly sure what he could do about that, but he supposed he could research the matter. "I think that'll be up to God more than us," he said, "but I swear I won't make demands of you that you're not willing to fulfill." He let out a sigh and shrugged. "In truth, I never expected to have kids.

I planned to live life on my own. I've already done the parenting thing with my siblings, and I wouldn't mind too much not repeating the experience." Although he found the thought of Abigail swollen with his child more compelling than he would have anticipated. "But if we did end up with a young'un or two, I'd pull my weight and not leave you to carry that load by yourself."

She eyed him skeptically. "You wouldn't expect me to give up the running of the bakery to stay home with our children?"

Hadn't he just said they'd be equal partners? Zach fought off a rising tide of disgruntlement, reminding himself that the main example of husbandly devotion she had to compare him to was a father who'd apparently treated his wife like a broodmare with no consideration for her own goals and dreams or even her physical health.

"Look. Raising kids is time-consuming and hard work. I know. I've been there. I imagine it's even harder with infants. Whether you had a bakery to run or not, I wouldn't abandon you to shoulder that load alone. When I say we'd be partners, that's what I mean. We'd share the family responsibilities. It's obvious that the bakery is important to you. I wouldn't expect you to give that up just because some little ankle biters showed up on the scene. What I *would* do is look for ways to help you. Reuben takes his kids to work one morning a week. We could work out something similar. Maybe rig up some sort of fenced play area in the kitchen for the youngsters when they're with you. I could even hire you some help if need be. You know, with all that extra money I'll be saving by living with you."

That earned him another shy smile, and Zach breathed a shade easier. Then a tiny frown wrinkled her brow. "You raised your siblings?"

"Adoptive siblings, but yeah." Honesty prodded him to paint

a more accurate picture. "Well, Seth did most of the raising where little Evie was concerned. I just kept their bellies full and a roof over their heads."

"Where are they now?" She looked concerned. Probably wondering if he'd dropped them off a cliff somewhere.

"Pecan Gap. Evie married last year. Seth too. They have neighboring farms."

Those lines in her forehead deepened. "But how could they be adults? You're not old enough . . ."

He ran a hand over his face. "I got an early start. But that's a tale for another time."

Hopefully a much later time. Never, would be his preference. Talking about his stint as a stand-in parent would inevitably lead to talking about how he'd managed to provide for said roofs and full bellies, and he'd rather Abigail not glimpse the darkness of his past. Better to focus on the here and now.

"If it's all the same to you," he said, "I'd like to take this here contract home and ponder it awhile." Maybe even seek the Lord's guidance, though he and the Big Man were still on rather shaky footing. "Seems like you might want some ponderin' time too, since I just sprang the whole relations thing on ya. I'll come by the bakery in the morning before you open, and if we're both agreed, we can sign it."

She blinked—twice. "Am I to understand that you're truly considering my proposal?"

What had the last twenty minutes been, if not consideration? He raised a brow at her. "You trying to talk me out of it?"

"No!" She wagged her head with a vigor that soothed his pride.

It was rather nice being a female's first choice, even if he'd originally planned to avoid the parson's mousetrap. Of course, if her second and third choice were Beekman and Ormandy, he couldn't exactly brag about being top of the list. The rungs on that ladder were pretty low.

"All right, then." He folded the papers in half and tucked them into the waistband of his trousers. Then he stood and held out a hand to help her rise. It seemed like something a gentleman would do. Not that he was much of a gentleman, but if she was gonna be his wife, he figured he should extend the courtesy.

Besides, at least four pairs of eyes were staring at them from the boardinghouse kitchen window, and he wouldn't give any of those busybodies reason to wag their tongues about anything improper.

Abigail's hand slid into his palm, and his fingers closed around hers. She had a strong grip, yet her touch felt nothing like an ordinary handshake. His skin warmed where it touched hers, and little pinpricks paraded up his arm. Not a sensation he was used to, but not one he disliked, exactly, either. He guessed he'd get used to it.

He steered her in such a way that kept her back to the boardinghouse, hoping she'd fail to notice their audience.

"I guess I'll see you in the morning, then?" she said as she retrieved her hand from his and used it to smooth out her skirt.

"Yes, ma'am." Zach nodded, trying to convince himself that the thought of sacrificing his freedom didn't leave him a tad bilious. "Bright and early."

Her lips curved in a tiny smile, and then she nodded and left him in the boardinghouse yard, watching her hips sway side to side as she made her way down the street.

Maybe he should have signed the papers without giving himself time to think about the consequences. But no. If he was going to tie himself to a woman for life, he needed to make sure he wouldn't balk at the yoke.

He still had his freedom. He could choose the path his future took. If he chose Abigail, there'd be no going back. No bellyaching about being tied down. No whining with the fellas at the saloon about clipped wings. It would be his choice, and he'd make the best of it, just as he'd been making the best of whatever life threw at him since he was a kid.

Zach tossed a quick glance at the sky before starting the trudge home. *You just can't leave me alone, can you? You keep throwing family at me, even when you know my track record for messing it up. I thought you were smarter than that.*

Apparently not.

Zach sighed, his gaze turning south. Was it too late to catch that boat to go visit the queen?

"He'll do it. You'll see." Rosalind grinned as she set plates on the tables near the front window. As if the outcome had already been decided.

Abigail knew better. If the matter had been decided, Mr. Hamilton would not have needed the night to consider things. Her hands shook slightly as she placed a selection of sticky buns in the display case. *His* sticky buns. Not until this morning had she realized that she thought of them that way. She'd been doing so for weeks, apparently. Now, thanks to her impetuous marriage proposal, he'd probably start breakfasting elsewhere to avoid the awkwardness. Which would be for the best. Especially if she managed to convince Elmer Beekman to take his place, a prospect that didn't sit as well with her as it once had.

After her conversation with Mr. Hamilton yesterday, and their discussion of *intimacies*, Abigail just couldn't picture anyone other than him as her husband. Especially not Mr. Beekman and his breath of doom. But if Mr. Hamilton's night had been anything like hers, he was probably questioning why he'd ever considered her offer in the first place.

Whenever Abigail had awakened during the night, which had been *far* too often, she'd prayed. At first she'd begged God to convince Mr. Hamilton to agree to her scheme. Then, as the night grew darker and her doubts and insecurities grew louder, she'd asked him simply to save her bakery. When morning came and she rose exhausted from a restless night of little sleep and no reassurances, her petitions deteriorated to a humble plea that God provide a way for her and Rosalind to survive.

"Look!" her sister exclaimed as she leaned close to the window. "Here he comes now . . . wait." Her smile dimmed. "That's not Mr. Hamilton crossing the square. It's Marshal Burton. Carrying a box of tools."

Abigail straightened. Tools? That didn't sound good.

"Unlock the door." Abigail flapped her arm at her sister as she scurried around the counter. "Hurry!"

Rosalind bustled to the shop entrance and turned the key in the lock, her face full of questions Abigail didn't have time to answer. She swept past her sister and pulled open the door.

"Marshal," she greeted, a wide smile masking the terror floundering in her chest. "We don't open for another fifteen minutes, but I'd be glad to make an exception for the man who keeps Honey Grove safe. What can I bring you? A cinnamon roll, perhaps, or a croissant?"

The lawman mounted the boardwalk in front of her shop and tipped his hat. "I'm sorry, ma'am, but I'm not here for breakfast. I've been tasked with posting a public notice stating that the Taste of Heaven Bakery is conducting business illegally and will have all operations shut down by the end of the week." His gaze softened with regret, but his eyes never flinched as he delivered the devastating news. He handed the printed notice to her to examine.

The glaring headline of *City Violation* jumped off the page in print so large that people would be able to read it from halfway across the square.

She shook her head, slowly at first, then with greater speed as reality forced its way into her numb brain. "You can't do this." She glanced up from the paper. "The council gave me until the end of the month to comply with the ordinance. My time's not up. If you post this inflammatory notice, you'll do irreparable harm to my reputation and the reputation of this bakery when I've done nothing wrong."

Marshal Burton bent sideways and set his box of tools on the boardwalk with a jangle of metal. He stuffed a few nails in his trouser pocket, then grabbed a hammer and straightened. He took the notice from her hands and laid it flat against the siding next to the door.

"If you have an issue with the notice, you can take it up with Mayor Longfellow. He's the one who gave the order. He said you had failed to communicate any plan regarding coming into compliance, so he thought it best to warn the public of the upcoming closure."

"The council never asked for any communication. They just gave me a deadline. I do have a plan in place to bring the bakery into compliance, but I need to finalize a few details first. Give me until Friday. If I haven't addressed the issue by then, you can post the notice. Posting it now would be prejudicial and malicious."

The marshal dug a nail out of his pocket and set it at the top right corner of the page. He slanted a glance at her. "Anything in this notice untrue?"

"Not precisely," Abigail hedged, "but it paints an inaccurate picture of the situation."

He shrugged and swung the hammer. It connected with a bang that sounded far too much like a nail being driven into a coffin—a death knell for her business.

"Please," she begged, taking hold of his arm. "Don't do this."

"Sorry, ma'am," he said, gently but firmly removing her hand from his arm. "It ain't my call to make. You're gonna have to take it up with the mayor."

But not before all her morning customers saw the notice and spread the tale. Even if the mayor relented, it would be too late.

❀————❀

Zach strolled up Sixth Street at a leisurely pace. At least that was what he told himself he was doing—strolling. It wasn't cowardly feet dragging if a man was simply enjoying a lovely summer morning. Zach blew out a shaky breath and tried to focus on the sunshine and the cool breeze, but every time that breeze swirled around his face and neck, he had to fight the urge to scrub at his skin. After spending most of the night tangled in a nightmare where snakelike ropes coiled around him from head to toe, he was a little on edge.

Get a grip, man. You're not marching to the gallows. Though he had to admit he'd welcome a reprieve if Miss Kemp changed her mind. He'd prayed she would let him off the hook, take the decision out of his hands, but his gut told him she wouldn't. She was fighting for her livelihood and her family. Powerful motivators. Ones Zach understood far too well. Yet he couldn't help but hope for a miracle. After all but giving her his word yesterday during their conversation, he didn't feel like he could call things off and still be a man of honor. But if the lady's wishes had changed? Well, that was an entirely different matter.

As he neared the square, a commotion outside the Taste of Heaven made him pick up his pace. Was that the marshal? What was he doing? And why was Abigail trying to pull him away from her shop?

Zach broke into a jog and pounded up the boardwalk steps.

The marshal paused his hammer mid-swing and turned to assess who approached. Apparently determining Zach wasn't an immediate threat, he continued his swing and pounded a nail deep into the bakery's siding. His sprawled hand kept Zach from being able to read the words printed on the paper the lawman was posting, but if the tears welling in Abigail's eyes were any indication, it wasn't good news.

"What you got there, Marshal?" Zach's gaze bounced from Abigail to marshal.

"A public notice," Burton said before shifting his hands so he could dig in his pocket for another nail. As his hands moved, the heading of the notice was revealed.

Zach frowned. "Violation?" His gaze swung to Abigail.

"Mayor Longfellow thinks I have no plans to comply with the city ordinance banning women from owning businesses." Her voice shook slightly, but she held her own, her eyes flashing enough fire to keep the tears at bay. "He instructed the marshal to post an inflammatory notice about my being in violation despite the fact that the deadline the council dictated is several days away. He won't take it down without the mayor's permission, but I won't be able to get in to see the mayor until after nine, and in the meantime, all my morning customers will see this—this *slander* and believe me to be unethical."

Zach slid between Abigail and the marshal. "Take it down, Burton. She has until the end of the month."

The marshal sighed and pivoted to face Zach, leaning his shoulder against the wall to keep the bottom edge of the notice from flapping in the breeze and possibly tearing free. "Look, Hamilton. It's my job to enforce the law in this town, even laws I don't particularly agree with. So unless you can change the law in the next few minutes or show me a falsehood in the document the mayor drew up, you're out of luck."

Zach hardened his jaw. "Step aside and let me read it."

The marshal eyed him as if he thought Zach might light the notice on fire or something. "I already examined it and found nothing illegal or incorrect. Neither did Miss Kemp." He tipped his head toward Abigail. "But give it your best shot." He straightened away from the wall, keeping one hand on the bottom corner of the paper to hold it in place. "Just know that if you tear it down, I'll take you in for obstruction of justice."

As much as he wanted to rip the page away, Zach knew that wasn't the way to win this round. Burton played by the rules. No bluffs. No trickery. And he held everyone else at the table to his standards. There was no room for sleight of hand or distraction techniques. A player had to rely on finesse and strong gameplay. Zach's father might have taught him how to cheat, but he'd also taught him to out-strategize anyone who came to his table. That was what Zach aimed to do.

He read the notice from beginning to end, then went back to the top, searching for a loophole, for anything he could use to convince the lawman to remove the notice. At the start of the second read, his gut clenched the way it did when instinct flared faster than reason. He jerked his gaze back up to the first line and read it a third time.

Due to a failure to comply with city ordinance . . .

. . . a failure to comply . . .

Zach turned to the bakery's owner, the winning strategy crystalizing in his mind. "That offer you proposed yesterday still on the table, Miss Kemp?"

Her eyes widened slightly, and her forehead crinkled. Her gaze moved from him to the marshal then to the notice tacked to her wall. She nodded. "It is." Her attention flew back to Zach, her light brown eyes brimming with a depth of hope that made him nervous. A woman putting such store in him was bound to end up disappointed, but perhaps not today.

"Then I accept." Zach backed away from the notice and braced his feet apart as he pivoted to face the marshal. "There you go, Burton. I found your inaccuracy. There is no longer a failure to comply on Miss Kemp's part."

The marshal raised a brow. "How do you figure? Her name's still on the deed."

Zach laid down his trump card. "But come Friday evening . . ." He cast a quick glance at his bride-to-be to make sure he'd gotten the timing right. Upon receiving her nod, he continued. ". . . she'll be carrying a man's name."

"Yours, I suppose?" Burton asked.

"Yep."

The marshal turned to Abigail. "That true, ma'am? You planning to sign your deed over to this fella?"

She glanced at Zach, her expression emitting equal parts gratitude and trepidation. Apparently, he wasn't the only one unsure about this plan. Nevertheless, she stood her ground and looked the marshal straight in the eye. "Yes, sir, I am."

Burton shook his head. "I suppose this is one of them *details* you were tellin' me about earlier?"

Abigail nodded, sidling closer to Zach. Odd how that action made him want to stand a little taller and scowl a little fiercer at the lawman who had caused her such anxiety this morning. And drawn a crowd. An amazing number of neighboring shopkeepers had decided this was the perfect time to sweep their walkways. Zach angled his body a little more perpendicular to the shop wall to block even the closest neighbor's line of sight to the notice.

"Technically, you're not in compliance until ownership changes hands," the marshal said.

Zach took a menacing step closer and opened his mouth to

argue, but Burton shot a staying glance his way and held up his hand before Zach could utter a word.

"But since the mayor's main concern was notifying the citizenry about the upcoming closure, I suppose we can forgo posting the notice if there will no longer *be* a closure."

"Oh, thank you!" Abigail beamed a smile that had her dimples flashing and Zach's gut tightening.

Burton yanked the notice down and crumpled it in his fist. He bent over, dropped his hammer into the tool box at his feet, then grabbed the handle and straightened. He pointed a finger first at Zach then at Abigail.

"I'm warning you, though. Hamilton's name better be on the deed by the end of the week, or not only will I shut down this business, I'll bring the two of you up on charges for making fraudulent claims. Understand?"

"Yes, sir." Abigail nodded then glanced at Zach.

He gave a slow nod of his own. Not slow enough to show the lawman any disrespect, but enough to let the marshal know he wouldn't be intimidated.

"All right, then. I'll be on my way." Burton tipped his hat, then set off down the boardwalk in the direction of the nosy neighbors. He gave Zach a telling look as he passed, making it clear that he'd run interference with the other shopkeepers, but it would be up to Zach to get Miss Kemp inside.

Seeing as how that matched his thought process precisely, Zach fit a hand to Abigail's lower back and steered her to the bakery door—one that opened as if by magic and closed the instant they cleared the threshold.

Rosalind Kemp released the handle and plastered her back against the door. Her face was pale, but a wobbly smile brought a touch of life to it. "Looks like we have two days to plan a wedding."

CHAPTER

11

Abigail attempted to treat Friday like any other day. She rose before dawn to knead and bake. Opened Taste of Heaven promptly at seven, served Zacharias Hamilton his sticky buns and coffee at seven thirty. Not an easy task when the delicate butterfly flutters he previously inspired had turned into a company of deranged bats swooping through her abdomen.

For the last two mornings, after their tense encounter with the marshal, they'd continued their ritual as if nothing had changed. She delivered his order, poured his coffee, and accepted his payment all without a word. He tipped his hat and nodded at her before he left, just as he always did, though she swore an added intensity heated his gaze.

Probably probing to see if she had changed her mind.

Well, she hadn't. She couldn't afford to. And truthfully, she wouldn't want to even if her bakery wasn't in jeopardy. Never would she have guessed that she could land a husband like Zacharias Hamilton. She looked forward to the shock on Sophia's face when Zach escorted her to church on Sunday. She could almost hear the sputtering disbelief now.

Yet as Abigail locked the bakery door at three that afternoon, she had to admit that she didn't want Zach as her husband simply to foil the city council or silence Sophia Longfellow's spiteful comments. She wanted Zach as her husband because she liked and respected him. And even better, she could sense his respect for her. After growing up with a father who never found her good enough because she'd been born the wrong gender, her soul thirsted for validation. A validation Zach had given when he signed her contract without a single argument about her retaining control of everything related to running the bakery. Only time would tell if his words matched his character, but he didn't seem the type to back out on his word once it was given.

Climbing the stairs to her living quarters, her stomach swirled over what was to come. In two hours, she'd be standing before a preacher with a man any woman would covet. A man she'd bribed with sticky buns, a free place to live, and the possibility of *relations*.

Good grief. What kind of foundation was she building for this marriage? Her steps stuttered, and she braced herself against the stairway wall. Doubts and second thoughts assailed her like an invisible maelstrom, churning her insides until she thought she might retch.

Then a gentle whisper echoed above the storm. *If I am the cornerstone, whatever you build will stand firm.*

A shiver passed through her, stilling her panic.

Her eyes slid closed. Yes. Jesus must be the cornerstone. That was the only way this crazy, unconventional relationship would work.

Help me, she prayed. *Help me lean on you, not on myself. Not even on Zach. Only you are strong enough to make a marriage out of a business transaction. You've already performed one miracle by convincing Zach to wed me. Now I ask for another. Let friendship grow between us so we can be true partners. Teach me how to be a blessing to him instead of a ball and chain, and give me the courage to be the wife he needs.*

Friendship. She could be content with that. The little girl inside her might crave love and fairy-tale romance, but the grown woman living in the real world knew better than to set herself up for disappointment. Friendship would be lovely. Having a man she could depend on, one who would stand by her side and support her, one she would support in return. That was what she needed. What she wanted.

Feeling more in control, Abigail straightened her posture and marched the final two steps to the landing and on to her bedroom. But when she walked through the open door and spied the bed, her confidence evaporated.

Husbands and wives shared beds. It was the natural order of things. Her parents had shared this bed before her mother passed. It had seemed big then, from a child's perspective. Now, as she stared at it, the wooden frame shrank before her eyes.

Zach would never fit. He was a large man, tall and broad. And she . . . well, she was no slender willow branch. More like a solid chunk of oak. They'd be practically on top of each other.

Abigail wagged her head back and forth, the motion growing more pronounced as reality set in. No. No, this would not do. They couldn't share the bed, wedged together like biscuits in a pan. She'd never sleep. His presence disturbed her equilibrium when an entire dining room stood between them. With nothing but a thin nightdress and perhaps a blanket to separate them, she'd likely develop some kind of nervous disorder.

"Abby, are you ready . . . oh." Rosalind flounced into the room, took one look at Abigail's face, and grasped her sister's shoulders, quickly angling her away from the bed.

Abigail tried to focus on her sister, but her mind remained in a fog of blankets and overlarge men.

Rosalind gave her a strong shake. "Abby. It's going to be fine."

At her sister's firm statement, the last of the fog cleared. "I know. It's just . . ." Her gaze shifted to the ceiling. "Everything's hitting me all at once." She sighed and tilted her chin back down to find refuge in Rosie's kind eyes. "I thought I was prepared. I have a plan, after all. It's not as if I didn't know what was coming. But . . ."

"But knowing in theory is different than knowing in experience."

"Precisely." The tension in Abigail's neck eased at her sister's words. Rosalind understood. Maybe not all the details of the situation, but she understood the gush of uncertainty.

Perhaps better than Abigail did. Abby was used to being in charge. Bending ingredients to her will, managing the business, running the family. But today, as soon as she conquered one obstacle, another appeared to lay her flat. Hadn't she just been praying in the stairwell? Was her faith really so weak that she couldn't hold on to her assurance for more than a minute? Thank God for Rosie.

Abigail pulled her sister into an embrace. "I'd be lost without you."

Rosalind returned her hug, then stepped back with an expression that warned she was ready to lecture. "You're the strongest woman I know, Abby. You'd be *fine* without me. Not that you'll be getting rid of me anytime soon," she hurried to clarify. "I plan to hang around long enough to make sure this new husband of yours behaves himself."

"That's good." Abby smiled despite the momentary panic that had stabbed her heart at the thought of her sister leaving.

It would happen one day, she knew. But today was not the day to ponder that eventuality.

"Perhaps I should move back into your room for a while," Abigail said, latching on to the notion as if it were a rope tossed to a drowning swimmer. "Zach and I need time to get comfortable with each other before we . . ." Her eyes said what her tongue couldn't, focusing back on the bed.

She and Rosie had shared a room until their father died three months ago. It would be a simple matter to resume that prior arrangement. Yet when Abigail looked to her sister for confirmation, she found reluctance instead of the automatic agreement she'd been expecting.

"If you don't want to give up your privacy," Abigail said, "I'm sure I could figure out something else."

"Of course you're welcome to bunk with me again," Rosie assured her with a bright smile.

Abigail's big sister instincts flared. That smile had been a tad *too* bright. "Are you sure? I feel like there's something you're not telling me." She clasped her sister's hand. "I've been so preoccupied lately—first with the city council, then with this crazy wedding—but I'm still your sister. Still here if you need me."

"It's nothing to worry about," Rosalind said with a wave of her hand. "I haven't been sleeping particularly well, is all. I know how important it is for you to get a good night's rest, getting up before dawn like you do. I don't want to disturb you."

Abigail probed Rosie's gaze. There was something more lingering beneath the surface, something her sister didn't feel comfortable sharing. Because she didn't want to add to Abigail's current load? Or did her desire for secrecy stem from deeper motives?

As much as Abigail wanted to press for answers, two hours before her wedding wasn't the time. She'd have to revisit this later, after things had settled a bit. And in order for things to settle in a timely fashion, she really needed to ensure her new husband had his own quarters.

"You won't disturb me," Abigail said, the tightness in her chest finally starting to loosen with the conception of a new plan. "I'll be asleep before you come to bed. You could toss and turn, and I probably wouldn't even notice." She'd been sharing a bed with Rosalind nearly her entire life, after all. Knew the sound of her breathing, the way she tended to pull the covers when she rolled, even the little rocking motions she made when she had trouble falling asleep. None of that had the power to disturb her while she slept.

But Zach? *Everything* about him had the power to disturb her.

"I have a bath drawn for you in the washroom," Rosalind said, gently changing the subject. "Go freshen up, and I'll get your dress laid out for you."

Abigail complied, grateful to leave the room—and the bed—behind. Whether she was ready or not didn't really matter at this point. She had an appointment with a preacher in less than two hours, and she wouldn't allow a few qualms about sleeping arrangements to throw off her schedule. Two hours left barely enough time to bathe, dress, fashion her hair, and walk to the Sinclair home with the cake she'd made this morning. She might not be marrying for love, but no daughter of Edward Kemp could wed without a cake.

Quit thinking and get moving, Abby.

Preparation plus performance equaled prosperity. Her father had drilled that sentiment into her head since the first day he allowed her into his kitchen, and she'd taken it to heart. Staying busy kept her focused, kept her on track in accomplishing her goals. It was during the quiet moments when doubts and insecurities crept in to poison her thoughts. Productivity provided an antidote, so she dosed herself heavily, attacking her bath with a vigor that ensured no hint of uncleanliness lingered anywhere on her person. She brushed her still-dry hair with relentless precision, counting out one hundred strokes both to occupy her mind and add shine to her tresses. Then she marched back into her room, purposely stared down her enemy clothed in a quilted counterpane, and headed for the wardrobe to retrieve her best Sunday dress.

Only her pale green walking costume with the puffed sleeves and ribbons at the hem was not hanging on the hook of the wardrobe door where she'd left it that morning to air. In its place was a confection of silk and satin in the palest pink. Silver embroidery decorated the skirt in a pattern Abigail instantly recognized.

"Do you like it?" Rosalind asked from the doorway.

Her eyes misting faster than she could blink the moisture away, Abigail turned to face her sister. "You remade Mama's wedding gown? When?"

"In the evenings after you went to bed. I've been working on it every night since you came up with this crazy scheme." Rosalind winked and strolled into the room. "It's a good thing you go to bed so early. I never would have finished otherwise."

"It's beautiful!" Abigail exclaimed as she turned back to the dress and stroked the soft fabric. "But you shouldn't have. Mama's dress was to be yours."

For a bride who was marrying for love. She didn't say the words, but they hung in the air between the sisters. Their mother might have been weak-spirited, but not even Abigail could deny that she'd loved her husband. She had literally sacrificed her life for him, and amid all the grief of dead babies and physical exhaustion, she never said an unkind word about the man she married. She was true to him to the end.

It wasn't right for Abigail to wear Mama's dress. Not when her own marriage was based on business. Besides, her mother had been slender like Rosalind. There was no way her big-boned plumpness would ever fit into it. Unless it had been drastically altered.

"Don't be silly," Rosalind said as she swept past Abigail and gently took the dress down from where it hung on the open wardrobe door. "Every bride deserves a beautiful dress." Her sister's gaze bored into Abigail's. "You only marry once, Abby, and there should be no regrets. You might be getting married in a parlor instead of a church and with a handful of witnesses instead of the packed pews you deserve, but you will have flowers and a dress and a handsome groom. Everything you need to create memories that will warm your heart twenty years from now when you look back on this day."

The sweetness of the picture Rosalind painted so overwhelmed Abigail that she couldn't speak. She hadn't allowed herself to imagine her wedding as anything other than a practical arrangement. But now—she sniffed and rubbed the tears from her cheeks with the back of her hand—now she just might have a new picture to paint.

"Let's try it on," Rosalind said, undoing the closures at the back and bunching up the skirt to fit over Abigail's head. "I made it to your measurements, but since I didn't fit it to you, there might be a few places to adjust."

The gown, of course, was perfect. No one turned a needle like Rosalind. Abigail backed up to see more of herself in the mirror above the bureau. Her sister had cleverly opened up the bodice, removing all of the material through the chest and arms that never would have contained Abigail's bounty. She'd replaced it with soft ruched silk that looked like a cloud at sunrise. Short, puffed sleeves. A scooped neckline. Plenty of gathers to cover her bosom in a way that flattered instead of making her look like a cow in need of milking.

Since their mother had been a few inches taller than her oldest daughter, Rosalind had managed to let out the waist and lift it to fit just beneath Abigail's breasts, allowing the skirt to fall in graceful lines and hide the roundness of her belly and hips. The hem didn't quite reach the floor, but that would actually be a blessing, since she'd be walking to the Sinclairs'.

Rosalind stepped back and examined the dress from top to bottom with a critical eye. "It's a little short and could use a tuck beneath the arms. Maybe a—"

"Stop." Abigail laughed in delight. "It's gorgeous. I've never worn a dress so fine."

Rosalind grinned. "You do look beautiful, sis."

"Thanks to your genius with a needle."

"No," Rosalind argued, "it's all you. I just provided the frame."

Determined not to cry a second time, Abigail took refuge once again in tackling what needed to be done. "Let's get to work on my hair."

Forty-five minutes later, with a coat covering her beautiful dress and enough pins in her hair to hold her tresses steady even in a gale-force wind, Abigail stepped out into the alley behind the bakery with her cake box in hand and her sister at her side.

A masculine throat cleared nearby. Abigail looked sharply to her right and found Reuben Sinclair standing near the bakery's back wall.

He doffed his hat and made a sweeping gesture with his arm. "Your carriage awaits, milady."

A roughhewn buckboard stood in the street at the end of the alley. Tall, sturdy, and built to carry loads of lumber, not brides in fancy gowns. But to Abigail, it couldn't have looked finer had it been gilded with gold.

She'd been dreading the walk, dreading the chance of being stopped and questioned. A keen observer would note the unusual style of her hair and could easily spy the hem of her dress beneath her coat. Most people would probably be more concerned with their own business than that of a random passerby, but if Sophia Longfellow caught sight of her, Abigail would be sunk. Reuben Sinclair had just removed that possibility.

"How kind of you, sir." Abigail smiled with genuine delight. "A ride in your carriage sounds lovely."

The lumberman gave her a sheepish look as he took the cake box from her and offered his arm. "My wife insisted."

"Your wife is a wise woman," Rosalind said as the three of them made their way to the buckboard.

"That she is." Reuben carefully set the cake box in the back, then handed Rosalind up first, allowing Abigail to sit on the outside, where her dress would be less likely to be crushed.

The ride to the Sinclair home took barely five minutes, yet it felt like days. Abigail had trouble gauging their progress, since she kept her gaze downcast to avoid making eye contact with anyone milling about town, and every time she glanced up, she was amazed at how little ground they'd covered. They eventually arrived at their destination, however, and Audrey Sinclair greeted her at the door. She showered Abigail with smiles and compliments as she ushered her into the parlor. At their entrance, the two men seated inside rose to their feet. She knew the older one must be Brother Samuelson, the minister, but she couldn't pull her gaze away from Zach to verify.

His gaze had melded with hers the instant she crossed the threshold, and for a moment, Abigail forgot to breathe. He was dressed in a black suit coat and trousers, a white shirt visible at his neck above a black vest. Whiskers from a day's growth of beard shadowed his jawline, giving him a rugged appearance.

He didn't say a word. Just stared at her. Yet his attention didn't make her feel self-conscious. All she felt was warm.

Of course, the warmth might be due to the fact that she was still wearing her coat.

Her hands moved to the buttons, and her lashes dipped to veil her eyes from his. She worked the first button free, then the second, but a commotion from outside stalled her progress. A loud knocking. Persistent. Pounding.

"Zach!" a muffled voice called. A *female* voice. "Zach, are you in there?"

A groan echoed from the man across the room, but Abigail was more concerned with who was outside. The woman seemed awfully determined. As if she had some prior claim to Abigail's groom. A knot twisted in Abigail's belly, and her hands fell away from her coat. Turning her back on Zach, she stepped into the hall in time to see Audrey Sinclair open the front door.

A beautiful auburn-haired woman thrust her way inside, took one look at the people gathered in their finery, and threw her arms wide. "Stop the wedding!"

Zach stalked out of the parlor and into the hall to confront his sister. This was exactly why he hadn't wired her until this morning about the wedding. Well, this and the fact that he wasn't completely sure the ceremony would actually take place. But when Abigail gave no indication at breakfast that she planned to back out, he'd sent the telegram. Evie never would have forgiven him if he'd kept such information to himself, and she'd already forgiven him for more than he deserved, so he wasn't about to press his luck.

Evie wrote to him every week, keeping him up-to-date on family matters and pestering him about writing more often. He made a point to write once a month, not that he had much to say. His letters rarely contained more than a paragraph or two. Lumber work just wasn't that riveting, and it wasn't as if he had a social life to report on. Usually he spent the majority of his letter talking about Reuben and his brood. He guessed that would change once he gained a wife and sister-in-law. Maybe, if he was really lucky, he could convince Abigail to take over the correspondence for him. Females were better at that sort of thing, anyway. 'Course, most females didn't run a bakery on their own. He probably shouldn't ask for that favor just yet.

"Quit causin' a scene, Evie," he groused as he wove between the spectators to reach his sister. He braced himself for either a hug or a swat, both reactions equally likely to occur. The swat came first.

Evie's palm bounced off his bicep, her blue eye shooting sparks at him even as her brown eye warmed in welcome. They hadn't seen each other in over a year, and Zach had to admit that he felt a nearly irresistible urge to wrap her in a bear hug. Not that he would. One Hamilton making a scene was plenty.

"I wouldn't have been forced to rely on such theatrics if you had given me more than a few hours' notice that you were getting married. *Married*, Zach! And I almost missed it." Her forehead creased, and her gaze darted to the parlor doorway and back, her haunted look piercing his hide. "I *didn't* miss it, did I?"

All right. Maybe he should have given her a little extra notice. But he'd told her she didn't have to come, that it was more of a business partnership than an actual marriage. As if that would matter to Evie—the girl who put family above everything. He should have known his little sister would move heaven and earth to get here in time.

"Nah. You didn't miss it."

A smile broke out across her face bright enough to light the entire house. "Good! Because there's no way I'd let you get married without your family by your side."

That was when the hug hit. Evie hurled herself at him, forcing him to catch her. It was a trick she'd been using since she was a kid to get him to hold her, since he wasn't exactly the affectionate sort. Although when he wrapped his arms around her, a warmth infused his chest he hadn't realized he'd missed.

"Ah, Zach? You gonna introduce us to your company?" Reuben

sounded as though he were stifling a laugh. At Zach's expense, of course.

Zach set Evie away from him and turned to his best friend, only to catch a glimpse of Abigail from the corner of his eye. A very pale Abigail who looked as if someone had just stolen her bakery out from under her.

Zach's gaze zipped past Reuben to land on the face of his bride, though her attention seemed fixed on Evie, not him. "This is my sister, Evangeline Fowler."

Abigail blinked a couple times, then finally managed to meet his eyes. Her brows arched in question, even as her expression warmed with an ember of hope. "Your sister?"

"Yep." Zach jabbed a thumb in the direction of the front door without really looking at the man standing just inside. "And that fella over there's her husband, Logan."

Abigail's attention darted toward the doorway, a hint of dimple finally coming out of hiding.

"Don't forget me." Zach's adopted brother, Seth, pushed past Logan and slipped through the mingling crowd.

"Seth!" Zach grinned and held out his hand even as he scanned his brother with a critical eye for any sign of distress. Seth's asthma had nearly killed him as a kid. A couple times as an adult too. Thankfully, he seemed healthy enough at present, though Zach couldn't help but start cataloguing anything in the house that might cause an attack to flare up. Old habits died hard.

Seth gripped Zach's hand and pulled him in close to slap his back. "Good to see you, Zach."

"You too. How's Christie?" Zach asked as they separated.

"Glowing." Seth grinned, and Zach swore his brother's chest puffed out an extra inch or two. "Another month, and you'll be an uncle."

"Hard to believe." Zach had gotten a little practice playing uncle with Archie, the baby brother of Seth's wife, who'd come to live with them before Zach left the homestead in Pecan Gap, but the thought of Seth actually having a kid of his own—well, it made Zach feel like maybe he hadn't completely screwed up Seth's and Evie's futures.

As good as it was to see his family, and as much as he wanted to catch up with them and revel in the reunion, this moment wasn't just about him. He held out a hand to Abigail. "Seth, Evie . . . Logan," he added as an afterthought when Evie's husband came up behind her and placed a possessive hand at her waist. Zach and Logan shared a complicated past, but like it or not, the man was family now. "This is Abigail. My bride."

Her hand slid into his, and the feel of her skin on his roughened palm sent a surge of possessiveness stabbing through him. He tightened his hold and drew her into the circle of his family. After today, she'd be part of this circle, too.

"Hello," she said, her voice quiet and a touch shy, making him want to wrap his arm around her and offer shelter.

"I'm delighted to meet you, Abigail." Evie smiled wide and bright, though her face held a trace of trepidation as well. Usually when people met Evie for the first time, her mismatched eyes spooked them. One dark brown, the other vividly blue. It could be a tad unnerving. Zach would have warned Abigail so she'd be prepared, but he hadn't expected Evie to show up tonight.

He snuck a peek at Abigail's face from the corner of his eye. Thankfully he saw no judgment or discomfort. Only a touch of nervousness, which was to be expected when meeting a sister-in-law for the first time.

"Zach has told me a little about how you came to be a family," Abigail said, her smile bringing those dimples to the party again. "I look forward to getting to know each of you." She smiled at Seth and Logan in turn, her confidence growing. "Let me introduce you to my sister, Rosalind. Rosie?" Abigail craned her neck around. "Come meet your new family."

As Rosalind stepped forward to greet the newcomers, Evie poked Zach in the side and whispered, "I like her."

Zach said nothing, but his chest expanded—much, he imagined, like Seth's had earlier.

I like her too.

After a quarter hour of introductions and a surplus of chatting that had no end in sight, Zach prodded the minister to get on with things. Brother Samuelson made some quip about an eager groom, eliciting a chuckle from the room and a blush from the bride, but it did the trick. People starting milling into the parlor.

The preacher took his place by the hearth, and Zach moved to stand beside him. He turned to locate Abigail and promptly lost his grip on his jaw. It hung loose from its joists as Zach absorbed the beauty of the woman before him.

She had removed her coat and handed it to her sister, accepting a small bouquet of bright pink flowers from Reuben's wife and giving Zach his first unobstructed view of her wedding finery. His practical, businesswoman bride looked like a princess from a storybook.

Zach forced his jaw closed and managed a swallow despite the rapidly shrinking collar at his throat. He'd known she was pretty, but this? This woman was fit for a prince, and he—well, he was fit for mucking a prince's stables.

"Smile, idiot, before you scare her off," Reuben muttered from somewhere to Zach's left.

Smile. Yeah, he could do that. Maybe.

Zach's lips twitched, but the effort must have fallen short, for when Abigail reached his side, she lifted up on tiptoes to whisper in his ear. "There's a back door through the kitchen if you want to make a run for it."

She smiled, and his tension evaporated. He reached out, captured her hand, and fit her palm into the crook of his arm. "No one's gonna be running anywhere, Miss Kemp."

He might not be ideal husband material, but his daddy had taught him never to question good fortune. You just snatched it up when it was in front of you and did your best not to lose it in the next hand.

Zach nodded to Brother Samuelson. "We're ready."

The preacher did his duty and spat out all the necessary words. A bucketful of unnecessary ones as well, but Zach endured without fidgeting too much. Abigail's hand on his arm made the pontification bearable.

At the appropriate time, he promised to stick by her for better or worse, to cherish her, and to keep himself faithful unto her for all his days. Abigail did the same, even agreeing to obey him when the minister insisted, though she added a caveat of obeying "in domestic matters" under her breath that only the three of them heard, making Samuelson raise a brow and Zach cough to cover an ill-timed laugh.

Then came time for the ring. *Please, God, let it fit.* The last thing he wanted to do was embarrass his bride on her wedding day. Too small, and he wouldn't be able to get it on her finger. Too large, and he'd insult her.

Zach reached into his trouser pocket and pulled out the smooth gold band he'd purchased that afternoon. He'd studied Abigail's hands the past couple mornings when she served him breakfast in her shop, taking her measure as best he could without actually touching her. She had strong, working hands. Capable fingers. Wider than her sister's but thinner than his own meaty paws. In the end, he'd decided to purchase a band that fit the widest part of his smallest finger.

Holding his breath when the minister directed him to place

the ring on her finger, Zach slipped it past the first knuckle. He had to muscle it over her second knuckle, which brought a film of perspiration to his brow as doubts jabbed at him, but once the ring made it over the mountain, it slid into the valley with no resistance. Silently thanking God for answering his prayer, he let out the breath he'd been holding and spoke the required words. "With this ring, I thee wed."

"I now pronounce you husband and wife." Brother Samuelson grinned his approval. "What therefore God hath joined together, let not man put asunder."

Zach set his jaw at the preacher's words. No man would be putting anything asunder in this marriage. He guarded what was his, and as of this moment, Abigail Kemp was his.

"You may kiss your bride."

Abigail's eyes widened slightly as Zach bent his head. He hated that their first kiss was up for public consumption, but if she expected him to give her a polite buss on the cheek, she was fixin' to be disappointed.

He wanted no doubt in anyone's mind, especially his new wife's, that this marriage was real. So he cupped her face between his hands, burrowed his fingers into the fancy hairdo at the back of her head, and slanted his mouth over hers.

CHAPTER

13

Abigail's pulse hiccupped as Zach lowered his face toward hers, and when their lips touched—mercy, but her knees nearly buckled. He was kissing her. Honest-to-goodness kissing. As if he meant it. As if this marriage were something more than a business arrangement. As if he actually had feelings for her.

His hands on her face held her upright. Strong. Insistent. Yet tender at the same time. And when his fingers moved through her hair, shivers coursed down her neck and over her shoulders. For the first time in her life, she felt beautiful. Desired.

By Zacharias Hamilton.

Leaning into him, she kissed him back. His hold on her shifted, gentled, even as his kiss deepened.

Until the clapping started. And the hooting. And the whistling.

By the time Zach pulled away, Abigail's cheeks smoldered. She tried to hide by ducking her head, but Zach tucked her arm into the crook of his and forced her around to face the gathering.

Brother Samuelson's voice rang out behind them. "I now present to you Mr. and Mrs. Zacharias Mitchell Hamilton."

Mrs. Zacharias Hamilton. The name felt surreal. But where had the *Mitchell* come from? Zach's middle name? She'd never attended a wedding where the groom's middle name was used in the pronouncement. She slanted a questioning look at her new husband, but he was too busy dragging her over to the well-wishers to notice.

She had so much to learn. About him. About his family. She slanted another glance at him, her tongue darting out to moisten her lips. About how to kiss properly.

Would he be expecting such liberties on a regular basis? Anticipation swirled in her belly. She wouldn't be opposed to a few kisses every now and then. Not if the sample she'd received was an accurate indicator of what could be expected in the future.

Fortunately, now was not the time to ponder her new husband's expectations in regard to physical intimacies. Family and friends waited to celebrate, and heaven knew Abigail could use the distraction.

As the men circled around Zach and engaged in a raucous round of backslapping, the women flocked to Abigail and spirited her off to the kitchen, where aprons were passed around and food was set out.

Being in the kitchen settled Abigail's nerves as nothing else could. Audrey Sinclair tried to stick her in a corner, claiming the bride should not be allowed to work, but Abigail insisted. She sliced cheese, poured water, and set platters on the table. Basically any task with a low probability of soiling her dress. While Audrey finished frying the potatoes and Rosalind made fresh coffee, Abigail unboxed her cake and started slicing.

"That looks delicious," Evie declared, coming up beside her. "Do you use a boiled icing or an unboiled one?"

Abigail smiled. "Unboiled. But I do melt the chocolate ahead of time. It incorporates better than grated chocolate."

"I'll have to remember that."

Pausing with her knife above the cake, Abigail glanced at her new sister-in-law. "Does Zach like chocolate?" She hated admitting that she didn't know the answer to that question, but she needed to start learning his preferences sometime. Having his sister at hand afforded the perfect opportunity. "The cake itself is white, but chocolate just seemed to fit him better."

As if a man's coloring determined his flavor preferences. She gave her head a tiny shake. Perhaps she'd been working in the bakery too long, matching people with food based on appearances.

"I'm not sure." Evie shrugged. "We rarely had chocolate around the house growing up. But if you made it, I'm sure he'll love it." She touched Abigail's shoulder and grinned. She really was a cheerful sort. And those eyes—so expressive. Abigail found it hard not to stare.

Forcing her attention back to the cake, Abigail brought the knife down for the next cut. "Will you be in town long? I'd love the chance to visit with you. To learn more about your brother." She lowered her voice. "You might not realize, but our marriage is a bit . . . unconventional. We haven't actually courted, so beyond his preference for sticky buns, his skill with lumber, and his penchant for rescuing bakers in distress, I really know very little about him." Pulling the knife from the cake, she pivoted to face Evie. "I want to be a good wife to him. I swear I'm not just using him to get out of a bind." Shame bent her gaze downward. "Well, I am, but—"

A hand on her arm stopped her rambling. Slowly, Abigail lifted her face to meet the vivid eyes of the woman before her.

"I've prayed for you," Evie said. "For more than a year now."

Abigail's brow scrunched. More than a year? How was that

even possible? She'd never met Evangeline Fowler before today, and judging by the commotion Evie made when she first arrived, Zach's sister hadn't known about her brother's nuptials until this morning.

Evie laughed at her consternation. "Oh, I might not have known your name, but God did." She smiled and pulled two chairs from the table, then motioned for Abigail to sit. "Ever since Logan came into my life, and Christie into Seth's, I've pleaded with the Lord to bring the right woman into Zach's life as well." Her expression softened. "He gave up his future to take care of us when we were kids. He made sacrifice after sacrifice to ensure we had food to eat and a place to lay our heads." She met Abigail's gaze. "Some of those sacrifices carried prices he's still paying."

Abigail wanted to ask. Heavens, how she wanted to ask. But a crowded kitchen with children rambling about wasn't the place. And really, the story should come from her husband, not his sister. Perhaps in time . . .

"You," Evie pronounced with a tap to Abigail's knee, "are the answer to those prayers."

Abigail started to shake her head, but Evie stopped her with a wagging finger.

"Nope. No arguments. I asked the Lord to bring the right woman into Zach's life, and He brought you. Therefore, *you* are the right woman. Never doubt it."

Could it possibly be true? In Abigail's selfish quest to find a husband to save her bakery, had Providence brought her into the life of a man who needed *her* as a wife? Abigail's chin came up a notch, the idea shifting her perspective and planting a sense of purpose in her heart.

If Zach needed her as much as she needed him, well, that opened an entire realm of possibilities.

Abigail reached for Evie's hand. "You *are* staying a few days, right? I have a hundred questions for you."

Zach's sister laughed. "I'd love nothing better than to tell stories on Zach all weekend, but I'm afraid we're heading back to Pecan Gap in the morning. Seth refuses to be away from Christie for more than one night." She leaned forward, a twinkle shining in her blue eye. "She's expecting their first baby."

"How wonderful!" Abigail smiled even as her spine sagged in disappointment. She was venturing into an unknown country, and the most experienced guide available was leaving her to flounder about on her own.

"You ladies ready for me to call the men?" Audrey Sinclair shot the question over her shoulder while sliding sizzling potato slices onto an already heaping platter.

No! I need more time. But, of course, that wasn't what Abigail said. She rose from her chair, smiled, and resumed slicing the cake. "Sure."

Audrey sent her daughter Dinah to fetch the men from the parlor, and voices soon echoed through the hall as the herd approached.

Evie stood and leaned in close. "I will give you one piece of advice, though."

Abigail turned her head, cake forgotten. "What?"

"Don't expect him to tell you how he feels," Evie murmured, glancing toward the doorway as the voices increased in volume. "Look for his feelings in his actions. That's where they live." The men poured into the kitchen, and Evie waved to her husband. "Zach's more of a grunter than a sharer," she said in parting, "but don't let that fool you. His heart is as big as they come."

Abigail knew he had a big heart. He never would have let

her talk him into this arrangement if he didn't. But would she ever be able to claim a piece of that heart as her own?

She stared at the man standing just inside the door, the man chatting with a brother he'd obviously missed, yet a man who also seemed to sense her regard, for he turned his head and pinned her with his dark blue eyes.

Her skin tingled, her stomach danced, but she held his gaze. She expected one of his nods, like the ones he gave her when leaving the bakery—acknowledgment with just a hint of personal connection—but instead of dipping his chin, he moved his feet in her direction.

Belly tightening, she turned back to her cake and positioned her knife, even though plenty had already been sliced.

"You make it?" The warm, masculine voice of her new husband rumbled close to her ear.

She pasted on a smile as she lifted her head to face him. "Yes."

Goodness, he was close. Bare inches separated them. She jerked her attention back to the cake, her hand trembling slightly as she moved the knife to cut the last piece. With all the guests cramming inside, the kitchen had grown crowded. When little Ephraim wiggled his way through the guests' legs to get to his mama by the stove, Zach bumped up against Abigail. The contact was brief but sufficient to scorch her with memories of his touch on her face. His kiss.

"Can I have some?" he asked.

She spun to face him, knife still in hand.

He dodged backward. "Whoa. Easy there." Gently, he circled her wrist with one hand and extracted the cutlery from her with the other. "I didn't think having dessert before supper was a fatal request." His lips twitched slightly. "Guess I can wait 'til afterward like the rest of 'em."

Cake. Of course. He'd been talking about cake. Not kisses.

She brazened a smile. "Sorry about that. I'm a little jumpy."

He raised a brow. *A little?*

She shrugged, silently conceding the point. "I think it would be permissible for the groom to receive special treatment on his wedding day." Something flashed in his eyes, but she ignored it. Her imagination had gotten her into more than enough trouble already. Reclaiming the knife that Zach had placed on the table after confiscating it, she slid the flat of the blade under the widest piece of cake and moved it to a nearby plate. "Just don't let the children catch you, or Audrey will rap your knuckles." She collected a fork and handed over the dessert.

"I'll hide over here in the corner." He moved around the table to a spot a few strides away against the wall. Fitting his back into the corner's crease, he sliced off a large piece of cake and lifted it to his mouth.

As people milled closer to the table and started filling plates, hiding seemed like an excellent notion. With no appetite to speak of, Abigail picked up one of the glasses of water she'd filled earlier, then abandoned her post by the cake and moved to assist Zach in holding up the far wall.

"Good cake," he said as he shoved another bite into his mouth.

She guessed that meant he liked chocolate. Abigail grinned to herself. He made no further effort at conversation, and she was glad. It was nice just to stand next to him without worrying about what to say.

Although there was one question she'd been pondering. Something a wife should know about her husband. "Is Mitchell your middle name?"

The bite of cake must have lodged in his windpipe, for he suddenly started coughing. Much like he had when she'd first proposed, as a matter of fact.

Alarmed, Abigail took the plate from him and pressed her water glass into his hand. "Here. Drink this." She worked a hand between him and the wall and thumped his back.

Apparently her husband was allergic to marriage proposals and personal questions. He'd managed to overcome his marriage allergy right enough, so hopefully he'd recover from the questions as well. Because there was a whole bucketful waiting for answers, and she didn't intend to remain ignorant.

CHAPTER

14

Zach guzzled every last drop of water from the glass his new wife handed him, needing the time to compose an appropriate response. One that would answer her question without opening up his past for further investigation.

"Are you all right?" Abigail touched his arm.

He nodded, taking quick stock of the rest of the room. No one else seemed to have noticed his episode, or at least they were putting up a good front of being unaware. Except Logan, who was chuckling under his breath. At least until Evie smacked him with the back of her hand. Sisters did have their uses.

Gripping the empty drinking glass, Zach ran the pad of his thumb over the rim, memories assailing him. Riverboats. Orphan trains. A sacrifice he'd never deserve. "Mitchell's the surname I was born with," he finally admitted. No need to go into more detail about his sire. A famous riverboat gambler as a father might impress saloon rats, but it wasn't exactly the heritage a proper woman like Abigail would appreciate. "Hamilton's the name Evie, Seth, and I adopted when we became a family. It was the name of Evie's blood brother who died in the derailment."

"Derailment?" Abigail's brown eyes exuded compassion, but Zach wouldn't be drawn in. The fewer details he offered, the better. She might feel pity for a bunch of orphans surviving on their own, but her charity would shrivel and die if she learned all he'd done to aid that survival. Better to turn her soft heart in another direction.

"Orphan train." Zach dropped his gaze to his boots. He didn't like to think of that day. The broken glass. The blood. The wrong boy dead. "Hamilton saved my life in the crash." He rumbled his throat to clear out the thickness. "Made me promise to watch out for his sister. So I did." Not always in the way Hamilton would have wanted, Zach knew, but he'd done his best. "Evie's a Fowler now, and Seth reverted to Jefferson when he married, but I want to keep Hamilton. Honor the kid who saved my life." And hide the man he didn't want to be.

"So you use both names." A practical statement from a practical woman. He hadn't realized how much he appreciated that side of her until now. She understood without the frills of emotion flapping around and distracting from the core truth. She simply nodded as if his choice to carry a name that didn't belong to him made perfect sense.

He met her gaze. "I keep both for legal purposes, but my name is Hamilton. *Our* name is Hamilton."

A dusky pink flushed her cheeks at the possessive tone of his voice. The force of the statement had surprised him as well, but he didn't regret it. She needed to know where he stood. Vows had been spoken. Abigail was bound to him now, and he to her. Yes, they had some details to iron out between them, but time would work out the wrinkles.

He hoped.

Because if it was left up to him, things might stay bumpy. He wasn't exactly one of them smooth lothario types who could put a woman at ease with a pretty compliment and gallant manners. Though he did have a knack for planing lumber until it leveled enough to be useful. Zach stood a little straighter. Charm and flattery made flimsy building materials for crafting a life with someone. Much better to use something with actual substance. Most women cared more about flocked wallpaper than the hidden beams supporting it, but hopefully his practical little baker would prove an exception.

Brother Samuelson skirted the food table and made his way toward them, Bible tucked under his arm.

Abigail stepped forward to greet the preacher. "Thank you for a lovely ceremony, Parson. And on such short notice. I hope we didn't interfere with your schedule too badly."

"Not at all." He smiled at Abigail, then slanted an arch look at Zach.

The two of them had engaged in a rather vigorous *discussion* about the rushed nature of the wedding. Samuelson had expressed several qualms. In fact, he'd refused to perform the ceremony at first, but Zach had explained the need for haste and given his promise to provide for and protect the Kemp sisters. That assurance, plus the grilling the preacher had dished out for the next quarter hour, finally convinced Samuelson to reconsider. He'd shoved a heap of scripture at Zach about weaker vessels and one flesh and loving one's wife as Christ did the church, then promised to keep the wedding secret and appear at the appointed time. The look he aimed at Zach clearly insinuated that he'd held up his end of the bargain. Now it was Zach's turn.

Samuelson refocused his attention on Abigail. "Joining lives together in holy wedlock is one of my favorite duties. So much hope for the future."

"Well, we appreciate you officiating." She dipped her chin,

then jerked it back up as if she'd just hooked an elusive fish. "Can I fix you a plate, Parson? Surely you'll stay and eat. It's the least we can offer in compensation."

Not really, Zach mused. He'd already paid the preacher handsomely not only to enact the hitching but to deliver proof to the city council so there'd be no doubt that Abigail had met the terms of their ridiculous ultimatum. He and Abigail had a meeting scheduled at the bank Monday morning, as well, to add his name to the bakery's deed. The council would have no leg to stand on after tonight.

"Thank you for the offer, Mrs. Hamilton, but I promised my wife to be home for supper."

Mrs. Hamilton. That was going to take some getting used to—having a missus. Hearing his name attached to someone other than a sibling. Not that he minded sharing his name with Abigail. He respected the spunky not-afraid-to-do-what-had-to-be-done-to-protect-her-family woman. Understood the impulse, the determination. Oh, and she wasn't too hard on the eyes either.

"I'll stop by the mayor's office on my way home," the preacher intoned in a lower voice. "Let him inspect the marriage license while I testify to the validity of the union."

Abigail looked dismayed. "The mayor?" She turned to Zach, her eyes pleading. "Couldn't we . . . send a note or something to one of the aldermen instead? No need to bother the mayor tonight."

Why was she in such a dither? She was the one under the deadline. "Any other council member would still have to report to the mayor. I figured it'd be better to cut out the middle man and go straight to the fellow in charge."

The preacher aimed a solicitous look at Abigail. "Would you prefer I wait, ma'am?"

She nibbled her lower lip for a moment, then shook her head. "No. My husband is correct. It's much more efficient to inform Mayor Longfellow directly."

So why did she look so doggone depressed by the idea?

"Thank you for tending to the errand for us, Brother Samuelson," she said.

The preacher bobbed his head. "My honor, ma'am." He pivoted and offered Zach his hand. "See you in church on Sunday."

He had a surprisingly strong grip for a fellow who made his living with his mouth. Zach firmed up his shake, making it clear he wouldn't be dictated to, even by a preacher man. He'd be in church, but not because the minister expected it. He and the Almighty had a rocky relationship, but the Big Man had proven he could be trusted. Zach's backside would warm the pew because he owed it to the God who'd seen him through hard times, not because Samuelson wielded guilt like a soldier did a sword.

Just to be contrary, Zach left the comment hanging and his grip clenching. Samuelson didn't back down, though. He probed Zach's gaze as if trying to see into his soul. Zach tensed.

"We'll be there," Abigail assured the preacher, casting Zach a curious glance before turning her dimples on Samuelson. No man could resist those. Including preachers, it seemed.

The minister released Zach's hand and sketched a small bow in Abigail's direction. "Excellent. See you then."

Zach felt the weight of his wife's attention, of questions hanging in the air between them—questions he'd prefer not to answer. At least not here. So, like any good card player whose gut told him a bluff wouldn't win the hand, he folded and left the table. Or escaped *to* the table, in his case.

"Gonna get some food." He strode past Abigail without meeting her gaze. It wasn't cowardly; it was strategic. At least that was what he told himself as he started piling his plate full of potatoes, ham, and other items the ladies had set out for consumption.

Thankfully, his wife didn't remain abandoned for long. As soon as he moved to the food table, her sister scurried over to fill the vacancy. Almost as if she'd been waiting for an opening.

His own urge to hide dissolved as his wife and sister-in-law put their heads together and whispered between furtive glances cast in his direction. What were they discussing?

Zach stepped toward them, only to be waylaid by Logan offering his congratulations.

"Finally found a woman willing to put up with you, huh?" Logan thumped Zach's shoulder blade, nearly sending his freshly piled potatoes cascading to the floor. "Smart of you to snatch her up before she changed her mind."

Zach grunted in response, earning a chuckle from Evie's husband.

"Smooth talker." Logan smirked. "No wonder you swept her off her feet."

"Shut up, Fowler." Zach cast a glance his wife's way. She nodded at something her sister said, and Rosalind immediately cut a swath through the crowd, heading for the door.

What was going on? Why would Rosalind leave her sister's wedding celebration?

The only one with answers was making her way into the main part of the kitchen, where the majority of the guests had gathered. Zach moved to intercept, but his brother-in-law stepped into his path.

"Eva wanted me to check with you about accommodations," Logan said.

Zach bit off a growl as Abigail stopped to talk to Audrey Sinclair, who stood at the dry sink, stacking dishes. His wife added his cake plate to the pile, but not before lifting the last bite into her mouth. She took a moment to scrape the remaining icing off the plate too and licked it off the fork. The same fork he'd used. His chest clenched. It was stupid to notice, to care about something so inconsequential. He and his siblings had shared more than utensils in those rough early years. Yet her sharing his plate and fork felt intimate somehow. It was something families did, not business partners.

"Zach?" Logan's voice cut into his thoughts. "Accommodations?"

Right.

"You can stay at my place." His rent was paid up through the end of next month, since his plans for the future at the time of payment had not included accepting a marriage proposal. Going from confirmed bachelor to pronounced husband in less than a week left a few ripples in a man's pond. "Seth can make a pallet on the floor."

Logan leaned in close. "She's going to want details, you know."

Of course Evie wanted details. Not that Zach had many to give. But his sister wouldn't be satisfied with anything short of the full story.

"I know you'll be occupied elsewhere tonight," Logan said, pitching his voice low, "but she hoped to corner you in the morning before we skip town."

"Have her stop by the lumberyard." Weary of his least favorite brother-in-law—no contest, since the only other fella with the title was four-year-old Archie, who knew better than to stick his nose where it didn't belong—Zach thumped Logan on the shoulder and sought out his wife.

An hour later, the food had disappeared and the conversation had lulled, cuing Zach to make an exit. Audrey had already snuck away to put the younger children to bed, and Rosalind had never returned after her abrupt departure, so all of Abigail's support had deserted her. Evie headed her direction, no doubt intending to fill the gap, but Zach didn't want her pressing Abigail for the details she craved. His sister could grill him all she wanted, but he didn't want her saying anything to make Abigail uncomfortable.

Besides, he'd already spotted his wife stifling two yawns. She was tuckered out. Hadn't eaten anything, either. He'd have to see about making her a sandwich or something when they got back to her place. *Their* place, he corrected. The rooms above the Taste of Heaven Bakery belonged to him now too.

Decision made, Zach marched up to Abigail and captured her hand. "Time to go, wife."

Abigail's eyes widened slightly, and her throat worked as she swallowed. Evie aimed one of her baby kitten scowls at him, but he ignored her, choosing to focus on his bride instead.

She smiled an apology at his sister even as she stepped closer to him. Choosing him. Accepting him. Even when he sounded like a growling bear.

"Please stop by the bakery before you leave town tomorrow," Abigail urged. "Family eats free."

Evie grinned. "We will. Thank you."

They made their good-byes to the rest of the gathering, then finally escaped into the quiet of the evening. At half-past seven, the sun hung low but still lit the sky. Zach helped Abigail into the lumber wagon, his small trunk of belongings already stashed in the back.

Neither spoke on the way to the bakery, which suited Zach

just fine. He'd had enough yapping in the past couple hours to last him a week. Though he wouldn't mind a few hints about what was going through his wife's mind.

Was she quiet because she liked the peace, or was she scared of what he might do when they got home? On their wedding night. He'd promised not to press her for any relations until she was ready, and he was a man of his word. So she shouldn't be worried. But then, how would she know if his word meant anything until he proved it to be solid? It wasn't like he could offer references or anything.

Thankfully the ride was a short one—his brain couldn't take much more of the guess-what-your-new-wife-is-thinking game—and he parked the wagon behind the bakery and helped Abigail down. She looked real pretty all spruced up, sneaking shy glances his way. Made a man wish he hadn't made promises to wait. But he had, so he would.

He moved to the side of the wagon, collected his trunk, and hefted it to his shoulder. "I'll take this inside, then return the rig to Reuben." That would give her time to get comfortable having him in her home.

"All right." She strolled to the back door and opened it wide, making it easier for him to enter. She then led the way upstairs, and they met Rosalind in the hall.

"Everything's in order," Rosalind reported, her hair a bit mussed and her fancy dress traded in for a plainer one. She cast a quick glance at Zach, then disappeared into a small bedroom to his right.

Not quite sure what to make of that, he held his tongue and followed Abigail to a larger room to the left. A room, he was relieved to see, that held a bed big enough for two. They might not have a customary wedding night planned, but he'd been looking forward to sleeping next to his wife. Even if she insisted on stuffing some kind of bolster between them. They'd still be close, and *close* would be needed if he hoped to woo her over to the more intimate side of marriage.

"You can place your belongings in here." Abigail stepped inside the room and held the door for him as he entered.

He set his trunk at the foot of the bed and glanced at the bureau across from the bed and the wardrobe to the left. Not a trinket in sight. He knew Abigail was a practical woman, but even a practical woman had brushes and hairpins and such, right?

"Make use of any drawers you like," she said.

He turned to her. *Any* drawers?

She started backing out of the room. "I'll be sharing Rosalind's room. A man needs his privacy, after all. His space." She dipped her chin, clearly aware that privacy was the last thing a husband wanted on his wedding night. "All of my things are already moved, so make use of whatever you like."

She waved her hand at the furnishings, but his gaze never wandered from her eyes. At least he knew what the sister had run off to do.

He stalked toward her. She retreated into the doorway.

"I usually retire around eight o'clock," she babbled, "since I get up at four to prep the ovens and prepare the sweet breads. I wouldn't want to disturb you." She backed into the hallway.

He wasn't about to let her get away. Not without some kind of understanding between them. He lengthened his stride and caught her about the waist.

Abigail's palms flattened against his chest. Her eyes widened, but only in surprise, not fear, thank the Lord. "I-I'm very tired," she protested.

He raised a brow. The excuse was weak, even if she had gotten up at four o'clock that morning.

"Good night, husband." She actually managed to make that sound like a command. Impressive.

Zach grinned. He liked her take-charge side. It showed gumption. Grit. But that didn't mean he'd be leaving the field of battle with his tail between his legs. He had his own supply of grit.

"You don't have to share my bed until you're ready, Abigail, but tonight you vowed to obey me . . . in domestic matters." He let that sink in for a moment. They had been her words, after all, not his.

She stiffened. Her mouth pursed, no doubt preparing to issue a severe dressing down aimed at putting her arrogant husband in his place. Well, this husband knew his place, and it wasn't across the hall from his wife. At least not in a permanent arrangement.

"A good-night kiss," he said before she could lash into him.

She blinked.

"Before you go to bed each night, I want a kiss." If he couldn't have the closeness of sleeping beside her, he'd just have to manufacture it another way. And since memories of their wedding kiss had been plaguing him all night, it was the first strategy that came to mind.

She cocked her chin upward. "A kiss."

"Yep."

"I suppose that's a reasonable request."

It was actually more of a demand, but if it made her feel better to call it a request, he'd go along.

"All right. I agr—"

He didn't let her finish. Just swooped in and claimed her mouth. Man, but he'd been wanting to do this again. He held her close, relishing the feel of her against him. The taste of her lips. The softness of the skin at her nape as he supported her head while deepening the kiss.

Slowly, he separated his lips from hers and peered into her face. Her lashes fluttered open, revealing beautifully dazed brown eyes.

It might not be the wedding night a man dreamed about, but it was a block to build on.

She was avoiding him. She knew it. Rosalind knew it. Zach probably knew it too. Yes, she had a bakery to run, but that didn't explain why she'd sent her sister upstairs with a plate of sticky buns and a mug of coffee at precisely 7:20 a.m. Abigail told herself she was being a considerate wife, anticipating her husband's needs and meeting them with efficiency. Yet as much as she wanted to believe that lie, she recognized the delusion at its core. Her actions didn't denote consideration, they revealed her insecurity.

If he ate upstairs, she wouldn't have to face him in the shop with memories of their good-night kiss zinging through the air between them. None of her customers even knew she had married. What would they think if Zacharias Hamilton entered the shop from the kitchen instead of the front door? Her cheeks would fire hotter than her ovens.

Better to have Brother Samuelson announce their newly wedded state at church tomorrow. Then everyone would know, and Zach could stroll into the shop from whichever direction he liked.

Of course, that did nothing to solve the problem of how

she was supposed to act around him. Logic dictated that he was the same person he'd always been, so she should carry on as she had in the past. Unfortunately, rational thought failed to keep her heart from palpitating whenever she saw him . . . or heard his voice . . . or even just thought about him. It was a wonder she had only spoiled one batch of muffins this morning instead of all five.

Marriage to a man with a penchant for kissing was proving to be a trial. Maybe the newness would wear off in a few days, and she would regain control of her mind. At the moment, her husband held it hostage.

Was he in the sitting room enjoying his breakfast, or had he already left through the alley to head for the lumberyard? Would he leave without telling her good-bye? Did she *want* him to tell her good-bye?

Oh, for pity's sake. Get your head back in the bakery where it belongs. Abigail bit the inside of her cheek as she focused on the customer standing at the counter. Had she asked for one croissant or two? Sometimes the schoolmarm bought a second pastry to have for lunch, but Abigail couldn't recall what she'd said. Her hand hovered over the croissant shelf, so hopefully she had at least that much correct.

Abigail placed one croissant on the square of butcher paper on the counter, then decided to admit her distraction. "I'm sorry, Miss Eider. Did you ask for one or two?"

The teacher offered a friendly smile. "Just one today, thank you."

Praise God for kind patrons. Abigail returned her smile as she wrapped the pastry in paper and handed it over. Just as Miss Eider dropped a pair of copper coins into Abigail's palm, the bakery door flew open, jangling the bell with enough force to cause every customer to turn and look.

Sophia Longfellow swept inside, her overly puffed sleeves clearing her path more effectively than a pair of flanking guards. People backed away as she marched toward the counter. Even Miss Eider skittered sideways to let the mayor's wife pass.

"Tell me it isn't true, Abigail." Sophia's dramatic utterance echoed throughout the shop with all the subtlety of cannon fire. "I knew you were desperate to save your shop, but I never thought you would go so far as to—to *sell* yourself to some man."

Silence instantly smothered the shop. No teacups clattered against saucers. No spoons rattled in coffee mugs. No chairs scraped against floorboards. The room had gone so still, Abigail swore she could hear dozens of eyes widening in shock. Her own among them.

Sophia enjoyed lashing Abigail with that barbed tongue of hers, but never in so public a forum. Never with such deliberate intent to destroy her reputation. Abigail held her head high beneath the assault, but the cruelty of it sliced her heart to ribbons. They had once been as close as sisters.

Preening under the attention, Sophia took full advantage of the silence. "Dearest Abigail." She reached across the counter and clasped Abby's balled hand, Miss Eider's coins still clenched inside. "Mr. Gerard was more than willing to purchase your shop at a fair price. You had other options. There was no reason to—"

"Enough." Zach's deep masculine voice reverberated behind Abigail. The single word was soft, but it carried such menace that even Sophia looked uneasy. She released Abigail's hand and straightened her posture.

Suddenly Rosalind was at Abigail's side. Was her sister the

reason for Zach's sudden appearance? She had been in the kitchen fetching a fresh pot of coffee when Sophia had barged in.

While Abigail was thankful for her new husband's support—more than she wanted to admit—she couldn't allow him to fight her battles for her.

With her sister at her side and her husband at her back, Abigail's confidence renewed. "My reasons for marrying Zacharias are my own and none of your concern, Sophia." Abigail made sure to enunciate *marrying* very clearly as she spoke. Best to chop the gossip off at the knees before Sophia's purposely vague insinuations took root. "He's a good man, and I am especially blessed to claim him as my husband." She glanced up to address the room at large, raised her voice, and forced her lips to curve upward in what she hoped was a smile. "We intended to share the news tomorrow at church, but since Mrs. Longfellow has spoiled the surprise, I might as well announce that yesterday evening, I officially became Mrs. Zacharias Hamilton."

She lifted her left hand and showed off the gold band circling her third finger. It still felt odd there, rubbing against her other fingers. Foreign. As if it wasn't really hers. She'd nearly taken it off while kneading her loaf dough that morning, not wanting to coat it in flour paste. But at the last minute she decided to leave it on. Dough residue would wash off, and not wearing it seemed disloyal to the man who had given it to her.

"Congratulations to you both." Miss Eider smiled with genuine warmth, and the tightness in Abigail's chest eased a fraction.

Zach played his part well, stepping up to her side and wrapping an arm around her shoulders.

"Way to go, Hamilton!" some loud fellow at the back called.

The room erupted with laughter and applause after that, transforming a potential scandal into a celebration.

A situation that left the mayor's wife silently fuming, though she hid it well. Were it not for the slight pursing of her lips and the narrowing of her eyes, Abigail might have believed her smile solicitous.

"So, have the two of you been courting, then?" Sophia just couldn't leave it alone, could she? "You never mentioned having a beau, and I haven't seen you together at church or about town."

"Really, Sophia," Rosalind said, sweeping around the counter and saving Abigail from trying to formulate an answer to that web of a question, "such a Nosy Nellie." She made a *tsk*ing sound and playfully hooked her arm around Sophia's tightly corseted waist. "Abby and Zach have been married less than a day. Let's give them some time to breathe before peppering them with questions, shall we?"

Rosalind forcibly drew Sophia away from the counter, covering her exertion with a smile that was even more sugary than her counterpart's.

"But I'm concerned for her," Sophia protested, trying to turn back even as Rosalind continued to gracefully drag her toward the door. "I fear she's being taken advantage of—"

"By Zach?" Rosalind laughed. "You can't be serious. That man is the best thing to happen to our family in years."

Rosalind had Sophia nearly to the door. Abigail had never realized her sister was so strong. Or so clever. She'd sidestepped every one of Sophia's verbal traps, responding but not actually answering any of her questions.

Zach squeezed Abigail's shoulder as if equally impressed. Or maybe his fingers just twitched. How would she know? Instinct told her it was more than a random tic, though. She felt connected to him in this moment, allies on the field of battle, appreciating the skilled maneuvers of a younger soldier.

"This is too much." Sophia planted her feet and jerked away from Rosalind's hold. "I won't be ushered out like some kind of pathetic street urchin. I'm concerned about my friend."

"Tell you what," Rosie said, smile never wavering, "why don't you come by later this afternoon? Say, around four o'clock? After the bakery is closed for the day. That way you and Abby will have plenty of time to talk. In *private*. A place of business isn't really the appropriate venue for this conversation, wouldn't you agree?"

It was all Abigail could do not to cackle with glee. The look on Sophia's face! Hoisted with her own petard. She'd *wanted* to make a scene. Why else would she time her entrance to co-incide with the peak of the breakfast crowd? But thanks to Rosie, if she pressed the issue now, she'd appear insensitive and rude. Sophia cherished her reputation almost as much as her husband's position. Staying would endanger both.

Sophia glanced around at the staring patrons. "Of course." She manufactured a touch of abashment. "I was just so swept up in my concern for Abigail when Chester told me the news this morning that I dashed over without a thought." Her gaze shifted to Abby. "Forgive me, Abigail. I didn't intend to disrupt your business."

Mouth tight, Abigail stepped away from her husband. Zach's support buoyed her, yet Sophia needed to see that she wasn't intimidated. With the public looking on, Sophia no doubt expected Abby to demure, to accept her apology as if no harm had been done. But harm had been done. Or at least intended.

Shrugging off the insult was not acceptable, yet neither was lashing out like a shrew. So Abigail took a page from her new husband's book and said nothing. She just stared at her former friend until the quiet grew oppressive and Sophia glanced away.

The victory might be small, but it was a victory nonetheless, and it felt good to watch Sophia sashay out the shop door unsatisfied. Their war wasn't over—Abigail could feel that truth biting into her like a cramp in the side—but she'd won this skirmish, and that was enough for now.

"Are you all right?" Zach's voice rumbled gently in her ear as the door closed and chatter in the shop resumed.

She nodded.

He touched her elbow and drew her away from the counter. "I can leave work early, be back by four, if you want."

Abigail frowned for a moment, then recalled Rosalind's invitation to Sophia. She smiled, touched by his offer, but shook her head. "There's no need. She won't come. Not if there won't be an audience."

Zach raised a brow, questions nearly popping from the furrows in his forehead. Yet he didn't ask them, because he recognized this wasn't the time. She had a business to run, and he had his own vocation to see to. He'd already stayed later than usual.

"We'll talk later," she promised. And maybe they would. He was her husband now, after all. Her problems were his problems, just as his were hers. Yet she didn't want to burden him so soon after saying their vows and make him regret tying his life to hers. It wasn't fair for her to be the only one making deposits into that particular account.

He looked at her hard, as if privy to her thoughts and not pleased with their direction. "We *will* talk," he said, his tone giving no quarter. "We're partners now, Abby. Whatever affects you affects me too."

"All right."

At her agreement, his face cleared. "I'll see you this evening."

KAREN WITEMEYER

She nodded absently, giving him a good-bye smile as he turned and exited through the back.

One thought echoed louder than any other in her mind as he left. He expected her to share her troubles with him, but would he share his with her?

CHAPTER

16

Dear Evie,
Weather's been nice. A little on the warm side, but

Zach groaned and crumpled the paper. His sister didn't care about the weather. She wanted to know how he and Abby were getting along. He knew this because she'd left strict instructions before heading back to Pecan Gap, demanding letters on a regular basis with details about how the courtship was progressing.

He scratched at an itchy place beneath his chin, grimaced, then pulled a second piece of paper from the desk drawer.

Courtship was a slow business. Especially when one's wife retired an hour after supper every night. But if he didn't put a few words to paper soon, Evie was likely to sic Logan on him. The last thing Zach's courtship needed was the sins of his past hanging around in the flesh.

He situated the clean sheet of writing paper in the middle of the walnut desk and dug around in his brain for a handful of words to satisfy his sister's curiosity. He came up empty. Grinding his molars, Zach twisted his pen between his fingers and glanced at the walls for inspiration. They were the only masculine walls in the entire house, but like a friend who didn't want to get involved in personal affairs, they offered no input.

He thought he'd been prepared to move into a feminine household. All he needed was a bed, after all. Maybe a chair and a place to put his feet up. The surroundings didn't much matter. Or so he'd thought. But after nearly a month of lacy curtains, roses blossoming on the walls, and female undergarments dangling above the bathtub in the washroom, he'd started feeling a tad claustrophobic. Even the pitcher and basin on his washstand had been smothered with blue flowers. A matching shaving mug had been set out for him, as if that made the collection more masculine somehow. His plain white mug had supplanted the botanic blight the first morning of his residence, but he'd hesitated to replace the remainder of the set.

Abigail seemed the practical sort who wouldn't balk at a plain white ewer and basin, but if he hoped to woo her into sharing the room with him, he didn't want to do anything that might deter her from feeling welcome there. If she liked floral washbasins—which she must, since petal-bearing specimens adorned everything from seat cushions to dinner plates in this home—he wouldn't banish them from his room. He'd just try not to look at them. A strategy that had earned him several nicks on the thumb while rinsing his razor blade over the past four weeks.

Thank the Lord for Edward Kemp. He might have been an insensitive clod when it came to appreciating his daughters, but he'd managed to carve out a corner of masculinity in the sea of flowers that was his home. A tiny study at the end of the hall boasted dark wood paneling. A desk and chair stood at the rear, in front of a narrow bookcase. A lumpy armchair and scuffed lamp table sat near the entrance. A thin brown rug with worn edges adorned the floor. The room was a cave, especially at night, but like all good caves, not a single leaf or bud bloomed anywhere within. The perfect male retreat.

So why couldn't Zach relax enough to write?

Clenching his jaw, he dipped his nib in the ink and threw a handful of words onto the blank page.

Evie,

Things are good here. Folks in town were surprised to learn of the wedding at first. The mayor's wife tried to stir up a scandal, but that passed.

Abby had been right about Mrs. Longfellow. She hadn't shown up to talk in private that Saturday afternoon. In fact, at church the following morning, she had gone around telling people how disheartened she was that Abigail hadn't come to her for advice before taking such drastic action. What woman of sound moral character would choose marrying a virtual stranger over a straightforward business arrangement? If she wanted to hold on to her little bakery that badly, all she needed to do was partner with one of their local businessmen, a partnership the mayor's wife would have been more than happy to orchestrate.

Thankfully, Audrey Sinclair caught wind of Mrs. Longfellow's rumor-weaving and countered with some well-crafted information of her own. She'd gushed to all who would listen about the intimate wedding ceremony she had hosted in her parlor. About the way the couple had stared into each other's eyes as they recited their vows, and especially about the kiss Zach had planted on his new wife at the end. Obviously Zach's daily visits to the Taste of Heaven Bakery all these months hadn't been solely on account of the sticky buns. He must have been developing a taste for something even sweeter.

Zach hadn't denied the story when acquaintances ribbed him about pining after the young baker. He'd just shrugged and accepted their teasing as his due. Maybe a dab of truth lived in the tale. There had been something about Abigail from the beginning that had drawn him, made him anticipate seeing her each morning. He'd never named it or put any effort into understanding it, but that didn't mean it hadn't existed.

Even good old Beekman unwittingly aided their cause. The man himself was too decent to gossip, but Maggie Rayburn, his landlady, had cheerfully spread the tale of how she'd witnessed Zach run Elmer Beekman off when he'd found Abigail speaking privately with the deacon near the boardinghouse oak tree. Why would he do that, if not out of jealousy? Then after an extensive *private* conversation, Zach had taken Abigail's hand, and the two had walked away together. Yes, Miss Maggie insisted, the secret lovebirds had definitely been courting.

Mrs. Longfellow's insinuations had gradually withered beneath the town's desire to believe in a secret romance. Zach still wasn't sure why the mayor's wife was so bent on blackening Abby's name, though. All his wife had told him was that the two of them had been close friends as children and that a mistake Abigail made drove a wedge between them. She'd looked so heartbroken that he hadn't wanted to press for more details, but something told him this rift was only going to tear wider, and he'd need to be armed with the facts of what happened if he was to offer his family adequate defense.

Turning back to his letter, Zach inked his nib and scribbled a few more lines.

It's a good thing I cart lumber around all day, or I'd be several pounds heavier by now. It's hard to go hungry living in a bakery.

In truth, he ate like a king. Abigail packed him a lunch every morning, usually a sandwich and a piece of fruit. Ham or roast or sometimes a couple of hard fried eggs with bacon between thick slices of the best bread he'd ever eaten. Hearty yet not dense, just the right texture to fill a man's belly and keep him going through the afternoon. And there was always something for dessert. A couple cookies, a slice of cake, even a fruit tart had been known to make an appearance in his lunch bucket, causing more than one scuffle with Reuben when his partner tried to nip a treat without permission. When Zach complained about his friend's thievery, Abby started packing extra sweets in his tin. She did love to feed people.

The courting is

Zach paused, unsure of what to write. *Frustrating* was the word that immediately jumped to mind, but that wasn't fair to Abby. She was holding up her end of the bargain and sharing kisses with him every night—kisses he looked forward to from the moment his eyes opened in the morning. She fed him. Did his laundry. Well, Rosalind did most of the laundry and household chores while his wife worked in the bakery, but Abby was the one who mended the tears in his trousers and the holes in his socks. The one who read from the Bible every evening after supper. The one who asked him how his day went at the lumberyard and smiled as if "fine" was a brilliant response.

One of his biggest fears before saying his vows was that once she had a claim on him, Abigail would start making demands on him as well. Demands for conversation. Before Evie had left town, she'd given him a stern lecture about how womenfolk liked to know what their menfolk were thinking, and worse yet, feeling. Zach had dreaded those first few evenings with his wife and sister-in-law. But all his worry had been for naught. Abigail never pressed him for conversation. She'd ask questions, enough to let him know she was actually interested in the answers, but she never grew testy about his brevity. Never huffed or glared or rolled her eyes like his sister did when she found his responses lacking. She simply accepted what he was willing to give. And, ironically, her acceptance of his silence made him want to share more.

Zach scratched a few more words onto the stationery.

The courting is going well. Abby and I are getting to know each other, and I can honestly say that I have no regrets. She's a good woman.

Zach scanned what he'd written so far. Nearly ten lines. Might be a record. He grinned, proud of his efforts, then inked the pen a final time.

All my best to Seth, Christie, and little Archie.
Oh, and tell that husband of yours that my offer to shoot him still stands if he gets out of line.

He had to get at least one dig in. Evie was smart enough to see through her big brother's bluster to read the fondness between the lines. Logan might have been a no-good scoundrel with nothing but revenge on his mind when he'd first crossed their paths last year, but Zach couldn't deny that Logan had been good to his sister. Good to all the Hamiltons, actually. Shoot, if it wasn't for the guilt that stabbed Zach's gut every time he looked at him, he might actually *like* his brother-in-law.

Shaking his head, Zach signed his name to the bottom of the letter and set it aside to allow the ink to dry. The onerous task of letter writing complete, he turned his mind to other pursuits. Namely, how to carve out some private time with his wife. He liked Rosie and all, but if a man wasn't sharing a bed with his wife, he needed to find other avenues for conducting his wooing. Reuben had suggested the opera house, but Zach didn't see how sitting in a theatre with a room full of strangers would aid his cause. He needed time alone with Abigail.

Maybe they could go for a ride out to some pretty spot in the country. Reuben hadn't grown up around here, he and Audrey having moved to the area about five years ago to be closer to Audrey's sister, but surely he'd know a few good courting spots. Maybe even someplace with flowers. Abby liked flowers.

Zach thought of renting her a horse, but he had no idea if she knew how to ride. A buggy would work, but he'd rather just take her up with him on Jack. Ride double. It might raise a few eyebrows, but who cared? They were married. Zach's pulse quickened at the idea of holding his wife close. Tucking her against his chest. Her hands gripping him for support.

Like a predator catching scent of his prey, Zach lifted his head and readied muscles that had gone stiff from sitting. His blood thrummed. His mind spun with plots and plans. No slapdash effort would do. If he was going to elevate his courtship, he'd best make sure the results were impressive.

First thing tomorrow, he'd get Reuben's recommendations on scenic locales in the area, then he'd corner Rosalind and see if he could convince his sister-in-law to aid his cause.

Only . . . someone else cornered her first.

⊶——⊷

Monday afternoon, an hour before his usual quitting time, Zach left the lumberyard armed with directions to the three best courting spots in Honey Grove. He marched up Seventh Street, heading to the wagonyard where he stabled Jack, but a familiar head of blond hair in the alleyway snagged his attention.

Rosalind, a market basket filled with parcels wrapped in butcher paper slung over her arm, shook her head adamantly at a disreputable-looking fellow that Zach didn't recognize.

Protective instincts flaring, Zach turned into the alley.

"You're mistaken," Rosalind said, lurching back toward Sixth Street.

"I don't think so, love." The man stepped into her path and blocked her escape. He pulled something about the size of a playing card from his pocket, studied it, then looked back at Rosie's face. "You're her, all right. Wait 'til I tell the boys. They'll all want to come take a gander."

"Let me pass."

Zach couldn't see Rosalind's face, but the shakiness of her voice had him striding forward. She attempted to skirt around the stranger, but the vermin grabbed hold of her arm.

Zach broke into a run, jaw set and fingers clenched.

This man had just made a date with his fist.

CHAPTER

17

"Let her go." His growled demand echoed through the alleyway as Zach advanced.

The man's eyes widened, then narrowed into angry slits as he jerked Rosalind closer to his side. "Back off, buddy. I saw her fir—"

Zach grabbed the man's arm and yanked him away from Rosalind. The card he'd been holding fluttered to the ground as he brought up a fist to defend himself. He jabbed. Zach dodged.

Rosalind dropped to the ground between them, and Zach nearly stepped on her hand. "Get out of the way, Rosalind."

But she didn't. Not until her flailing in the dirt produced the fallen card. Worried about knocking her head with his knee, Zach looked down, giving his opponent an opening.

The man's fist connected with Zach's jaw, snapping his head sideways. Rosalind gasped and finally scooted out of the way. Icy calm penetrated Zach's veins. With his sister-in-law out of the equation, he could give his full attention to his assailant.

The man retreated a step, but not far enough. Zach swung. His knuckles collided with the man's cheekbone with satisfying solidness. The fellow staggered backward until he bumped up against the butcher shop wall. Zach advanced, grabbed his shirtfront, and pinned him there.

"Go fetch the marshal, Rosalind."

The man made no move to strike another blow, but he glared at Zach belligerently. "You laid hands on me first, mister."

Zach twisted the cotton shirt a notch tighter in his fist. "You laid hands on the lady first, *mister*. Around here we don't take kindly to brutes forcing innocent young women into alleys and assaulting them."

"Innocent? Ha!" The man practically spat the words. "She might be female, but she sure ain't innocent. One look at that picture she crawled through the dirt for will tell you that much." He smirked, and a vile laugh escaped his throat. "Hope you weren't planning on buying that particular cow. She's probably been givin' her milk away for free to gents all over the county. Right under your nose too."

Zach's hands were full of the man's shirt, so he lifted him a few inches off the ground and head-butted him right in the face.

"Ow!" Blood spurted from the man's nose. Good. Maybe the idiot would shut up now.

A handful of passersby were gathering at the end of the alley and peering in. Rosalind must have seen them too, for she started backpedaling.

"Let him go," she said, her voice quiet and quivering.

Zach twisted to look at her. Pale face. Wide, shimmering eyes. White knuckles gripping that confounded card.

"Please, Zach. Just let him go."

Zach frowned. The maggot deserved jail time, or at the very least a few more blows to the head. Or the groin. That would be more fitting for someone who said such vile things about a girl barely old enough to wear long skirts.

Unfortunately, Zach couldn't mete out the appropriate punishment without becoming guilty of assault himself, now that the man was subdued. So, with a sideways shove, Zach released him, taking what satisfaction he could from the blood dripping down the fellow's face.

"Get out of here," he muttered, silently daring the slimy toad to take another shot at him. One swing, and Zach would be justified in smacking him into the ground.

Unfortunately, his adversary seemed to have come to the same conclusion and opted for self-preservation. After stumbling a couple steps, he righted himself, rubbed the blood from his mouth and nose with a swipe of his sleeve, and shot a scalding glare at Zach that worried him about as much as a dart from an ant's peashooter. Then, with a sarcastic tip of his hat to Rosalind and a smirk begging to be wiped off his face by Zach's fist, the man turned and strolled away.

"You all right?" Zach asked, pivoting to face his sister-in-law.

She nodded, but she looked about as all right as a kicked puppy.

He reached a hand toward her. "Here, let me—"

"No!" She covered the card she held with both hands, pressed it to her chest, and twisted away from him.

"—take your basket," he finished, approaching her with the same care one would exude near a skittish mare. His hand closed around the basket handle and gently lifted the weight off her arm. "I ain't got no interest in relieving you of anything else."

As soon as she realized her precious card was safe from prying eyes, everything about her drooped. Her shoulders sagged, and her arms loosened, allowing him to collect the shopping basket from her. But her defenses crumbled as well, for her eyes started leaking and her entire body shook.

Not tears. Please, Lord. Anything but tears.

140

A messy, gasping sob was the answer to that prayer.

Panic pumped blood double-time through his veins. He scanned the alley for help and found nothing but curious on-lookers who didn't need to be sticking their noses in Rosalind's private business.

Not having a clue what to do to make the tears stop, he opted for the one thing he *could* figure out—how to protect her privacy.

"This way." Wrapping his arm around her shoulders, he bundled her close and marched away from Sixth Street. He'd been aiming for the wagonyard when this whole debacle unfolded. He might as well take her there. Hide her in Jack's stall until the tears dried.

Dried. Handkerchief. Something else he could do.

Zach jostled the market basket up to his elbow, crammed his left hand into his trouser pocket, and pulled out the solution to all feminine distress. Feeling slightly less inept, he shoved the white cotton at Rosalind as they trudged toward the end of the alley.

Thanking the Lord for a less crowded walkway on Seventh Street than Sixth, Zach lengthened his stride and steered Rosalind around the handful of folks out and about. They garnered more than a few strange looks, but Zach just scowled and kept moving. No one approached.

Once they reached the wagonyard, Zach waved off the stable-boy with a shake of his head and bustled Rosalind into the livery barn, relieved to note they had the place to themselves. Well, except for a mule team and a pony or two lazing about in their stalls. They stuck their heads over the half doors to see what all the fuss was about when the humans clomped down the center aisle, but otherwise paid them no particular attention.

Jack nickered a welcome, bobbing his head as Zach approached, but his longtime mount picked up on his mood and grew solemn in a heartbeat. The quarter horse, solid black except for the white star on his forehead and socks on his hind legs, backed away from the door and made room for his human visitors. Zach dropped the market basket outside the stall and shuffled Rosalind into a front corner. Then, moving to his horse, he clasped Jack's halter and patted his neck as he backed him up a few steps.

"Good boy," he murmured softly as the animal obeyed his instructions. "Gonna have to postpone our ride, I'm afraid." He kept his voice low, not wanting Rosalind to feel bad about interrupting his plans. *He* had no regrets. Family came first. Always. Even before courtship.

Right now, his sister-in-law took precedence over his wife.

With Jack settled and as out of the way as one could manage in an average-sized stall, Zach stepped away from his horse and joined Rosalind at the front near the door. Not wanting to crowd her, he positioned himself across the stall, casually leaning against the wall behind him.

Her head bowed, she stared at the ground, the card she'd been grasping so tightly having disappeared. Into a pocket, most likely.

Not really sure what to say, Zach opted for his favorite tactic—silence. She'd open up when she was ready. And if she didn't? Well, he'd make it clear that she had his protection. No matter what.

She was family.

"It's not true," she finally said, her voice quiet, her gaze still glued to the floor, her hands worrying the ends of the damp handkerchief twisted between her fingers. Slowly her chin came up, and pretty blue eyes reddened from tears begged him to believe her. "I haven't . . . *been* with anyone." Her head wagged back and forth, and fresh tears threatened. "I wouldn't. I swear."

Zach frowned, insulted she would think it necessary to deny that particular charge. She was barely more than a kid. "Of course you haven't," he snapped. "Anyone with half a brain knows that filth was a lie. You're as innocent as the day is long."

Her gaze dropped back to the ground, and she bit her bottom lip. "No." She shook her head, and Zach's gut clenched. "No, I'm not."

She'd probably kissed a fellow behind the schoolhouse or something. Didn't mean she wasn't still an innocent. A girl as pretty as her had probably had opportunities to kiss dozens of boys over the years. Not that she would have. Zach might not have known her all that long, but he'd seen her character up close and personal the last month. She worked nearly as hard as her sister, running things at home while Abigail ran the bakery. Delivering the widow bread. Even watching Audrey Sinclair's brood on occasion to allow the busy mother to get a little shopping done without the chaos of toddlers constantly underfoot.

Girls as pretty as Rosalind tended to use their looks to get *out* of work, flirting and teasing to entice men into doing things for them. But not Rosalind. He rarely even saw her talking to men, now that he thought about it. She always flocked with other women at church and hung close to the bakery during the week.

"I did something," she whispered. "Something wrong." Her knuckles whitened at the force of her grip on the handkerchief. "It was for a good reason, or at least I thought so at the time. Papa needed medicine. He was so sick. So weak. When Julius offered to pay me . . ."

Zach's throat tightened and bile rose. Surely she hadn't . . . *Please, God.*

". . . to pose for a few pictures . . ."

Air whooshed from his lungs in relief. Yet the dread knotting his gut refused to completely abate.

". . . I thought it would be safe. He swore that no one within a hundred miles of here would ever see them. And the money paid for the medicine my father needed. Abby was so busy trying to keep the bakery going. Papa's care fell to me." Rosalind's head jerked up. "She doesn't know." She stiffened, a zealous light entering her eyes. In three steps, she crossed the stall and gripped Zach's wrist with icy fingers. "She can *never* know."

"Can't say that I agree with you there," he said. "Secrets have a way of eating away at a family, even when we think keeping 'em hid is doing the folks we care about a favor. Trust me. I know." He'd learned that truth the hard way with Seth and Evie. 'Course, he couldn't deny his reluctance to spill all his skeletons onto Abigail. He would, he told himself. Eventually. After they got to know each other better. A boat needed to be sturdily built before a fella started rocking it.

Rosalind didn't seem to agree, though. Her fingernails dug into his skin, and if her head shook any harder from side to side, it was bound to pop plumb off.

"Don't worry." He patted her hand a couple times, then gently pried her claws out of his hide. "It ain't my story to tell, so I won't be flappin' my gums about it. But if family's gonna stick together, they need to know what they're fighting."

"She wouldn't understand."

"Maybe not." Zach sure didn't. A sweet girl like Rosalind posing for naughty pictures? Didn't make a lick of sense. Even if it was for her pa's medicine. "But she'd stand by you, regardless."

Rosalind shrugged, obviously recognizing it was true but still not wanting to admit her mistakes to the one person whose opinion she valued most. He understood the sentiment.

One thing was painfully clear. That Julius fella had manipulated her, exploited Rosalind's worry about her pa's health and trapped her into doing something she never would have done

144

otherwise. The girl had been barely seventeen, for pity's sake. Alone and unprotected with her father at death's door. No one to watch out for her.

No wonder she had begged Zach to marry Abigail. She needed a protector. Had probably been needing one for a while. Well, now she had one—one who recalled a particular promise she'd made to reveal *everything* about her problem once he married her sister.

"So I take it this is the mistake you warned me about, the one you worried would bring danger to Abigail's doorstep?"

The poor girl's body wilted in on itself. She nodded.

Zach inhaled a deep breath and made himself as comfortable as possible against the wood slats at his back. He wouldn't be going anywhere for a while.

"Guess you better start at the beginning."

CHAPTER

18

Rosalind let out a sigh, then scooted around to plant her back against the wall beside him. Taking her cue, Zach stared straight ahead instead of at her and waited.

"There's not much more to tell," she hedged.

Zach bent down, picked up a piece of straw, and twirled it between his thumb and finger, signaling he wasn't in a hurry. That usually did the trick with Evie. She hated the quiet almost as much as she hated him not giving her an easy exit from a difficult conversation. It didn't work as well on Abigail. His wife seemed to enjoy the quiet. But maybe her sister would be—

"He was a traveling photographer," Rosalind blurted.

Ah. More like Evie than Abigail, it seemed. Zach hid his satisfied smile behind one of the bland masks he'd mastered during his poker-playing days.

"He set up a portrait studio in a storefront a couple blocks from the bakery. Families came into town from miles away to have their pictures taken. One fellow even brought his horse into the studio, if you can imagine." Her lips curved slightly, and she tilted her face toward his.

Zach grinned in reply, but they both knew she was only delaying the distasteful part of the story.

"Julius ate at the bakery most mornings and tried to convince Abby and me to come sit for him. But we had Papa to worry about and money was tight, so we turned him down, even when he offered us a discount." She scuffed the sole of her left shoe against the straw-littered floor. "He was always very charming and gracious. Wore a tidy brown suit with a chocolate brown tie and a bowler hat. He never flirted with me, at least not the way most men do. No winks or suggestive comments. No excessive compliments or bragging. Just earnest conversation and attentive listening. When he looked at me, I had the oddest feeling that he was . . . *absorbing* me, as if I were a painting or a piece of sculpture." She shook her head. "It's foolish, I know. But he was an artist, and his interest flattered me more than it should have."

Zach stuck the straw in his mouth, needing something to chomp down on before his lips opened and his opinions on artists and their flattering attention disgorged all over the girl at his side. Julius might need his camera tossed off a cliff, but Rosalind didn't need to feel worse about a situation she no longer had any control over.

"A few days before Julius planned to leave town," she continued, "he ran across me coming out of the drugstore. The doctor had diagnosed my father with heart failure earlier that morning. He'd said there was nothing we could do beyond keeping him comfortable, but I couldn't just let him die. He was my father, and his care was *my* responsibility. So I consulted with the apothecary, and he advised me on a few patent medicines that promised invigorating results. They were costly, however, purchased mostly by his wealthier clientele, but I wouldn't be deterred. I told him I'd be back the next day with the funds.

"I intended to take coins from the till that night after Abby went to bed. Then I ran into Julius. Seeing my distress, he took me aside, and I poured out my troubles. I couldn't help it. I felt so overwhelmed. So alone. That's when he mentioned his side business. Photographic cards. If I posed for him and signed a document that granted him permission to replicate my image, he'd pay me enough to purchase the medicine Papa needed."

A regular Good Samaritan. Zach's molars ground the straw to stringy bits. He could have offered to buy the blasted medicine for her, but no. The photographer had seen an opportunity to make a profit, and he'd taken advantage.

"For the first time in my life, I felt as if my appearance might actually have value beyond superficial packaging. As if, like Esther, God had graced me with beauty in order to fulfill a higher purpose—saving my father."

So naïve, yet the longing in her voice resonated. How often had he wanted to believe that he was created for some higher purpose? For a while, he'd found that with Seth and Evie. His efforts had been imperfect, and he'd gathered more than his share of regrets along the way, but his purpose had been crystal clear: Provide. Protect. Then they outgrew their need for him, and he'd floundered.

Until the Kemp sisters. They'd given him a cause higher than himself to serve. He might still be figuring things out with Abigail, but he knew his job. Provide. Protect. Maybe if he fulfilled his purpose well enough, Rosalind would gain the freedom to find hers.

"I followed him back to his studio," she recounted, "and he showed me some of the photographic cards he'd made of other girls. Young. Pretty. The photographs were improper, to be sure, but not sinfully immodest. At least that's what I told myself. All the girls wore undergarments. Their hair might be unbound and their poses a tad wanton, but Julius promised that my pictures would be different. Special. He wanted to capture my vulnerability. Preserve my purity."

Preserve his profits, more like. Zach spit out the mutilated straw. Most decent men would feel guilty even looking at a print of a partially clothed woman in a salacious pose, but a print of a young girl with innocence shining in her eyes? It would stir protective instincts and conjure fantasies about rescue and marriage. The clever fiend would make a killing.

"I signed the paper and sat for the photograph."

Zach hated the flat tone of her voice. So defeated. So filled with self-derision. He couldn't let that stand.

"You made a poor choice." He wouldn't sugarcoat it, but neither would he allow her to define herself by it. "So have I. More than once." He cocked his head in her direction, but she kept her gaze glued to the ground in front of her. "Can't undo what's been done," he said, "but you *can* change how you handle the consequences."

That brought her chin up. Her brow furrowed as she tilted her head toward him. "What do you mean?"

He pushed away from the wall and turned to face her more fully. "Don't let this mistake shape who you are. Deal with it, make recompense where you can, but don't let it dictate your future. You are a strong young woman with a kind heart. Don't let it change you into a weak little girl cowed by guilt and fear of discovery."

Zach tried to ignore the taste of hypocrisy on his tongue. It was a miracle he hadn't smacked her to the ground, swinging that protruding log from his eye while he lectured her on how to clean the speck from hers. Practicing what he preached might not be his forte, but with any luck, Rosalind would surpass his less-than-stellar example.

"But if people find out, my reputation will be ruined."

He stared hard at her. "So?"

"So?" She jerked away from the wall, fire lighting her eyes. "*So?* You may not care what people think of you, but you're a man. Your life isn't dictated by the opinions of others. If word gets out about these photographs, my friends will turn their backs on me. Decent men will scorn my company, and indecent ones will proposition me like that fellow in the alley. I will be gossiped about and looked down upon. No one will ask me into their homes or trust me to watch their children. I'll be a pariah." Tears moistened her eyes. "And because of her relation to me, Abigail will suffer as well. The bakery will suffer. People won't patronize the shop of a woman with an immoral sister. They'd view it as a contamination of their standards."

"You won't be a pariah. Or a contamination. Not to the people who matter."

For the first time since meeting Rosalind Kemp, the truth of her youth hit him square between the eyes. Evie had instigated a few similarly dramatic scenes during her teen years, certain the world was going to end. But it never did. The world kept spinning, and she kept putting one foot in front of the other until things improved. Granted, Rosalind's situation had a little more kick to it than anything Evie had faced, but his sister had dealt with ostracism too, thanks to close-minded people judging her by her mismatched eyes instead of her character. He'd borne witness to Evie's pain and understood what Rosalind stood to lose.

Zach put a hand on her shoulder. "No matter what happens with the bakery, I'll take care of you and your sister."

She twisted away from his touch. "That's not enough! I want a future. And without my reputation, I won't have one." Clapping her arms against her sides, she turned her back on him.

"So we build you a new one."

Rosalind cast a disbelieving look over her shoulder. "As if that's possible."

Zach took a step in her direction. "Why not? We could move to a new town where no one knows us. Maybe even a new state."

She shook her head. "Abigail would never leave the bakery."

If the worst came to be, she might not have a choice. "Your sister is good enough at what she does to be successful anywhere. And if forced to choose between you or the bakery, she'd choose you every time."

"But she shouldn't have to choose!" Rosalind spun to face him, cheeks red and eyes flashing. "Don't you see? It's not fair for her to pay for my mistake. I won't let her!"

"Well, we'll just have to pray it doesn't come to that, then, won't we?" Zach crossed his arms over his chest.

He had no satisfactory answer to her problem, and he hated that. Hated not being able to fix things for her. He couldn't just smash his fist into the photographer's jaw like he had the fellow in the alley. He didn't even know where the scoundrel was. And with Rosalind's signature on that paper, he had no legal high ground, either.

"Look, Rosie, we can't control the future. All we can do is deal with the present. And right now, your reputation is intact, so frettin' about what *could* happen does you no good. What might do you some good, though, is learning how to handle yourself should any other fella try to lay hands on you."

A spark of interest flared in her gaze, clearing away the foggy hopelessness that had been dulling the blue of her eyes. "You'll teach me?"

"Yep."

Thank God for something he could actually do. He was about as good at using words to soothe female worries as he was at walking on water. But fighting? *That* he could do. After scrapping his way through the majority of his life, he had enough experience to make her a prize-winning bare-knuckle brawler if she wanted.

"Taught my sister," he said, making no effort to disguise the pride in his voice. "Figure I can teach you too."

"When can we start?"

Zach fought off a grin. He didn't want her to think he was laughing at her. In truth, he was downright impressed by this newfound gumption. She was gonna need plenty of that to face whatever trouble came from those picture cards.

"Tomorrow. Noon. Meet me at the field behind the church. Should be a private enough spot for a few lessons."

"Thank you, Zach," she said as she jumped forward and flung her arms around his neck.

Unprepared for such an attack, he froze. With his arms still crossed in front of him, he couldn't exactly hug her back. And while she *was* family, it just didn't feel right to hold another female close when he and Abigail still had distance to navigate between them.

Thankfully, Rosalind released him nearly as quickly as she'd grabbed him. A smile on her face, she opened the stall door and swept out into the heart of the stable. Whisking up the market basket, she waved her fingers at him. "Until tomorrow."

Well, actually she'd see him tonight at home, but he didn't correct her. Just nodded as she traipsed away, chin high, her world no longer facing imminent collapse.

Too bad his own world felt a little shaky. He'd just made a date with the wrong sister.

CHAPTER

19

"Are you sure one loaf will be enough, Mrs. Putnam?" Abigail smiled at the tiny gray-haired lady carefully wrapping a bread cloth around the sourdough loaf Abigail had just given her. "You're the last stop of the day, and I still have this pair of rolls that will go to waste if you don't claim them." She tilted her basket so the rolls tumbled toward the side closest to her friend.

It probably wasn't right to have favorites, but Lydia Putnam was such a little firecracker that Abigail always saved her for last on her widow bread delivery days.

Lydia raised a brow and pointed an accusing finger, one that tremored slightly with palsy. "I know your tricks, Abby Jane. Forcing your leftovers on a poor old lady who can't defend herself."

"Can't defend yourself?" Abigail gave a snort of disbelief. "You could hold off a stampede with a cast-iron skillet and a hatpin."

"Hoo! Now yer talkin'." Lydia smacked her palm against the top of the pie safe that stood waiting for its new acquisitions.

"If they'd a-had me at the Alamo, Elizabeth Crockett wouldn't have ended up a widow."

"I don't doubt it." Abigail smiled.

Lydia and her husband had helped settle Hood County decades ago, surviving Indian raids and harsh conditions, and meeting the famed Mrs. Crockett after she and her son claimed land in Acton. Lydia's connection to the famous frontiersman's wife was significant in this area, seeing as how Davy Crockett himself was responsible for naming Honey Grove. The story went that on his way to the Alamo, he set up camp in a copse of trees filled with honeybees and found the area so pleasing that he carved his name and the name *Honey Grove* into one of the trees, intending to return. Unfortunately, he didn't survive the Alamo, but a few years later, a dear friend of his, Samuel Erwin, purchased land near Crockett's camp and preserved the name. Honey Grove was born. Needless to say, Lydia was inordinately proud of her connection to the Crockett family and found a way to work Elizabeth Crockett into a conversation at least once per week.

"I can still shoot a squirrel in mid-leap, you know."

A slightly terrifying thought, when one considered the way the dear lady's hand shook, but Abigail couldn't naysay her. Not when she'd enjoyed Lydia's squirrel stew last week when she brought a pot by the shop as a belated wedding gift. It might have taken her three weeks to bag that squirrel, but she'd done it.

Lydia set the carefully wrapped sourdough in the pie safe, then reached for the dinner rolls. "Are these wheat?"

Abigail nodded. "With a touch of honey."

"So not only are you trying to fatten me up, you're trying to sweeten me up, too." She *tsk*ed and wagged her head. "If you have your way, folks around here won't know what name to put on my headstone when I finally turn up my toes." But she accepted the rolls and added them to the pie safe. "How're things going with that new husband of yours? Big strapping fella. Just like my Abe. Makes a woman feel safe, a man like that." She patted Abigail's arm as her teasing gaze turned serious. "Don't waste a moment, girl. As much as we love 'em, they don't live forever."

Abigail swallowed. Was that what she was doing? Wasting moments? She and Zach had been married a month, and nothing significant had changed between them. They had settled into a routine. They told stories about their families. Shared their likes and dislikes. Their friendship was growing, but their courtship had hit a plateau. Flutters didn't attack her belly every time she spied him across the room anymore. Not unless the room was her bedchamber, and Zach was approaching her doorway to claim his good-night kiss.

If it weren't for those kisses, she might not know she was a married woman. Of course, she only had herself to blame for that predicament. Zach's kisses promised deeper delights if she would only dig up the courage to welcome them.

Maybe tonight. Her pulse raced at the thought, filling her chest with those flutters she thought had abandoned her.

Could she really do it? Share his bed and become his wife in more than name? Did she *want* to?

Yes . . . and no.

Her feelings had certainly deepened. How could they not? Her husband had a kind streak she hadn't expected from the gruff loner. He might never quote poetry like a lovesick swain, but he showed his care for her in other ways. Just last week, he'd snuck into her room one evening before dinner to confiscate her shoe and fix the heel that had come loose during the day. He'd returned it without a word, leaving her to find it the next morning. Not only was the gesture considerate, but it proved he paid attention to the smallest details about her. He cared enough to notice and actively sought ways to please her.

He made sure to keep all the hinges oiled and doors well-hung, as well. When she'd teased him about his clever attempt to keep her early morning movements from disturbing his sleep, he'd looked completely confused. He'd done it to protect *her* sleep. It was why he never wore his boots upstairs. He didn't want to wake her. Now every morning when she went down to fire the bakery oven and saw his overlarge footgear standing against the kitchen wall by the stairwell, her heart stirred.

Yes, her heart desired greater intimacy with her husband, but uncertainties lingered. What if children came along before she was ready? Would Zach help out as much as he'd promised? Would she be able to handle motherhood *and* the bakery? Surely if the Lord gave her children, he'd also give her the strength to raise them well amid her other responsibilities. Wouldn't he? Or would God expect her to sacrifice her career for her family? A shiver coursed over Abigail's skin. She'd sworn not to lose herself like her mother had, becoming nothing more than a breeding machine for her husband.

Baking was her life. Her identity. But wasn't *wife* part of her identity now too? The more time she spent with Zach, the more she wanted to be both—baker *and* wife. Her determination and passion for her culinary art had given her the strength to overcome opposition from first her father and now her community. Perhaps her passion for her husband could overcome obstacles as well. She wouldn't know until she tried.

"Here I thought I needed to apologize for getting lost in my memories of Abe, but you're just as distracted as I am, ain't ya?" Lydia chuckled. "Having a good man will do that to you."

The older woman winked, bringing a blush to Abigail's cheeks, but even her embarrassment couldn't stop her from noticing the wistful look in Lydia's gaze as she smiled. Love still glowed within her for the husband who had been gone nearly a decade.

Would she and Zach ever share that level of devotion?

Not if she never found the courage to become a real wife to him.

Lydia gave Abigail a gentle nudge with her elbow. "Quit standin' here yakkin' with an old lady and get on home to that man of yours. Whip him up something special for dinner and tell that sister of yours to come pay me a call. She can help me with the quilt I'm workin' on."

"I–I couldn't just foist her on you like that," Abigail stammered. Had Lydia somehow figured out that she and Zach had yet to truly become man and wife? She hadn't said anything, but maybe there was something about the way she talked or acted that gave her away.

"Sure you can!" The nudges became a little more forceful as Mrs. Putnam pushed Abigail toward the kitchen door. "I need the company and you don't."

Abby's feet dragged as she shuffled forward against her will. "But I . . . I wouldn't want Rosalind to have to walk home alone after dark." There. That excuse sounded reasonable. Thoughtful even. Very big sister-ish.

Lydia cackled and shook her head as if Abigail had just added salt instead of sugar to her cake batter. "Oh, Abby Jane. It don't have to be *dark* outside for a woman to love her man. All you need is a little privacy, a spirit of adventure, and a heart full of love. I'll supply the privacy. You supply the rest. And if Zacharias Hamilton is half the man I think he is, you'll be thanking me the next time you bring bread."

Good heavens! What was she supposed to say to *that*? Never would she have imagined she'd be discussing marital relations with an eighty-year-old woman on bread day.

"We'll see," Abigail hedged, suddenly very eager to reach the door. She twisted her lips into what she hoped would pass for a smile and darted out into the sunshine.

Escape the only thing on her mind—well, not the *only* thing; a growing part of her consciousness remained stuck on that spirit of adventure Lydia had alluded to—Abigail hastened down the road, head down, gaze fixed on making sure her legs continued placing one foot in front of the other. With her discombobulated state of mind, there was no guarantee her limbs would actually work properly.

As it was, she missed the turn onto Sixth Street from Main and had to do an about-face in front of Dora Patteson's millinery shop. Hoping no one had noticed her awkward pivot, Abigail avoided making eye contact with the pair of women chatting at the corner, parcels in hand. However, today was apparently not the day for inconspicuosity, if that was even a word, for as soon as she rounded the corner, her name rang through the air. And in the voice Abigail least wanted to hear.

Biting back a groan, Abigail looked up to find Sophia Longfellow dragging a reluctant Mary Bowen across the street to intercept her.

"Tell her, Mary," Sophia demanded, pushing the unfortunate woman at Abigail. "Tell her what you told me."

Mary shook her head. "I don't think . . ." She bit her lip.

Sophia waved her hesitation away as if it were a puff of insignificant vapor. "Nonsense. She needs to know. 'Forewarned is forearmed,' as they say. *Not* telling her would be the bigger sin."

The only one forearmed in this conversation was Sophia. As usual. Abigail looked from one woman to the other, not liking what she saw. Guilt was etched into Mary's face, satisfaction on Sophia's. This didn't bode well.

"They also say 'ignorance is bliss,'" Abigail muttered as she tried to sidle past. Her rattled brain didn't have the wits to do battle with Sophia this afternoon.

"Even when it has to do with your husband being seen in the arms of another woman?"

Abigail's head jerked up as her stomach plummeted to her toes. Her gaze locked with Sophia's.

"You don't have to make it sound so tawdry," Mary protested, though her voice lacked confidence. "The woman was her sister."

Rosalind? Oh, thank heaven. Abigail managed a shallow breath, though her heart still pounded painfully against her breastbone.

"Even worse!" Sophia declared. "Betrayal by family, by a *sister*, cuts the deepest."

The old hurt rose to slap Abigail across the face, the destruction of a friendship between two young girls who had sworn an oath binding them as sisters of the soul. But it was fear of a new hurt that pulverized her heart like a pestle in its mortar, breaking off bits from the whole and grinding them into dust.

She shook her head. "I'm sure there's nothing to get so worked up about, Sophia." Of course there wasn't. Rosalind would never go behind her back. "It's only natural for Rosalind and Zach to be seen in town together from time to time. They are related by marriage, after all. It would be odder if they didn't stop to speak to each other."

"From what Mary tells me, there was very little speaking going on." Sophia lifted her chin and raked Abigail with a pitying glance. "Your husband had his arm around little Rosie, clutching her tight against his side as the two of them marched down the street. Her head was tucked against his chest."

Abigail worried her lip, desperately searching for a logical explanation. An *innocent* explanation. "Maybe she . . . turned her ankle and needed his support."

Sophia snapped her focus to her friend. "Was Rosie limping, Mary?"

Abigail silently pleaded for an affirmative response, feeling only a twinge of guilt for wishing an injury upon her sister.

The apologetic, slightly embarrassed shake of Mary's head broke Abigail's dam of hope, though, and released a flood of insecurities.

"Not only were they seen walking together in an intimate fashion," Sophia announced, "but they disappeared into the stable at the wagonyard and remained inside . . . alone together . . . for *ages*."

There was an explanation. There had to be. Abigail turned an imploring gaze on Mary, begging her to refute Sophia's story.

"I'm sorry." Mary couldn't meet Abigail's gaze. "My brother works at the stable, and he said the two of them were in one of the back stalls together for at least twenty minutes. Maybe longer."

Abigail's heart shriveled in her chest like a plum left out in the sun, leaving nothing but a wrinkled black prune in its place.

"I told you, you should have sold the bakery," Sophia declared. "If you were free to devote your time to your husband, his head wouldn't have been turned by your sister. Rosie's always been the pretty one. You know that. Yet, like a fool, you just kept on working those horrendous hours. Neglecting the man you married." She gave a disparaging click of her tongue. "For all you know, they've been carrying on right under your nose in the evenings after you retire."

"Stop it!" Abigail shook her head and backed away. "Zach is a good man. An honorable man. And Rosie is my sister. She'd never betray me like that. You're a cruel woman to even suggest such a thing."

She turned and raced toward the bakery. It wasn't true. It couldn't be. Rosie would never hurt her that way.

Then again, Rosalind *was* the pretty one. Men had always preferred her.

No! She wouldn't let her mind travel that path.

Yet as she ran home, her thoughts kept turning down that road again and again. What had Rosalind and Zach been doing for *twenty minutes* in that stable?

She tried to silence the suspicious whispers, truly she did. She set about making dinner, ordering her mind to attend only to the task in front of her. But as she chopped the sausages Rosalind had purchased at the butcher's shop and dropped them into the pan to sauté with some potato and onion, the whispers grew too loud to ignore. So when her sister came into the kitchen to retrieve a crock of butter, Abigail seized the opportunity.

"I heard you ran into Zach today while you were running errands."

Rosalind's head jerked up, but her gaze darted away. In guilt? "Yes, I, uh, ran into a bit of a—a situation . . . and Zach helped me out." She shrugged. "Nothing of consequence."

Nothing of consequence? Nothing of consequence had her cuddling up to Abigail's husband in the broad light of day and disappearing into a stable for *twenty minutes*?

"What kind of situation?" Abigail struggled to keep her voice light and her tone merely curious, even as her grip on the spoon handle tightened until pain radiated up her arm.

Butter crock in hand, Rosalind traipsed back toward the stairwell, obviously eager to make her escape. "Oh, there was just some stranger in town who got a little too friendly toward me. Zach happened to witness the scene and stepped in to scare the fellow off. No harm done. I promise." She backed into the stairwell. "Nothing to concern you."

Rosalind smiled, spun around, and flew up the stairs. Too bad that smile was the same one she always used when trying to talk her way out of trouble.

Abigail's heart throbbed. The spoon loosened in her grasp and knocked against the side of the skillet, splattering grease onto her hand. With a hiss, she yanked her hand away from the pan and rubbed it against the front of her apron. Rosalind was hiding something from her.

Abigail said little through dinner, opting to watch her companions instead. The guilty little glances Rosie shot at Zach when she thought Abigail wouldn't notice. The pointed looks he jabbed back. Not exactly lover-like, but they hinted at something between them. A shared secret.

Something about stables, no doubt.

Abigail lurched to her feet. Rosie exuded a small gasp at her abrupt movement. Zach halted his fork halfway to his mouth and raised a brow. Abby could feel the heat of their eyes on her, but she didn't care. She needed to get away. Now.

"I'm not feeling well," she said, her untouched plate adding credence to her statement. "I'm going to bed."

"It's not even seven yet," Rosie protested.

"I know, I'm just . . . tired."

Tired of pretending nothing was wrong. Tired of being on the wrong end of family secrets. Tired of not being the woman men preferred.

Leaving her dishes on the table, she fled the room, only to be stopped by a warm hand on her arm just outside her bedroom.

"Abby?" he said, his voice rich, rumbly, and setting off newfound flutters in her belly when he had absolutely no right to have that kind of effect on her. Not when he was keeping secrets from her. "Are you all right?"

No, she wasn't all right. Two hours ago she was seriously considering sending Rosalind to visit Lydia and inviting herself into her husband's bed. Now she couldn't even manage to look him in the eyes.

He must have noticed, for he cupped her chin with his hand and drew her face around. "Abby?"

Her lashes shuttered her gaze from him. "Please, Zach, I just want to go to sleep."

"All right."

But he didn't release her. Instead his free hand came up to cup the other side of her face. He lifted her toward him. His breath fanned across her cheek.

No. She couldn't do this. Couldn't pretend their courtship was real.

Just as Zach's lips lowered to hers, she twisted her face away.

CHAPTER

20

When Zach's lips skittered off the edge of Abigail's jaw, hurt
hit him square in the chest. Followed by confusion. Then a
spark of anger.

Straightening, his hands fell away from her face. "You're
upset."

She offered no comment, just spun around and made for
the doorway.

Not so fast, chickadee.

Zach clasped her wrist and halted her escape. She glared at
him over her shoulder and gave a tug on her arm, but he held
firm.

"Let me go." Defiance flared hot in her golden eyes as she
tugged a second time.

He stepped closer so her tugs wouldn't strain her arm, but
he didn't release his grip. "Why didn't you let me kiss you?"

In answer, she jerked her arm again, harder this time. He
opened his hand, not wanting to hurt her.

Abigail darted into her room and flung the door at the jamb
with enough force to splinter wood—or injure a man's foot, if

he happened to be fool enough to stick it in the way. Zach bit back a groan as the door ricocheted off the side of his stocking-clad foot. Wishing he hadn't left his boots downstairs tonight, he tried to ignore the throbbing, but his clenched jaw must have given him away, for when his wife yanked the door open to glare at him for interrupting her grand exit, a flash of regret crossed her face. It only lasted a moment, but at least he knew she cared a little about his well-being.

"Remove your foot from my door," she demanded.

He shook his head. "Not until you explain."

Chest thrust forward, eyes flashing, chin proudly erect—she was beautiful. Full of fire and spice. He wanted to snatch her off her feet and carry her to his bed to see what else they could set aflame. Too bad the passion she displayed at the moment most likely leaned toward bashing his skull with a bread tin.

"The physical truly is all you care about, isn't it?" she said.

Zach gave a guilty start. Had she read his mind?

"Fine. A bargain's a bargain. You want a kiss every night? Have a kiss." Anger laced her words, but not so much that he failed to hear the sorrow in the crack of her voice.

Before he could blink, she jabbed her face at him and poked his cheek with all the finesse of a woodpecker drilling for worms. Thankfully, the reaction time of his arms was faster than his brain, for the instant she attacked, he grabbed her about the waist. Her palm splatted against his chest as she caught her balance, and a quiet sob squeezed out of her.

That sob scraped his heart raw. But he couldn't let this wound fester. Especially if he was the cause. Which he must be, even if he didn't understand what he'd done.

Their marriage might not be conventional, but that didn't mean he didn't care how it fared. How *she* fared. He'd vowed to cherish her, and judging by her obvious dissatisfaction with him at the moment, he'd missed that mark by a pretty wide margin today. He needed to adjust his aim, but until he could figure out which way the wind blew, he risked making things worse.

She no longer fought him, but her tucked chin hid her face, making it impossible to gain clues from her expression. He had a sneaking suspicion there might be tears. He hated tears. Never knew what to do to make them stop. He steeled himself for dripping eyes and set his jaw.

He'd warned her he wasn't marriage material, but she'd wed him anyway. Too late for either of them to back out now. Zach might not know much about being a husband, but Brother Samuelson had given him a list of verses to study up on the matter. He distinctly recalled one of them stating that they weren't to let the sun go down on their wrath. So tears or not, he'd find a way to cut through this wrath and defuse it before letting Abigail dodge off to bed.

He slid a hand under her chin and gently inched her face upward. Damp lashes blinked back pooling moisture. His gut knotted, but he didn't stop. He caressed her jawline and forced his gaze to hold hers. "I don't care about one missed kiss, Abby," he said. "I care about *why*. Why did you turn away from me? From us?"

"Because I was foolish enough to believe that you might be coming to care for me. But those kisses we share don't really mean anything to you, do they? They're just to pacify your manly needs. Isn't that what you said? That men tend to focus on the physical side of relationships?"

Zach winced, his thoughts from a moment ago rising to convict him.

Her head fell back down, her shoulders sagging. "That's what I thought. If you cared for me at all, you wouldn't keep secrets from me."

Secrets? Zach's hand fell away from her face, dread clinching in his gut. What had she heard? He didn't think anyone in Honey Grove knew about his past, but things like that didn't stay hidden forever.

He cleared his throat, determined to face whatever consequences had risen up to bite him. He owed her that much.

"Ask me," he said as he braced himself for the bullets she would fire. They might blow this marriage to bits, but he'd made a vow, and he aimed to hold up his end of the bargain.

She slowly lifted her chin, hope warring with hurt in her golden-brown eyes. "What were you and Rosalind doing alone together in the stables?"

Zach blinked. He'd braced for a shotgun blast, and she'd hit him with a slingshot. The question bounced off his chest with such insignificant impact that it left him a bit stupefied.

"What?"

"Today. In town. You and Rosalind were seen together . . . *embracing* . . . and–and disappearing into a stable for . . . extensive periods of time. Alone. I asked Rosalind about it, gave her a chance to explain, but she offered only evasive responses and nervous gestures. Then at the table, I saw the way you two looked at each other. Guilty glances. Secrets. It's obvious that you're hiding something from me."

Zach's mind spun, searching for a way out of this tangle without hurting either sister, but he hesitated too long.

"I never should have forced you into this marriage." Her gaze slid back down to the floor, and her toe kicked at a knothole in the floorboard. "It wasn't fair to you. My hours in the bakery keep me from being the attentive wife a husband deserves. And while I don't believe the foul rumors that are circulating about how you and Rosalind are carrying on behind my back, I understand why they are easy for people to believe. She's so much prettier than I am. Sweet-natured and charismatic. You could have had the sleek, spirited Arabian filly, but you got stuck with the dumpy plow horse instead."

"Stop."

Her head snapped up at his sharp tone.

He worked his jaw back and forth, his temper flaring with a heat he hadn't expected. Busybodies and their small-minded pettiness. Yet it irked him that Abigail had allowed them to get under her skin. And what was she thinking, calling herself a plow horse? If a man had made such a comment about his wife, he would have flattened the scoundrel.

"Stop belittling yourself, Abby. And stop apologizing for trapping me in this marriage. I'm a grown man who's been making his own decisions since I was thirteen years old. No one trapped me into anything. I came into this marriage as a willing partner and spoke my vows without any duress. And if I ever hear you compare yourself to your sister in such an unflattering way again, so help me, I just might bend you over my knee and take a paddle to your backside."

Eyes wide, she blinked at him as if he'd started spouting Chinese. Well, maybe a little Chinese would finally straighten out her thinking.

Hoping he was on the right track, he jumbled together the rest of what he had to say and tossed it at her before she could close the door on him for good. "Some cad harassed your sister in town today, and I put my arm around her in an effort to protect her from prying eyes, just like I would shelter Evie if she had been the one involved. I took her to the stables because I couldn't think of anywhere else in the immediate area where we would be assured some privacy. Rosalind needed to tell me a few things without a bunch of busybodies around to eavesdrop."

Abigail's forehead scrunched. "What would she tell you that she couldn't tell me?"

"I promised to keep her confidence, so I can't say, but I did encourage her to talk to you. Told her you would support her no matter what."

"Of course I would!" That fierce light he loved so much flashed in her eyes.

"Just like I will support *you* no matter what."

She tilted her head, her gaze searching his.

He gently gripped her upper arms and rubbed her shoulders with his thumbs. "I vowed to stand by your side for better or worse, and I meant it. But there's more than a wedding vow holding me to you, Abby."

She blinked, then nodded. "Our contract."

Good grief. Was she really so blind to her own value? He shook his head. "I haven't given that piece of paper a second thought since we wed."

Her brows rose slightly as she scanned his face for clues. "Then, what?"

"*You*, Abby."

Her head tipped back. "Me? I–I don't understand."

And that was the problem. One he needed to rectify. No more patiently waiting for her to get used to him. Time to stake his claim in a way she wouldn't be able to doubt.

"I didn't marry you to save your bakery."

"Y-you didn't?"

"Nope." His grip on her arms tightened slightly, urging her to pay attention. Words weren't exactly his specialty, and he didn't want to have to repeat himself. "If some other female had proposed marriage to me in order to keep her sewing shop or laundry business, I would have turned her down." He gave her a sharp look. "Even Rosalind."

Her breath stuttered a bit as she inhaled. "Why?"

"Because I'm selfish. I ain't about to tie myself to a woman for the rest of my days when I hold no affection for her."

She swallowed. "Are you saying that you . . . care for me?"

"I'm saying that of all the women in this town, you're the only one who could have tempted me to say yes."

"But why?"

Could she not just believe him and be done with it? How much explaining did a man need to do to convince his wife of his affection? He felt sweat gather between his shoulder blades. He was no good at making pretty words. The more he opened his mouth, the greater his chances of mucking things up. But she was looking up at him with such a mix of confusion and expectancy. He knew that if he failed to give her an answer, he'd undo any progress they'd just made.

"Your dimples," he blurted.

Oh, good one. Zach fought not to roll his eyes at his ineptitude. He dropped his hands from her arms and shifted his weight. "I like looking at them, all right? When you smile, your cheeks crease and it makes me feel . . . I don't know . . . lighter."

That had to be the stupidest attempt at flattery ever uttered. Even he could hear how defensive and grumpy he sounded. But she didn't scoff or grunt in disgust. No, she smiled, letting those little creases dance for him, and something shifted inside him, making him feel—yep—lighter.

So he tried again.

"I like your hands too."

She held her palms out in front of her and flipped them over, as if trying to see what he could possibly appreciate. He brought his own hands up and traced the lines of her fingers, the pads of her palm. "They're strong hands. Not afraid of hard work. Yet delicate and gentle too."

She watched his hands move over hers, her fingers quivering at his touch.

He searched for another compliment to give, gaining a bit of confidence at her response. But the next several parts of her anatomy that jumped to mind as being exceptionally admirable were not exactly appropriate to mention.

Slowly, her focus lifted from their hands back to his face, and he saw the craving there. The hunger to believe she could be wanted for herself.

Come on, man. Think of something.

"Your clothes."

Her nose scrunched, and she cast a quick glance down at her plain, dark blue frock. "My clothes?"

"Not your clothes, exactly," he hedged, trying to find the words for what he meant. "More the fact that you don't really care about how they look."

She frowned.

He knew he would screw this up if he kept opening his mouth. "That didn't come out right." He let go of her hands and paced. "What I meant was that you don't waste time gussying yourself up."

"And you *like* having a plain wife?"

"You're not plain!" Zach groaned. Could he dig this hole any deeper? "I'm no good at this, Abby." He blew out a breath and gazed at the ceiling. "I'm trying to compliment you on being practical and concerned about things that actually matter instead of superficial fripperies, all right? Cut me some slack."

A strangled sound erupted from his wife. He slanted a glance at her. Abby's hand covered her mouth as her eyes twinkled with mirth. He scowled, which only made her eyes brighter. Ornery woman.

"So what you're saying," she said, dropping her hand from

her mouth and stepping closer to him, "is that you like that I'm a businesswoman, even if that means I don't have time to gussy myself up for you."

He harrumphed. "You don't need any gussying. You're plenty pretty without all the rigmarole females call fashion."

Her fingers fiddled with the shirt button in the middle of his chest. His pulse kicked up.

"And you don't think I'm a neglectful wife because I go to bed early and leave you to your own devices instead of doting on you hand and foot?"

"Shows you're sensible," he said as her fingers worked their way up to the next button. "A well-rested woman makes better company than one who's short-tempered 'cause she didn't sleep enough. Besides—" He paused to clear his throat. She had walked her fingers up to the button just beneath the opening at his neck, and concentration was becoming scarcer by the moment. "My, uh, hands and feet work just fine. Don't need you waiting on me." Her finger slipped inside his collar, and her cool skin brushed against his heated neck before dodging away to lay against the fabric of his shirt. "Though I'd, uh, not be opposed to a little doting every now and then."

"Zach?"

"Hmm?"

Her head tilted up. "I'm ready for that good-night kiss now."

Thank heaven. He could finally do something with his mouth that didn't require words.

Zach clutched his wife to him and claimed her lips with such intensity, such heat, that their connection would surely be seared into her memory, cauterizing all doubt.

And just in case a few worrisome breaches remained, he kissed her again.

CHAPTER

21

The following morning, Abigail hummed as she pulled her second batch of sticky buns from the oven. Memories of the kiss she'd shared with her husband last night zinged through her mind and energized her work.

Zach had been kissing her good night for a month, but as much as she'd enjoyed every one of those kisses, none of them had left her as staggeringly altered as the ones they'd shared last night. Perhaps it was because they'd shared more than a physical connection. They had laid their hearts bare to each other, exposing the raw and ugly places. Anger, jealousy, and self-derision had swirled within her, yet Zach hadn't shrunk back. Even when the muck inside her spilled out onto him. Instead, he stepped into the fray, fought for her—for *them*. With the most backward, inelegant, completely wonderful compliments she'd ever received. No poet could stir her heart as completely as her husband grousing at her to cut him some slack because he couldn't get the words out right.

Abigail grinned as she flipped the round baking pan over and coaxed the sticky buns onto the worktable. The sweet concoction of maple syrup, brown sugar, and nuts she'd lined the pan with glistened atop the buns in sheer perfection. Judging the dozen buns with an expert eye, she picked out the two best from the batch and set them on a plate for Zach. She'd carry them upstairs as soon as she finished organizing her bakery trays for the morning. Perhaps instead of simply leaving his breakfast for him, she could seek him out and share a pleasantry or two before they went their separate ways.

As if her thoughts had conjured the man she sought, a stair creaked and a pair of large feet worked their way down. Unable to look away, she watched as long legs appeared, gradually stretching up into a solid, well-muscled chest. When his face finally cleared the stairwell wall, her breath caught. His midnight-blue eyes locked directly onto hers as if he'd known precisely where she stood.

"Mornin'." His low voice rumbled, and her skin registered the vibrations with delightful tingles of awareness.

Her lips curved upward. "Morning."

He didn't say more, just took a seat on the third stair and reached for his boots. He winced slightly as he shoved his right foot in, and Abigail immediately recalled the abuse she'd dished out with her bedroom door last night.

"Sorry about your foot." She took a hesitant step toward him, her gaze climbing upward as he stood.

His intense regard didn't flicker one iota at the reminder of her less-than-commendable behavior. It just kept radiating heat in her direction. "It'll heal."

Goodness. She wouldn't need her oven the rest of the morning if this heat between them kept up.

Clearing her throat, she ventured a step closer. "You're down early today. I just pulled the sticky buns out of the oven."

"Thought I'd start breaking my fast here in the kitchen." *With you.* His mouth didn't say the words, but his eyes did.

Abigail wasn't accustomed to such overt masculine attention. It made her jittery and altogether uncomfortable. Yet she refused to duck her head as instinct demanded. Zach had emboldened her last night, made her believe she might actually be worthy of a man's regard despite her unconventionally round shape. Perhaps even *because* of it. And wasn't that a mind-altering thought? Zach might actually prefer abundant curves to wispy waists and delicate features. As much as that contradicted her previous experience with men, she could no longer deny the possibility. After all, there had been nothing polite about Zach's most recent kisses. They had been passionate. Barely contained. Not the kisses of a man simply doing his duty.

"I'd like that," she said, finally turning away from his sizzling gaze to collect the sticky buns she'd set aside for him. She carried the plate to the small table she kept in the kitchen, then fetched a mug from the cupboard and filled it to the brim with coffee from the freshest pot on the stove.

The bakery would open for business in about thirty minutes, and Rosalind would soon bustle between the kitchen and the shop as she tended to customers. But for now, Abigail and Zach had a few private moments.

"Sit with me?" Zach held out the second chair.

She nodded. All of her breakfast items were done and cooling. She'd need to arrange them on the trays and move them to the display case in the shop, but that could wait a few minutes.

Abigail seated herself across from him, her gaze raking his features while he turned his attention to his breakfast. Broad shoulders encased in blue cotton, nearly black hair in need of a trim curling slightly behind his ears, tanned swarthy skin, dark whiskers shadowing his square jaw. He hadn't shaved. He must have changed his morning routine to accommodate having breakfast with her. Her heart warmed at the thought.

175

She watched as he sipped his coffee, deciding that she liked his dark scruff. It enhanced his rugged appeal. Made him look just the tiniest bit dangerous. Though not to her. Never to her. He was her protector, only dangerous to those who threatened what belonged to him. And *she* belonged to him. While some independent women who ran their own businesses and made their own decisions might balk at that rather primitive idea, the concept secretly thrilled Abigail, because she knew that *he* belonged to *her* as well. Equal partners. Mutual respect. Belonging wasn't ownership, it was relationship. A relationship she very much wanted to build with Zacharias Hamilton.

He'd finished his first bun while she wool-gathered. Embarrassed to have made no effort to converse, Abigail frantically dug around for something to say, latching on to the item most on the town's mind of late.

"Will Mr. Sinclair be closing the lumberyard early this Saturday for the Fourth of July celebration?"

"Yep." Zach wiped his mouth with the back of his hand, then reached for his coffee. "If we can get the order for the James Gilmer house filled by Friday, we'll take the entire day off."

She smiled. "That's wonderful! I'm glad you'll have time to relax and enjoy the festivities."

The coffee halted halfway to his mouth. "I thought we'd be enjoying the festivities together."

"I'll be there," Abigail hedged. "Eventually."

Zach set the coffee cup down with a *thunk* and shot her a frown.

"Holidays and special events bring so many people to town that the businesses on the square remain open late into the afternoon." She shrugged in apology. "I make some of my best profits in the hours before and after the Fourth of July parade."

"Then I guess you better give me some pointers on how to help in the shop."

Help in the . . . ? Abigail blinked. Surely she'd misunderstood. Zach didn't know the first thing about baking, and he certainly wasn't the sociable type to chat up customers while they stood in line. And picturing him in an apron was ludicrous in the extreme. Her father might have worn one, but Zach? Abigail bit back a giggle.

"You can tutor me tonight and tomorrow," Zach said, "but not on Thursday."

She tilted her head. "Why not Thursday?"

Heat flared in his eyes again as his gaze caressed her face. "I'm abducting you."

Her pulse tripped. "Abducting me?"

"Mm-hmm."

The beast left it at that, picking up his second sticky bun and tearing off a large bite instead of explaining himself.

"Should I notify the marshal?" Abigail quipped while he chewed.

Zach quirked a half grin and shook his head.

What is he planning? Whatever it was, he seemed in no hurry to relate the details. Unless, of course, he simply enjoyed prolonging her torture.

He leaned forward and took another bite of his bun. Yes. Definitely enjoying the torture.

Time to shift the balance of power.

Abigail manufactured a bored little sigh and got up from the table. "I suppose I'll find out on Thursday." She waved a hand as if completely uninterested in what would transpire that evening. "I better get my pastries into the shop."

She turned her back on him. A mistake. Before she managed two steps, he'd abandoned his chair and wrapped an arm around her midsection, hauling her backward against his chest. She gasped at the sudden contact.

All right. Not a mistake. Abigail smiled, keeping her face aimed away from him. She was exactly where she wanted to be.

His face bent close to her cheek. So close that she felt the rasp of his whiskers against her skin. Then his voice rumbled low in her ear. "I'm stealing you away, wife. Getting you alone. Taking you up on my horse and carrying you off into the countryside, where we'll feast on a dinner packed by the Commercial Hotel, walk along a pretty little stream, and watch the sun set behind the trees."

Her heart beat faster than a hummingbird's wings, as much from his nearness and the low, seductive murmur of his voice as the actual description of her *abduction*.

Unable to speak and barely functional enough to breathe, she made no comment, just leaned her head back against the hollow of his shoulder.

"Still want to invite the marshal?"

Her eyes slid closed, and she gave a small shake of her head, which earned her a growly chuckle from her very-pleased-with-himself husband.

The click of the door leading to the shop brought Abigail's eyelids to attention. She stiffened in Zach's arms as Rosalind strolled into the kitchen.

"It's nearly opening time, Abby. Where are the—oh." Her sister drew up short, her eyes widening, then crinkling as a smile blossomed across her face. "Never mind. I'll, ah, just wait to open until you're ready." With a sharp pivot, she made a hasty exit and left Abigail alone with her husband.

Her sister's dancing eyes and obvious delight in finding the two of them together soothed some of Abigail's embarrassment, yet it also brought the unanswered questions from last night back to the front of her mind.

"Zach?" She twisted in his arms and leaned away from his hold.

"Hmm?" He seemed reluctant to let her go. His fingers lingered at her waist.

"Is Rosalind in some kind of trouble?"

Zach's hand fell away from her hip, and she felt the loss so keenly that she almost wished she hadn't asked. Yet this was her sister. If something was wrong, Abigail needed to know.

Her husband straightened and blew out a breath as he scratched at a spot beneath his chin. "It's not my story to tell," he said, "but I promise that I will do everything I can to ensure no harm comes to her."

"No harm?" How serious *was* this? Abigail's chest tightened. "Does this have something to do with the man who accosted her yesterday?"

"It's more complicated than that, but I really can't say more. You need to put the questions to her."

She would. At first opportunity. Abigail rubbed her arms, suddenly chilled.

"Oh, and in case some interfering busybodies decide to come tattle on me again," he said as he casually reached behind him to grab the last bite of sticky bun from his plate, "I should let you know that your sister is meeting me behind the church today at noon for some lessons on personal defense." He popped the bun into his mouth.

"Personal defense? Zach, you're scaring me." Abigail fisted the fabric of her apron. "Is she in danger?"

He shook his head as he swallowed. "Nah." But his eyes hinted that might not always be the case. "She's spooked after yesterday. Learning how to protect herself will restore her confidence." He grabbed his coffee and swigged down the last of it. "Besides, it's foolish for a woman not to know how to protect herself." He plunked down the cup. "I made sure Evie knew where all a man's vulnerable spots were and how to get to them. I'll teach Rosalind the same." He eyed her speculatively. "I could teach you too, if you want. It never hurts to be prepared."

"Focus on Rosalind for now."

He gave a sharp nod, then reached out to squeeze Abigail's shoulder. "I'll be watching out for her," he vowed.

Abigail nodded. Then, needing more than words to calm the worry exploding in her heart, she pressed her cheek to his chest and wrapped her arms around his waist. He embraced her in turn, dropping a kiss on her forehead.

Oh, Rosie. Have I been so busy taking care of the bakery that I've failed to take care of you?

Abigail pointed to a patriotic display behind the clerk's head. "I'll take ten yards of bunting, a spool of paper festooning, and a dozen of your small muslin stick flags."

The clerk glanced behind him, then turned back. "Those are actually our medium-sized flags. Three and a half by six. They're only two cents more per dozen than the tiny two-by-three-inch ones."

"All right, let's do the medium size." She'd give the decorations away to local children after she closed her shop on the Fourth, and they'd have much more fun waving the larger size around.

Wilkins, Wood & Patteson Dry Goods had to be the most festive store on the square. Red-white-and-blue displays filled the windows and shelves. They carried the largest selection of dress goods all year round, but in July, they were the exclusive purveyor of the bunting officially approved by the Honey Grove City Council. Every business on the square had to purchase the same bunting to present a uniform appearance, but Abigail was just now getting around to purchasing her required length. Thankfully, Rosalind had volunteered to deliver the widow bread this afternoon, which freed Abby to take care of this errand. Though, in truth, if she and Zach hadn't discussed their plans for July Fourth this morning, she'd probably still be procrastinating.

Decorating was not her forte. She could braid a beautiful loaf and ice the perfect cinnamon bun, but drape bunting and hang streamers? She didn't possess the patience nor the talent for such an undertaking. Thank heaven for Rosie. Her sister would have the bunting gathered and swathed in the time it would take Abigail to add a single length of paper festooning to the three shelves of her display case. Rosie was a marvel.

The clerk folded the cloth he'd finished cutting, counted out her flag sticks, and removed a spool of festooning from the display behind him and plunked it onto the counter next to the rest of her order. "Anything else today, Mrs. Hamilton?"

A handsome ewer and basin set in a display at the end of the long counter caught her eye. Several different razors and shaving soaps were artfully arranged atop draped toweling around the masculine basin. The ewer matched its counterpart, both solid white with a smooth finish and a single stripe of midnight blue around the rim. The blue reminded her of Zach's eyes.

She'd noticed his plain white shaving mug on the washstand in his room when she went in to dust and clean the rugs. Her mother had selected the floral set she'd shared with Abigail's father, and after she died, Papa hadn't had the heart to replace it. But that didn't mean Zach should be forced to face such femininity every time he washed. Now that she thought about it, she was amazed her burly husband had not banished the entire set at once.

"How much for that ewer and basin set?" Abigail nodded at the display of red razor boxes stacked around the white-and-blue porcelain. Even their ordinary goods had been made to look patriotic.

The clerk smiled, obviously eager to make another sale. "Three and a quarter for the entire ten-piece chamber set."

"Oh, I don't need the entire set." She blushed at the thought of buying her husband a chamber pot. They might be growing closer, but they weren't *that* close. Not yet. "Just the ewer and basin, please."

The clerk's smile dimmed just a bit. "The two pieces alone will run you two dollars, ten."

She raised a brow at the price. That was two-thirds the overall cost for only two-tenths the pieces.

"My manager doesn't like to break up sets," the clerk explained with an apologetic shrug. "And those are two of the largest pieces of the set. You sure you don't want all ten for only a dollar fifteen more? It really is the better bargain."

Abigail shook her head. Paying more for something she didn't need did not constitute a bargain. Not for a woman on a budget. "No, thank you. I'll just take the two pieces we discussed."

"Very good, ma'am. I'll fetch some from our inventory in the storeroom so I don't break up the display. I'll be back in just a moment."

She smiled, thankful he wasn't the type to press her for a larger sale against her wishes. But the instant he disappeared from behind the counter, a woman pounced like a lioness waiting for a weakened gazelle to separate itself from the herd.

"Abigail! Oh, you poor dear. I just heard." Sophia Longfellow snatched up Abby's hand, her voice carrying in a loud stage whisper.

Abigail snatched her hand back. "Stop, Sophia. Just stop." Whatever she was about to say, Abby didn't want to hear it.

Sophia reared back, eyes wide at Abby's blunt statement. She blinked once, then recovered her poise, a tiny pout slipping into place, as if she were the wronged party. "Stop what, Abigail? Being a concerned friend?"

Abby sighed and shook her head. "You stopped being my friend a long time ago." Her heart ached as she forced herself to accept that sad truth. This perfectly coifed, fashionably dressed woman before her was not the Sophie of Abigail's childhood. The one who'd been her partner in adventure, who'd run around in pigtails, muddy boots, and torn hems—that girl no longer existed. "For years I hoped we could mend our fences and at least get to a place of cordiality if not friendship," Abigail admitted, "but you've made it clear that is not an option."

"*I've* made it clear? I've done nothing but look out for your interests."

Abigail held her chin up, determined not to be cowed. Guilt would not blind her this time. She wouldn't scurry away to wallow in her insecurities again. She knew the truth, and it was past time to give it voice. She met Sophia's gaze straight on. "You tried to destroy my marriage. How is that in my best interest?"

Sophia's eyes narrowed. "I did no such thing. I've only tried to protect you from that philandering man you call husband. Just today he was seen out behind the church with his arms around your sister! That's twice in as many days. The man has no shame!"

Several patrons had taken an interest in items on shelves closer to the front of the store, their eavesdropping intentions clear. Heat rose to Abigail's cheeks, but she refused to back down. Sophia had disparaged Zach, and that, she would not allow.

Head high, heart pumping faster than a locomotive at full steam, Abigail stared down her former friend and ensured her voice carried to all those who cared to listen.

"Zacharias Hamilton is an honorable man and a good husband. Anyone who knows him at all will attest to his character. Yesterday my sister was accosted by a man in town, and Zach came to her aid. Today he met with her at noon to teach her how to defend herself against such villainy should a similar situation ever arise in the future."

Sophia shook her head as if she believed Abigail's faith too blind for her own good, but when she opened her mouth to offer her opinion, Abby cut her off. She wasn't about to let her spew more of her poison.

"You have good reason to bear me a grudge, Sophia, but I won't allow you to speak ill of my husband. He has done you no harm and doesn't deserve your scorn nor the scorn of anyone who listens to your perverse twisting of the truth."

Sophia gasped, as did a few of the ladies close enough for Abigail to hear. But she wouldn't back down now.

"Neither of us can change the past, as much as we might wish we could." And heaven knew how much Abigail wished she could. "All we can do is move forward with grace and build the best future we can. You have a life with Chester, a political career to navigate, and a town to help run. More than enough to keep you busy. Leave me and Zach alone."

Sophia lurched toward Abigail, her expression hardening in an instant, though she was careful to keep her face angled away from the other patrons. Abigail drew back slightly, shocked at the vitriol in Sophia's gaze.

"Chester isn't the life I wanted," Sophia hissed in a voice that, for once, *wouldn't* carry. "You know that." Her fingers grasped Abigail's wrist and tightened like a shrinking manacle. "An eye for an eye, Abby. Isn't that what the Good Book teaches? You stole my future from me. I'm returning the favor."

After a final squeeze that nearly cut off the blood flow to Abigail's hand, Sophia released her, pasted on an utterly false smile, and twirled back into the main part of the store. "Our Fourth of July celebration is going to be the best yet, don't you agree, Mrs. Timmons?" She waltzed over to the woman closest to the counter, who held a conveniently located mortar trowel in her hand as if she were seriously contemplating trading in needlepoint for bricklaying as her hobby of choice. "Now that our dear Abigail has finally purchased her bunting, we're guaranteed to have the finest-looking square in a hundred miles. Have I told you that the city has purchased fireworks for the occasion? Chester insisted. He does love a good show."

As Sophia deftly drew the attention of the other shoppers, Abigail turned from them and stared unseeing at the top of the counter where her parcels lay. She absently rubbed the sore spot on her wrist, but the throbbing of her arm was not half as painful as the throbbing in her heart. Mercy. She'd known Sophia harbored a grudge against her, but she had never imagined her former friend actually wished her ill.

"Are you all right, Mrs. Hamilton?" The quiet murmur of the clerk brought Abigail's chin up. Kind eyes met hers, and the softness there nearly undid her.

She blinked away the moisture gathering faster than she would like behind her lashes and smiled. "Yes. Thank you." She fiddled with her purse strings, the obstinate things tangling instead of opening. "How much do I owe you?" Her purse refused to cooperate. Stupid strings. Must they set themselves against her too?

The clerk set the basin and ewer he'd fetched on the counter and reached for her hand. Unlike Sophia, his touch was gentle and feather-light atop her fingers. "I'll write up a bill and send it around to the bakery later today. Don't worry about it now."

Her fumbling fingers stilled. She met his gaze, her own blurry with tears she refused to let fall. Yet she had the feeling that should one escape, her only witness would not hold the transgression against her.

"Thank you." The words were too small to represent the flood of gratitude rising within her, yet he accepted them with a nod that somehow communicated he understood the wealth behind the words.

He removed his hand, stepped back, and recorded her purchases on a sales slip. "Let me summon a delivery boy to help you home with your purchases."

Normally she would turn down such an offer. The ewer and basin weren't so heavy she couldn't manage, and a delivery boy would expect a tip, an extra expense she usually opted to avoid. But seeing as how she couldn't even manage to open her own purse strings, having someone else carry her items gave them a better chance of arriving home unscathed.

"That would be much appreciated."

By the time the boy arrived, Abigail had her emotions in check and her eyes dry, or at least no longer threatening imminent rainfall. She'd even managed to unknot her purse strings enough to extricate a coin for when the lad completed his duty.

A duty that was interrupted less than two storefronts down the boardwalk when Mary Bowen scurried up from behind.

"Abigail. Wait."

Waiting was the very *last* thing Abigail wanted to do. Goodness, could she not just be left alone to lick her wounds and try to get her head on straight before Zach came home?

She kept walking.

"Please, Abigail." Mary huffed a bit as she caught up. "I want to apologize."

Not pour salt in her wound? Abigail cast a sideways glance at Mary. She looked sincere. Abashed, even. Abigail slowed.

The delivery boy fell back a couple paces, giving the ladies a modicum of privacy.

"I never should have told Sophia what I saw yesterday. She twisted it into something ugly that I knew wasn't true. I barely slept at all last night, fretting about not standing up to her when she started spinning her tales." Mary nibbled on her bottom lip and glanced at the ground before meeting Abigail's eyes. "But *you* stood up to her today. Back there in Wilkins's store. I heard you. We all heard you. It's like you're a completely different person from who you were yesterday. You didn't let her intimidate you or sway you into believing anything bad about your husband. You just stopped her in her tracks and stood up for what was right. It was . . . amazing."

Abigail's feet ceased moving altogether. Amazing? *Her?*

But Mary wasn't done. "What changed?" she asked, a hungry look on her face as if she too wished to transform overnight. "How did you find the courage to stand up to her?"

"I didn't find it," Abigail said, a shy smile on her face as she recalled Zach shoving his foot in her door, demanding they talk things through and siphon out the poison before it infected their marriage. "It found me."

Mary's forehead scrunched.

Abigail knew she wasn't making any sense, but she didn't really care. Her equilibrium was coming back into balance, and it felt so good that she nearly laughed.

"I had a long talk with my husband last night," Abigail explained, "and he made me realize that I have to choose which voices to believe. I can believe the ones that tell me I'm not good enough or brave enough or pretty enough and let them skew my perception of events, or I can push aside that clamor and seek out the voice that tells me I am fearfully and wonderfully made."

Mary blinked, her face blank.

Abigail did laugh then. "If you want to be brave, Mary, choose to be so ahead of time. I knew I couldn't listen to Sophia any-more, not if it was going to hurt my marriage, so I told myself that the next time she tried to shame me or my husband, I would stop her before she could plant any negative thoughts in my head. That's what I did. You can do the same thing. Just make a plan and stick to it when the time comes. It's hard, and it might hurt." A lot. "But it's worth it."

Especially if it meant strengthening her marriage.

Perhaps she should apply that principle to another area of her life. Might she be less afraid of sharing Zach's bed if she made a plan ahead of time?

It couldn't hurt to try.

CHAPTER

23

With nervous energy zinging through her at the prospect of actually *planning* to become a true wife to her husband, Abigail tossed her patriotic purchases on the kitchen worktable, paid the delivery boy for his trouble, then took the new pitcher and basin upstairs.

She stepped into the master bedroom, and a shiver danced along her arms. *Don't be a ninny. It's not like you're planning to don your nightclothes and wait for him under the covers. You're just surprising him with a gift.* A gift that might eventually lead to covers and what occurred under them, but she'd best not jump too far ahead on this planning thing. She'd lose her courage before she even began.

Bread won't rise unless the baker first activates the yeast. Another of her father's favorite sayings. In other words, take one step at a time and trust the process.

Only she didn't know the process. Not for becoming a man's wife. Nor for handling the arrival of children that might follow sooner than she'd like. Once she took this step, there'd be no going back. Changes would come. The bakery could no longer be the center of her existence. Her dreams would have to adjust. Could she do that?

Sophia mourned the future she'd lost so much that she'd let it embitter her. Would the same happen to Abigail if she could no longer manage the bakery? Would she come to resent her husband, her children?

There was no question in Abigail's mind that Zach would be a good father. Just look at Evie. He'd raised his adoptive sister, and she adored him. And his treatment of Rosie only bore that out further. Protective yet at the same time empowering her to face her problems on her own. He didn't see women as lesser beings. He respected their abilities and would defend them like a hero of old.

So it came down to trust. Did she trust God either to postpone pregnancy or to work out a way to preserve her career aspirations if she pursued intimacy with Zach? She knew what the right answer was supposed to be, yet she wavered, unsure of how reality would play out. Not only where children were concerned, but with the intimate act itself.

Abigail sat on the corner of Zach's mattress, biting her lip when the bed frame creaked. If she knew more about what to expect or had a recipe to follow, it might be easier, but Mama wasn't around to ask, and as frank as dear Lydia was, Abigail couldn't imagine seeking such personal advice from someone outside of family.

She'd tried looking in the Bible, but the majority of the marriages chronicled there consisted of Husband X taking Bride Y into the family tent and—*boom*—wifedom. Sometimes on the very day the two met. There was the lovely story about Jacob loving Rachel and working for her for seven years, but nothing about courtship was revealed, only work. And the whole bride-switch trickery with Leah brought up too many uncomfortable notions about older, less attractive sisters.

Which meant Abigail would be making up this recipe on her own.

Heaven help her.

Abigail stood and crossed the room to the washstand situated to the left of the wardrobe. After transferring what water remained from the old ewer to the new, Abigail wiped the old pitcher dry with a towel, moved it and its matching floral basin to the floor, and arranged the new set nicely in the center. She tidied Zach's shaving mug, brush, and razor, then hung the damp towel on the rack to dry. Satisfied with the increased masculinity of the items, she turned her attention to finding a place to store the old set.

The wardrobe made the most sense. The last time she'd checked, Zach hadn't stored anything on the high shelf above the hanging rod. The pitcher would be too tall to stand upright, but she could lay it on its side next to the basin.

She opened the wardrobe door, her gaze skimming over her husband's Sunday suit coat and the two starched shirts that hung on the rod. Such ordinary items, yet they stirred her heart. These were the clothes of a hardworking man. A good man. A man willing to fight for the well-being of their marriage even though she had yet to share any wifely intimacies with him.

A man who planned to abduct her the day after tomorrow. Abigail's stomach fluttered, and a quiet giggle bubbled free. Maybe she didn't have to plan much after all. Her husband obviously had some schemes in mind already, so perhaps she could simply go along with whatever he devised.

Then again, did she really want to be a passive partner in this marriage? Zach might be the one instigating their romantic rendezvous, but that didn't mean she couldn't wage her own war to capture his heart. For that was what she wanted: his heart. He desired physical intimacy, loyalty, and trust from her. She wanted love.

Abigail bit her bottom lip as she stretched up on her tiptoes and slid her mother's basin onto the top wardrobe shelf. When had a practical solution for saving her bakery turned into an emotional campaign for a love match?

The minute Zacharias Hamilton said yes. That was when.

Add a month's worth of delicious good-night kisses along with companionable evenings, the zealous championing of little sisters, and a large smashed foot in her doorway, and Zach had perfected the recipe for love. At least on her side. Now she just had to discover the secret recipe for claiming his heart in return. Equal partners, that was the bargain they'd agreed to. If she were going to fall head over heels, it was only fair that he do the same.

Rising up on tiptoes again, Abigail tipped the pitcher sideways and slid it onto the shelf next to the basin. Halfway in, though, it stuck on something. She scooted it to the right until it cleared whatever had been blocking its progress, then tucked it securely onto the shelf. Afraid she might have inadvertently pushed one of Zach's belongings to the back of the wardrobe where he wouldn't be able to find it, she fetched a chair from the corner and climbed atop it to retrieve whatever she'd displaced. Reaching in nearly elbow-deep, Abigail felt around in the shadows until her fingers brushed against a small leather case. She pulled it to the foreground, intending to simply leave it there for her husband to find when he needed it, but curiosity stirred.

Zach had left this entire shelf empty save this one item. Was it important to him? But if so, why had he pushed it so far back that it couldn't be seen? It seemed an odd contradiction.

Taking it down, she examined the small case, running her fingers over the initials embossed on the top flap. *J.M.* Who was J.M.? The M could stand for Mitchell, she supposed, the surname Zach had been born with, but what about the J? His father perhaps? Grandfather? The leather looked old, well-worn at the corners. Whoever it had belonged to had used it often. She eased a finger under the flap and slipped the loop free of the button holding it in place. She peeled back the flap and found a rather ordinary deck of playing cards.

Her brow furrowed. An odd memento. She'd expected to find a tintype of Zach's family or a pocket Bible or something else of sentimental value.

"Abigail? Are you here?" Rosalind's voice echoed up the stairwell, startling Abigail badly enough that she nearly lost her balance on the chair.

"Upstairs," she called, then frantically closed the card case and thrust it back onto the shelf. It wouldn't do to be caught snooping through her husband's belongings. Besides, she had much more important business to discuss with her sister.

Abigail scrambled off the chair, returned it to its designated corner, and exited the room just as Rosalind hit the top stair.

"Mrs. Gillespie insisted I accept a half dozen eggs in exchange for the delivery last week and today. I added them to our supply."

Abigail grinned. "She's such a sweetheart. I've told her she's doing us a favor by taking the day-old bread off our hands, but she insists on bartering whenever she's able."

"Pride is a delicate thing," Rosalind said. "She doesn't want to admit to accepting charity."

Abigail met her sister's eye. "It's hard for some people to accept help from others."

Rosalind frowned, obviously sensing Abby's double meaning.

"Come sit with me in the parlor, Rosie." Abigail laid a gentle hand on her sister's arm. "Zach won't be home for another hour, and it's been a while since we've talked."

"Talked? About what?" Rosalind's voice rose slightly, and an expression came over her face that reminded Abigail of a rabbit caught in a snare. "What did Zach tell you?"

"Frustratingly little," Abby admitted, "but enough for me to know that you've been carrying something on your own for far too long. Whatever it is, I want to help."

Rosalind pivoted sharply and crossed her arms over her midsection.

The self-imposed distance slashed at Abigail's heart. Perhaps she shouldn't push. Rosalind obviously didn't want to talk, and she feared driving a wedge between them if she forced the issue. But then she remembered Zach's foot in her door. The easy path rarely brought healing. Her sister carried a secret that had her seeking out lessons in defending herself against attack. Abigail couldn't just let the matter drop.

She circled her sister until she could see her face. "I'm sorry, Rosie. Sorry that I've been so wrapped up in bakery business that I failed to notice what you were going through. I let you down, but I'm here now, and I want to support you. To help you however I can."

Her sister pressed her lips together as she shook her head. "I can't tell you, Abby." Her voice rasped as if she'd wandered too close to a campfire. Her eyes reddened, and her chin quivered. "You'll be so ashamed."

Abigail vowed that no matter what her sister revealed, she'd show no shock and offer no recriminations. Only compassion.

"You're my sister." Abigail squeezed Rosalind's arm. "I love you. No matter what. You stood by me after what happened with Benedict. Let me stand by you now. Please."

Rosie's face crumpled. Her arms uncrossed, and tears slid down her cheeks. Abby didn't hesitate. She wrapped her sister in a hug and held on tight. A sob exploded from Rosalind's chest, and her arms came around Abby's waist. She bent her head to Abby's shoulder and let the tears fall.

After long minutes of mutual tears and murmured comfort, the two sisters finally made their way to the parlor and sat side by side on the settee. True to her vow, Abigail listened to Rosalind's tale with objective stoicism. At least on the outside. She nodded encouragingly and held Rosie's hand even as horror and heartbreak flared in equal measures in her breast.

Her baby sister had been manipulated by an older man, tricked into compromising herself in the guise of helping her dying father. Yes, she bore responsibility for her foolish choice, but it seemed grossly unfair that she should be the only one to pay the consequences. A man who profited from a young girl's desperation deserved to rot in jail, even if his actions weren't technically illegal. They were morally reprehensible and should be punished.

Yet even as outrage heated her blood, Abigail knew that railing at the corrupt photographer would do her sister no good. It wouldn't change what had happened, wouldn't remove the encroaching danger Rosie faced, and wouldn't help her move forward. So instead, Abigail held tight to her sister's hand and made sure Rosalind knew she wasn't alone.

"We'll get through this, Rosie. With God's help, no problem is insurmountable."

"God and your husband." Rosalind managed a small smile as she dabbed wetness from her cheeks with the back of her hand. "Zach taught me the most wonderful things today, Abby." Her eyes lit up, and she bounced a bit on the settee as she turned to face her sister more fully. "Did you know that a man has weak spots a woman can exploit? Like gouging at his eyes or stomping the heel of our shoe onto the top of his foot. An elbow to the soft spot under his ribs can knock the wind out of him."

She demonstrated with a short, quick jab of her elbow into the air above the settee's arm. "And a knee to, well, you know . . ." Pink colored Rosalind's cheeks. "Zach said if you jab as hard as you can, a man will double over and give you the opportunity to run away. Apparently an injury to that . . . area is quite debilitating."

Abigail blinked, not sure how to respond to such frank commentary. "Well. I suppose that's . . . good to know."

"He insisted I hit him. Full strength. I didn't want to at first. I was afraid I'd hurt him. But he insisted. He said I needed to know what kind of force to use. The poor man will be sporting a few bruises tonight." As her enthusiasm built at the retelling, Rosalind's natural optimism returned. Tears dried, and the temporary blotchiness of her complexion dissipated to reveal her usual peaches and cream. "He did protect his eyes and other . . . sensitive areas," she said, "but I lost count of how many times he took my elbow to his midsection and my heel to his foot."

"Oh dear." Abigail looked guiltily at her sister. "I hope it wasn't his right foot. I already abused that one quite shamefully with my door."

"During your argument last night?"

"You heard?" Abigail nibbled her lip.

Rosalind nodded. "It's a small house." She patted Abigail's knee. "But I also spied a rather enthusiastic kiss when I peeked down the hall after things quieted down, so I assumed the two of you worked everything out."

Heat flared in Abigail's face.

Her sister grinned at her discomfort. "So, will you be moving out of my room soon?"

Abigail shrugged. "Possibly."

Rosalind laughed. "It's about time."

"I didn't realize you were so eager to kick me out." Abigail pushed her sister's shoulder.

"Never." Rosalind's face grew serious. "And if I had any qualms about how he might treat you, I'd lock you in with me. Zach might be a little grumpy, but he has a good heart."

"He's not grumpy, he's just . . . not talkative."

"And you're completely besotted."

Abigail met her sister's gaze. She couldn't verbalize her agreement, but the warmth in Rosie's eyes told her she didn't have to. They both knew Abigail was well on her way to falling in love with her husband.

"You made a good choice, Abby." Rosalind's hand enveloped hers.

"I know."

She just wished she knew if Zach felt the same way. He obviously believed in making the best of any situation he found himself in and was doing an admirable job of making the best of their marriage, but if he could go back in time, would he make a different choice?

CHAPTER
24

Zach pushed open the bakery's back door and made sure not to limp when he entered the kitchen. He couldn't have the womenfolk thinking him battered by a little afternoon sparring. But the show was for naught, since his womenfolk were nowhere to be seen.

Clicking the door shut, Zach glanced about the kitchen. Empty. No pots on the stove. No food on the counter. Abigail usually had supper ready when he dragged in from the lumberyard, but the only evidence that she had even been home recently came from a haphazard pile of red, white, and blue decorations on the worktable.

With no one around to impress, he rolled his shoulder to ease its stiffness and rubbed at the sore spot beneath his ribs as he hobbled over to the stairwell. "Abigail?" His voice boomed up the stairs. "You home?"

Footfalls echoed above him a moment before a pair of lovely ankles encased in familiar brown leather half boots appeared at the top of the stairs. Zach enjoyed the view afforded by his wife's slightly raised petticoats as she bustled down to greet him.

"I'm so sorry. I lost track of t—"

He grabbed her by the waist, cutting her off mid-word while she was still two steps from the bottom. As she squealed in surprise, he spun her around, his achy shoulder and tender rib cage forgotten. The bruises on his instep smarted, however, when his off-balance bride stumbled over his feet to find purchase as he lowered her to the floor. He ignored the insignificant twinge. After their breakfast discussion of abductions and box dinners, he'd been fantasizing all day about having her in his arms and all to himself.

Slightly breathless, Abigail peered up at him with a delightfully dazed expression, her dimples winking at him. "My! Had a good day today, did you?"

His mouth tugged up at one corner. "Havin' a good one now."

Her lashes dipped to hide her tawny eyes. The shy smile she sported widened, deepening the creases around her mouth, which immediately put him in mind of kissing. Too bad the click of additional footsteps on the stairs warned that their privacy was about to disintegrate.

Not one to let a good hand go unplayed, however, Zach slid his palm from Abigail's waist to the middle of her back, pressed her up against him, and planted a kiss on those plump lips just as they formed an O of surprise. The kiss was quick but mighty sweet. So sweet, he had to turn away to collect himself before greeting his young pupil.

Rosalind's gaze darted from him to her sister, the light in her eyes glinting as she pieced together what she'd interrupted. "I think I'll, uh, take these decorations upstairs," she said as she crossed to the worktable and started piling fabric and streamers into the crook of her arm.

That sounded like a good plan to him. Unfortunately, his bride disagreed.

Abigail dashed over to her sister's side and laid a staying hand on her arm. "No, that can wait. We need to get supper started. Zach's bound to be hungry."

Yep. Though what he hungered for most wouldn't be found in any pot.

"No need to go to any trouble," he said, casually stalking his wife until he stood a mere foot from her position. She shot a look his way, and her teeth peeked out to nibble on her bottom lip. "We live in a bakery. I'm not gonna starve. Just slice up some of that ham from last night, and we can make sandwiches."

"But you had that for your lunch today."

He shrugged. "Filled my belly then. Imagine it'll do the same now."

Something flared in her gaze. Interest? Appreciation? Whatever it was, it had him itching to get her in his arms again.

"Why don't you go wash up?" she suggested as she turned to retrieve some bread from the cabinet that held their personal stores. The bread was a day old—all fresh baked goods went to paying customers—but it was still some of the best Zach had ever tasted. "I'll throw together some sandwiches and meet you upstairs."

"I'll just take mine to my room," Rosalind said, mischief dancing in her eyes as she shot him a conspirator's smile. "That way I can baste this bunting on the Singer machine before you turn in for the evening, Abby. Get an early start on all that gathering."

"There's no rush." Abigail glanced over her shoulder, her brow furrowed. "It'll keep until tomorrow when you have more daylight."

"I don't mind. Besides, it'll do the two of you good to have some time alone together without me hanging around like a third wheel."

Zach had to give the girl points for directness. Abigail would have a hard time wiggling out of that one.

"You're not a third wheel, Rosie. You're family."

Apparently not a hard enough time. Zach bit back a sigh. Was she still nervous to be alone with him? Or was she just trying to be a good sister and not allow her sibling to feel excluded? He thought he had seen something in her gaze earlier, something that seemed more open to physical closeness, but maybe it had been his own desire reflecting back at him, showing him what he wanted to see.

"I know," Rosalind said, turning to her sister. Something passed between them that Zach couldn't quite decipher. "But I could use a little time alone tonight anyway. To sort my thoughts."

Abigail touched Rosalind's arm, her gaze never leaving her sister's face. Then she nodded, and everything was decided.

It looked like he'd get his wife all to himself after all.

With a little extra pep in his step, Zach headed for the stairs, barely pausing long enough to yank his boots from his feet. "Guess I'll go wash, then."

Neither of the sisters paid him any mind, but that didn't matter. He had an engagement with his wife to prepare for and a good two hours of her company to enjoy before she retired. He aimed to make the most of it.

After hustling up the stairs, Zach pushed open the door to his room and crossed to the wardrobe, his fingers working shirt buttons through their holes. A clean shirt was in order. One smelling more of soap than sawdust and sweat. A man who intended to sit close to his wife on the settee while she read aloud after supper needed a clean shirt. Maybe a shave as well.

Nah. That'd be too obvious. He could practically see her mind whirring as she tried to figure out the implications of a clean-shaven jaw in the evening. Better not get ahead of himself. He'd save that for the abduction.

Zach grinned. Wooing one's wife might require more effort than he'd originally anticipated, but the hunt invigorated him. He might have to continue the abduction tradition even after she was fully his. Keep things interesting.

Not paying much attention, he yanked open the wardrobe door with one hand while shrugging his other shoulder out from under his suspender. As the strap fell away, his gaze caught on a foreign object on the top shelf. Two objects, as a matter of fact. The horrid floral basin and ewer that normally adorned his washstand. Why would they be in his wardrobe?

Zach freed himself from the second suspender and leaned back to see around the wardrobe door. There on his washstand stood a white china ewer and basin set with nothing but a band of dark blue to break up the plain display. No fluted edges or decorative handle. Just a straightforward, simple design without a single flower in sight.

He rubbed at an itchy place on his chest that just happened to be directly over his heart.

She'd thought of him. Fondly, apparently. The itch deepened into an ache. His practical wife had spent her hard-earned money on something completely unnecessary. The old wash set had been functional. Ugly, but functional. Yet she'd purchased a new one simply to please him.

His pulse ratcheted up to high speed even as he warned himself not to read too much into the gift. It didn't mean she'd developed feelings for him, although the thrill that surged through his blood at the thought had his hands fumbling as he tugged his shirttails free of his waistband.

Leaving the wardrobe door open, Zach moved to the washstand and fit his palm to the ewer handle. He poured a stream of tepid water over his other hand into the basin, enjoying the experience far more than the act warranted. Setting the ewer on the stand, he dried his wet hand on his trousers, then stripped out of his work shirt. He wadded it into a ball and tossed it at the basket on the far side of the wardrobe. It fell dead center, which only enriched Zach's good mood. Lathering his hands with a cake of soap, he washed his face, arms, and torso, then toweled dry.

Soft voices in the hall told him the women were finished in the kitchen, which meant Abigail would be waiting for him in the small sitting room off the parlor that served as their dining room. Alone.

Zach grabbed the first clean shirt he came to and threw it over his head. As he stuffed his shirttails into his trousers, his gaze caught on the corner of the leather case that hung over the edge of the top shelf.

His hands stilled.

She'd found his cards. Not that he'd been trying to hide them from her, but the thought of her touching that tainted part of his past brought the acrid taste of bile to the back of his throat. He wanted to erase that bit of history, scrub it away as he had the sweat and dirt from his hands, so that it wouldn't defile her. But it was a part of him. A part she deserved to know about. But when? They were just starting to gain their footing in this marriage. Surely it'd be wise to fortify the foundation before he started shaking the walls.

Zach tucked in the remainder of his shirt with more deliberate motions, the frenetic edge of his energy dissipating beneath the sober turn of his thoughts. As he buttoned the shirt placket and stretched his suspenders over his shoulders, he knocked the rust off his spirit and sought wisdom directly from the source.

"I know you and me got unfinished business between us," he

murmured in a low voice that barely wiggled the air, "but Evie's always sayin' as how the Bible teaches that if a man wants wisdom, he needs to ask for it. So, that's what I'm doin'. I've got a good thing goin' here with Abigail, and I don't want to ruin it. Don't want to lose her good opinion and affection before they have a chance to put down roots. Yet we vowed there'd be no secrets between us. And there are. Big ones. So what do I do? When is the right time to crack the lid on this can of sardines?" Zach reached for the leather card case and with one finger, pushed it back from the shelf edge until he could no longer see it. "Any recommendations you have to offer would be appreciated." He rapped his knuckle twice on the shelf edge. "Thanks."

Feeling a tad better now that someone much smarter than him was on the job, Zach closed the wardrobe door and gave himself one more check in the mirror above the washstand. He gave his hair a quick comb with his fingers, frowning at the chunk that insisted on falling over his forehead. Then, after making sure his turndown collar lay straight, he firmed his abdominal muscles against the sudden surge of nerves hot-footing it inside his gut and made his way to the sitting room . . . and his wife.

CHAPTER

25

Abigail found it difficult to eat much of her sandwich, what with the intense looks her husband kept shooting at her from across the table. He didn't seem to suffer the same affliction, polishing off two ham sandwiches, the majority of the watermelon salad she'd tossed together, and the largest of the cinnamon buns she'd saved for his dessert.

Dropping her napkin over her unfinished supper, she stood, collected her plate, and reached for the salad bowl. "I'll just clear these away, then join you in the parlor."

Zach rose to his feet. "Leave 'em." His fingers traced the curved table edge as he came toward her. "I'll clean up after you go to bed."

A man volunteering to do women's work? Her father had never washed a dish in his life, as far as Abigail knew.

Her astonishment must have shown on her face, for Zach chuckled softly, the rich sound dancing along her nape and causing her skin to tingle. "I lived alone for nigh on a year before we hitched up. I ain't allergic to dishwater."

"But . . ." She couldn't make herself put the plate down. It just felt wrong somehow. Irresponsible.

Then he took the plate from her and removed her only excuse to stall. Though why she felt the urge to stall, she couldn't figure out. She *wanted* to spend time with him. Hadn't she been planning that very thing? Apparently spending time alone with one's husband was more easily accomplished in theory than in reality. Nerves and insecurities barely existed in the hypothetical world, but here in the sitting room, they swarmed around her head like angry bees with stingers poised.

"Join me in the parlor?" Zach extended his arm.

Her belly fluttered, and some of the bees dispersed. How could she resist such a gallant invitation?

Nodding, she placed her hand on his arm and allowed him to lead her from the room. When they entered the parlor, she tried to slip free in order to fetch the Kemp family Bible that she usually read from after dinner, but Zach captured her fingers and tugged them back into place on his forearm. He gave them a little pat, a silent instruction not to stray again, then picked up the Bible himself from the bookcase and promenaded her over to the settee.

She usually sat in the rocker by the lamp where the light was better, but not tonight. Tonight her husband had different plans. Plans that included the two of them on the settee, his large frame taking up most of the room. Not that she minded. She enjoyed the close quarters, her limbs pressed up against his. Though how she was supposed to find the breath needed for reading aloud was a mystery yet to unfold.

Zach handed the Bible to her, the thick tome thumping down onto her lap. Then he did the oddest thing. He pivoted in his seat. Away from her.

Maybe he wasn't as keen on getting close as she'd thought.

Abigail tried to scoot closer to the arm on her end of the settee, but he glared at her.

"Wrong way."

"I thought you needed more room." Her hips *were* rather wide, after all. Even she and Rosalind had little elbow room when they shared this small sofa.

"Nope."

He bent toward her and dragged her against his side, fitting her hips quite snugly between the back cushions and the outer edge of his thigh. His arm came around her shoulders, securing her position while at the same time comfortably supporting her neck. One of his legs remained firmly planted on the floor, but the other stretched out, his calf coming to rest on the settee's opposite arm. She followed his example and balanced her ankles as well. Shoes didn't belong on the furniture anyway.

Little by precarious little, Abigail relaxed against her husband. He smelled good. Like soap and something a little musky. He gave no further instructions. Offered no topic of conversation. He just sat there, breathing. As if he'd accomplished everything on his list.

Get wife into parlor—check. Snuggle close on settee—check. Let wife make next move . . .

He might be waiting awhile on that one, since his wife had no idea what kind of move she should be making. The only thing she *was* sure about was that she liked being close to him. Feeling wanted. Accepted. No performance required. No expectations to meet.

She'd spent her whole life trying to prove herself worthy in her father's eyes, to earn his approval and thereby justify her existence. An impossible task when he only found value in sons. Yet toward the end, he'd depended on her more and more. He'd never gone so far as to verbalize pride in her ability to run the business, but the criticisms had faded, and she'd convinced herself that was almost the same thing as praise.

As much as she enjoyed simply sharing Zach's company, however, the idleness ate away at her peace of mind. She needed to *do* something. The mending basket sat across the room out of reach, and Zach had declared the dishes off-limits. So unless she wanted to start picking lint off the sofa upholstery, she had one option. Start reading.

Abigail fingered the Bible's cover as she snuck a sideways glance at her husband. His attention seemed to be focused on a spot on either her neck or shoulder. She couldn't tell which, but he seemed quite absorbed. Hopefully his attention was based on admiration and not on a spot of dirt or a sandwich crumb that had become lodged in the pleats of her blouse. Ordering herself *not* to investigate the misplaced crumb theory—she'd barely eaten enough to create crumbs in the first place—she tightened her grip on the Bible and turned her thoughts in a more pious direction.

She thumbed through the pages until she found her place in Romans where she'd left off the evening before, but as she smoothed the page, her heart tugged her toward a story that had come to mind earlier today. Failing to recall exactly where it was located, she flipped through Luke until she found the passage she sought in chapter ten.

Not quite willing to jump straight into the section that pricked her heart, she began reading aloud at verse twenty-five, the parable of the Good Samaritan.

The coziness of their position made her modulate her voice to a soft timbre appropriate for such intimacy. As she read, Zach stroked her arm. Then her neck. Then the tendrils of hair behind her ear. By the time she reached the story her heart had led her to, she was pretty sure he had ceased listening. She'd nearly ceased listening herself, what with all those distracting, tingle-inducing caresses, but as she began verse thirty-eight, her concentration sharpened.

> "Now it came to pass, as they went, that he entered into a certain village: and a certain woman named Martha received him into her house. And she had a sister called Mary, which also sat at Jesus' feet, and heard his word. But Martha was cumbered about much serving, and came to him, and said, Lord, dost thou not care that my sister hath left me to serve alone? Bid her therefore that she help me. And Jesus answered and said unto her, Martha, Martha, thou art careful and troubled about many things: But one thing is needful: and Mary hath chosen that good part, which shall not be taken away from her."

Abigail fell quiet. She stared at the words on the page without really seeing them. She didn't need to see them. They throbbed in her chest, convicting her, rebuking her.

"I'm Martha," she admitted quietly.

Zach's fingers stilled at her nape, but they didn't pull away. They simply came to rest, their warmth continuing to radiate against her skin. "Yep, you are. You work hard, aren't afraid to take charge, and value practicality. All good qualities."

"Not when all that work blinds me to what is truly important." She brought her chin around to look into his face. "I let Rosalind down, Zach. I was so focused on making the bakery a success that I left her to deal with our father's illness on her own. Worse, I never noticed the strain it was putting on her, nor the attention that scoundrel Julius paid her. If I hadn't been so consumed with work, she might not have felt so alone. I would have noticed . . . could have talked her out of . . ."

The tears she'd worked so hard to hold at bay during her

conversation with Rosalind finally found their freedom with Zach, as if his strength gave her permission to let down her guard.

"Hey. Come here." Zach shifted positions, scooping her up and setting her across his lap. He ran the pad of his thumb over her cheek to wipe away the moisture. "None of that."

He *did* look a bit panicked, now that she got a closer look at his eyes. Adorable man. Her lips twitched in the beginning of a grin.

"That's better." His heartfelt relief added another layer of balm to her soul. "We can't change the past," he said, stroking the side of her face. "All we can do is strive not to make the same mistakes in the future."

"You sound as if you're speaking from experience."

"Yep."

She waited for him to elaborate, and for a moment she thought he would. But then he gently guided her head to lie in the crook of his shoulder. It was a comfortable spot, one that could easily lull her into not caring that he was holding something back from her. Curiosity begged her to ask questions, but caution kept her lips sealed. Zach had been waiting patiently for her to open up to him physically. She supposed she owed him the same courtesy regarding emotional intimacy.

After all, she harbored a secret or two of her own.

Zach resumed his stroking, this time focusing his attentions on her arm. He did love his touching, and my, but she was quickly becoming addicted to his caresses.

"I'm glad Rosalind told you about the photographs," he finally said, breaking the silence and changing the subject in a rather neat maneuver.

Abigail sighed. "Me too. I just wish I could do something to fix it for her."

"You can stand by her. Might not fix the problem, but it'll give her the courage to face it."

She nuzzled a little closer and slid her palm up to rest over her husband's heart. "I know, but the Martha in me wants to *do* something."

"Don't you go sellin' Martha short, now," Zach said, a smile in his voice. "As I recall, she was the one who ran out to meet the Lord on the road after her brother died, while her sister stayed home with the mourners. Martha confessed Jesus as the Christ and believed he could do anything through his Father's power. That there's a woman of faith."

"Yes, well, she also told Jesus the body would stink after being in the tomb for four days when the Lord ordered the stone rolled away."

Zach chuckled. "Gotta love a practical woman. Best kind to have around in a crisis. Keeps a man grounded."

Grounded was all fine and good, but Abigail suddenly found she wanted to be the one to enable Zach to fly.

CHAPTER

26

"Hey! Watch it." Reuben ducked an instant before the planks Zach carried on his shoulder slapped him across the eyes. "You trying to take my head off?"

"Sorry," Zach mumbled, fighting the instinct to swerve back to correct his error. Doing so would bring the wood around again and take Reuben out from behind, completely invalidating his apology. "I didn't see you there."

"Didn't see me? I'm right in front of you." His partner placed a hand on the planks, as if not quite trusting Zach to keep them still, and slid up their length until he stood less than six inches from Zach. Reuben stroked his jaw and raised a brow. "How could you possibly miss this good-looking mug?"

"Guess the angelic shine blinded me," Zach said, completely stone-faced.

Reuben busted out a laugh, then slapped Zach's free shoulder. "My pulchritude *is* legendary, but I'm pretty sure it wasn't me who has you distracted." He winked. "Tonight's the night, right?" He waggled his eyebrows. "The picnic, the sunset, holding her close on horseback . . . You've been planning this little escapade for days. I'm amazed you haven't sawn off a finger or two by now."

"Need 'em to steer the horse."

"Uh-huh." Reuben rolled his eyes. "Try not to overwhelm her with your gushing sentimentality when you're out there tonight."

Zach sidestepped his know-it-all partner and dropped the fresh-cut boards onto the planing pile. "Abigail's a practical woman." One of the things he liked best about her. "She doesn't need gushing sentimentality."

He brushed the sawdust from his hands and turned, only to spy Reuben's wagging head and pitying expression, clearly indicating his opinion of Zach's intelligence. Or lack thereof.

"*All* women need gushing sentimentality, my friend. Well, maybe not gushing, and certainly not anything insincere, but a woman wants sweet words from her man. Even if she tells you she doesn't—trust me, she does." Reuben swaggered forward and grabbed Zach's shoulder. "After being married to Audrey for close to a dozen years, I've picked up a few pearls of wisdom. One of my favorite being that sweet words inspire warm feelings. And warm feelings from one's wife open many a desirable door." He released his grip on Zach's shoulder to thump him on the back.

Zach had to admit that he craved what his friend had. Not just the physical intimacy that Reuben's waggling eyebrows obviously referred to, but the closeness he had with his wife. A closeness that allowed him to know what she needed without her even having to say it aloud.

Zach had never experienced that kind of closeness with another person. Maybe with his mother, but he couldn't remember her. He'd idolized his father, the legendary riverboat gambler who taught his son card tricks and knew a hundred schemes to outplay an opponent. Yet despite the good times they shared, Zach would not consider them close. Jedidiah Mitchell had intentionally held himself apart from his son. Most likely for Zach's protection, but the barrier had existed all the same. He had separated himself from a boy too young to follow him into high stakes saloons in good times and too vulnerable for the dark alleyways and underhanded deals in bad times. Then there was Grandfather. With his cane and his resentment and the cotton he forced Zach to work until his fingers bled and his back gave out. A thousand miles wasn't enough distance between them, even if the man was surely dead by now.

Zach had closed himself off after escaping Grandfather's farm and become a loner, depending on no one but himself. Until the Children's Aid Society got their hooks into him. Even then, he'd walled himself off. Didn't socialize with the other kids in the orphanage. Bucked the system as often as possible in the hopes of getting kicked out. It would've worked too, except they opted to rid themselves of him by sticking him on one of the orphan trains headed west and trying to farm him out as free labor under the guise of adoption. No way was he going to work another farm, though, so he did what he did best—sabotaged himself. Acted belligerent, disrespectful, and downright mean to make sure no one wanted him. His size and stature made it difficult to dissuade those in the market for a field hand, but a well-placed threat to kill them in their sleep usually did the trick.

Then the train derailed, and Hamilton Pearson saved Zach's life, losing his own in the process and leaving his four-year-old sister without a protector. Evie and her mismatched eyes, Seth with his sickly constitution—Zach couldn't leave them to fend for themselves. They'd never make it on their own. So, at thirteen, Zach became head of the Hamilton family. A family more real than any he'd had blood ties to. Yet even with his adoptive siblings, he'd still held part of himself back. He'd been the oldest, the one the others depended on for survival. So he'd ensured they survived. No matter what that entailed, taking pains to protect them from any taint he accrued along the way. His secrets preserved their innocence, yet they also prevented true closeness.

Could he really have such a thing with Abigail? Or would she pull away once she learned the truth about his past?

"Easy, man. If that frown gets stuck, your wife will never get on that horse with you."

Zach blinked at Reuben's words. His partner's tone teased, yet his eyes held a concerned light that proved their friendship went deeper than business.

"Abigail's too resilient to be scared off by a little frown." The thought cheered Zach a bit, boosted his confidence. She *was* resilient. She'd handled her sister's mistakes with grace and a fighting spirit. Surely she'd handle his the same way.

If she loved him.

Did she love him?

His gut tightened. He wanted her love. Wanted her to accept him. All of him.

Did that mean he loved *her*?

He liked her. Admired her. Desired her. But love? He wasn't sure what that was. He loved Seth and Evie, he supposed, if love meant feeling unswerving loyalty, wanting whatever was best for them, and being willing to fight to the death to protect them. He felt those things for Abigail, yet he felt them for Rosalind too. Because they were family. But the craving he had for Abigail went deeper than his signature on a marriage license. Deeper than a sense of responsibility and fidelity.

He wanted to throw open the cellar door and let all his secrets escape so her light could shine into his dark places. Yet at the same time, he wanted to padlock that door shut and never risk her disappointment.

Was that love? If so, he couldn't fathom why poets waxed on about it being such a blissful state. As far as he could tell, it was about as blissful as riding an unbroke horse, a bone-rattling endeavor where one held on for dear life, unable to recognize if he was making progress until either the horse quit buckin' or the ground smacked him in the face.

'Course, he was probably doing it wrong.

"Do I need to kick you in the pants to get you moving?" Reuben threatened. He swept his hand out in an exaggerated gesture, pointing toward the office. "The door's that way."

Maybe Zach did need a kick in the pants if it meant getting out of his own head.

"I'm going," he said, glaring at Reuben for good measure. He couldn't have him thinking Zach actually appreciated his interference.

He'd made it halfway across the lumber shed floor when Reuben called out to him. "Zach?"

He turned, expecting a smirk or eyebrow waggle, anything but the supportive comradery etched into his friend's face.

"Remember. She chose you."

Zach nodded, then resumed his walk to the door. His back a little straighter, his chin a little higher, and his stride carrying a touch more strut than he'd sported a moment ago.

⊰────⊱

Every time a man on horseback passed her shop window after closing time, Abigail's heart rate tripled and her breathing grew ragged. When traffic in the square picked up just before five o'clock, she'd been forced to cease polishing her eatery tables and retreat to the kitchen in order to preserve her sanity. Repeated incidents of anticipatory palpitations were quite detrimental to one's mental health.

How exactly was a woman supposed to prepare for an abduction? Especially when said abduction involved her handsome husband on a noble steed. The husband who'd left her that morning with a blazing kiss and a promise to steal her away the next time he saw her. The husband who was fast becoming the center of her world.

Needing something to occupy her hands if not her mind, she grabbed a broom and started sweeping. Dust was never fully eradicated, after all. Even if one had swept the same area a mere hour before.

She shuffled the broom in small strokes, careful not to sweep too vigorously. It wouldn't do to dirty the hem of her second-best skirt, the same one she'd worn when she proposed to her husband all those weeks ago. The russet color hid most dirt, her clothes being as practical as their owner, but it hadn't been pragmatism that led her to change into this ensemble. It had been pure sentiment. Zach probably wouldn't notice or care, but putting on this particular outfit made her feel less like a Martha and more like a wife ready to be wooed. Possibly even one who would do a little wooing of her own.

Abigail had swept her way around the worktable when the sound of boots thumping on the back stoop stole her breath. Zach!

A picture of what she must look like flashed through her mind. She didn't want her husband to find her like this, broom in hand like a scullery maid. She wanted to look enticing. Elegant. Inviting.

Dashing around the worktable, she tossed the broom at the corner with a clatter and made for the stairs. If she could just get to the top, she could turn and come down again, making an entrance like a debutante at a ball.

She grabbed a fistful of skirt, her heart pumping as she raced up the stairs. But before she could make it halfway, a strong arm snatched her from behind. Abigail gasped as her feet lifted from the stairs. Her back connected with a warm, wonderfully familiar chest, and her gasp transformed into a delighted giggle.

"Zach!" She swatted at the arm banded around her middle. "This wasn't supposed to be a *literal* abduction."

The slight abrasion of his afternoon stubble tickled her neck as he leaned his face next to hers. "Wasn't it?"

Shivers coursed over her skin. Heavens. What was she supposed to say to *that*?

Thankfully, he didn't seem to require a response. He simply scooped up her dangling legs and started marching toward the back door.

Mercy, but he was strong. One would think she barely weighed a hundred pounds, the way he carted her around with so little effort. For the first time in her big-boned, full-figured life, she actually felt . . . delicate.

Until he neared the door and made no move to put her down. Then all she felt was panic.

She grabbed him about the neck with both arms and tried to pull herself up out of his hold. "You can't carry me outside."

He grinned at her, his eyes sparkling with mischief. "Wanna bet?"

"Zach, please." She kicked her heels against his hip, her growing panic overriding her delight in his possessive display. "I don't want to be a spectacle."

"Not to fear, Mrs. Hamilton. I have everything under control."

No one had everything under control. To prove that point, Abigail did the only thing she could think of to knock her man off balance. She grabbed his face, dragged his lips toward hers, and kissed him for all she was worth.

All forward motion ceased. Interior motion, however, sped up to an alarming rate as her husband turned his full attention to their kiss. Heart pumping faster than the piston on a speeding locomotive, Abby twisted in his arms to face him more fully. He complied with her unspoken request and gentled his hold. Her legs slid free, and her feet came to rest on the floor as his hands splayed over her back.

She should feel triumphant at accomplishing her goal, but there wasn't room for triumph with all the other feelings rushing through her. Desire. Passion. Belonging. Love.

Abigail lifted up on her tiptoes and trailed her hands down from his face to his shoulders then his chest. His muscles quivered beneath her fingertips.

Zach's lips slanted more fully over hers, drawing her into him, and all rational thought fled. Heavens, but she loved this man.

Just when she thought her knees would complete their transformation into jelly, Zach lifted his face from hers. He panted slightly, making her own breathless state much less embarrassing.

"Guess I woulda lost that bet," he murmured with a half grin.

Abigail smiled, feeling light and flirty and happier than she'd been in ages. She danced away from her husband, catching his hand as she went. Opening the door to the alley, she tugged him after her and cast a playful glance over her shoulder as she went. "Two can play at this abduction game, you know."

Heat shot from his dark blue eyes. "Yes, ma'am."

Feeling like a fairy-tale princess, Abigail allowed her husband to set her upon his horse and then leaned back against him once he mounted behind her. No longer able to dredge up much concern about what others might think of a professional businesswoman in the arms of her husband in broad daylight, she relaxed and even smiled as her husband absconded with her in full view of the town.

With the sun warm and lovely overhead, they left the bustle of Honey Grove behind and meandered through the countryside. Birds serenaded them while a gentle breeze strummed the tree-tops like a guitar. It was the single most beautiful day of her life.

Until Zach turned his horse east along *the path*.

Abigail stiffened. *No. Please. Anywhere but there.*

But where else could they be headed? It was the only place *the path* led.

You can do this, Abby. It's been years. It probably doesn't even look the same.

Only it did. Exactly the way it appeared in her nightmares. The giant live oak towered over the innocent meadow like a merciless monster ready to destroy the lives of whoever ventured too close.

She pushed backward against her husband, no longer leaning against him in lazy, romantic abandon but actively pushing, desperate to get away from the Death Tree that loomed closer with every step of the horse's hooves.

CHAPTER

27

Zach slowed Jack with a gentle tug on the reins. Something was wrong. He scanned the area but found no threat. No disturbance. Just prairie grass, trees, and the pretty little stream he'd planned to sit beside as he picnicked with his wife.

Only the woman who had moments ago been so pliant and soft as she snuggled against him had gone as stiff as a 4×4 hickory post. Worse, she seemed to be trying to crawl over his shoulder to get away from something. The only thing in front of them was a tree. It might be a tad on the tall side, but it wasn't like it was going to pull up its roots and start chasing them.

What had his sensible wife so spooked?

"Abigail?" Signaling Jack with his legs to halt, Zach released the reins and took hold of his wife.

"Not here, Zach," she murmured. "Anywhere but here."

Again he scanned his surroundings. It was one of the prettiest spots in the area. Reuben brought Audrey here on special occasions. Apparently it used to be a trysting place for young couples years ago, but few people came out here anymore. That made it private. Secluded. The perfect place to woo one's wife.

Unless, of course, one's wife was terrified of the tree standing guard over the small meadow.

"Easy, Abby." He tugged her back down into his lap and tried to soothe her by rubbing her arms, but she wasn't in the mood to be soothed. She continued squirming and twisting away from the view in front of them. Finally, he smartened up enough to turn the horse so she didn't have to see the giant oak. That calmed her a little. "We don't have to have our supper here," he said. "If you want to go, we'll go."

"No."

No? Lord help him. He'd never understand females. "You want to stay?"

Tremors hit, quaking her hard enough for him to feel them. He wrapped his arms around her and bent his face close to hers. He might not understand what was going on in her head, but a mighty squall was battering her hull, and if he couldn't figure out how to shelter her from it, he aimed to be her anchor until it passed.

She twisted in his lap and pressed her cheek to his chest. "I'm sorry. I–I'm ruining everything." Her voice cracked.

"Nothin's ruined," he barked, then winced at his curt tone. Not exactly the compassionate response a woman fighting unseen demons wanted from her man. Time to shut his trap.

Thankfully, her tears never really got started. His little warrior harnessed her trembling with a few deep breaths before lifting her face.

"Can . . ." Another deep breath and a brave jutting of her chin. "Can we get down for a minute?"

Zach nodded, still subscribing to the idea that holding his tongue increased the odds of not screwing things up. He swung his leg over Jack's rump and settled on the ground while keeping a steadying hand on Abigail. Then he lifted her down beside him.

"Do you believe things happen for a reason?" She didn't look at him when she asked. In fact, she took a step away from him and fisted her hands. Slowly, she pivoted to face the tree that seemed to be the cause of her distress.

Not knowing what else to do—and not wanting to risk disaster by opening his mouth—Zach stepped up behind her and placed his hands on her shoulders. *I'm here*, he tried to convey. *I've got your back.*

"Of all the places you could have brought me, you chose this spot. I think it's a sign."

Yeah, a sign that he shouldn't have taken romantic advice from his sawdust-for-brains partner.

"A sign that we shouldn't deepen our physical intimacies when secrets linger between us."

Zach stiffened. Did she know? Had she somehow figured out who he was and what he'd done when she found his father's playing cards? He fought not to pinch her shoulders as tension radiated from his neck down through his back, shooting along his arms all the way to his fingertips.

Her shoulders lifted beneath his palms as if in response to the weight of his fear. But no. She was only inhaling. A heartbeat later, the air released from her lungs, and her shoulders sagged back into place.

"There's something about me you don't know, Zach. Something that might . . . might change your opinion of me."

It took a minute for her words to penetrate his dread-filled brain. Once they did, his relief was so great, he almost forgot that his wife was on the cusp of telling him something important. Scraping his focus off himself and placing it back on her where it belonged, he gave her shoulders an encouraging squeeze and rubbed gently at the tightness he felt beneath his thumbs.

"See that tree?" She raised her right arm and pointed with

a shaky finger at the oversized live oak forty yards in front of them. "That's where I killed my best friend's beau."

⸙———⸙

Abigail stopped fighting the memories of that day and let them pound into her with all their fury. Zach held her fast as the waves buffeted against her, his stalwart strength an anchor in her storm.

He hadn't left her. His hands might have stuttered for a brief second at her revelation, but they never left her shoulders. Even now they massaged and supported, silently encouraging her to continue her tale.

It had been a day much like this one. Sunny. Warm. Ripe for adventure. For love.

Sophia's mother never allowed her daughter to gallivant around with Benedict Crowley unescorted. She had set her sights higher than the son of the local blacksmith for her daughter, and she made sure to protect against any scandal that might hasten Sophia to the altar before she was old enough to be dangled in front of a more suitable man. A mature man already established in business or politics. One with clout. Power. Not a grubby urchin who spent his afternoons shoveling horse droppings.

At fifteen, Sophie was well aware of her mother's plans, but she and Abby had made a pact to protect each other from cold, heartless unions. They'd marry for love or not at all—Sophie to escape the social climbing of a mother who cared more for appearances than affection, and Abby to avoid becoming a broodmare to a man like her father who only saw value in sons.

So when Ben Crowley started courting Sophie, Abby gladly played chaperone. It was an easy task, since they'd all grown up together and were fast friends. And if Abby harbored a secret crush of her own on Benedict, well, she was careful not to let it show. Friends didn't steal beaus from one another. Not that she could have even if she'd wanted to. A dumpy girl like her could never compete with Sophie's beauty. Even at fifteen, she had an elegance about her that drew attention.

When Sophie suggested they all climb the old oak that day, Abigail had readily agreed. Tree-climbing was one of the few things she actually did better than her friend, and she couldn't pass up the chance to impress Ben with her skill. It didn't take long, however, to figure out that Sophie had made the suggestion in order to finagle time alone with her beau. While Abby darted up the tree like a squirrel, Sophie lingered behind, not making a move without Ben's hand to steady her. After securing a spot on the lowest layer of limbs, Sophie declared she couldn't go a bit higher and begged Ben to keep her company.

"But you go ahead, Abby," she had called with a smile. "Show Ben how far you can go." Then she'd clasped Ben's hand to make sure he remained at her side. "She really is the best climber," Sophie told him.

And that had settled things. Abby couldn't leave the challenge unmet, even knowing that it had only been issued to give Sophie a chance to lean against Ben and have him hold her while they pretended to watch the climb.

When Abby had ascended halfway to the top, she'd stopped to wave at her friends. Only they were no longer watching. They had eyes only for each other. Lips too, apparently, for their faces were plastered together.

Feeling embarrassed, envious, and a tiny bit betrayed, Abby ripped her gaze away from her friends and took refuge in climbing. Higher and higher she scaled, face tipped upward to catch the breeze.

Until that breeze caught her. A gust, really. A strong one that shook the tree, nearly tearing the limb she held from her hands.

A scream tore from her throat as she scrambled for a better grip. For secure footing.

"Abigail!" Benedict called from below. *Far* below.

She looked down for the first time. Her mind spun in dizzy circles. Her vision blurred. Her equilibrium teetered. Whimpering, she traded her handhold for wrapping her arm around the branch. Why had she climbed so high?

"Abby!" Sophie's voice this time. "I can't see you!"

Sophie sounded truly frightened. Abby tried to answer, to reassure her friend that she was all right—at least for the moment—but she couldn't seem to find sufficient breath. The branches that had seemed so close and easy to grasp before now seemed miles away as she tentatively reached a foot down to a lower limb.

Another gust blew. The tree swayed. Abby gasped and instantly retracted her leg. She couldn't do it. She'd fall.

Sophie peered up between the branches, a hand shading her eyes. "You're too high, Abby! You need to come down."

Leave it to Sophie to try to boss her out of the tree. Abby would have smiled at the ridiculousness of that tactic, but she was too terrified to move a muscle—even the little ones in her cheeks.

"She's on this side, Ben," Sophie instructed. "Hurry! The wind is picking up."

"I'm coming," Ben shouted up to Abby. "Hold on."

Holding on was about all she *could* do at the moment. Everything else seemed impossible.

Closing her eyes, she alternated between praying for God to still the wind and lecturing herself for not paying closer attention to her surroundings.

Her arms grew weary as she waited for Benedict to make his way up to her, and she began to shake as if she were just another leaf on the tree. Thankfully, the blacksmith's son was tall and strong and climbed nearly as well as she did.

"I'm here, Abby." The touch of his hand on her ankle infused her with hope and security. Ben wouldn't let her fall.

Yet when she opened her eyes, she didn't see her rescuer. She saw the ground, blurry and far, far away.

"I can't," she moaned, hating her weakness but not knowing how to circumvent it.

"Look at me," Ben urged, his voice warm, calm, steady.

Abby forced her eyes open again and found Ben's face. He smiled, and the wind seemed to lose some of its vigor.

"I've got you." He tightened his grip on her ankle. "I'll get you down."

She believed him. How could she not? Benedict Crowley was the most noble boy in school. Kind, honest, trustworthy. And he was here. With her. She couldn't disappoint him.

So she gave a little nod and loosened her hold on the branch near her shoulder. With Ben's steadying hand, she managed to make it down to the branch he stood on, and immediately wrapped an arm around his waist and buried her face in his chest. "Thank you."

For one blessed moment he hugged her back, and Abby's heart sang.

Then Sophie called up to them and broke the intimacy that Abigail had no right to enjoy. "Is she all right?"

"She's fine." Ben winked at Abby and reached for a new handhold. "We're coming down."

"Good." Then almost as an afterthought, Sophie added, "Be careful!"

Ben stayed right by Abby's side as they worked their way down. Patient. Understanding. Never once did he scold her for climbing too high or complain about her timid descent.

Instead, he repeatedly offered reassuring touches to her arm or shoulder, praised her for the progress they'd made, and insisted there was no hurry. She could take as much time as she needed.

The belittling voice of her father that had been castigating her in her head ever since she realized her folly slowly faded from her mind, replaced by Ben's steadfast encouragement. She could do this. *They* could do this. Together.

Then they dropped onto a branch weakened by mistletoe. A sickening crack. Ben's wide eyes. His arm snaking about her waist even as he grabbed for another handhold. But there was no time.

The limb broke. Their feet hit the air. They fell. Sophie screamed.

Ben held Abby tight against his chest, taking the brunt of the damage as they banged off limbs. One slammed against his skull. His neck flopped. Then they hit the ground. Ben first. Abby second, her friend's body cushioning the blow.

Abby was battered and disoriented, and everything that happened next was a blur. Sophie crying. Asking Abby if she was all right. Then pushing her off of Benedict. Screaming. Blood. Brokenness. And one sentence that rang in Abby's head over and over.

"You killed him! You killed Ben!"

Silent tears ran down Abigail's face as the past shifted back into the present. Zach still stood behind her, listening. At some point during the retelling, he'd ceased rubbing her shoulders and instead wrapped his arms completely around her torso, surrounding her with his strength, his acceptance.

She turned her head to find his eyes. "I killed him, Zach. Not on purpose, but it's my fault he's dead."

Zach glanced away from her, and pain ripped through her breast. What had she expected? That his holding her meant acceptance? That there would be no consequences? She was responsible for a young man's death and guilty of keeping secrets from her husband.

"I should have told you before we married," she said, facing forward again to keep from seeing the disappointment, the betrayal in his eyes. "You had the right to know who you were taking to wife. We should be able to get an annulment, if that's—"

Zach spun her around so fast, her words cut off in midair. His glare was fierce enough to fire her bread oven without kindling. She tried to back away from him, but he wouldn't let her. He grabbed her upper arms and refused to let her budge.

"I don't want an annulment," he growled.

That declaration should have made her happy, yet he seemed almost savage as he said it, leaving her confused and aching. He probably felt trapped, figuring an annulment would reflect poorly on him. But it wouldn't. This was her failure, not his.

"I'll testify to withholding the truth from you before we wed. No one will blame you for not wanting to be married to a killer."

"You're *not* a killer." He shook her.

"Not legally, I suppose. Yet I *am* responsible for a young man's death. If it wasn't for me, Benedict Crowley would still be alive. I don't expect you to understand—"

"But I do." His voice broke. In a flash he released her and stepped back. His gaze rammed into hers for a split second before it darted away, but not before Abigail caught a glimpse of the torture dwelling in her husband's soul. "I killed a man too."

CHAPTER

28

How had a picnic designed for courtship turned into an exercise in stripping the skin from each other's souls? Zach blew out a breath and gripped the back of his neck, as if the action would anchor him when his entire being was adrift.

This wasn't how the evening was supposed to go. He and Abby were supposed to be sitting on a blanket by the creek, eating fancy hotel food, and sharing kisses. Not standing in the middle of an emotional briar patch, confessing secrets that held the power to destroy everything they'd built.

Yet in the midst of that poisonous bramble, a gentle hand alit on his arm, and his barbed surroundings retracted some of their thorns.

"Zach." It wasn't a demand but an invitation. One he couldn't resist.

He looked down at his wife and nearly wept when he saw compassion shining in her soft brown eyes. Like a drowning man grabbing a lifeline, he reached for her, cupping her face in his hands and bringing his mouth down upon hers.

His kiss was rough, desperate, afraid. Even so, she made

no effort to pull away. In fact, she clasped his shoulders and rose up on her toes to meet him. He could taste the salt of her tears, reminding him that she'd already blazed the trail. Brave, wonderful woman. He'd offered to help her run from her fears, but she'd turned and faced them. Faced *him*. He could do no less.

Curbing his rising passion, Zach softened his hold and eased his lips from hers. Abby's eyes were slow to open, and with her moist mouth still upturned, he found her impossible to ignore. He had to press two tender kisses to her lips before he found the strength to pull away.

"How do you deal with it?" he asked, his voice scratchy and hoarse, the words he never spoke aloud scraping against his throat as he forced them out. "The guilt of knowing your actions hastened a man's end?"

Abigail's breath shuddered, but her hand slid down his arm, over his wrist, and into his palm. Her fingers twined with his, and for the first time in nine years, the weight on his soul lessened just a little.

She didn't answer immediately. Instead, she started walking toward the creek, turning along the grassy shore to follow the stream's winding path. She dragged him along with her. Not that he minded. It felt good to move, to have an outlet for all the pent-up emotion ricocheting around inside him.

"It's not easy," she finally said. "Especially when Sophia won't let me forget."

Zach nodded. "Mine hits me fresh every time I see Logan."

Her steps faltered as she craned her neck to look at him. "Evie's husband?"

"Yep." Zach cleared his throat. "His father is the man I killed."

"Oh, Zach." Those beautiful eyes swam not with disappointment or accusation but empathy—a commodity he'd never thought he'd find. "How awful for you. Is that why you moved to Honey Grove? To keep from having to see him every day?" Suddenly her eyes sparked. "He didn't make you leave, did he? To keep you away from Evie? He seemed pleasant enough at the wedding, but if he's keeping you from your sister, I'll grab my frying pan and–and . . ."

He grinned, then bopped the end of her nose. "No need for frying pans, sugar. At least not where Logan is concerned. I might take one to Mrs. Longfellow one of these days, but that's another matter."

How had he managed to hitch himself to the one woman in all of creation who not only understood his past but stood ready to fight for his future? The miracle of it made his head spin. All he could do was thank God for antiquated laws and prejudiced council members. If Abigail hadn't proposed to him . . . well, he didn't want to contemplate how bleak life would be without her.

"Logan's a good man," he said as they resumed their stroll along the water's edge. "We might not be the best of friends, but he's good to Evie, and he's forgiven my part in his father's death."

"Have you forgiven yourself?"

The quiet question slipped between his ribs to stagger his breath.

Abby squeezed his hand. "That's the hardest part, I've found."

A thickness crept up Zach's throat. "How do you manage it?"

"Little by little. I take comfort in scriptures that talk about how God removes our transgressions from us as far as the east is from the west, how he will remember our sins no more, how he urges us to cast our cares on him. But to be honest, whenever I see Sophia, the guilt twinges in my heart and tempts me to believe that I'm not worthy of such forgiveness."

That was a feeling he could relate to. He didn't even have to see Logan in the flesh. He thought about it every time he spied his father's card case. He *wanted* the shame, though. Wanted the reminder of the consequences so he'd never repeat his mistake. But for the first time, he wondered if locking one foot in the past had kept him walking around in circles without really making any forward progress.

"After the accident," Abby continued, "I stopped going out in public. I saw accusation everywhere I looked, though in truth it was more in my own mind than in the eyes of others. Thank the Lord for Lydia Putnam. She refused to let me hide away. When I stopped attending church and delivering her widow bread, she started barging into the bakery kitchen when Papa was on break. Rosalind abetted the ambushing, of course, allowing Lydia behind the counter where only family was permitted. At first Lydia tried to cajole and reassure me that the accident wasn't my fault, but when that met with no success, she changed tactics. I still remember the day she marched into the kitchen and slapped her Bible down on the worktable with enough force to make the yeast bowl rattle. She jabbed a crooked finger into my face and said, 'Abby Jane, quit being a hypocrite.'"

Zach's head jerked toward his wife as she wagged a finger in the air, reenacting the scene. "A hypocrite?" he echoed, disbelief thick in his voice. *He* might deserve that moniker, but not Abigail. "Seems harsh."

Abby smiled. Not a wide smile that exposed her dimples, but a soft, gentle one of fond remembrance. "She asked me straight out if I had sought the Lord's forgiveness for my poor choice in climbing that tree. When I said yes, she asked me if I believed the Bible to be true. When I said yes again, she snorted and said that if I believed the Bible to be true,

I wouldn't be hiding away and wallowing in guilt when the Word clearly stated that there is no condemnation for those who are in Christ Jesus.

"Guilt leads us to confession and repentance, she told me, but after we take it to the cross, we're supposed to leave it there, not carry it around with us. Jesus's burden is light. Guilt is heavy. Satan is the one who wants to increase our burden, to weigh us down with shame and despair, to steal our joy and the strength of the Lord that goes with it. Believing his lies instead of God's truth makes us weak. Made me a hypocrite."

Zach's gut clenched. What did that make *him*? A heretic?

For years, Evie had bugged him about his lack of singing in church. Told him he looked like a grumpy bear when he just sat there with his mouth shut and his arms crossed. She took him to task for not praising the God who had provided for them.

He appreciated the Almighty well enough and understood the blessings he'd received even when he didn't deserve them, which was most of the time. He sure as shooting didn't deserve the woman walking beside him, the one sharing her heart, her pain, and her vulnerabilities with him without making a single demand in return. The one who innocently believed all he lacked was to leave his guilt at the cross when, in fact, he'd never made it to the cross in the first place.

He didn't sing in church because the Good Book taught that he wasn't to offer worship without first being reconciled with a brother who had a grievance against him. He figured having a grievance with the Big Man himself made the crime an even larger offense. Didn't Jesus define a hypocrite as one who worshiped with his mouth and honored with his lips while his heart was far from God? Zach thought that by refraining from worship, he was keeping himself from being a hypocrite.

Maybe he was, but holding back certainly did nothing to span the gulf between him and the Almighty. Why the Big Fella hadn't just given up on him by now was a mystery Zach couldn't fathom.

"But . . ." Zach drew Abigail to a halt, struggling to push the words through his rapidly constricting throat. "What if . . . I ain't sorry? What if I haven't confessed because I know I'd do it again if I found myself in the same situation?"

He braced himself for her horror. Her judgment. But all that came was a crinkling of her brow and a tilting of her head. She didn't even say anything, just took a page out of his book and waited, trusting that he'd offer the explanation she deserved. She had more faith in him than he did in himself. It left him humbled even as it gave him courage.

He tugged his hand free of hers, then stripped out of his coat and laid it on the ground. Maybe he was just stalling, but he suddenly felt compelled to sit. As if that would make the tale easier to tell. It wouldn't, but it *would* make it harder for his wife to run away from him once he was finished.

He lowered himself to the grass, propped up a knee, then held his hand out to her in invitation. Angel that she was, she didn't hesitate. She settled atop his coat, folded her legs to the side, and braced one arm behind her for support. The other arm stretched toward him, her fingers coming to rest upon his thigh in silent encouragement.

"I was just thirteen when Seth, Evie, and I left the orphan train to make our own way. I'd spent a year livin' on the streets in New York before gettin' shoved into an overcrowded found-ling home, so I thought I knew what it took to survive. I knew what it was like to go to bed hungry. I could handle that. What I couldn't handle was watching Seth and Evie go to bed hungry. It like to tore my heart out. So I decided I would do whatever it took to make sure they had food in their bellies and a roof over their heads. I hired myself out as a stable hand so we could sleep in the livery. Did odd jobs for farmers in exchange for potatoes or anything else I could get my hands on. When I couldn't find work, I stole what we needed. And as soon as I could pass for a man, which was around fifteen or so, thanks to an early appearance of facial hair and longer than average legs, I started putting my daddy's gambling skills to work and made myself a place at the poker tables."

"Your father was a gambler?"

Zach met her gaze and offered a self-deprecating grin. "Yep. Best on the Mississippi. No card game invented he couldn't win." He paused, his grin dissolving. "One way or another."

She nodded in understanding, the edges of her mouth turning down just a bit in disapproval. But then, she *should* disapprove. Any person with a functioning moral compass would consider cheating wrong, and Abby's compass pointed true north.

"For years, we scraped by," he said. "Surviving but never able to get ahead. Evie was growing up in stables and back storage rooms, surrounded by men with foul mouths and shifty eyes. Seth's asthma was worsening with the continued exposure to unsanitary conditions. It got so bad that we nearly lost him a time or two. I needed to get them somewhere safe. Somewhere clean. They needed a home. So when the opportunity presented itself to get them that home, I didn't hesitate."

He grabbed a clump of grass near his hip and tore it from the ground. If only tearing the ugliness from his past could be accomplished as easily. Squinting up at the sky, he opened his hand and let the grass float away on the breeze. Then, after blowing out a breath, he returned to his story.

"Word had spread around Pecan Gap about a card sharp

who enjoyed luring men into deep play by dangling the deed to his family's ranch as bait. When he was sure he had a winning hand, he'd up the ante with that deed, causing the others to either match it or fold, sacrificing the high stakes pot. Most folded. He walked away with hundreds of dollars each time. Until I earned my way into the game. I used every trick my daddy taught me. I out-sharped the sharp. Boosted his confidence, fed him the cards that would inspire him to wager the deed, then stole it out from under him by feeding myself the winning hand.

"I won that house for Evie and Seth and never gave a second thought to the family who'd be forced to leave." Zach stared at the ground. He couldn't look at Abby when he admitted the worst. Couldn't watch the esteem die in her eyes. But he owed her the truth. "The day after I stole his house, Rufus Fowler committed suicide. Left his wife and kid not only without a home but without a man to provide for them. I destroyed that family. What happened to the Fowlers eats away at my soul, but I can't repent if I don't actually regret the sin I committed. My baby sister gained a safe place to grow up, and my kid brother got a healthy environment that healed his lungs. How can I regret that?

"I left gambling behind that night and swore to God that I'd never return, that I'd never pick up the cards again for personal gain. And I haven't." Zach ran a hand over his face. "But even knowing the destructive outcome of that night, if I had it to do over, I'd make the same choice."

He finally forced himself to look Abigail in the face. Her hand remained on his leg. She hadn't pulled away from him, but he knew this would change the way she saw him.

"You would undo what happened to Benedict Crowley," he said, a tender smile curving his lips as her chin trembled and her eyes misted. He didn't blame her for losing faith in him. How could he, when he'd never been worthy of it in the first place? "You'd make a different choice and preserve his life because you have a good heart. A righteous heart. You deserve absolution. I don't."

CHAPTER

29

Abigail leaned close to her husband, an ache throbbing in her chest. *Zach*. So stoic, so strong and capable. Yet wounded, and determined to hide that wound from the world. Even from family.

But not from her.

Her heart so full of love she could barely stand it, she shifted up onto her knees directly in front of him. His eyes followed her, watching, waiting to see what she would do. His fingers twitched on the hand that dangled over his knee, almost as if he wanted to reach for her, but he made no move.

So she made it for him. She captured those fingers and clasped their joined hands to her thumping heart.

"None of us deserve absolution, Zach. It is a gift freely given. A gift that is waiting for you too. All you need to do is accept it."

"How?" His voice rasped. "Confession without repentance gains me nothing. And I can't repent if I'm not sorry."

"You *are* sorry," she insisted, every protective instinct roaring to life inside her. "You're so sorry it's eating you up inside."

He shook his head and dropped his gaze to the ground. "Not

sorry enough to regret my actions. They achieved the ends I needed. They saved my brother's life and gave my sister a home."

What could she say to that? Without repentance there could be no forgiveness, yet she could see the craving in him, the weariness of carrying this burden. Her soul longed to help him, but how?

Lord, show me what to—

Before she could complete the prayer, a whisper of an idea swirled through her mind.

"What if something else could have achieved those same ends?" she asked. "Would you regret your actions then? If there had been another choice?"

Zach stiffened, and the edges of his mouth turned down. "There was no other choice. Playing *what if* is pointless."

"There's always another choice." *Open his heart, Lord. Let him hear me.* "When Rosalind agreed to let that photographer exploit her, she did it because she thought she had no other choice. It was the only option she could see to earn the money she needed to buy medicine for our father. But just because it was the only option she could see doesn't mean it was the only option available."

Zach said nothing, just stared at her hard enough that she wanted to squirm. She could practically hear the justifications in his head, claiming that Rosalind's situation was different. Yet it wasn't. Not really. Not at the core.

"Rosalind believed it was her responsibility to care for our father, just as you believed it was your responsibility to care for your siblings."

"They *were* my responsibility." Zach yanked his hand away from her, and the harsh movement felt as if he were tearing himself from her heart.

Nevertheless, Abigail held her course, an inner voice warning that if she gave up now, she might not get a second chance. "Yes, they were your responsibility, but not yours alone."

"What are you talking about? I was all they had." Tension radiated off him. He grabbed at the grass with a fist.

"No." Abigail kept her voice soft. Gentle. He didn't need accusation. He needed truth spoken in love. And, oh, how she loved him. "No, Zach. You weren't all they had. They had God."

A muscle in his jaw ticked.

"God always provides other options for his people when they are tempted to take an unrighteous path. But if we depend only on ourselves to solve our problems, we narrow our vision and see none of those options. Rosalind could have come to me, she could have taken her worries to the church, or she could have left the outcome solely in God's hands, even if that meant losing our father sooner than we wished. She did none of those things, however, because she never saw them as options. She was convinced that the burden was hers to bear alone. She was wrong. And so were you."

Zach clamped his jaw so tight that his teeth hurt. What did she know? She hadn't been there. She didn't know what it had been like.

"Did you ever ask for help?" Why did she have to keep prodding at him? Digging into his sore spots? Why couldn't she just leave it alone? "Approach the minister of the local church to see if someone would take Seth in for a short time until his health improved?"

"And risk some do-gooder breaking up our family?" Zach slashed his hand through the air. "Not a chance!"

"So you let fear about what *might* happen dictate your actions."

"What do you know about it?" he shouted.

Shame rammed him in the gut. He had actually shouted. At his wife. The woman he'd sworn to honor and protect. The woman whose opinion mattered to him more than any other.

"Abby. I'm sorry. I . . ." What could he say? He had no excuse. None. He'd lost control.

But instead of shrinking back from him, she smiled. What kind of woman smiled when her bear of a husband roared at her like a wild man? She should be running for the horse and leaving him to rot, not scooting closer and placing her hands on his shoulders.

"I know quite a lot about it." Her fingers felt small and delicate against his shoulders as she squeezed, yet he recognized her strength. "I've chosen fear over faith more times than I can count," she admitted. "And every time I did, I ended up with regrets. When I chose faith, I didn't always get the outcome I wanted—my mother still died, as did my father—but I never regretted my choice, because I felt God beside me, holding my hand and lending me strength.

"You're a good man, Zacharias Hamilton. I admire your dedication to your family, your willingness to sacrifice anything to protect and provide for them. For *us*. But I love you too much to sit back and watch this old wound fester and destroy your soul."

Zach's head snapped up, and his gaze zeroed in on her like a sharpshooter eyeing his target. Had she just said she loved him?

Her cheeks reddened beneath his scrutiny, and her lashes lowered, hiding her eyes from him, but he didn't look away. Couldn't. Not with her words surging through his brain like a flash flood banging ten-foot tree limbs against his skull.

I love you too much . . .

Did she mean it? Every instinct honed at the poker tables told him it hadn't been a bluff. Information she hadn't intended to expose—yes. But not untrue.

His pulse ratcheted up to a full gallop, and light-headedness assailed him. "Abby, I . . ." His throat tightened around the words, refusing to let them out.

They were words he'd never said. Not since the day his mama died. Love made a man vulnerable in a world that required armor and a shield to survive. His father's world demanded he hide all emotion to prevent his weaknesses from being exploited. The harshness of his grandfather's world had beaten all softer places from him until only calluses remained. Evie and Seth had reminded him he still owned a heart and taught him how to use it, but not even they had managed to bring forth that three-word utterance from him. Some lessons were just too ingrained. Evie had taken to saying it for him in that teasing way she had, and he'd never denied the charge. But that was as close as he'd come.

His silence condemned him, and razors scraped his shoulders as she pulled her fingers away and sat back on her heels. He followed, unable to stop himself from leaning forward, from preserving whatever closeness he might scavenge.

Her eyes remained downcast, however, refusing to look at him, stealing the sunshine and leaving him cold.

"Just . . ." She pushed to her feet and brushed at her skirt. "Just promise me you'll think about what I said."

As if he'd be able to think about anything else.

"Pray about it too."

He blinked, then realized she hadn't been talking about her declaration of love but about the subject that had prompted it.

"I will," he promised, his voice gruff, raw.

He might not be able to give her the words she deserved to hear, but he could give her this. No matter how pointless he found the exercise, he'd do it. He owed her that much.

Abigail finally met his gaze, some of the red fading from her cheeks. "Thank you."

He swallowed and managed a nod.

A dimple peeked out just a bit before she turned away from him. "I guess our abduction is good and ruined, isn't it?"

Not if he could help it. He hopped to his feet and whistled to Jack. Abby startled at the shrill sound, and when she caught sight of his horse trotting straight for them, she dodged behind his back.

Zach stood a fraction taller as her hands took hold of his waist. All the secrets they'd shared hadn't destroyed her trust in him. She still looked to him for protection and security.

She'd stayed. Even when he had uncovered the putrid gash in his soul. There was no drawing back in horror and disgust. No forfeiture of hope, declaring him a lost cause. Not his Abby. She'd rolled up her sleeves and set to doctoring the nasty thing, scouring and prodding in places no one in their right mind would venture. It might have hurt like the very devil and left him with fresh bruises that still throbbed, but he could see the heart behind it. The *love* behind it.

"The sun hasn't set yet," he said as he reached for Jack's reins. He patted the horse's neck, then bent to retrieve his coat from the ground. "I say we give it another try." He shook the dust and grass off his coat, then stuffed his arms in the sleeves and grinned at his wife, hoping it would cover his nervousness.

Don't give up on us, he silently begged her. *Not today or any day hereafter.*

He checked the saddle, made sure everything was still secure, then turned and held a hand out to Abigail. "What do you say? I'll let you do the abducting this time. Give you the reins and let you take Jack wherever you want to go."

Even if it's back to the bakery. But please don't go back to the bakery. Not yet.

Her eyebrows lifted in matching arches. "Anywhere?"

"Yes, ma'am. I'm your captive. Completely at your mercy."

Both dimples appeared, full and deep and adorable as her lips split in a flirtatious smile. Zach's pulse stuttered, then pounded into a full-out sprint.

"All right, then." She slipped her hand into his. "Let's go."

CHAPTER

30

"So . . ." Rosalind's singsong voice tickled Abigail's ears as her sister swept through the connecting door from the shop to the kitchen. The last of the breakfast crowd must have cleared out. "Are we moving you out of my room today?"

"Rosie!" Abigail, face aflame, yanked off a piece of yeast dough and threw it at her sister's chest. It splatted with satisfying force but proved an ineffectual deterrent, for her sister simply peeled it off and threw it straight back. The dough ball smacked Abigail on the left cheekbone and stuck there like some kind of unnatural growth, which set Rosie to giggling.

Abigail only managed to hold her disapproving big-sister scowl for a moment before cracking a smile herself as she wiped her face clean.

"Come on, sis. Spill the details," Rosalind urged as she came around the worktable, grabbed Abigail's hand, and dragged her to the table where Abby and Zach shared breakfast in the mornings. She held out a chair for Abigail. "I want to know *everything*," she said as she waited for her sister to sit. "The two of you were out awfully late last night."

Abigail ducked her head, knowing the teasing joy dancing

in her sister's eyes would dim when she learned the truth. "The marriage is still unconsummated."

"What? What happened?" Rosalind moved to the vacant seat and flopped into it with an unladylike thud. "I thought for sure . . ."

"So did I," Abigail admitted. Yet she couldn't be disappointed. Not really. Their evening might not have gone according to plan, but something important happened nonetheless. Something that might do more to bond them as a couple than the physical intimacy she had anticipated. For what good was physical closeness without emotional and spiritual connection? Better to take the time to lay the proper foundation than to rush to build on shaky ground.

Rosalind's face turned mulish. "Tell me."

Abigail sighed. "He took me to the old oak."

Rosalind drew back, her jaw loosening. "Not the—"

Abigail nodded.

"Oh, Abby. How horrible! But surely he couldn't have known."

Abigail's lips twitched at the memory of Zach's consternation as she tried to climb over him in the saddle in her irrational need to get away from that tree. "He had no idea, poor man. He'd just been on the hunt for a pretty spot to eat and watch the sunset. He probably thought he'd hitched himself to a loon by the time we finally stopped."

Rosalind leaned forward again and clasped Abigail's hands. "Did you explain?"

Abby nodded. "I almost took the coward's way out, but he deserved to know the truth." She met her sister's gaze straight on. "I didn't want secrets between us."

Rosalind nodded, her eyes conveying her keen understanding of how secrets could wreak havoc with relationships. "How'd he take it?"

"You should have seen him, Rosie." A full smile stretched

Abigail's cheeks wide. She probably looked like a lovesick calf, but she didn't care. "He never left my side. He stood at my back, hands on my shoulders, through the entire retelling. He cast no blame at my door, yet he didn't sweep things under the rug either. He understood, Rosie. Understood my feelings of responsibility, my regret." Because he'd felt them himself. But that story wasn't hers to tell.

Tiny creases appeared across Rosalind's forehead. "If he didn't turn away from you, why did you leave him to sleep alone?"

Abigail quirked a brow. "Why do you assume *I* was the one to leave?"

"He's a man." Rosalind rolled her eyes. "And I've seen the way he looks at you. Zach has wanted you in his bed since the day you wed him."

"Rosie!" Goodness. She might as well just paint her face red and be done with it, as often as she'd blushed lately. "What would you know of men and their wants?"

"More than I should."

The wry comment stabbed Abigail with guilt. How could she be so careless with her words? After all the trouble with scoundrels her sister had endured?

Rosalind must have read the regret in Abigail's expression, for she smiled and waved a hand above the table as if sweeping the thoughtless words away. "I've had to deal with men's stares since I turned fifteen. Even before the whole photography debacle. I know how to distinguish polite interest from the less noble variety, and I recognize admiration when I see it. Zach is crazy about you, Abby. There's no way he turned you away."

He might not have turned her away, but he didn't extend an overt invitation either, and she'd been too unsure about where they stood to make a move on her own.

They'd managed to resurrect their evening to some extent. She'd taken him to a pretty little spot north of town. They'd eaten their supper on a grassy knoll, surrounded by a smattering of red and yellow firewheels still in bloom despite the summer heat. Conversation had been minimal. Zach had seemingly exhausted his store of words, and she'd felt silly feigning interest in the weather when all she could think about was his lack of response to her accidentally telling him she loved him.

Well, that wasn't entirely true. He'd responded. Everything about him had sharpened, heightened. His voice had even quaked slightly when he'd said her name. For one glorious moment, she'd thought he was going to share his heart with her, to reciprocate in kind. But then the words died in his throat, and the fire in his eyes dulled to an apologetic ember.

Evie had warned her. Explained that Zach wasn't one to talk of feelings, but Abigail wanted the words. Or at least *some* words. He didn't have to speak of love, but he could have said *something*. All he'd needed to do was ask, and she would have gone to his room. But he'd held his tongue, and she'd lost her courage.

⎯⎯⎯⎯⎯⎯

All she'd needed to do was take one step, and he would have swept her up in his arms and made her his wife. But her feet had rooted themselves to the floor. And when they finally moved, it had been in the wrong direction. Away from him.

Zach unloaded fresh lumber from the sawmill's train car, welcoming the pinch of the planks against his neck and the weight on his shoulder as his piled the load twice as high as usual before tromping the twenty yards to the wagon near the depot platform.

What had he expected? That she'd just ignore all he'd told

her and fall into his arms? Him being such a Romeo, and all. He'd grunted more than talked after they left the giant oak. It was a wonder she'd managed to stay awake until the sun went down.

Zach heaved the heavy load from his shoulder and dropped it into the wagon with a loud clatter. The heads of nearby rail hands swiveled to stare, but he ignored them. So what if he was handling the job with less finesse than usual? If they'd been living with a kindhearted, beautiful woman for five weeks without a single night of wedded bliss to alleviate the ever-increasing want, they'd be cranky too.

He'd known there would be a price to pay for telling her about his past, but the price she'd asked of him wasn't the one he'd been prepared to pay. He'd expected withdrawal or anger or accusations of betrayal. Even disappointment. Evie had given him practice with that one. Watching the light go out of his sister's eyes when he admitted to cheating and scheming a man out of his home had nearly killed him. She'd eventually forgiven him, and while Evie might not look upon him with hero worship any longer, she loved him, accepted him, and even respected him. He'd hoped that with time, the same would hold true for Abigail—that she'd move past the hurt and disappointment to a place of acceptance and love.

But she'd gotten everything out of order. She already accepted his past, even sympathized with it. And she loved him—a circumstance he still had trouble wrapping his mind around. Yet her love and acceptance didn't absolve him from his sin. Instead it demanded an even higher price than he'd expected. He'd been prepared to reconcile with *her*, but she'd asked him to reconcile with *God*.

"There he is," a male voice boomed behind Zach. "Just the man I was looking for."

Zach shoved the last two rough-hewn planks from his load to lay flush against the driver's end of the wagon bed, then pivoted to face Honey Grove's mayor.

"Longfellow." He offered a nod but not his hand. For one, his work glove was covered in sap and dust and all manner of ungentlemanly debris that the dapper mayor in his fine suit would no doubt wish to avoid.

However, the second reason was the more compelling of the two. Longfellow's wife had hurt Abigail. Repeatedly. And while that crime belonged to her and not her husband, Zach had a hard time respecting a man who willfully turned a blind eye to his wife's cruelty, or worse, allowed her to manipulate him into doing her dirty work for her. Because Zach was fairly certain, now that he knew the history between Sophia and his wife, that Mrs. Longfellow had been the one pulling the city council's strings to enforce that ridiculous law against women owning businesses in town. She was the only one with anything to gain from Abigail losing the bakery.

The older man with gray at his temples and crow's feet around his eyes smiled his politician's smile. "Mr. Hamilton, I have an offer for you that I think you'll find quite advantageous."

Uh-huh. Zach knew that look—the look of a man holding three kings and trying to convince his opponent that the two pair in his hand could win the pot. Zach wasn't buying, but he wouldn't mind calling the bet to get a read on the mayor's agenda. One could often learn more from a well-played loss than take-all win.

"What did you have in mind?" Zach lifted his hat from his head and rubbed the sweat from his brow with his shirtsleeve. Longfellow's gaze followed the movement, but Zach's remained locked on the mayor's face, taking in the eyes, the tightness around the corners of his mouth, the too-smooth forehead of a man practiced in creating an illusion to instill confidence in others, whether or not that confidence was warranted.

"The Honey Grove City Council regrets having to take such a hard line with your wife upon her inheritance of her father's bakery, and we wish to do something to make amends."

Zach crossed his arms over his chest and stared down at the shorter man. If Longfellow thought Zach was going to fawn all over him in gratitude for the crumb he was offering, he was fixin' to be disappointed.

The mayor cleared his throat, slightly nonplussed, but gamely continued on. "We'd like to add a last-minute float to our parade lineup. One specifically designed to honor the prettiest young lady in the city—the Honey Grove Queen Bee."

"Not sure how that's supposed to make amends to my wife, unless you want to make her the queen." And if they did? Zach wasn't sure he particularly liked the idea of other men ogling his woman, but having the town name her Queen Bee might go a long way toward proving to his self-conscious wife that she could compete with any female when it came to beauty.

Chester Longfellow cleared his throat. "No, ah, the council decided that only unmarried young women would be eligible for nomination. Your sister-in-law, Miss Rosalind Kemp, was unanimously voted in as our queen." At Zach's darkening glare, he hurried to spill more words, as if that would help matters. "We thought that if Miss Rosalind agreed to represent Honey Grove, we would show our gratitude by allowing the Taste of Heaven Bakery to sponsor the float she rides on. The bakery's name would be printed on signs hanging over the sides of the wagon. And perhaps instead of tossing penny candy to the children, Rosalind could toss dinner rolls. Give them a taste of heaven, as it were." He snickered at his play on words, but when Zach failed to crack even a hint of a smile, he cleared his throat and resumed his attempt at persuasion. "Your partner, Mr. Sinclair, has already agreed to donate lumber for the signs, and my lovely wife insisted on providing additional bunting. It would be great advertising, don't you think?"

What he thought was that Rosalind would never agree. Not after the run-in she'd had with that clod in the alleyway. There was no way she would want to be the focus of hundreds or even thousands of staring eyes.

Zach kept his arms crossed and his scowl affixed. "You got a backup candidate if Rosalind's not interested?"

The mayor's brow crinkled. "Why would she not be interested? This is a huge honor. Her name in the paper, her face declared the fairest in the land. She'll be the envy of every girl in town."

Zach shrugged. "All that may be true, but Rosalind has a mind of her own. If she don't want to stand around in the back of a fancified freight wagon and wave her arm off for an hour, I ain't gonna force her."

"Well . . ." Longfellow straightened his shoulders and jutted his chin. "I'm afraid that if Rosalind fails to agree, we'll just have to postpone our first annual Queen Bee float until next year. We don't have time to vote in a replacement."

And whose fault was that? Dumb question. Zach knew exactly who was behind this sudden Queen Bee nonsense—Sophia Longfellow. What he failed to grasp was why. Had she finally realized that her unjust treatment of Abigail reflected poorly on her and was now making a last-ditch effort to repair her reputation? Or did she have something more malicious in mind?

CHAPTER

31

That night at dinner, Zach broached the topic of the parade float.

"I'll leave it up to you gals to decide what you want to do," he said as he helped himself to a second scoop of potatoes. "Far as I'm concerned, the council can sit on their float till next year. No telling what their true motives are in making the offer so late in the game."

"It *would* be good promotion for the shop," Rosalind hedged, her level of enthusiasm less impressive than her sense of duty to the family business. "Hundreds turn out for the parade." Her throat worked a long swallow.

Abigail reached across the table and touched Rosalind's hand. "No advertising is worth your peace of mind. If you don't feel good about it, we won't do it. End of discussion."

Man, but he admired his woman. Zach hid a grin by stuffing a bite of potato into his mouth. He'd known she'd choose the good of her sister over the good of the bakery, but it was mighty satisfying to see her prove him right.

She glanced up at him as that thought traipsed through his

mind. He stopped mid-chew. Her eyes held his, a question in them. Was she seeking his approval? His chest tightened. He'd told them the decision was theirs to make, yet she sought to include him. Treated him like family. Like the head of the house. Even when their pre-wedding agreement stipulated that he had no legal footing in bakery business.

He gave a small nod.

Abigail's lips tipped up slightly at the corners, as if having his agreement lightened her load. As if she needed him. Wanted his support, his opinion. Him. The unrepentant cheat who couldn't manage to straighten out his own life.

Lord, I ain't never gonna be worthy of her, but if you and I can find a way to work out our differences, I might at least come a little closer to being the man she deserves. David asked you to make him a clean heart. I ain't no king, but I'm gonna ask for the same treatment. Can't seem to get the job done on my own.

"I'm not a baby to be coddled," Rosalind said, her chin jutting out despite the dread in her eyes. "If smiling and waving to a crowd will drum up business, then what is there to discuss? Sales are bound to increase if people actually get a sample of your baking. They won't seek out your shop simply because they get hungry, they'll seek it out because they've had a taste and they want more." A spark of excitement flared, bringing new life to Rosalind's gaze. "And since they'll have seen me on the float, if they spot me again, they'll know to look for more treats. I can set up a stand at the opposite end of the square to sell smaller items like your honey-glazed biscuits. Then, if people want to make a larger purchase, I can direct them to the shop."

Zach turned his attention to his wife and found her nibbling her lower lip. He swore he could hear her thoughts warring with each other as she balanced risk for her sister with reward for the bakery. He understood the protective urge that compelled her to take no chances, yet stifling a sibling's freedom to decide her own destiny rarely turned out well. He'd dangled off the edge of that particular cliff more often than he'd care to admit. Thankfully, Seth had never stomped his fingers and sent him hurtling into the ravine of broken relationships, but they'd come dangerously close a time or two.

"The idea has merit," he ventured, not quite sure if opening his mouth was a wise move at this point but opting to do it anyway. "Your honey biscuits are nearly as good as your sticky buns. They'd go fast." He scratched at his chin where his afternoon stubble was growing in. "I could rig a box frame for a booth and attach the signs from the parade wagon to the top and bottom to help with visibility."

"That's a great idea!" The last traces of trepidation disappeared from Rosalind's face as she scooted to the edge of her seat to face him. "Do you think the Sinclairs would let us hire Simeon and Dinah to help? No one can resist a child. The kids could walk on either side of the float with baskets of goodies to hand out. Then later they could be our runners if we need to replenish our supply of biscuits at the booth. The twins could ride with me on the float so they don't feel left out."

And to deflect attention away from her too, no doubt. Good strategy. Give people something else to look at than just the pretty girl at the center. Ash and Zeb's antics would no doubt provide ample distraction. But before Zach could say as much, Abigail's drinking glass clinked against her plate and interrupted Rosalind's enthusiastic scheming.

Zach's head came around. His wife looked like a herd of cats had stampeded over her lap, leaving her dazed and confused. It took two tries for her to find the proper place to set down her glass.

He leaned around the table corner and clasped her shoulder. "Abby?"

She blinked, then slowly focused on his face. "I don't know if I can do it."

"Do what?" Let her sister risk exposure?

"Bake enough biscuits. I worked all afternoon to have enough goods to accommodate the usual surplus of customers. There's not enough time to put out a couple hundred biscuits for the parade, let alone double that to supply paying customers afterward. I'm not even sure I have enough flour."

Zach's mind spun as he started to piece together Sophia's scheme. She was setting Abigail up for failure. Late notification to ensure time was short, stores closed so she couldn't resupply her ingredients. She probably planned to do a slipshod job on the bunting for the wagon too.

He clenched his jaw. He shouldn't have waited until after work to bring this idea to Abigail. He'd shaved her time even more. Well, he'd just have to fix that problem. Because his wife was *not* going to fail. Nor was she going to shoulder this load on her own.

"I'll go to the Sinclairs' tonight. Get Reuben to help me put together a booth. Paint the signs. Ask Audrey about the kids and see if she has any flour I can buy from her. I'll stop by the Longfellows' house on my way, tell the mayor we accept his offer and collect the bunting so Rosalind can do the decorating. Then, tomorrow, I'll get up with you, and you'll put me to work."

Abigail's brows arched. "But you can't—"

He cut off her protest with a shake of his head. "I sure enough *can*. I'll fetch and carry whatever you need. You make the dough, I'll cut out the rounds and slather 'em with the honey butter sauce. If I can use a jigsaw, I should be able to handle a biscuit cutter. And I got decent painting skills, so you don't have to worry about me missing spots. Every top will be covered. Rosalind can run the shop with whatever goods you've already got on hand. Anything else people may want will just have to be listed as sold-out. Most folks'll be home preparing for the day's activities anyway. In the meantime, you and I will make so many biscuits, we'll have to cart them around in a wagon bed."

His wife stared at him, her brown eyes wide. Then, without a word, she pushed her chair back, rose to her feet, and came to stand directly in front of him.

A little worried he might have gotten himself in trouble by being too presumptuous—after all, his knowledge of running a professional kitchen wouldn't cover a nailhead—he leaned back in his chair and braced himself for whatever she might dish out.

Braced for anything except the kiss she planted on his mouth. At the dinner table. In full view of her sister. Her palms cupped his jaw as her lips touched his. By the time his dull wits processed what she was doing and urged him to respond, she had pulled away. But then she spoke.

"I love you, Zacharias Hamilton."

His heart gave a donkey kick. She'd said the words. Again. On purpose. And in front of a witness.

And again, his tongue glued itself to the roof of his mouth. Only this time she didn't seem to expect anything from him. Even if he could have managed to spit out a word or two, she didn't give him the chance. Just started rattling off orders of her own, their kiss apparently galvanizing her practical nature back into working order.

She straightened to her full height, and the affection in her gaze hardened into tactical alertness. "If Audrey agrees to let the children help with distributing the baked goods during the parade, I want you and Reuben flanking their movements at all times—one with each child. I don't want any overeager spectators grabbing at their baskets or crowding them in any way. Their safety must be paramount."

Zach nodded. Couldn't argue with good sense.

"After the parade, you stick to her like glue." Abigail pointed to her sister, the intensity in her face giving neither Zach nor Rosalind any room to quibble. "The square will be filled with wagons and folks milling around, most of them men. Rosalind is not to be left alone. Agreed?"

"Abby . . ." Rosalind whined, but a sharp look from her sister cut off the complaint.

Zach drew his wife's attention by pushing to his feet. "Agreed." He'd hoped to spend more of the holiday with Abigail than her sister, but he'd learned a long time ago that life didn't always give you what you wanted. Watching out for Rosalind was the right thing to do. And the best way to support Abigail, which, after all, was his main concern.

"Good." Abigail nodded her satisfaction, then pivoted sharply back toward the table. "I'll clear the dishes and prep the kitchen for tomorrow."

She started stacking plates in the crook of her arm, barely pausing long enough for Zach to scrape the last bite of potato from his before adding it to her collection. Her brown eyes danced with teasing light as she snatched his plate away before he could get his fork out of his mouth. The dimples he adored flashed, and the task before them suddenly felt much less daunting.

"Rosalind, if Audrey has no flour to spare, you might ask Mrs. Putnam," Abigail said as she piled dishes into the dumbwaiter that would lower them to the kitchen. "Be sure to pay her more than it's worth, though. Or if she refuses money, take note of the amount so we can replenish her supply with interest. I won't have dear Lydia going hungry because of my predicament."

"Don't worry," Rosalind said as she rose and reached for the serving dishes. "I'll find the flour you need and generously compensate whoever donates."

Abigail nodded, collected the glasses and the few miscellaneous items remaining on the table, then signaled her sister to lower the dumbwaiter and left to meet it downstairs in the kitchen.

As Rosalind worked the pulley, her gaze zeroed in on Zach.

"Be careful with her heart," she said in a low voice. "Abby might be a practical-minded businesswoman, but her heart has taken a lot of abuse through the years. It's bruised and battered, but it's still a priceless treasure." Her blue eyes narrowed slightly. "Treat it as such."

Zach held her gaze without flinching. "I will."

He knew the value of the gift Abigail had given him. Knew he didn't deserve it. Yet he vowed to guard her heart with every ounce of his strength and do everything in his power to shore up those bruised places and keep from adding any new damage. A challenging task for a rough fellow who knew next to nothing about healthy relationships, but one he'd endeavor to accomplish nonetheless.

Rosalind held his gaze for a long, measuring moment before giving a nod. "Then let's go to the Sinclairs'. Abby needs that flour, and we need to make that float something she'd be proud to have carry the bakery's name."

Once they were out of the house and on their way, Zach gave his sister-in-law a considering stare. "You sure you're all right with the whole Queen Bee thing?"

Rosalind didn't break stride, just rolled her shoulders as she marched down the street. "Can't say I'm looking forward to it, exactly, but I can bear a little discomfort for Abby's sake. She's been making sacrifices for me for years."

The girl had grit.

"Keep your eyes peeled when you're on that float," he cautioned. "I can't help but think Sophia Longfellow's got some kind of trick up her sleeve with this last-minute addition."

He'd already pictured several unpleasant possibilities. Spooking the float horses. Recruiting delinquents to throw rotten vegetables. Sabotaging a wheel or axle. Humiliation seemed the most likely goal, based on past experience.

Rosalind's brow crinkled. "You might be right, but I don't think she intends any harm toward me. She always aims her vitriol directly at Abby. I wouldn't put it past her to try to discredit the bakery in some way, though."

A horrible thought jumped into his mind, and he pulled up short.

Rosalind slowed and turned a perplexed look on him. "What?"

"You don't think she found out about those photo cards, do you? Even if Sophia hasn't attacked you in the past, instigating a large scandal with ties to the bakery could be an effective way to destroy the business."

Rosalind paled. "I-I don't think she knows." She shook her head, her gaze dropping to the street. "I've only ever been approached by out-of-town men. No one local." She inhaled a breath and lifted her chin. "Sophia and Chester run in elevated circles, well separated from the rail hands and cowboys who drift in to visit the saloons." A touch of color returned to her face along with a determined glint in her eyes. "If Sophia planned to start a scandal, I don't think she would have named me Honey Grove's Queen Bee. That associates me with the town, and more directly, with the council, including her husband."

Zach nodded, the knot in his gut loosening a smidgeon. "I'm sure you're right," he said, offering a smile he hoped looked brighter than it felt.

Rosalind's logic was sound, but revenge had a tendency to warp a person's mind when allowed to fester for long periods of time. One couldn't trust logic to win out over vengeance.

He'd be keeping a close eye on Mrs. Longfellow.

"Whatever that woman has in mind, we'll just have to beat her to the punch. Take away her opportunities to cause mischief. You and me will see to the wagon decoratin'. I'm not letting Sophia Longfellow anywhere near that float until the parade is over." The more elements he controlled, the more protection he could offer his family.

Unfortunately, he couldn't control everything. And the variables dangling out of reach made him nervous.

CHAPTER

32

Abigail rose earlier than usual the following morning, her bed-side clock registering ten minutes before four o'clock. Thankful for the nervous energy that had made sleep elusive despite her weariness, she drew back the covers and crawled out of bed, taking care not to disturb her sister.

It had been after eleven last night when Rosalind finally came to bed. Even later for Zach, Abigail imagined. Her husband didn't seem the type to take his rest before his work had been completed, and he'd set himself a mountain of tasks. Building a booth, painting signs, decorating a wagon for the parade. As Abigail splashed water on her face, she considered letting him sleep. Surely he was exhausted.

She dressed in her navy blue work dress and pinned her hair in a simple braided wreath around the back of her head, then picked up her shoes and eased the door open. She tiptoed into the hall, but her efforts were for naught. Zach had taken his own measures to ensure he wasn't excluded from this morning's activities.

His door gaped wide, and the moment she clicked hers shut,

rustling echoed from his bed. The rope supports creaked and drew her gaze as he swung his legs over the edge of the mattress. As she watched, unable to look away, Zach stood, yawned, and stretched. And heavens, what a stretch. He slept without a shirt, giving her a spectacular view of muscles, swarthy skin a few shades lighter on his chest than his neck and forearms, and a smattering of dark hair that her fingers itched to explore.

Rumpled and eyes half-lidded, he prowled toward her. Abigail's mouth dried in an instant. She'd always found her husband attractive, but gracious. He was magnificent.

His gaze caught on the shoes she carried. He raised a sleepy brow to notify her that she'd been caught, then slanted her a slow, cocky grin, obviously proud of himself for outsmarting her. Not a single iota of disappointment manifested in her over her defeat. How could it when she had such a vision to feast her eyes upon? And even better was the evidence of the heart of the man before her. Selfless, dedicated, committed. She doubted he'd had more than four hours' sleep, yet here he stood, ready to do biscuit battle on her behalf. No wife could ask for a better champion.

"I'll be down as soon as I throw a shirt on," he said, his voice thick with the rasp of sleep.

Words failed her, but she managed a nod, thinking all the while that a shirt would be a shame.

"Abby?"

"Hmm?" Slowly, she dragged her gaze away from his chest to find his eyes. His extremely fierce, suddenly wide-awake eyes.

That cocky grin slid back into place a heartbeat before he grabbed her waist and pulled her tight against him. Her shoes dropped to the floor, and her palms flattened against the muscular expanse that had so mesmerized her.

"Mornin'." Then his lips captured hers. Passionate yet gentle, the kiss ended far too soon to her way of thinking. But then, they did have a couple hundred biscuits to bake.

Was it too late to change her mind about the float? Spending the day with her husband in non-baking pursuits suddenly seemed a much better use of her time.

Thankfully, Zach possessed more sense. He brought his hands up to cup her shoulders and planted a kiss on her forehead. Then he bent to retrieve her shoes, handed them to her, spun her around, and gave her a little push toward the stairwell.

She wobbled forward, casting a glance at him over her shoulder as she went. Something warmed his eyes. Something deeper than passion. More intimate than the teasing quirk of his smile. Something that had her heart swelling to near painful proportions.

Love. Oh, please let that be love. But how would she know? She had zero experience with suitors and knew nothing about interpreting a man's romantic regard.

Her feet stumbled, and she jerked her attention forward. If only he would *say* something.

"Careful," Zach called softly.

Not exactly the something she'd had in mind, but she supposed it would do. For now.

⸻

It took more than the couple minutes he'd needed to dress before Zach was ready to make an appearance in the kitchen. Not because he wasn't hurrying. He'd thrown on his clothes in record time, forfeited the comb for a quick run of his fingers through his hair, and ignored his razor completely. They had too much to accomplish this morning to waste time with superfluous niceties.

Yet it was that very need for efficiency that had him pausing at his door and reaching for the Bible on his dresser.

His mind had completely derailed when Abigail stood mute before him, staring as if he were a well-baked cake she wanted to devour. It had taken every ounce of self-control he possessed—which had been precious little while still in the hazy, post-dream realm that favored fantasies over reality—not to sweep her off her feet and carry her to his bed. He'd settled for a quick kiss and the glorious torture of her hands upon his skin. Not even scrubbing the cotton of his shirt over his chest had erased her touch.

This morning is about Abigail and the bakery, not about you. Get it together.

Inhaling a deep breath, he flipped open the pages of his Bible. A few *thou shalts* and *thou shalt nots* should straighten him out. Not really caring where he ended up, he thumbed to a spot near the back of the book. He jabbed his finger at a verse and read, ". . . for it is better to marry than to burn."

He jerked his gaze toward the ceiling, his hands thrown out in incredulity. "Really?"

Zach had never thought of God as having a sense of humor, but the Big Man must be elbowing the angels right now and guffawing with the heavenly host over the fool mortal who'd done the marrying part yet was still combusting over a pair of dimples.

Fine. Next time Zach and Abigail stood at the threshold of consummation, he wouldn't wait for her to take the first step. He'd take the reins and drive her straight to his bedroom. Where she belonged.

Oddly enough, that resolution restored a bit of his control and allowed him to bank passion's flames down to manageable embers. Those embers would be free to blaze later when he and Abigail didn't have a mountain of biscuits to bake.

Maybe the Big Man was doing more than laughing it up with the seraphim, after all.

Zach traipsed down the stairs, stopped long enough to put his shoes on, then entered his wife's domain. A long white bib apron covered the dark blue of her dress. With her sleeves rolled to her elbows, she worked biscuit dough in a giant bowl.

Zach strode over to the worktable. "Where do you want me?"

Pink colored her cheeks, shooting ideas through his head that threatened to bring his carefully banked embers back to life. He hadn't intended anything intimate by the question, but he couldn't help but be pleased that his wife's mind had veered that direction. It was nice to know he wasn't the only one battling the heat.

Abigail lifted her wrist to her forehead to rub at an itch, leaving a white flour mark on her skin. "I measured out butter and honey last night," she said, pointing with her elbow toward the stove that stood against the south-facing wall. "The butter's melting on low heat. Give it a stir every now and then, and when it's completely melted, add the honey from that small bowl and stir it into the butter for the glaze. I should have the first batch of dough ready for you to cut out by then."

"Got it."

Wanting to see one more blush before getting down to work, Zach came up behind Abigail, wrapped his arms around her middle, and planted a kiss on her cheek. He was rewarded by blooming pink roses creased with dimples. And a vigorous shooing of dough-encrusted fingers.

"You're supposed to be helping, not hindering," Abigail scolded, though her smile took all the sting out of her words.

"Right." All business now, Zach crossed to the stove, picked up the wooden spoon lying on the cabinet top, and gave the half-melted butter a stir.

Abigail scattered flour on the worktable and plopped a sticky mass of goo into the center of it. She kneaded it with the heel of her hand, folded it, kneaded again, added flour, rolled it around, then kneaded again. Her movements were elegant in their efficiency. If he'd tried to wrangle that sticky mess, he'd end up looking like he'd just crawled out of a paste jar, but she commanded the dough like a master potter working clay. She glanced up, caught him staring, and smiled before turning back to her dough wrangling.

Helping a woman make biscuits should *not* make a fellow this happy. But when the woman was the fellow's wife, and she smiled at him as if he were the noblest hero of her acquaintance—well, it couldn't be helped.

Zach shook his head at his rapidly deteriorating cynicism. Much more of this, and he'd be in danger of taking up his little sister's habit of breaking into song at random intervals. A snort escaped him at the thought.

"What?" Abby aimed a quizzical look in his direction.

"Nothing," he muttered, waving a hand to clear the air of ridiculous notions. Though to be honest, the more time he spent in Abby's company, the less ridiculous singing seemed. He'd probably croak like a toad after nearly a decade of no practice, but he couldn't deny that the urge to try had emerged from a long-enforced hibernation.

Cutting off a rumble in his throat that some might interpret as a hum, Zach focused on stirring butter and making the glaze.

After an hour, he and Abby had perfected a rhythm. Mix dough, cut biscuits, bake, baste, cool, repeat. The moment a batch came out of the large industrial bread oven that stood against the east wall, Abigail had a biscuit-laden sheet pan ready to take its place. Zach's hands felt like they were encased in gloves made of flypaper thanks to all the honey, but at least he didn't have to worry about dropping the basting brush.

By the time Rosalind came down to open the shop, they'd stockpiled twelve dozen biscuits in cloth-covered baskets.

"Don't forget to eat," Rosalind cautioned him as she neared the stove, where he stirred yet another batch of honey butter. She carried a coffeepot in each hand that she'd filled at the sink and set them on the hot part of the stove. When she opened the coffee tin to retrieve the grounds she'd milled last night, the scent hit Zach hard in the gut, setting his mouth to watering.

"I've already snitched a couple biscuits," he admitted softly, "but I sure could go for a cup of that coffee when you get it ready."

Rosalind smiled at him. "First cup's yours."

Living in an all-female household did have its advantages. Coffee made by someone who knew what they were doing, for one. Having it delivered, for another.

'Course, there were disadvantages too, Zach recalled five hours later as he paced the length of the upstairs hall for the sixth time. How long did it take to throw on some clothes, for pity's sake?

The parade started at two o'clock. The float had to be lined up in its assigned position at one. Rosalind was supposed to report to City Hall at one thirty. Mayor Longfellow planned to declare her Queen Bee of Honey Grove for the Fourth of July Parade as part of his oration to kick off the festivities. But here it was, nearly twelve thirty, and she and her sister were still in their room, fussing with who-knew-what while he paced the hall. Again.

He'd washed, shaved, put on his Sunday suitcoat, double-checked the biscuit baskets, and even made his bed. He *never* made his bed. At least not voluntarily. That was how desperate the situation had become.

After the eighth pass down the hall, Zach huffed out a breath and knocked on the door to Rosalind's room. "You gals almost ready? We gotta get goin'."

"Almost," his wife called. She'd closed the shop in order to help Rosalind dress. Why a grown woman needed help dressing, Zach couldn't fathom, but he considered sending out for reinforcements, since two didn't seem sufficient for the task at hand.

Abigail planned to attend the mayor's speech and watch the start of the parade before hurrying back to reopen the shop. The parade route would start at City Hall, make its way down Hickory to Sixth Street, circle around the square, then head east down Main to finish up in front of the Christian Church. Once the parade vacated the square, spectators would disperse. Those who'd traveled a significant distance would seek provisions to see them through the journey home. Locals planning to stay for the fireworks that evening might be in the market for a snack to keep their energy up. Hence the biscuit stand.

Zach, however, was going to need a lot more than a biscuit to get him through the rest of the day if those two didn't speed things—

The door opened. Zach spun around at the sound of the hinges.

"It's about t—" The complaint died on his tongue as his wife stepped through the doorway. She'd abandoned her work apron and changed her dark blue shirtwaist for a white lacy confection with a pleated front that highlighted her abundant curves. She'd tied a red sash around her waist that set off her blue skirt with patriotic flair and had somehow folded a scrap of leftover paper festooning from the shop's decorations into a circle thing that looked remarkably like a flower. It was pinned to her blouse like a brooch. She'd also magically woven red ribbon through the braid on her head, a ribbon he was certain hadn't been there when they'd been working side by side that morning.

"Isn't she stunning?" Abigail asked as she turned her face away from him.

She? He only saw Abigail.

When Abigail gestured behind her, Zach finally noticed Rosalind stepping into the hall. She didn't make his heart pound like Abby did, but he had to admit that she was a right fine-looking female. They must have taken curling tongs to her hair, for it hung in blonde ringlets down her nape in a way that reminded him of the fancy women in New York who used to bring donation baskets to the orphanage at Christmas. Her clothes were much fancier than her sister's too. All white and frilly. She'd taken some of the bunting fabric and fashioned an overskirt that draped down her front and pulled up into a big bow at the back. She wore a straw hat decorated with more of those red, white, and blue paper flower things.

For someone who'd known for less than twenty-four hours that she was going to be the star attraction of the Fourth of July parade, she'd done an impressive job of improvising a patriotic ensemble that would no doubt put Sophia Longfellow to shame.

Abigail shot him a look that felt remarkably like a kick to the shin. Obviously, she expected him to say something. And not to her.

He smiled at Rosie. "I've never seen a prettier Lady Liberty."

Abby beamed at him, making him stand a little taller, since he'd somehow managed *not* to stick his foot in his mouth. Then she took her sister's hand. "You're beautiful, Rosalind. No one deserves the title of Honey Grove's Queen Bee more than you."

Rosalind ducked her chin. "I just hope all this hoopla is worth the effort."

"It will be," Abby assured her. "You'll see. We'll break all kinds of sales records today. I just know it!"

Zach wanted to share her optimism, but his instincts warned that trouble lay ahead. And his instincts were rarely wrong.

CHAPTER

33

"There you are, Miss Kemp." Sophia Longfellow separated herself from the group of aldermen's wives in front of City Hall and crossed the street to meet Abigail and Rosalind. Her face pinched, Sophia clicked her tongue in displeasure. "If you're going to represent Honey Grove, you really ought to have a care for punctuality. The photographer's been waiting for an age."

"Ph-photographer?" Rosalind's gaze darted to the men gathered beneath the clock tower at the front entrance of the stone building. "No one told me anything about a photographer."

Abigail touched her sister's arm, scanning the crowd herself. Thankfully, the man holding the box camera and tripod was Alexander Westman, the local portraitist who doubled as the photographer for the *Honey Grove Signal*, the local paper. An older gentleman, a church deacon, nothing like that perfidious Julius. Nevertheless, Abigail felt a tremble course through her sister, and her steps slowed.

"Of course there's a photographer," Sophia said as she whisked Rosalind away from Abigail's side and drew her toward the group of women who were timidly edging near. "We commemorate every Fourth of July with a photograph of our civic leaders prior to the mayor's speech. You know that."

"Yes," Rosalind replied, pulling her arm from Sophia's grasp, "but no one mentioned that I would be a part of it."

Sophia rolled her eyes. "You're the first Honey Grove Queen Bee. Of *course* you'd be in the picture. Really. I thought you Kemp girls were sharper than this."

Abigail inserted herself between Sophia and Rosalind. It was a tight squeeze. She might have belly-bumped the mayor's wife a bit as she forced her way in, but one did what one must when defending one's sister.

Pasting on a smile, Abigail demanded Sophia's attention as she planted herself directly in her path, bare inches from her face. "I'm terribly sorry we're late. The fault lies entirely with me. I was so excited by the idea of a Taste of Heaven Bakery float that I rose well before dawn to bake treats for the occasion. I'm afraid all that cooking caused us to fall a bit behind schedule." She turned a woeful gaze toward the parade committee ladies. "If only we'd had more than a single day's notice. Decorating the float wagon and preparing the treats that Mayor Longfellow so cleverly suggested we distribute left little time for guessing the city council's unspoken expectations."

Abigail slanted a hard stare at Sophia, one that made it clear that picking a fight with her was fine, but condescending to a nervous seventeen-year-old girl was *not*.

Sophia's eyes narrowed as she glared back.

"All is forgiven," Mrs. Jones announced, bustling forward and wrapping an arm around Rosalind's waist. The kind older woman smiled as she steered Abby's sister closer to City Hall. "It never hurts to make the menfolk wait a minute or two, does it, ladies?" Like hens, the others circled around the young chick. "Have to make sure they appreciate all the effort we go through to make ourselves beautiful, don't we? And just look at the results. My goodness, Rosie. I've never seen you look so fine. And look at that clever use of bunting cloth on your skirt! Never in a thousand years would I have thought of employing such a technique, yet the result is utterly charming. You, my dear, are going to be the star of our parade."

Rosalind offered a hesitant smile but still cast a glance over her shoulder that pleaded with Abigail not to leave her alone. Abby turned to follow, then stopped and, recalling the verse from Romans about heaping burning coals on an enemy's head by treating them with kindness instead of evil, she tossed out a parting shot.

"I haven't had the chance to thank you, Sophia, for recommending Rosalind as Queen Bee. I know the council would never have thought of such an idea without your direction. And allowing the bakery to sponsor the float?" She pressed a hand to her bodice. "What a generous gesture. Thank you."

Before Sophia could do more than blink owlishly, Abigail pivoted and strode toward the ladies who were fitting a bright red sash over Rosalind's torso. Was it wrong of Abigail to hope that her coals of kindness were singeing Sophia's perfectly coifed head? Probably, but she figured that verse had been recorded in scripture for a reason. Enemies of the mean-spirited, shrewish variety seemed particularly singe-worthy, in her estimation.

⸎————⸎

"This windbag's speeches get longer every year," Reuben grumbled near Zach's ear. "I can't believe you dragged me down here."

They had left the float wagons farther down Hickory Street and skimmed the edges of the crowd that had gathered to hear

Mayor Longfellow's oratory on the history of Honey Grove and the blessings of freedom.

Zach couldn't care less about the speech. He'd come to lay eyes on the orator's wife. Sophia Longfellow stood on the dais a few steps behind and to the right of her husband as he gave his address, her bright red dress drawing Zach's attention and animosity like a matador's cape taunting a bull. Her smug expression made his skin itch.

"I can't see, Papa." Zeb yanked on his daddy's pant leg. "Lift me up." Reuben grumbled about there not being much worth seeing, but he reached for his son anyway.

"Me too, Mr. Zach." Ash didn't bother asking permission. He just grabbed Zach's arm as if it were a rope and planted a foot on his leg, ready to make the climb.

Before the scamp could get his second foot off the ground, Zach bent down and scooped him up. He settled the boy on his shoulders and grabbed his ankles to keep the little daredevil from attempting any unsupervised dismounts.

Would he someday be lifting his *own* son onto his shoulders to watch the parade?

The thought rocked Zach back on his heels. Abby was in no hurry to have children, but odds were good that when they finally stopped sleeping in separate beds, a child would eventually result. His gaze skittered over to where his wife stood, off the dais but close to her sister, who was positioned behind the mayor on his left. Zach's gaze fell to Abigail's belly, and an image of it rounded with a babe sprang to mind. His chest tightened as something primitive, protective, and downright prideful sprang to life inside him. Then Ash grabbed hold of his ears, and the feeling dissipated beneath the prick of little fingernails.

As Chester Longfellow brought his remarks to a close, Reuben gestured with his head that he and Zach needed to get back to the float. Zach nodded, though he shot a handful of glances Sophia's way as he went. That woman had something up her sleeve. He just didn't know what.

Audrey Sinclair waited at the float wagon with Dinah and Simeon. She had tied paper streamers to the bottom of the basket handles to make them more patriotic and even twisted some into a wreath for Dinah's hair. Thankfully, Simeon had escaped the decorative additions. For the most part, anyway. A red, white, and blue armband circled his left sleeve.

"There you are!" Audrey rushed forward and held her hands out to the son on Reuben's shoulders. "The parade is fixing to start."

Reuben lifted Zeb down and handed the boy over to his mama. "We've got plenty of time. The band's not even playing yet. The crowd has to thin out after the speech before we can go anywhere."

"Even so, it's better to be early and prepared than late and scrambling." She aimed a pointed look at her husband that clearly warned against arguing.

Being an intelligent man, Reuben nodded.

Being a somewhat clever hombre himself, Zach kept his mouth shut altogether, turned Ash over to his mother's care, and got out of the way.

While Audrey fussed over her children's clothing and gave the twins last-minute instructions about behaving themselves on the float, Zach double-checked all the rigging and extracted the driver's promise that the team would be held to a walk for the duration of the parade. The alderman in charge of the queen's float was a staid fellow in his forties with grown daughters of his own. He didn't seem the sort to willfully put a young woman in harm's way.

"Here's the lady of the hour," Reuben announced, stepping

forward to greet Rosalind and Abigail as they wove between the people setting up the float ahead of them in line. Rosalind looked a bit dazed, surely from all the unwanted attention she'd endured for the last hour, but her step was steady and her chin held high.

Audrey unfolded from her crouch where she'd been spit-polishing Ash's cheek and clasped her hands together. "How beautiful you look!" She rushed over to Rosalind and wrapped the younger woman in a hug. "I might not agree with all of the decisions the council has made of late, but naming you the first Queen Bee of Honey Grove has my full support. There is no lady fairer of face or kinder of heart than our Rosie."

"Hear, hear!" Reuben stepped forward and gallantly held out his arm. "Might I assist you into your carriage, Your Majesty?"

His silly charm erased the dazed look from Rosalind's eyes and instead had them twinkling by the time he lifted first her, then her two lads-in-waiting into the wagon bed. Abigail reached over the side and handed each boy a stick flag and told them they were the official flag bearers for the float and must wave their flags with national pride and enthusiasm. This, of course, set the two boys off in a contest to see who could wave more vigorously.

While Rosalind laughed and gave the twins instructions on proper flag waving, Zach collected two biscuit-filled baskets from the wagon, sidling extra close to his wife as he did so.

She smiled shyly at him, and his chest muscles flexed in response, remembering the heated way she'd looked at him that morning. He might as well flaunt his good points. Heaven knew he didn't have many, so he'd better make the most of what he had. The way her gaze skittered along his arms as he curled the baskets over the wagon's side tempted him to find something even heavier to lift for her. Too bad there weren't any giant rocks in the middle of the road needing to be moved out of the way or a stack of lumber to clear out of their path. The best he could do was slow the basket-fetching down and soak up as much admiration as he could before it ended.

"Need some help there, speedy?" Reuben thumped him on the back and reached for one of the baskets, a crooked grin sprouting on his impertinent face.

Tempted to straighten that crook with his knuckles, Zach settled for a glare instead as he bypassed his smart aleck partner to hand the basket to the sweet little girl standing behind her daddy. "Here you go, Dinah."

She reached for the basket handle with both hands.

"It's not too heavy for you, is it?" Zach asked.

They'd opted for multiple smaller baskets that could be switched out during the parade instead of larger baskets that would cause the children's arms to tire. He and Reuben would handle fetching the replacements. Two extra baskets had been placed on each side of the wagon in readiness.

She shook her head. "I can do it."

Zach tweaked the end of her nose. "Of course you can."

As he turned to hand the second basket to Simeon, the band struck up the opening notes of Sousa's "The Liberty Bell."

"Hurry, children." Audrey clapped her hands. "Dinah on the left with your father. Simeon on the right with Mr. Zach. Don't give out the biscuits too quickly, now. Make them last."

Zach moved to take up his assigned position, happy when Abigail came with him. Though when he smiled down at her, he realized her attention was focused on her sister, not him.

"I'll watch out for her," he vowed.

She looked up at him, touching his arm. "I know."

"The mayor and his wife are in the buggy directly behind

the band, so there shouldn't be any trouble from that quarter while the parade is going on. But I'll keep an eye on them too."

"Thank you." Grabbing his shoulder for balance, she rose up on tiptoes and aimed a kiss at his cheek.

He bent sideways to close the distance for her, his heart thumping like one of those bass drums in the band. All too soon it was over, and his wife was letting him go.

"I'll take the back road down to the bakery and open the shop so we'll be ready for customers once the parade ends. I'll wave at you and Rosalind from the doorway."

He gave her a nod, then watched her scurry away, his heart starting up a second cadence when she glanced back at him and waved before turning the corner down Seventh Street.

✣────✣

Abigail hurried down Seventh with a giddy energy that a woman who'd risen before four in the morning shouldn't be feeling. Then again, any woman fortunate enough to be married to Zacharias Hamilton had to learn to expect flutters and tingles and excessive giddiness from time to time.

Biting her lip to keep her smile contained, she reached into her skirt pocket to retrieve the key to her shop. Entering the alley, she checked to make sure she had the key situated correctly for sliding into the lock. Before she could reach for the handle, however, the door flew inward, and a boy flew outward. He barreled past her, knocking her to the ground.

"Hey!" Abigail barely had time to register the fact that some little ruffian had broken into her bakery before a volley of muted gunshots firing inside her kitchen stalled her heart.

CHAPTER

34

Abigail's stomach tightened into a hard knot of dread as she scrambled to her feet. Her first thought was to run, but something about the gunfire inside struck her as odd. Sporadic. Some pops impossibly close together. Others delayed.

Bracing a shaky hand against the doorframe, she inched closer. Then, after taking a breath that was far too shallow to have any calming effect whatsoever, she chanced a quick peek inside.

No outlaws took shots from behind overturned worktables. No deputies returned fire from the stairwell. Her kitchen looked exactly as she'd left it.

Abigail's lungs finally began taking in sufficient air as she pressed her back to the wall of her shop. Not gunfire. Thank the Lord.

Another series of pops exploded. What *were* they? The sound of the band competed with the muffled bangs inside her shop as the parade entered the square.

The parade . . . the boy . . .

Firecrackers.

In her kitchen!

Suddenly more afraid for her bakery than herself, Abigail rushed through the back door. She twisted her head from side to side, trying to ascertain where the loud popping was coming from. If that boy had set off firecrackers in her kitchen or shop, the sparks could start a fire. Yet she saw nothing. No chains of red poppers flashing and dancing across her floor. Slowly she pivoted in a circle, closing her eyes as she honed her ears. There. In the back.

Her eyes opened. Horror tore through her chest. No!

Abigail lunged forward and yanked open her bread oven door. Sparks erupted from the oven, spitting over her chest and hands. With a gasp she jerked backward, batting at the specks on her blouse even as she raced for the kitchen sink. She turned the spigot and set her hands beneath the flow, the cool water easing the tiny pinprick burns on her hands. She splashed water on her face, then dampened a towel, opened it wide, and splayed it across her chest.

She gave herself a quick inspection to make sure she'd gotten them all, then dampened a second towel and ran back to the oven. She had to save it. Without an industrial oven, her business would fail.

Sparks continued to shoot out of the behemoth's mouth. She held the towels out in front of her like a shield, protecting her face as she inched closer. After tossing one of the towels over her shoulder to hang down across her front, she reached for the long-handled wooden peel she used for placing and removing her loaves from the oven. Keeping the second towel around her hand, she gripped the paddle-like tool and cautiously slipped it into the open oven.

The dancing string of firecrackers popped and jerked and shot sparks, defending its territory with all its might. Abigail jumped and yelped and danced a bit herself as she dodged the sparks, but she kept advancing. She had to. She couldn't lose her bakery. Not after all she'd done to save it.

Gradually, the popping slowed, and Abigail found an opening. Sliding the peel beneath the hopping firecrackers, she pushed the shovel-like paddle deep into the oven until she managed to hook the string on the handle section. Angling the handle upward so the firecrackers wouldn't slide down to hit her hands, she extracted them from the oven and let them dangle and dance on their string all the way to the sink, where she dropped them beneath the still-running spigot.

The crackers sizzled and hissed in protest but eventually fell silent under the water's onslaught. Abigail turned off the spigot, then slowly swiveled to face the victim. Her bread oven.

The acrid odor of burned gunpowder filled the room. No comforting, homey aroma of fresh bread. No sweetness from the honey biscuits. Just the smell of battle, of destruction, of death.

One foot after the other moved her across the room.

Please let it be all right. Please let it be all right. The mantra matched the beat of her footsteps. Yet as much as Abigail tried to cling to hope, she knew in her heart that things weren't all right. How could they be? A string of miniature bombs had just exploded inside her bread oven. An oven that had taken her father more than ten years to save up for.

Dark gray smoke hovered at the mouth of the oven. Abigail cleared it with a wave of her hand, then bent at the waist and peered inside.

Merciful heavens.

Tears flooded her eyes and nausea swirled in her belly. Even with her vision obscured by lingering smoke, she couldn't deny the truth.

Her oven—her livelihood—had been utterly destroyed.

⚑————⚑

Zach cleared his throat and scowled at a lanky teen who was trying to sneak a second biscuit out of Simeon's basket.

The youth jerked a guilty look toward Zach and pulled his hand back as if he'd been slapped. Then a mulish look came over his face, and he jutted out his chin. "It's for my sister."

Maybe it was, maybe it wasn't. When Zach had been this kid's age, he would have been doing all he could to snitch an extra biscuit for Seth and Evie. Of course, before he had siblings to worry about, he would've lied through his teeth to fill his own belly.

Zach slowed his step and eased into the edge of the crowd to get close to the belligerent kid. "We're gonna set up a booth at the north end of the square after the parade. Help us set it up and earn an extra biscuit for your sister. Spend the next couple hours drumming up business for us, and you'll earn a half-dozen biscuits along with enough ham to fill each of 'em."

The boy's eyes widened in his thin face. "Ya mean it?"

Zach raised a brow. "I don't say things I don't mean. You work, you eat."

"I'll be there, mister." The boy stood a little taller, his sleeves pulling up to expose his bony wrists.

"Good." Zach nodded at him, his chest tightening. He hoped the boy showed up. The kid could use a good meal. If he proved to be a hard worker, maybe Abigail could be convinced to let him help out at the shop a few hours a week. Run errands, carry wood, sweep. Surely there'd be something he could do. They could pay him in bread if she didn't want to spend the coin. The kid seemed more than satisfied with the payment Zach had offered for today's tasks.

They locked gazes for a moment, an unspoken promise

passing between them. Then, in a blink, the kid disappeared into the crowd. That was Zach's cue to get back to his own job. Thankfully, the parade moved so slowly that he caught up to Simeon in a handful of lengthened strides. His gaze darted over to Rosalind. She was still smiling and waving, though her grin was starting to look a mite tuckered. It drooped a little around the edges and didn't really touch her eyes, but Ash and Zeb made up for her waning energy. They waved their flags in wide arcs, and whenever Rosalind called out, "Try the best honey biscuit in Honey Grove. It's a taste of heaven!" the boys zipped from one side of the wagon bed to the other. It seemed to be a race to see who could reach the opposite side the fastest. Thankfully, there'd only been one collision so far and no blood. Reuben had checked.

The float finally reached the south end of the square and made the turn to head back up Sixth Street, in front of Abigail's shop. Zach stretched tall to see over the crowd swarming the boardwalks. He'd purposely chosen to work the right side of the wagon in order to be closer to his wife, and he'd been looking forward to the wave she'd promised him.

However, as they rounded the corner, the anticipatory smile creeping onto Zach's face slipped into a frown. Something was wrong.

The shop door was closed. Abigail was nowhere to be seen.

Maybe she was busy setting things up inside and didn't realize the parade had arrived. But how could she miss it? The band had just marched past her door.

He took a step toward the bakery, then checked himself. He'd promised to watch over Rosalind. Simeon too. She wouldn't thank him if he left his post. Yet when they crawled past the shop and there continued to be no sight of her, the unease inside him deepened.

Zach jogged over to the wagon and called out to Rosalind, "Can you see Abby?" She had a higher vantage point from inside the wagon bed and should be able to see over the heads of the people packing the boardwalk.

Lines etched her forehead as she peered at the shop window. She shook her head. "No. There's no movement in the shop at all."

"She's probably in the kitchen," Zach said, forcing a smile to his face that he didn't feel. No need to get Rosalind worried. She had enough on her mind already. "I'll go by and check on her when the parade's done," he said without really looking at Rosalind. Better that no one else knew of their concern. "You can stay with Reuben and start setting up the booth. I hired a kid to help."

"You did?" Rosalind's waving hand dropped momentarily before she picked it up and resumed her Queen Bee stance.

"Told him he could have a second biscuit if he helped set up the booth. More if he drummed up business for us." Zach met her eyes for a brief moment. "The kid seemed hungry."

That brought a dash of fire to her eyes. "I'll see he gets ample payment if you're not back yet."

He hoped he'd be back. Hoped whatever was going on with Abby was a minor hiccup and nothing serious. A stabbing fear jabbed his heart. What if she was hurt?

Tension radiated through him, lengthening Zach's stride. When he sped past Simeon, though, he realized his error, turned around, and marched back into position. He modulated his steps, his legs feeling as if they'd been shackled in heavy irons. This plodding pace was going to kill him.

Take care of her until I can get there, Lord. Send someone else if need be. Just . . . take care of her. Please.

It seemed like an eternity before the float made it to the ending point at the churchyard. The moment the alderman pulled the wagon to a stop, Zach had his hands around Rosalind's waist, lifting her over the side.

"Reuben, I've got to check on Abigail," he said after setting Rosalind down. "Something's not right at the shop."

His partner, who had hunkered down to congratulate his daughter on a job well done, shot Zach a look and immediately straightened. "Go. I'll set up the booth."

Zach paused long enough to place a hand on his friend's shoulder. He lowered his voice to a barely audible rumble. "I need you to guard Rosalind too."

Reuben raised a brow. "Guard her?" he asked in equally hushed tones.

"Just watch out for fellas who get too friendly or treat her disrespectfully. She's had some problems lately." He couldn't say more without violating Rosalind's privacy, but Reuben didn't need any additional explanation. His eyes had already gone hard.

"No harm will come to her."

The words were a vow, and Zach found he trusted them as much as if they'd come from Seth or Logan. He trusted Reuben completely. He couldn't fill one hand with the number of men he could say that about.

Feeling a thickness start to clog his throat, Zach cleared it away and squeezed Reuben's shoulder. "Thank you."

Reuben nodded. "As soon as Audrey collects the twins, the rest of us will get started on the booth. I won't leave Rosalind's side. You have my word."

"You're a good friend, Reuben Sinclair."

"As are you." Reuben cleared his own throat, then slapped Zach on the back. "Now go. See about your wife."

Zach turned to go, then recalled the boy he'd hired to help with the booth. "There's a kid—"

"I'll fill him in," Rosalind interrupted. "Go."

Deciding it was rather nice to have people other than himself to rely on, Zach lifted a hand in thanks, then took off for the bakery. His run slowed to a jog then a walk the closer he got to the square. The crowds were thick and milling every which way, making it hard for a big man to maneuver. Once he managed to get into the alley, though, his path cleared.

He noticed two things immediately. Glass had been broken out of the back windowpane, and the back door stood slightly ajar.

"Abby!" Terror seized him as he bounded through the back door. Had she interrupted a robbery? Been attacked by a thief who had used the parade as cover?

His hands balled into fists, ready to fight whatever threat awaited. But then a flash of blue caught in his peripheral vision. He turned his head just as Abigail lifted hers from where she lay crumpled on the floor. Red-rimmed eyes met his. Tears had left streaks in the soot and smoke stains on her face. Gray scorch marks marred her white shirtwaist, and the stench of gunpowder filled his nostrils.

Zach dropped to his knees and grabbed her arms. "Are you all right?" His voice cracked, but then, his heart was hammering against his ribs so hard that he was amazed he managed to form any words at all.

New tears filled her eyes, and tremors coursed through her as she shook her head. "It's gone, Zach. It's all gone."

CHAPTER

35

Abigail had never been so happy to see another human being as she'd been the moment Zach charged into her kitchen. She needed his strength. His comfort. Needed *him*.

Their position on the floor was awkward, but when he took hold of her upper arms, she fisted his shirt in her hands and turned her face into his chest. He was here. Fierce, kind, wonderful Zach. She wasn't alone. Thank God, she wasn't alone.

His hands released her arms, shifting to circle her back and slip beneath her knees. In a single motion, he lifted her from the floor and settled her against his chest, then paced across the kitchen to the breakfast table, where he scooted out a chair with his foot and sat down, holding her on his lap.

He fidgeted for a moment, then urged her face upward with a gentle tug on her chin. When she looked up, he wiped the tears and soot from her face with his handkerchief. He took such care, brushing the damp stray hairs behind her ear with a gentle finger and running the handkerchief over her face with the same soft strokes one would use with a small child. Part of her was embarrassed to be coddled in such a way, but a much larger part craved the tenderness. Craved the chance to let someone else be the strong one. Just for a moment.

Once he'd cleaned her face to his satisfaction, he handed her the handkerchief. She sat up a bit, turned her face away, and blew her nose. She crumpled the handkerchief into her hand—she couldn't exactly hand it back to him after soiling it in such a way—then sagged back against him and laid her head on his shoulder. For a blissful moment, she simply listened to him breathe. Deep. Steady. Her breaths started mimicking his pattern, and soon she found herself relaxing against him.

"What's gone, Abby?" Her husband's low rumble sharpened her mind and brought her back to the reality of her situation. Only this time, with him surrounding her, it didn't feel quite so bleak. "Did the thief empty the till?"

If only the damage had been that minor. The bakery could survive a day of lost profits, even the biggest profit-bearing day of the year.

She shook her head. "No. At least, I don't think so." She straightened away from Zach, her brow wrinkling as she craned her neck to peer toward the shop. As if she could somehow see through the wall, beneath the counter, and inside the cashbox if she just squinted hard enough. "I haven't actually checked."

He rested a finger on her jaw and lightly turned her face back to him. "Then what's gone? What happened?"

She told him about the boy, about the firecrackers, and about her beloved oven being gutted from the inside. She had to dab at her eyes a time or two, but anger built inside her as she recounted the tale, pushing her grief aside.

"Why would that child play such a horrible prank?" She tried to recall as many details about the boy as she could. He'd run her down so fast, most of the memories were a blur. He'd been a thin little thing. Cap pulled low on his head. Not too tall. He'd shoved at her when he barreled past, and his hands had jabbed into the lower section of her corset. "Do you think it was a dare of some kind?"

Zach's face gave away none of his thoughts. "Doubt it."

"Well, if it was just pure mischief, the little vandal should be locked up. I don't care how young he is."

Zach raised a brow at her.

Abigail huffed and slumped a bit. "All right. I care. But there needs to be consequences." She straightened, indignation sparking to life once again. "No matter his age, his actions were criminal. Costly. He can't be allowed to run amok, destroying people's businesses. He probably thought it a harmless prank, but that act ruined me, Zach. Without my father's oven, the Taste of Heaven will fail."

"It *won't* fail." A muscle ticked in his jaw, and his arms tensed. "I won't let it. I've got money put aside. Not a lot, but I could talk to Seth—"

"Absolutely not!" Abigail grabbed his arm. "I will not drag your family into my woes. That's why we signed that agreement before we wed. You are not liable for any of the bakery's financial troubles."

Zach glared at her. "I don't give a flying fig for that agreement, and you know it."

Did she? She took in his fierce face, his square jaw clenching, his gorgeous midnight-blue eyes glimmering with intensity.

Yes, she supposed she did know. This marriage had ceased being a business arrangement weeks ago.

Softening against him, she laid her head back on his shoulder and reached up to stroke his jaw.

"You're right. We're in this together. You and I will deal with the ramifications of today's destruction, but Seth and Christie are just getting started. As are Logan and Evie. I don't want to burden them with these troubles. We'll get through."

Somehow.

Some of the tension drained from Zach's body. He cradled her close and rubbed loose fingers over her sleeve. With her husband's presence to combat the despair that had dragged her to her knees earlier, Abigail's mind slowly started to spin again. She didn't have time to worry about how to handle the oven issue right now. Didn't scripture teach that tomorrow had enough trouble of its own? She wouldn't borrow any. She'd focus on today and what she could do with what she had.

What she had was a fully functioning shop stocked with delicious loaves and rolls. Not to mention the biscuit booth Rosalind would—

Abigail bolted upright. "You're supposed to be with Rosalind." She pushed away from her husband and scrambled awkwardly off his lap.

Zach stood more slowly. Deliberately. "Reuben's with her. I stayed by her side until the parade was over."

Abigail gasped. "The parade's over? Of course it's over. I need to open the shop. We need whatever profits we can bring in." She dashed toward the door that connected the bakery to the kitchen.

But Zach ran her down and snagged her around the waist. He spun her around to face him.

"What are you doing? I have to go!"

"I'll open the shop. You might want to change your, ah . . ." He gestured to her chest, a touch of red staining his swarthy cheeks.

Abigail glanced down and sucked in a breath. Good heavens. She was a mess. Tiny charred spots across her chest, damp fabric clinging to her curves. And there was no telling what her face and hair looked like. She'd scare off the customers before they could even get a look at her bread.

But Zach couldn't open the shop. He knew nothing about prices or running the till. He couldn't make recommendations or answer questions about ingredients.

As if he'd read her mind, he raised a brow in slight offense. "I was a professional gambler, Abby. I can run numbers in my head and keep track of multiple pieces of information at one time. Rosalind told me she keeps a price list in the cashbox. I might not do things exactly as you would, but I can make do for the ten minutes it'll take you to change."

Of course he could. He was the most capable man she'd ever met. She shouldn't have doubted him. Not even for a moment.

"You're right." She smiled an apology, then kissed his cheek. "Thank you, Zach. For everything."

He didn't say anything. Just nodded. But she was coming to understand his nods and grunts. This one warmed her heart. He understood that her thanks extended to more than his opening of her shop. Perhaps he felt a touch of gratitude too for the fact that they had each other, for better or worse. They might be facing the *worse* right now, but the fact that they could lean on each other in the midst of it moved it into the *better* category.

"I'll be back down in a trice," she promised as she scurried to the stairwell.

As soon as she spied herself in the mirror above Rosalind's dresser, she mentally thanked her husband again for not letting her open the shop in her current state. Gracious, she looked like she'd been sucked up into a twister. As she worked the buttons at her throat, she noticed that the odor of smoke had infused her clothing. No one wanted to buy baked goods from someone who smelled burnt. It killed one's credibility.

Would the acrid odor of spent firecrackers seep from the

kitchen into her shop? Abigail's hands paused in tugging her bodice from her skirt. With a sigh, she shrugged off the answer. She couldn't control where aromas wafted. She'd closed the oven door. The back window had been broken out, so maybe that would help the smoke dissipate. God had been known to bring beauty from ashes. Maybe he would direct the smoke into the alley instead of her shop. Maybe not. Either way, it was out of her control, and she couldn't spare the energy to worry about things she had no power to change.

After stripping down to her chemise, corset, and drawers, she scrubbed her face clean at the washstand and examined her hair. She didn't have time to redo the fancy braid and ribbon that Rosalind had fashioned for her, so she settled for smoothing back the loose strands and adding some extra pins. Thoughts of her sister urged her to hurry. Mr. Sinclair was a good man, but he had his children to watch out for. Rosalind needed Zach with her.

Abigail grabbed serviceable clothing from the wardrobe, no longer caring about festivity. The brown twill would work just fine. She'd dress it up a bit with her ivory calico shirtwaist with the tiny maroon flowers. It might clash with the red ribbon in her hair, but she couldn't be bothered with that. Rosalind needed Zach, and Abigail needed to sell bread. Who knew how long today's profits would have to last them?

CHAPTER

36

Zach might have oversold his abilities just a tad. Once he'd unlocked the front door, he gave a holler to let those within earshot know the bakery was open for business. He'd expected a trickle of people to wander in, not a gushing flood. All right, so twenty people wasn't really a flood, but for a man who had no idea what he was doing, it seemed like feeding a multitude of biblical proportions.

Thankfully, folks were in good spirits from the parade, and after he cracked a joke about having mercy on the ignorant husband until his wife arrived to take over, the patrons seemed more than happy to point to what they wanted in the display cabinet. Which—thank the Lord—was labeled on his side, so he could match the type of bread to the price list. After about ten sales, he started getting the hang of things.

"Hey, Zach!" one of the builders he and Reuben supplied lumber to called out from the back of the line, his booming voice carrying over the buzz of conversation.

Zach glanced up from wrapping a sourdough loaf in butcher paper. "Yeah?"

"She got you wearing an apron?"

Chuckles rippled through the crowd.

"Nah." A fellow from the sawmill who stood second in line called back the answer. "I can still see his trousers. But I want to know if he had anything to do with the baking. I prefer my bread made with flour, not sawdust. Get enough of that at the mill."

More laughter broke out, especially among the male patrons. Zach just grinned and held up a hand. "You got nothing to worry 'bout, Jenkins. Abigail made everything you see here."

"Good," an older lady said as she looked up from the display case, "because no one makes yeast rolls like Abigail Kemp."

"That's Abigail Hamilton now, ma'am," Zach corrected, satisfaction lacing his tone.

She eyed him as if taking his measure. "So it is."

Zach turned his attention back to the sourdough and let the rest of the conversation ramble on without him. His ears pricked every time a regular Taste of Heaven customer bragged to a newcomer about the outstanding quality of Abigail's baked goods and shared recommendations of their favorite items.

It made a man right proud to hear his wife praised so highly. It also made a man determined to ensure that his talented wife had whatever she needed to continue her business. As well as seeing that whoever was responsible for the vandalism was brought to justice. And not just the kid with the firecrackers, but whoever hired him to do his damage.

A kid pulling a prank might break a window and toss a chain of lit firecrackers into a random business and then run for the hills. But no youngster would break into a business, take the time to locate the most expensive piece of equipment inside, then sabotage that equipment. It was too deliberate. Required too much time. Entailed too much risk of getting caught with zero personal reward. Zach had checked the till. All the funds were accounted for, which meant the motivation to do the deed was being supplied by someone else. Someone paying and giving strict instructions on where the vandalism should be focused. Only one person had the motivation to single out Abigail and attack her with such calculated malice—Sophia Longfellow.

Hinges creaked behind him, and Zach glanced up from making change to see his wife sweep through the door. She wore a bright smile on her face, as if nothing out of the ordinary had occurred, and the pride already tightening his chest intensified.

Trying not to get caught staring at his wife, Zach forced his attention back to the woman with the rolls standing in front of him, her palm extended for the fifty cents he owed her.

"Here you go, ma'am." He dropped the coins into her hand.

As her fingers closed over the coins, she smiled, but not at him. "It's about time you trained your husband in the family business, Abigail. He looks good behind that counter."

Abby winked at him as she navigated into her customary position behind the counter. "Zach looks good *anywhere*."

His eyes widened. Had she just flirted with him in public? Heat climbed his neck even as an idiotic grin stretched his lips.

"That he does," the middle-aged woman said with a wink of her own as she stepped away from the counter to make room for the next patron.

"Too bad he's needed in the square," Abigail said, real disappointment coloring her voice. "Rosalind is running a biscuit booth. Two for a nickel. Zach will be helping her get everything set up. Be sure to spread the word."

"I'll do that," the woman promised with a wave and headed out the door.

Zach stepped close to his wife. "Time for me to go, huh?"

She glanced at him, the joviality in her manner slipping just a bit as she nodded. Man, but he wanted to stay with her. She shouldn't be alone after all that had happened.

"I'll be fine," she said, as if she'd read his mind.

She'd be *busy*. He wasn't so sure about *fine*, but this wasn't the time or place to argue. And he really did need to check on Rosalind. A lot of outsiders in town meant an increased chance for trouble.

So after making a note of the sale he'd just completed on the ledger next to the cashbox, he took his leave. He made sure to pull the door to the kitchen closed behind him. He'd only noticed a touch of smokiness in the air inside the bakery, and no one had said anything, but he wanted to minimize the effect as much as possible.

Once in the kitchen, he took a moment to examine the broken window, frowning over the glass littering the floor. He grabbed the broom from the corner and swept up the shards, not wanting Abigail to have to deal with it later. When they finished with the biscuit booth, he'd track down the marshal to report the vandalism, then bring the two wooden signs home and use them to board up the window.

After dumping the broken glass into the trash bin, Zach headed out to the square and met up with Reuben and Rosalind. The kid he'd hired with the promise of food was there too, nailing the signs into place as Reuben held them.

Rosalind stepped away from the biscuit baskets, leaving Simeon and Dinah to guard them, and met Zach a short distance from the booth. "His name's Nate," she said with a nod toward the kid. "Seems to be a good worker."

Hunger was a powerful motivator. He'd intended to ask Abby about hiring the boy on, but now with the oven trouble, well . . . Zach set his jaw. He'd just pay the kid out of his own pocket. He wasn't sure how Abby planned to move forward with the bakery being down an oven, but if he could lessen her workload in other areas, taking the boy on would be a bargain.

Once the last nail had been driven and the sign hung firmly in place, Zach approached the booth. "Nate, is it?"

The kid turned and gave a quick nod. "Yessir."

Zach smacked him on the back. "Glad to see you took me up on my offer."

"I'll be drummin' up business fer ya too." He shot Zach a man-to-man look, one that promised he'd uphold his end of the bargain as long as Zach came through on his. "I'm meetin' up with my sister in a few minutes over by City Hall. I'll get her to help too. With two of us working, we'll spread the word even faster." He turned a shy smile toward Rosalind. "You'll be sold out of them biscuits in no time, miss."

"Then you better grab a handful for you and your sister before you head off, shouldn't you?" Rosalind smiled at the boy, which immediately turned his cheeks red, but she pretended not to notice as she retrieved a basket and held it out to him. "Thank you for your help with the booth. You did fine work."

Nate might be shy around the pretty Rosalind, but he wasn't shy around food. Four biscuits disappeared into the small knapsack slung across his body before Zach could even blink.

"Live around here, Nate?" Zach asked.

The kid nodded, though his gaze turned wary. "Just outside town."

Zach wouldn't press for more details. Nate's living situation was his own business. If he turned out to be a good worker and trustworthy, maybe Zach would talk to Abby about offering him and his sister a place to stay—if they needed one. Cots in the kitchen would keep them much toastier in the winter than some abandoned shed or lean-to if they were on their own.

"Come by the bakery tonight around six. Bring your sister. We'll feed you supper and maybe talk about offering you regular work. If you're interested."

The boy stood straighter. "I'm interested."

"I got to clear things with the wife, first," Zach warned, not wanting to get the kid's hopes up too high before he talked things over with Abby, but she had a soft spot for widows and others who had no one to look out for them. Surely she wouldn't refuse a hungry boy work. "It's her bakery, but if she approves, you can start on Monday."

"Six o'clock. We'll be there, sir."

"Hamilton." He grinned at the boy and extended his hand. "Name's Hamilton."

Nate took his hand and clasped it with a firm grip that spoke well of his determination. "I won't let you down, Mr. Hamilton."

Zach squeezed the kid's hand to let him know that he had some proving to do yet, but that he'd receive a fair shake. Nate dipped his chin. Message received.

When the kid scampered off, Rosalind edged toward her position in the booth, but Zach stopped her with a hand to her elbow. "Hold up just a minute." He gestured his partner over as well. When they both stood close enough that he could speak without the wandering crowds overhearing, Zach broke the news. "There's been an incident at the bakery."

Rosalind sucked in a breath. "Is Abby . . . ?"

"She's fine. A young boy broke in and set off a string of firecrackers in the bread oven."

"No!" Rosalind's hand shot up to cover her mouth. "Is it salvageable?"

Zach shook his head.

Tears gathered in his sister-in-law's eyes, but Zach gave her a pointed look. This was not the time to fall apart. They had biscuits to sell and Abigail to support.

Rosalind blinked the moisture away and stiffened her spine.

Reuben scowled. "That makes no sense. What kid would vandalize an oven? There's no flash to show off, no bragging rights to claim."

"I got no proof, but my money says Sophia Longfellow's behind it. She bears a hard grudge against Abigail and is the only one with a motive to damage the bakery."

Reuben's brows rose. "The mayor's wife? Why would she—"

"Benedict Crowley," Rosalind said as if that would explain everything, but Reuben's face remained lined with confusion. A thoughtful look crossed her face. "I suppose the accident happened before you and Audrey moved to town. Benedict was Sophia's beau when they were in school. He died in a fall while rescuing Abby from a tree. Sophia's never forgiven her for it."

As they spoke, little Dinah approached and tugged on Reuben's sleeve. "People have started askin' about the biscuits, Papa. What should we do?"

Rosalind spun away from the men, pasted a cheerful smile on her face, and swept up the little girl's hand. "We should sell them, of course. Come on. Let's get busy." A few steps away from the men, she raised her voice and called out to the crowd, "Best honey biscuits in Texas! Two for a nickel!"

Reuben moved closer to murmur in Zach's ear. "Whatever you need, you've got it. Just let me know."

Zach nodded, his heart twisting in his chest at the gift of unconditional friendship and generosity. "Thanks. I'll need some time off to visit the bank on Monday morning. See about a loan."

Reuben grimaced and hissed in a breath. "Charlie Evans at the bank is Sophia's cousin. If she really bears as strong a grudge as you suspect, I doubt you'll get much help from that quarter."

Zach frowned as Reuben slapped him on the back and moved off to supervise his kids.

If a professional bread oven was as pricey as Abigail had implied, and the bank refused to offer him a loan, how was he going to set this issue to rights?

Short of a confession and restitution from the woman responsible, he could only think of one way—one that required breaking a vow nearly as sacred to him as the one he'd spoken on his wedding day.

CHAPTER

37

Abigail closed the shop at ten minutes before five o'clock after selling her last wheat loaf. Not one crumb remained. She nearly wept at the beauty of an empty display case, so thankful for the Lord's provision. Of course, the empty display case also terrified her, heralding the famine to come. She tried to focus on the current victory, but the looming possibility of defeat proved too big to ignore.

Would she be able to limp by for a while with the small cook-stove oven they used for their personal meal preparation, or would her customers grow impatient with insufficient inventory and less variety?

And what of the widows? She always baked extra so there would be leftovers for those in need, but there'd be no extra now for Lydia and the others. They'd survive without her baked goods, but she hated to think of them going without.

A rummaging sound came from the kitchen, alerting Abigail to Rosalind's arrival. Hopefully Zach's as well. Her heart beat a little faster in anticipation. She wanted his arms around her again, his fingers on her hair, his strength infusing her. The future looked much less bleak when he held her.

Forcing her lips into a cheerful arc, she pushed through the connecting door, the cashbox under her arm. "We sold out the shop! How did the two of you fare?" Her gaze skimmed over Rosalind, searching for Zach, but he wasn't there.

"He stopped to talk to the marshal," her sister said. "Wanted to report the vandalism." Rosalind crossed the kitchen and wrapped her arms around Abigail. "Oh, Abby. I'm so sorry."

Abigail slid the cashbox out from under her arm, dropped it onto the countertop by the sink, then embraced her sister more fully. Ordering herself not to turn into a watering pot for the second time that day, she patted Rosalind's back and eased from her hold. "Things might be tight for a while, but we'll manage."

They'd manage as a family. Zach would see to that. And while her independent spirit chafed at depending on a man for her livelihood, her heart knew that were the situation reversed—if Zach had been injured or sick and unable to work—she'd want him to accept her provision with grace, not grow embittered by dented pride. So if the worst happened and the Taste of Heaven closed, resentment would *not* sour her marriage. She'd count her blessings and move forward.

If she'd learned anything from her escalating troubles with Sophia, it was that dwelling on past pain and injustice poisoned one's soul. That was not a path she wanted to walk.

"By the way, we'll have two more for dinner." Rosalind grinned and moved to the icebox, where she pulled out the sliced ham they'd made sandwiches from earlier in the week. "Zach hired a young man to help set up the booth and drum up business. He did everything we asked of him without complaint. Quite mature for one so young. I doubt he's even fifteen yet. And,

Abby . . ." Rosalind turned a sorrowful look on her sister. "You should see how thin he is. That boy hasn't had a good meal in months. I'm sure of it. And what I wouldn't give to get hold of his clothes. His arms and legs have outgrown his sleeves and trousers by a good two inches. Any fabric lingering in those hems needs to be let out."

Abigail couldn't say with any great honesty that she was excited by the news of guests. This day had been trying in the extreme, and all she wanted to do was sit on the sofa with her husband and let him cuddle her cares away. Yet as soon as that selfish thought caught a foothold, her mother's voice floated through her mind, and in an instant, Abigail was a ten-year-old girl again, walking hand-in-hand with her mother as they made afternoon deliveries.

"Do you know why we deliver leftover bread to the widows, Abby?"

"Because the Bible says to care for those who are in need?"

"Yes. But there's another reason, one that benefits us."

"We don't have to try to sell day-old bread?"

Her mother chuckled. "No, you little goose. It reminds us that no matter how hard things get or how many disappointments we face, there is always someone who is facing an even more difficult path. Therefore we should count our blessings and remember that the best way to take our minds off our own troubles is to help someone else with theirs."

Abigail blinked back the moisture gathering in her eyes, spawned not by her own troubles this time, but by the realization of what her mother must have gone through. All those lost babies. A ravaged and failing body. Her mother had suffered more tragedy and disappointment than anyone of Abigail's acquaintance. Yet she'd given of herself again and again—to the widows, to her husband, to her daughters—and Abigail had arrogantly looked down on her for being weak. For losing her identity and becoming nothing more than a breeding vessel for her husband. But Abigail was starting to think that her mother had been stronger than all of them. Like the widow with the two mites, she'd given *everything*—physical, emotional, even spiritual as she tried to instruct a hard-hearted daughter in the ways of kindness and gratitude.

I'm sorry, Mama. You never deserved my contempt.

And from this moment on, Abigail would do more than protect her father's baking legacy, she'd ensure her mother's legacy lived on as well—a generosity of spirit that would not be quelled by hardship or loss.

"Well, I'm glad Zach put him to work, and I'm happy to feed him," Abby declared, making the words true in her heart even as she spoke them aloud. Zach was proving to be a lamb in wolf's clothing. All tough and gruff on the outside and soft as bread pudding on the inside.

"Nate's bringing his sister too," Rosalind said as she set the ham on the counter and reached for a skillet. "I haven't met her yet, but I know she's younger. Not sure by how much."

A young boy providing for a sister? No wonder Zach wanted to help him. They were kindred spirits.

"We might have to stretch the ham a bit," Abigail said, frowning as she judged how many portions they could get out of the small slab they had left. "I'll get a pot of water on to boil and start peeling potatoes. Maybe we can do some roasted carrots as well. What do you think?"

Rosalind nodded. "That along with the day-old rolls in the pie safe should be plenty."

"I think I have enough peaches in the cellar to throw together a cobbler too. Kids love sweets." As did grown men with big hearts.

They worked in tandem, and in less than an hour, the lingering gunpowder smell in the kitchen had been replaced with that of sizzling ham, roasted carrots, and buttery mashed potatoes.

Forgetting those things which are behind, and reaching forth unto those things which are before.

The verse rang in Abigail's mind and filled her with sweet satisfaction. It was amazing how much more hope one could feel when looking forward instead of back.

Zach stepped through the kitchen door just as Abigail pulled the carrots from the oven and slid the cobbler into the vacancy. Hearing the heavy tread of his boots, she spun to face him, a smile stretching her cheeks wide.

"You're home!"

He paused midstep, his forehead scrunching. "You're more cheerful that I expected."

"And you look worn to a frazzle." Abigail crossed the room, planted her hands on his shoulders, and lifted up to plant a kiss on his whiskery jaw. "Lack of sleep on top of all the excitement of the day have taken their toll. Why don't you head upstairs—"

"I ain't headin' upstairs, woman." He swatted her hands away when she tried to steer him toward the stairwell. "I wanna be here when the kid comes by." His scowl melted into an expression that tipped a little toward sheepish. "Rosalind tell you 'bout Nate?"

Abigail fought back a smile. *Bread pudding, indeed.* "She did."

"I plan to hire him to help you out around here." He held up a hand to ward off her arguments even though she wasn't making any. "I know things are a bit . . . unsettled at the moment, but you'll have more time to bake if he takes care of all the other jobs. I'll pay him out of my own funds, so don't worry about that." His eyes pled with her. "The kid needs a job, Abby. Honest money before he gets desperate enough to try for the dishonest kind."

She folded her hands in front of her and gave a solemn nod. "All right."

He opened his mouth, then stopped, his jaw hanging agape for a beat before he reshaped his lips to form a new reply. "All right?" He'd been barreling down the rails with such speed, the switch in the tracks must have thrown him momentarily.

"Yes, husband. All right." She tried not to smile, she really did, but he was just too adorable, getting all ruffled on this boy's behalf, a boy he didn't even know beyond a couple hours' acquaintance. "It sounds like a fine idea. I haven't figured out how to manage the oven's loss yet, but if I hope to keep the bakery open on any level, I'll need a lot more time in the kitchen, as I'll be baking in smaller batches on a tighter rotation. Having someone to run errands, wash dishes, and clean tables would be a blessing."

"Well . . . good, then. I'll tell him he can start Monday."

"Have him come by around one o'clock. I'll feed him—his sister too—then he can help Rosalind with the closing of the shop and work whatever jobs need to be done until suppertime, when I'll feed them again."

Abigail nearly laughed at the blank mask that locked down Zach's face. He managed to blink once, the only proof that he was, in fact, still alive behind all that stillness. No wonder he'd been such a good card player. Whenever something shocked him, his expression simply shut down, giving away no hint of his thoughts or feelings. Which meant he was thinking and feeling quite a lot, if she didn't miss her guess.

She patted his arm. "You might be paying his salary, husband, but I fully intend on fattening him up. His sister too. Can't have scrawny workers in a bakery. It's bad for business."

Abigail smiled and spun away, intending to help Rosalind load up the dumbwaiter, but before she could take more than a step, Zach's hand snagged her elbow and whipped her back toward him. Her palms flew up to brace herself against the wall of his chest. His arms immediately encircled her, trapping her against him. Not that she had any desire to go anywhere.

"You're an incredible woman, Abigail Hamilton." His voice came out a little thick, and his grip was a tad too tight, but the moment could not have been more perfect.

That was about as close to *I love you* as she'd ever heard from him. Close enough that she might as well give him credit for the sentiment.

"I love you too," she murmured softly, her gaze zeroing in on his lips, her heels lifting off the ground.

Rosalind's throat clearing across the room brought Abigail's feet back to a flat position, however.

"Our, ah, guests are here," Rosie said, making a valiant effort to hide her smile as she gestured with a tip of her head toward the back door someone happened to be knocking on.

Zach released Abigail, but before he moved away, he leaned close and rumbled low in her ear. "We'll continue that later. When you come to my room. *Our* room."

Heat radiated from her cheeks, and her heart fluttered so hard that she had to blink several times to clear the specks from her vision. She reached for the corner of the worktable, afraid her knees might buckle. There was no misunderstanding *that* invitation.

A heartbeat before he opened the door to admit their visitors, Zach glanced over his shoulder and captured her gaze. His dark blue eyes speared into her with an intensity that stole her breath. "Tonight, Abby."

He said it as a statement—a demand, really—yet she wasn't so far in the woolies that she failed to catch the plea for agreement.

It was that plea that gave her the strength to lift her chin and nod shakily at her husband. "Tonight."

CHAPTER

38

"I brought the signs and scrap wood you asked for," Nate said, wiggling the arm that held all the materials against his body.

Zach nodded at the kid, but in truth his mind was too busy thinking about his wife to care about wood scraps. Tonight she'd be fully and completely his.

"If ya got a hammer and a few nails, I can board up the winder for ya before supper." The kid shifted his weight, jiggling the boards. The soft clatter sharpened Zach's attention enough to kick his brain back into motion.

"Nah. Just lean the boards up against the wall for now. I'll tend to it later."

Nate moved to obey, revealing the little girl who'd been hiding behind him. She followed her brother, sticking to his side like sawdust to sweat.

"I don't wanna go in," she whispered, probably thinking the four feet of distance between her and the man in the doorway was enough to keep him from overhearing.

It wasn't.

"They're good people," Nate reassured her, taking his time

stacking the wood in order to cover the awkward conversation. He tossed a quick glance Zach's way, but Zach made a show of examining the dirt under his fingernails, giving the kids at least the illusion of privacy.

"Can't you smell that?" Nate asked. "Smells like fried ham. I bet they got taters too. Maybe even some more of them biscuits. You liked those."

The girl looked about ten or eleven and mule-stubborn. She crossed her arms and shook her head. "I ain't gonna do it, Nate. I ain't going in."

The boy sighed and gave up all pretense of stacking wood. He hunkered down to face his sister. "Mr. Hamilton offered me work, Ida Mae. Here at the shop. Real regular-like. We'd have pay we can count on. I can't afford to pass that up, and neither can you. So put on the manners Mama taught you and come to dinner. I'll make sure nuthin' bad happens to ya."

The girl didn't look too convinced, but she trudged along with her brother without fuss when he steered her back to the door.

Nate's gaze offered an apology when he returned to Zach. "This is Ida Mae." He turned to check on her, probably wanting to make sure she was using her company manners. His posture sagged a bit around the shoulders when he found her staring at her toes. "She's shy."

"That's all right. She don't have to talk." Zach winked at Nate and offered a friendly grin. "She just has to eat."

The kid smiled back, and the awkwardness faded. At least between the males. The little girl with the lopsided brown pigtails and threadbare blue calico dress refused to look up from her scuffed black shoes even once they moved inside. She kept her hackles up when Rosalind stepped forward to introduce herself, but she acted downright skittish when Abigail approached, dashing behind her brother as if afraid Abby were the witch from "Hansel and Gretel," ready to toss her into the oven. She kept darting nervous glances at the large useless bread oven on the back wall too.

Zach led the way to the sink and washed up for supper, leaving the tap running for Nate and Ida Mae. When Abigail went upstairs to receive the dumbwaiter, the little girl relaxed enough to watch Rosalind work the hand rope, seemingly fascinated by the box that disappeared into the wall. But once upstairs and seated at the table, she was back to trying to hide in plain sight, this time by staring at her plate with such intensity that she nearly missed grabbing the bread basket when it was passed to her.

"I can't believe someone set off firecrackers in your oven," Nate said between bites of potatoes after Zach gave a brief explanation of what had happened. "That's just downright mean."

"Needless to say," Zach continued, "my wife is going to have her hands full trying to make do with the small oven until we can replace the large one. So you may be asked to do all manner of strange jobs—from cleaning windows, to sweeping the boardwalk, to washing dishes. I know it ain't exactly the work a young man dreams about, but I'll pay you fifty cents a day for an afternoon's labor, and my wife said she'd feed both you and your sister at the beginning and end of your shift."

Nate's forkful of ham ceased its sprint to his mouth. "Pay *and* meals?" His brown eyes widened, and for a moment Zach worried they might tear up. But the kid was tough. He choked down his emotion like a spoonful of castor oil and carried on as if the offer hadn't been life-changing. "Sounds . . . fair."

Zach hid a grin behind his napkin as he pretended to wipe crumbs from his chin. It was more than fair, and they both knew it. If Zach had been able to secure regular work at that wage at Nate's age, he might have avoided the poker tables altogether.

Abigail caught Zach's eye from across the table and smiled, the warmth in her gaze proving she knew exactly what he was doing. He couldn't quite figure why her approval mattered so much to him, but his heart felt twice as full as it had a moment ago when he'd been focused solely on the boy at his left.

"Once school starts back up," Abigail said, aiming her words at Nate, "you can stop by the bakery before class and help set up shop. You'll be fully trained by then and will know what needs to be done. I'll have box lunches fixed up for you and Ida Mae to take with you. Then you can finish up your shift once school lets out. Education is a valuable resource, and I prefer my employees make good use of it."

There she went, being more than he expected again. He shouldn't be surprised. He knew Abby's heart, yet he'd experienced so little generosity while he was growing up that witnessing it in such abundance now took him aback. She'd lost her oven, might still lose her bakery, yet she was ready to provide for a pair of kids she'd just met. How could he not love such a woman?

Wait . . . *love*? Had that word actually traipsed across his brain?

"Why are you doing this?" Ida Mae's accusing tone cut across the table like a cleaver, effectively slicing off Zach's other thoughts. "What's in it for you?"

The girl still had her chin tucked into her chest, but her eyes glared up at Abby, who sat diagonally across from her.

"Ida Mae!" her brother whispered sharply. "What's wrong with you?" Nate shot an apologetic look at Zach. "I'm sorry. She's not usually like this."

"It's all right," Abigail said. "It's smart for a young woman to be cautious and ask questions. There are too many people in this world willing to take advantage of someone they deem weaker than themselves. I admire her courage in speaking up." She turned her attention from Nate to his sister. "Without my large oven, baking is going to take much longer than usual, and I really need help. Your brother has proven to be dependable and hard-working. God made our paths cross at just the right time." She smiled, but the little girl only scowled harder. "And since I happen to have a little sister of my own," she said with a dip of her head toward Rosalind, "I know how much older siblings worry about the younger ones in their care. So I figure if I feed you both, Nate will have less to worry about and can focus more on his work. Besides," she said with a teasing wink, "like I told my husband earlier, I can't have a Taste of Heaven employee who isn't properly nourished. It would be poor advertising."

"Properly attired too," Rosalind added. "If you'll both bring your spare clothes in on Monday, I'll let the hems out for you. Maybe even cut down a few of my old dresses for you, Ida Mae."

The little girl shot up from the table. "I don't want any of your old dresses! Or your dumb food, neither." She glared at Abigail.

Zach slowly stretched to his feet. He sympathized with the kid's plight, understood hiding fear beneath anger, but no one insulted his wife. Not even a little girl with a heart full of hurt and a tongue full of spite. "That's enough." He kept his voice soft, not wanting to frighten her further.

Abigail rose too, but her expression confused him. It didn't reflect hurt or insult or even patience. She looked ill. Shaken. Yet before he could ask her what was wrong, she seemed to find her footing. Her eyes never left Ida Mae's as she slowly rounded the table.

Now it was the girl's turn to look shaken. She backed away from Abby, circling her brother's chair and using him as a barrier. For a moment Zach thought the girl would duck under the table, but Abby did the ducking first. She bent down, her expression soft yet intense.

"I forgive you, Ida Mae."

Zach frowned. For what? Acting like a brat? This scene seemed too intense for such a small infraction. He glanced at Nate, but the kid looked as confused as Zach felt.

Ida Mae, however, seemed to understand completely. She vigorously shook her head.

"Nate can still work here," Abigail said. "You don't have to worry. I won't hold it against him. I won't hold it against you either."

The little girl started sobbing. Her brother's arm came around her shoulders. "I didn't want to do it, Nate. I swear!"

Nate's face scrunched. "What did you do?"

But Ida Mae was beyond talking, so Zach and Nate turned their attention to the only other person in the room who seemed to know what was going on.

Abigail straightened. Her gaze found Zach's, and he swore he could feel the heaviness of her heart tug on his own.

"Ida Mae set off the firecrackers."

CHAPTER

39

It had been niggling at Abigail all through dinner. Something familiar. Something she couldn't put her finger on. Until Ida Mae shoved away from the table and glared at her in guilty defiance. Then everything clicked. Because the *boy* who had run her down making an escape from her kitchen had worn the exact same expression. And the exact same shoes, now that she thought about it.

Abigail peered at Ida Mae's scuffed shoes peeking through the legs of Nate's chair. Yes, that single button on the side was rather unique, and Abigail was certain she'd seen it before.

"I thought you said a boy set off the firecrackers." Zach's question sliced through the silence that had descended after her proclamation.

"She wore trousers and a cap to hide her hair. Probably some of her brother's old clothes." A rather ingenious disguise. No one would think to accuse a girl of a boy's crime. Abigail wouldn't have either if the girl hadn't been sitting across the table from her for the last thirty minutes.

Nate took hold of his sister's arms and pushed her away from him, shock and sorrow etched into his face as he handed her a napkin to stem her tears. "Why would you *do* such a thing, Ida Mae?" The words were barely more than a heartbroken croak. "Why?"

The little girl sniffed and hiccupped but managed to make a few words comprehensible. "She said . . . send me . . . orphanage. I'd . . . never . . . see you . . . again."

"Who said?" Zach barked, making Abigail wince at the sharp tone.

Ida Mae cringed too. She tried to burrow closer to her brother, but Nate decided to imitate his new mentor. He pushed to his feet and took on a stern countenance. "Tell us, Ida Mae. Who told you to put the firecrackers in Mrs. Hamilton's oven?"

The girl shook her head. "I . . . can't. If I tell . . . she'll . . . send me . . . away."

Abigail nearly shook with outrage. To threaten a child in such a way—it was despicable. She'd never considered herself particularly maternal, but every ounce of her womanhood bristled at the cruelty Ida Mae had experienced, and compelled her to take action.

"Is this *she* Mrs. Longfellow?" Abby blurted. So help her, if Sophia had bullied this child into doing her dirty work . . .

Ida Mae's round eyes and indrawn, hiccupping breath was all the proof Abigail needed.

"Well, this will not be borne. I'm going to corner Mr. Hackamore at church tomorrow and quiz him over family law. Surely she can't strip a child away from her nearly grown sibling and send her to an orphanage without her consent."

"She might . . ." her husband started to argue, but Abigail wouldn't hear it.

"Then we'll just find a way around it. Find a local family to sponsor the children, employ them both here at the bakery, or even become guardians to them ourselves. Whatever it takes. These two will not be separated!"

A strange look came over Zach's face, and he blinked. Several times. Did he have something in his eye?

Ida Mae's sobs died. She and Nate just stared at Abigail. Rosalind was probably staring at her too. The condition seemed to be going around.

Maybe she *was* acting a bit rash, but the situation called for a little audacity. Sophia Longfellow had been making this town—this *family*—dance to her tune for too long. Someone needed to stand up and put a stop to her manipulations. She wasn't just spreading rumors and making innuendos anymore. She was destroying property and threatening children. A line had been crossed, and Abigail refused to cower. If she lost the bakery, she lost the bakery. She had a husband, a sister, two able hands, and a faithful God who'd promised never to leave them to fight their battles alone. Whatever the future held, they'd be fine.

Zach broke the silence by clearing his throat. "We'll need to talk to the marshal. Ida Mae can tell him what she knows."

Nate lurched to his feet, yanking his sister close. "But what will happen to Ida Mae if she admits her part in this?"

Feeling too militant to soothe his worries with a smile, Abigail opted to meet his gaze head-on. "I have no intention of pressing charges against your sister. You have my word." She lifted her eyes and fastened them on her husband. "But I have every intention of bringing charges against Mrs. Longfellow. Tonight."

Zach grinned. A rather piratey grin, one that brought flutters to her belly even as it promised trouble for whoever dared sail into his path.

Yes, they'd be fine, indeed.

◈———◈

Zach prowled the Longfellow parlor, senses on alert. Abby sat with the two kids on the sofa, holding one of Ida Mae's hands while Nate held the other. The poor girl was whiter than fresh milk, but she wasn't crying. She hadn't cried a drop since Abby's pronouncement that she wouldn't allow anyone to separate the Miller children. Ida Mae had believed her, apparently, and it had changed everything. She'd managed to give her testimony to the marshal once they'd tracked him down across the square, and she even named Sophia Longfellow as the instigator. Now they sat in their enemy's front parlor, waiting to confront the woman herself.

The marshal sat in an armchair near the hearth, the sack of soggy firecrackers Zach had provided as evidence draped in his lap. Zach paced past him and headed back toward the door where the servant had exited with promises to fetch her employers.

Feeling the warmth of his wife's gaze on the back of his neck, Zach turned his attention her direction and met her eye. She smiled, just a hint of dimple winking at him. It was more of a *we can do this* smile than the intimate, teasing ones he preferred, but it melted his heart just the same. She was an incredible woman—willing to fight for a pair of orphans she barely knew, one of whom had vandalized her shop. Normal people didn't do that. They minded their own business and turned a blind eye to what they didn't want to see. But not his Abigail.

Maybe she was naïve to believe that truth would win over power, but she was willing to make the stand, so he'd stand beside her. Fight for her. For the kids. The odds might be stacked against them, but Abby had beaten the odds before. Sophia Longfellow might have wealth and prestige on her side, but

Abby had the intangibles—passion, creativity, and a will of steel. His money was on Abby.

An agitated Chester Longfellow strode into the parlor, his attention locked on the marshal as the lawman rose from his chair. "You know I don't like to be disturbed at dinnertime, Virgil. And tonight of all nights. I have a fireworks display to oversee. Whatever criminal matter has come up, just toss the accused in jail, and we'll deal with it on Monday at a civilized hour."

The lawman didn't seem a bit ruffled by the edict. He just stroked his mustache with his thumb and forefinger and gave the mayor a nod. "All right. Will your missus want to pack a bag first, or should I toss her in the calaboose as is?"

"Toss her in the—what are you—?" Chester sputtered, his gaze taking in the rest of the room's occupants for the first time.

Zach moved to Abigail's side and offered his hand to help her up from the sofa. Ida Mae and Nate scrambled to their feet as well. Ida Mae looked a mite shaky, but with Abby and Nate anchoring her on either side, she held her own.

"Yer wife's the one bein' accused," Burton explained. "Malicious destruction of property and coercion."

"Nonsense!" Chester's words echoed with adamancy, but his eyes exuded a touch of anxiety. Of doubt. "How dare you accuse my wife of such crimes? She's a pillar of this community and above reproach."

The marshal just nodded. "That's why we're here, Chester. To give her a chance to answer the charges in private."

The mayor's face reddened. "To entertain such an outrageous notion . . . You're not fit to wear that badge, Virgil."

Unheedful of the fine carpet at his feet, the marshal took one step toward the mayor, then upturned the sack in his hands and let the chain of spent firecrackers thud to the floor. "These match the ones you purchased for the celebration?"

Chester leapt backward to protect his shoes, his nose scrunching in disgust at the mess. "I suppose. What does that have to do with anything? Vendors were selling these crackers all over town today."

"Your wife have access to your inventory?" The marshal calmly pressed for details instead of accepting the mayor's dismissal of the matter. Zach's opinion of the lawman rose another notch. Virgil Burton wasn't the mayor's lackey. He was digging for truth, regardless of the identity of the players.

"Of course she has access," Chester blustered. "She's the one who organized the vendors. She arranged for half the proceeds to be given to the church mission fund too. Now, would you kindly get that filthy thing off my rug?"

The lawman bent to do just that but stopped when tapping footsteps sounded in the hall.

"Chester, darling? What is taking so long?" Sophia Longfellow swept into the room, her hostess smile firmly in place even though her tone carried a disgruntled edge. "We're expected on the square in less than . . ." Her gaze swept past the marshal, stumbled over Abigail, and crashed into Ida Mae. ". . . an hour."

The slip in composure was brief but undeniable. At least to Zach. Had she been his opponent at the poker table, he would have pushed all his chips into the pot after that tell. But had Marshal Burton or the mayor caught it?

"Mrs. Longfellow." The marshal dipped his chin politely. "I have a witness who has testified that you coerced her into vandalizing Mrs. Hamilton's industrial oven."

"Witness? What witness?" She motioned to Ida Mae, then made a scoffing sound. "You can't mean this *child*?"

"A witness is a witness, ma'am, regardless of age."

Sophia ignored the marshal's statement and went on the attack. "This is your doing!" She pointed a finger at Abigail's face. "What did you do? Bribe this child to malign me? It's despicable." She glanced back at her husband, her eyes demanding his corroboration. "You know how she is, Chester. She's borne a grudge against me for years. But this . . . this is slander." She cast an imperious glare at Burton. "I demand you arrest her, Marshal."

Zach's blood roiled, but he managed to keep his mouth shut. Barely. He'd agreed to let Burton handle things, but if that shrew kept attacking his wife, he might have to renegotiate that stance.

The lawman didn't seem too impressed by Sophia's outburst, however. He let her steam blow right by. "I seen the oven, ma'am. It's damaged beyond repair."

Was that a flash of triumph in Sophia's eyes? Hard to tell with the quick lowering of her lashes.

"The girl admitted her part in the vandalism and named you as the instigator."

"Well, the girl's lying." Sophia turned her back on the group and flounced over to her husband's side. "The very idea that I would actually engage in *criminal* behavior is ludicrous." She slid her hand around her husband's arm as if solidifying herself as local royalty and looked down her nose at the marshal. "I'd ask if you have any proof, but how could you? I didn't do anything."

"Got these firecrackers." The marshal retrieved the soggy string from the floor. "Girl couldn't afford to buy them. Says you gave them to her."

"She's mistaken. Someone else must have given them to her. Or maybe she stole them. You said she admitted to the vandalism, so you already have proof of her propensity toward criminal behavior."

Nate lurched forward. "My sister's no thief! And the only

reason she set off those firecrackers was because you threatened to send her away to an orphanage."

"I did no such thing. Why, that's . . . barbarous." Sophia shot a look at her husband. "Chester, tell them."

The mayor shook himself slightly, then firmed his chin. "My wife is an upstanding citizen with years of dedicated service to this community. If the only evidence you have is this child's word and some expended firecrackers, your proof is sorely lacking. Now, if you don't mind, I have responsibilities to this town and must ask you to leave so that I may see to them. Good day, Virgil."

The marshal picked up his hat from where he'd hung it off the corner of the armchair, then dropped it into place on his head. "Mayor." He nodded to Sophia. "Ma'am."

Zach moved to his wife's side and placed a hand at her back as he steered her past the Longfellows. She slowed as she came even with Sophia. He pressed her back, trying to signal her to stay calm and keep moving. They needed to keep the high ground. Sophia was a master at manipulating public opinion. If Abigail lost her temper in front of witnesses, the whole town would hear about her instability before the night was out. Yet when Abby insisted on stopping, he stopped with her.

"Nate, take your sister outside." Abby let go of Ida Mae's hand. "I'll be there in just a moment."

The marshal held the door for the kids as they traipsed out, casting nervous glances over their shoulders. "Mrs. Hamilton?" His voice held a warning edge.

"I'll be just a moment, Marshal."

Zach nodded in an attempt to reassure him that Abigail wasn't about to scratch Sophia's eyes out. At least he didn't think so. Her voice sounded controlled. Almost conversational.

"Hamilton," Chester blustered, "I've asked you to leave. Take your wife and go."

Zach just stared at him. He wouldn't move a muscle until Abby was ready.

Sophia glared at Abigail, haughty as ever. Her eyes lit with triumph even as she gave a little sniff of disdain. Abby ignored the slight.

"Benedict is dead, Sophia."

The other woman gasped, her composure not just slipping but entirely disintegrating as her face lost its color. "We don't speak that name in this house."

"That's the problem." Abby held her head high, and pride nearly burst through the seams of Zach's chest. "We've closed ourselves off from that horrible day for too long. It's festered inside us both, killing our friendship and turning us into people we never intended to become. Losing Ben was a horrible tragedy, one that haunts me to this day. But we have to let it go, Sophia. We have to let God heal our wounds so we can move forward."

Pale yet shaking with rage, Sophia Longfellow raised an arm and pointed at the front door. "Get out of my house."

Abigail dipped her chin and moved to the door. Zach shadowed her every step of the way.

His wife had just slapped down an ace-king combination. Sophia might have thought she'd won the hand with her full house, but Abby's play changed the entire game. They weren't playing poker anymore but blackjack, and Abby's bold move had stolen the pot and scored big, if the look on Chester Longfellow's face was any indication.

Once they'd made their exit, Abby hurried over to check on Ida Mae, giving Zach the chance to draw the marshal aside. "Well? You gonna bring Mrs. Longfellow up on charges?"

The lawman shook his head. "Won't do no good. Chester's

right. It's her word against Ida Mae's, and no judge is gonna take the word of a kid over a woman of her position without evidence to back up the claim. My hands are tied."

Zach looked over to where his wife was hugging Ida Mae and praising her for her bravery. Nate met Zach's eye, and it was clear the kid knew. They'd lost this battle. Zach straightened his posture and watched as Nate followed suit. Just because they'd lost didn't mean the battle hadn't been worth waging. A man did what was right even when the odds were stacked against him.

A tightness pressed against Zach's ribs. A man also found a way to fix his wife's problems.

The firm *whack* of Burton's hand on Zach's shoulder startled him out of his darkening thoughts. "Go home, Hamilton," the marshal said. "Tend to yer wife. She's had a trying day."

Tend to his wife. Zach's pulse kicked into a gallop. He'd been planning to tend to his wife in a much different way earlier today. Even now, though, he wanted to hold her, comfort her . . . love her. But after all they'd been through tonight, would she keep her promise and come to his room?

CHAPTER

40

By the time Abigail made it back to the house, all her righteous indignation had leaked out through her tired feet, leaving her depleted.

Sophia only won the first skirmish, Abby told herself as she dragged her weary bones up the stairs while Zach took a few minutes to board up the broken window. The steps seemed twice as steep as usual and her feet twice as heavy. Or maybe it was her heart that weighed her down.

Abigail lifted her chin and tugged her mind into a more positive place. Sophia might not be headed to jail tonight, but that didn't mean they hadn't struck a significant blow. Marshal Burton seemed to believe their side of the story, and Zach thought Chester might harbor a few doubts about his wife as well, despite his verbal support. It would have to be enough. For now. She'd chew on the problem some more tomorrow, after she had a good night's sleep.

Her toe stubbed on the top step, and her eyes flew wide open.

Sleep. Good gracious. Tonight was the night she and Zach were supposed to . . .

Abigail swallowed hard, suddenly awake. She made her way down the hall to her bedroom, but the door had been pulled closed. She tried the handle. Locked.

What on earth? They never locked this door.

Rosalind had stayed behind to clean up dinner and was then meeting up with a group of friends to watch the fireworks. She wouldn't be home for at least an hour or two. But why would she lock Abigail out of their room?

A seed of suspicion took root, sending Abigail down the hall to the master bedroom. That door stood open. One of her nightgowns—the pretty one with the embroidered roses at the neckline—lay draped across Zach's bed. And there on the washstand sat her brush and hairpins. And the soap she liked. Her Sunday dress probably hung in the wardrobe as well. Rosalind had always been good with details. The romantic little schemer.

"Everything all right?"

Her husband's voice nearly scared a shriek out of her. When had the hammering stopped?

Abigail spun around, her cheeks flaming at the scene she knew he could see over her head. "It seems Rosie's ready to kick me out of her room." She grinned, trying to lighten the mood even as her pulse accelerated. "She locked me out."

Zach's dark blue eyes searched hers. "I can take the door off the hinges if you want to sleep there."

Heavens how she loved this man. Always ready to put her needs ahead of his own.

Despite her uncertainty about what the marriage act actually entailed and her embarrassment over what her husband might think of her shape without all the tucks and lifts of her corset, she knew in her heart that it was time. Yes, children might result from their union, but she'd leave that possibility in God's hands. It wasn't right to keep herself from her husband out of fear that she couldn't be both mother and professional baker. If children came, she and Zach would figure out the best way to handle that particular challenge in the same way they were handling their current challenges—together.

It was time to become Zach's wife in full and to show him exactly how deep her love ran.

<hr>

Zach could barely breathe as he watched his wife nibble on her lower lip. *Please choose me,* he silently begged even though he wouldn't hold it against her if she didn't. He hungered for her worse than he'd hungered for food during those lean years of his childhood, but he'd abide by her wishes. Abby had endured enough people foisting their will onto hers today. Her desires, her needs would come first.

Her fingers trembled as she reached out to touch his arm. She took one step closer and tilted her chin up, just like she did when he claimed his good-night kisses. Stuffing down his disappointment, Zach placed his palm on her hip and leaned toward her. It might not be what he'd hoped for, but a kiss from Abigail was still a pleasure to savor.

He lowered his head. However, before his lips reached hers, she spoke.

"I don't want to share Rosalind's room anymore," she murmured, her voice breathy and soft as her fingers squeezed his bicep. Her lashes lifted, and her brown eyes glimmered with shy invitation. "I want to stay with you."

"You're sure?" Heaven help him if she backed out now, but he didn't want any second thoughts getting in the way later.

When she gave a small decisive nod, a host of fireworks that had nothing to do with the country's birthday shot off inside his chest.

Digging his fingers into her hip, he tugged her closer. The movement caught her off guard, and her head fell backward. He took advantage and laid a trail of kisses on the soft skin of her neck.

"Thank you for choosing me," he rasped as he passed by her ear. Not only choosing him tonight, but choosing him all those weeks ago when she searched for a husband. He shuddered at how close he'd come to making the biggest mistake of his life by turning her down. Thank God for Rosalind. Without her push, he might still be an antisocial bachelor believing he was better off alone.

"I always choose you." Abby's vow slipped between his ribs to wrap around his heart. He pulled back slightly, and she met his gaze. "Always."

A surge of strength flooded his muscles, making him feel invincible. Perhaps even strong enough to return her love.

In a single movement, he swept his wife into his arms and carried her across the threshold. Her nervous giggle heightened his confidence as he marched forward, barely pausing long enough to kick the door closed behind him.

He might not have the words yet, but he'd make sure every touch, every kiss, every passionate embrace communicated his devotion.

⊰———⊱

Sometime in the middle of the night, Abigail rolled over and met cold sheets. She sought out her sister's warmth, but Rosalind wasn't there. And her pillow smelled decidedly masculine. Abby's eyes popped open.

Zach.

Memories assailed her. Gentle, patient loving. Her husband holding her close and brushing his fingers lightly over her back until she drifted off to sleep as the pop of fireworks reported in the distance.

Her husband. In all ways.

Abigail hugged the knowledge close but quickly grew discontent, wanting to hug her husband close instead. The man who was supposed to be beside her.

A quiet ruffling sound echoed by the window that overlooked the alley. Propping an arm beneath her, Abigail leveraged herself up and searched for Zach in the shadows. He stood by the window, his face turned away from her as he gazed into the darkness. In his hands were a set of playing cards, expertly slipping through his fingers like well-trained soldiers on the march.

Abigail's belly tightened, and she pushed back the covers. Padding on bare feet, her white cotton nightgown fluttering down to cover her legs as she moved, she silently approached her husband. "Zach?"

He didn't jump at her voice, so he must have been aware of her presence, but it still took long moments for him to stop riffling the cards and bring his face around to meet her gaze. When he did, the torment etched in his features broke her heart.

"I want to fix it, Abby. I *need* to fix it."

Her oven. He had to be talking about her oven.

He set his jaw, and his eyes hardened. "I'm your husband. It's my job to provide for you. To protect you. To ensure you have what you need." His right hand fisted, and he tapped the pad of it against the wall as his attention jerked to the ceiling. "I plan to ask about a loan at the bank on Monday, but Reuben warned me that the manager is related to Sophia and likely to turn me down, even if I had sufficient collateral. Which I don't. Without a loan, there's only one way I know to make the kind of money we need to replace your oven." He met her eyes again, his own pleading. "I wouldn't cheat this time, I swear. And I'd only wager my own funds. I won't put the bakery at risk. It might take a few weeks or months, depending on how deep the play is, but I think—"

Abigail pressed her fingers to his mouth to shut off the words bringing tears to her eyes. She shook her head, her chest throbbing. "No, Zach," she said softly as she dragged her hand from his mouth down to rest directly over his heart. "Put the cards away."

"But it's the only way I can fix this," he groaned.

"It's not your problem to fix."

His eyebrows slanted down in an angry V. "Don't you dare start quoting that contract to me again, Abby. The bakery might be yours, but you're mine, and that makes your problems mine as well."

She smiled at his grumpy possessiveness, only loving him more for wanting so badly to take care of her. But she fully intended to take care of him too, and his soul was worth much more to her than the bakery.

"I love you, Zach, and I trust you to provide what I need. But I don't need a new bread oven. My business might need that, but I don't. What I need is a husband who will support me through the hard times, who will hold me and encourage me and let me know that I'm not alone in the fight. The bakery may fail, or by God's grace it may survive the upcoming storm and come out the other side even better than before. Only God knows what the future holds. All we can do is learn from the past. And what I've learned is that choices have consequences. If you choose to return to the gambling tables, there will be a price—a price that no fancy oven is worth." She stroked the side of his face. "I want to hear you sing in church, Zach."

His eyes widened, and she knew he understood what she meant. She wanted no new barriers between him and God. Especially not on her behalf.

"I'm not ceding the battle," she said with a smile, sliding her hand from his jaw around to his nape so she could dip her fingers into his hair. "I might not be able to afford a new industrial oven, but I have enough money set aside that I can order a large cookstove from Montgomery Ward. If I place the order on Monday, they could have it delivered in a week or two. The bakery wouldn't need to be closed for long. In the meantime, I can work on refining our menu to focus on our best-selling items and eliminate the rest. At least temporarily. Who knows? Maybe I'll even take some time off. I can't remember the last time I had a few days to myself." She drew a line with her finger, tracing his collarbone. "Maybe even spend some extra time with my husband."

The cards fell from his hand and scattered over the floor as he reached for her. His arms came around her waist, and he tugged her close.

Her heart thumped a little harder, and her desire to talk grew weaker. But she had one more point to make, so she held back the fog of encroaching passion for one moment longer.

"The future is in God's hands, Zach. Not yours, and not mine. Trusting him to bring about what is best is the only choice we need to make."

Her husband made no reply except to lean down and nibble at her neck. Had he heard a word she'd said?

"Zach?"

He reached for the top button of her nightdress. "You talk too much, wife."

She was starting to agree with him, but she couldn't let the matter drop. Not yet. She pushed at his hand. "Zach."

He sighed and met her gaze. "I'll let God take care of tomorrow," he said, "but I've got a vision for the more immediate future in my hands right now, and I aim to see it fulfilled." He raised one of those piratey brows at her. "With your permission, Mrs. Hamilton."

Heat suffused Abigail's face, but she managed a tiny smile as she dipped her lashes. "Permission granted, Mr. Hamilton."

CHAPTER

41

"Are you . . . *whistling*?"

Reuben's disbelieving tone should have grated on Zach's nerves, but he couldn't find the wherewithal to shoot his usual scowl at his partner. The taunt simply bounced off Zach's back and lost itself in the sawdust at his feet.

Reuben dropped a load of boards fresh from the mill onto the stack waiting to be planed, then wagged his head. "I never thought I'd see Zacharias Hamilton reduced to vaudeville status. You gonna break out in song next?" He pulled the hat from his head and flung it over his heart in dramatic fashion, then started belting, "'Daisy, Daisy, give me your answer, do. I'm half-crazy, all for the love of you!'"

Zach threw his own hat straight at his partner's nose. Reuben broke off his song in order to duck, a chuckle rising up between them.

"So you're saying I *shouldn't* sign you up for the next local production at the opera house?"

"Not if you want me to keep bringing extra honey biscuits to work with me."

Reuben held his palms out in surrender. "Mum's the word. Can't risk losing those biscuits."

It had been four days since the loss of Abigail's oven. The Taste of Heaven was now only open for breakfast service, and the menu had been simplified to focus on quick breads: scones, muffins, popovers, and biscuits. Items that could be baked in smaller batches with shorter cook times in the single oven. Abigail had to maintain a steady run of baking through mid-morning to keep up with customer demand, but without having to knead, rise, and bake the yeast breads, she managed to make it work. Nate did all the fetching and carrying, dishwashing, and shop setup, freeing Rosalind to tend to customers in the morning and give Ida Mae sewing lessons in the afternoons, helping the girl make herself and her brother some much-needed new clothing.

The Miller kids, Zach had come to learn, had lived with their mother in a small house outside of town until she died from a rattlesnake bite last fall. They'd been on their own for nearly a year, squatting in their old house until the bank sold it to a new family at the start of the summer. A kid could survive without a home during the summer and early fall, but come winter, those two were going to need four solid walls separating them from the elements. Which was why Zach had convinced his previous landlord to extend his rental contract and allow the kids to live in his bachelor abode. He had to promise to keep an eye on them and repair any damage done to the place, but Zach didn't expect there to be any. Nate was as responsible as they came. He'd even insisted on having his wages cut to cover some of the rent. Integrity like that would take the boy far.

"Speaking of biscuits," Reuben said, gallantly retrieving Zach's hat, then ruining the kindness of the gesture by smashing it down on his partner's head so far that Zach couldn't see anything above his friend's knees, "isn't it about time for your wife to stop by with your lunch?"

"Yep." Zach adjusted his hat, his heart giving an extra thump as his mind drifted to Abigail.

"I want to hear you sing in church."

Those words had lingered in his mind ever since she'd uttered them. And truth be told, they'd brought him to his knees. She'd chosen him over her bakery. Shown him what it meant to trust God with her future instead of trying to shape her fate herself. It had humbled him. And challenged him.

He and the Almighty had been chatting regularly since that night and had finally come to an understanding this morning while Zach was driving out to one of the ranches north of town to deliver an order of fence posts. The quiet had provided plenty of thinking space, and after wrestling and rationalizing for nearly an hour, he finally admitted that the logic he'd gripped so tightly through the years was flawed. He *had* had a choice all those years ago, and he'd made the wrong one.

He hadn't trusted the Lord to take care of Seth and Evie. He'd only trusted himself. And that fear-driven arrogance had taken him down a path that led to a man's death and damaged his own soul in the process. He'd told himself that the end justified the means. But that had been a lie, one he'd swallowed so fast he hadn't even noticed the bitter aftertaste of brimstone. He'd noticed it today, though, when he finally released his grip and let God yank it from where it had burrowed into his gut. It burned all the way out, but peace had rushed in to fill the hole. A much friendlier traveling companion than guilt.

Zach would never admit it out loud, but when he'd made his confession from that wagon seat earlier today, he swore he heard angels rejoicing. Probably just the wind playing tricks on his ears, but that song had taken residence in his head with such stubbornness that he'd started whistling without even being aware of it until Reuben came in and harassed him.

"You think she'll have some of them lemon scones with her again?" Reuben asked, a dreamy look in his eyes. "I could eat a dozen of those things."

"Doubt it." Zach stepped away from his workbench and slapped Reuben on the back. "I told her you prefer bran muffins."

"You didn't!"

Zach chuckled at the horror on his partner's face. Reuben had proven a true friend. After Charlie Evans denied Zach's request for a loan as Reuben had predicted, Zach's partner offered him an advance on his wages. Zach had turned him down, of course. He'd never do anything to put the welfare of the Sinclair brood at risk, no matter how many assurances their hardheaded father gave him that they could afford it. The fact that the offer had been made at all was gift enough.

Reuben suddenly straightened, shifting his attention to the doorway. "Speak of the lady, and she appears."

Zach spun around and drank in the sight of his wife sashaying into the lumberyard, basket on her arm and smile on her lips. A smile aimed directly at him. Now, that was an invitation he couldn't refuse. He sidestepped Reuben and wrapped Abigail in an enthusiastic embrace that lifted her feet straight off the ground.

She giggled, then swatted his shoulder and ordered that he put her down.

He chuckled, slow to obey due to the joy spiraling through him. He'd expected that making peace with God would help him feel closer to the Almighty. He hadn't expected that it would make him feel closer to his wife as well. But it had. Holding her had always been a pleasure, but never this keen, never this . . . pure.

Never this . . . public. Maybe he *should* put her down. Reuben was their only audience, but still. A wife as precious as Abigail should be treated with the utmost respect and decorum. That was hard to do, though, when her brown eyes danced with the same excitement that spun like a whirligig in his own chest. It made a man want to take his woman home and lock out the rest of the world for the afternoon.

Swallowing a sigh, he set her on her feet, trying not to be offended when she left him behind to totter over to Reuben. The line she took was riddled with zigzags, though, proof that his attentions had left her unsteady. A fact he found immensely satisfying.

"I've come to bribe you, Mr. Sinclair," Abigail said. Zach followed, intent on claiming his place at her side.

Reuben held a hand over his heart. "I'm a man of integrity, my lady," he pronounced with great pomp. "No amount of bran muffins will persuade me to compromise my principles."

Abby flashed her dimples and pulled back the cover on her basket. "How about a stack of lemon scones?"

"Lemon scones?" Reuben made a grab for the basket. "Consider me bribed."

"Wonderful! So I can borrow my husband for about thirty minutes?"

Reuben held the scones up to his nose and inhaled. "Thirty minutes? For lemon scones, madam, you can have him for the entire afternoon."

The entire afternoon? Zach's pulse ratcheted up three levels, nearly causing him to miss the knowing wink his partner threw his way.

"I only need thirty—ooh!"

Zach snaked an arm around her waist and spun her toward the exit. "Don't argue with the man, wife."

Reuben's chuckle echoed behind them as they ducked into the office. Zach grabbed his coat off the hook by the door without pause and steered Abigail out onto the street.

"You can kidnap me first," Zach murmured as he slid his arms into his coat sleeves. "Take me wherever you like. I'll do whatever you need me to do. But after . . ." He smoldered a glance her way, making no effort to hide his thoughts. "I get to kidnap you."

Roses bloomed in her cheeks, and her feet stumbled over a wagon rut in the road. Zach took her arm as much for his pleasure as her support. He did love touching her.

"Zacharias Hamilton," she scolded even as she leaned into him, "behave yourself. We're on our way to Lydia Putnam's house. She and the other widows wish to give us something, and I won't have you distracting me with such . . . suggestive talk."

Zach shaped his features into a mien of forced solemnity and nodded as soberly as Brother Samuelson after one of his sermons on the dangers of sin. "No talk of kidnapping. Got it."

"Thank you." Her lips twitched in an almost-grin, one she managed to subdue. Unfortunately. "These ladies are dear friends, and whatever gift they have planned, no matter how small, we will receive it with a healthy display of gratitude. Remember the story of the widow's mite from the Bible. It's not the size of the gift that matters but the size of the heart doing the giving."

"I know." He covered the hand she'd placed on his arm with his palm, his teasing attitude shifting to one more serious in nature. When she tilted her head sideways at him, he slowed his step. "You have one of the biggest hearts of all, Abigail, and you've given me more than I dreamed possible. More than I deserve."

She shook her head and tugged him forward as if embarrassed

by his praise. But she needed to hear it. To believe it. He gave in to her tugging and picked up his pace, but he steered her down a side street where fewer people bustled along.

After they'd gone about a block, he drew to a halt near a large shade tree and turned her to face him. "You've given me your love and made me part of your family, Abby. There are no gifts more precious than those."

"Well," she said, her eyes not quite meeting his, "you've made me part of your family too."

But he hadn't given her his love. At least not in a way that allowed her to be certain of his feelings. Her unspoken words deafened him with that truth.

He wanted to tell her, *needed* to tell her, but the words that came out of his mouth made a different confession.

"I, uh, made my peace with God today."

Her gaze slammed into his, no longer shy but brimming with excitement. "Oh, Zach! That's wonderful!"

The woman so set on not displaying her affection in public wrapped him in a hug. It might have been quick and platonic, but he felt the warmth of it deep inside his bones.

"I'm so happy for you."

He shrugged. "It's because of you, you know."

She started shaking her head, but he refused to let her belittle her part.

"You showed me that I *did* have a choice all those years ago, that I could have let God take the lead instead of charging forward on my own terms. I could have trusted God with Seth and Evie's welfare the way you are trusting him with the bakery. But I didn't. I want to change that. With you. With our family. I see you working with all your strength to preserve what is important but always in a way that honors the Lord. I want to do the same. With God's help, I will from here on out."

Abby rubbed at her eye with the back of her hand even as she beamed a smile at him. "Does this mean I'll hear you sing at prayer meeting tonight?"

"Yes, ma'am. Though I gotta warn you, the bucket I carry my tunes in is pretty rusty. Probably has a few holes in it too."

"Then you'll fit right in with the rest of us. There's a reason God told his people to make a joyful noise, you know. Musical prowess is not a requirement, just an engaged heart." She patted his chest to emphasize her words, and he snatched the opportunity, trapping her hand and pressing it even closer to the organ that belonged to her.

"Church ain't the only place my heart's engaged." In truth, it was about to beat its way out of his breast this very minute.

Her gaze sought his, her indrawn breath begging him not to disappoint her. Not in this.

"I . . . love you, Abby."

She froze, her face completely expressionless.

Had he done it wrong? He'd said the words out loud. His throat still vibrated from the effort.

A tear rolled down her cheek. Then another one.

Confound it! He *had* mucked it up. He never should have opened his big mouth.

"C'mon, Abby," he cajoled as he dug out his handkerchief and thrust it at her. "No cryin'. What will the widow ladies think?"

She ignored the handkerchief, lifted up on tiptoes, and wrapped her arms around his neck. "They'll think I'm married to the most wonderful man in the world, and they'll be right. Oh, Zach. I love you too. So much."

She kissed his cheek—a quick peck that ended before it began. But that stamp of approval inflated his confidence to the point that he strutted all the way to Widow Putnam's house, waving and tipping his hat to everyone he met because nothing could be finer than loving Abigail and having her love him in return.

Once they arrived at the modest home several blocks down Main Street, Mrs. Putnam ushered them into her parlor, where a dozen or so ladies nibbled on sandwiches and tea. The moment the Hamiltons entered, however, the ladies set their refreshments aside and rose to their feet. All but the two eldest, anyway. Elmira Welch was eighty if she was a day and had well earned the right to keep her seat, and Zach was pretty sure Gertie Donaldson had dozed off. But everyone else smiled at them in welcome, a secretive gleam lighting their eyes that made Zach a tad nervous.

Lydia Putnam cleared her throat and pivoted to face Abigail. "Abby Jane, we were all madder than hornets when we heard about that woman sabotagin' your oven."

By Sunday morning, news of the vandalism at the bakery had spread far and wide, and by Sunday night, rumors of Sophia Longfellow's alleged involvement in the crime had tickled nearly every ear in town. Zach wasn't sure how word had gotten out about Sophia. Perhaps the marshal had related the tale to someone, or one of the Longfellows' servants might have found the gossip too juicy to resist passing along. However it started, the story had certainly soured public opinion toward the mayor's wife.

Mrs. Putnam pulled a scrap of paper from her skirt pocket, unfolded it, and held it out at arm's length as she squinted at the words. "For years," she intoned, "you and your family have given back to this community by supplying baked goods to those of us in reduced circumstances. Not only did you feed our bodies with your visits, but you fed our souls as well, always taking the time to ask after our families and our health. It is only right that we do something to give back a measure of what you have given to us."

She folded the paper back up and shoved it into her pocket. "Ella Sue wrote them fine words." She nodded to a tall slender lady at the back of the parlor. "Every lady here had a part in this effort."

"What effort is that, Miss Lydia?" Abby's sweet smile revealed her genuine love for the ladies present. Whatever pittance they'd come up with, he had no doubt she'd thank them as if it were a king's ransom.

"We took up a collection, girl. For a new oven."

"That's so kind. You didn't have to—"

"Don't you act all demure, now, Abby Jane." Lydia Putnam was a fierce little thing, shaking her bony finger at Abigail as if she were an errant child. "You need a new oven. A *proper* oven. And while we might not have gathered enough funds to cover the entire cost, we figure we'll get you pretty close." She turned to the fireplace mantel behind her, took down a small battered paperboard box, and handed it to Abby. "We collected eighty-seven dollars and thirty-two cents."

"Eighty-seven . . . ?" Abigail's eyes widened to the size of silver dollars, and her jaw dropped, leaving her words to dangle unfinished.

Zach stepped closer and fit his hand to the small of her back, though truth to tell, he felt just as stunned as his wife looked. How on earth had a group of penniless widows raised that kind of money in a matter of days?

Lydia Putnam crossed her arms over her chest, looking exceedingly pleased with herself. "We might not have more than a handful of coins to rub together between the lot of us, but God blessed us with other gifts we could put to use. We got feet to carry us, hands to knock, and faces that remind even our grumpiest neighbors of their grannies, aunts, or sisters."

"And enough stubbornness not to take no for an answer," one of the ladies called out from the back of the room.

Laughter filled the air as Mrs. Putnam shrugged. "God gave me more than the average helping of that particular attribute, I must admit. Gotta use what we've been given, right?"

A lady in blue stepped forward. "We knocked on every door in town."

One in brown added, "We even staged a protest at City Hall."

Abigail slanted a glance at Zach before turning back to the ladies beaming in pride in front of her. "A protest?"

"Yep," Lydia confirmed. "All fourteen of us marched down to City Hall yesterday and parked outside Mayor Longfellow's office. We refused to leave until he heard us out. He tried to dodge us by hiding in his office, but he had to come out some-time, and when a meeting with the school board demanded his attention, we nabbed him."

"You should have seen Lydia." The lady who'd written the speech made her way to the front of the pack. "When we asked the mayor for a donation, he tossed his spare change at us and tried to walk away. Lydia wouldn't have it. She ignored his bluster when he demanded we leave, called his bluff when he threatened to send for the marshal, and then took him to task for know-ingly letting a criminal walk free just because she was married to him. She accused him of being a co-conspirator and betraying his constituents."

"Well, I didn't use those words, exactly." Was the feisty ma-triarch actually blushing? "Not even sure I know what half them words mean, Ella Sue."

"You communicated just fine, as far as Mayor Longfellow was concerned," Ella Sue insisted. "He sputtered worse than an overboiled teapot, adamantly denying he had any knowledge of the crime."

"But Lydia wouldn't let him dodge," the lady in brown said. "She insisted an honorable man would do the right thing and make restitution to the wronged party. A man who cared about his city would protect its citizenry."

The lady in blue took over the telling. "All the commotion drew a sizeable crowd, and in a matter of minutes, Mayor Longfellow folded like a paper doll. He ended up donating *fifty* dollars from his personal account to our oven fund."

More than half of what had been collected.

"It's a miracle." Abby trembled beside him, her emotions perilously close to the surface.

Zach anchored her to his side with an arm about her middle even as his own thoughts spun. God had provided. They'd trusted him to take care of things, been content to wait as long as necessary, and then he'd done this—worked a miracle through a gaggle of women who could barely eke out their *own* existence. Their need was greater than any need he and Abigail faced, yet these women gave freely, without thought for themselves. It humbled him and made one thing abundantly clear in his soul.

"God is good."

Zach scanned the females standing before him, then turned to his wife, the beautiful woman looking up at him with so much love, he swore he felt it seep into the pores of his skin. He tightened his hold on her waist and whispered the words again so that only she could hear.

"God is good."

Epilogue

Ten Days Later

Abigail never thought she'd actually be pleased to have a kitchen full of sweaty, grunting men, but she had to admit that they made a lovely frame around her new Montgomery Ward cookstove.

"A little more to the right," she directed as her husband and Reuben adjusted the heavy cast-iron range. "There! Nate, does the exhaust pipe line up properly?"

The boy, who'd been left in charge of the hollow pipe, jumped back onto the chair he'd been using and fit the large *L*-shaped cylinder to the rear of the stove, then twisted to see if the end would connect to the wall in the same place as her old industrial oven. Abigail said a quick prayer. This was the fourth time they'd adjusted the position of the cookstove, and she had a feeling that if it didn't match up this time, Zach would just cut a new hole in the wall.

"I think if I twist it around a little . . . yes! It fits."

"Wonderful!" Abigail clapped her hands even as she sent a silent thank-you heavenward. "I'll pour the celebratory lemonade while you gentlemen finish up the final connections."

Reuben exhaled an exaggerated groan, pressing his palms into his lower back as he slowly straightened his posture. "How long until you order the bigger oven? I think I'm going to need a year or two to recover from installing this one."

"Milksop," Zach grouched good-naturedly as he squished his large frame behind the oven to secure the exhaust pipe.

Reuben shrugged off the insult and handed Zach a wrench. "What can I say? Old age is setting in. Making me frail."

Zach snorted. "You're about as frail as a slab of granite."

Reuben made a fist and examined his bicep. "You think so?"

Abigail rolled her eyes. Men. They had their foibles, but they had their good points too. She and Rosalind never would have managed this stove on their own. Filling three glasses of lemonade, she thanked God for bringing these particular men into her life. A dear friend always ready to lend a helping hand, a boy with a big heart and a head that soaked up knowledge wherever he went, and her husband—the man she couldn't imagine living without.

Who would have guessed that a ridiculous, antiquated city ordinance would bring her the biggest blessing of her life?

But as for you, ye thought evil against me; but God meant it unto good. The words Joseph had spoken to his brothers after their jealousy led them to sell him into slavery resonated in her heart as if they were her own. Sophia had intended her harm, but God had used it for good. He'd given her a true partner in life, one who saw her as an equal, who respected her and loved her even with her abundant curves and independent mindset. Her bakery profits might be down, but the profits that truly mattered had surpassed all expectation.

Taking a glass in each hand, she made her way to where the men were huddled around the stove—Zach working the wrench, Nate holding the pipe, and Reuben offering unsolicited advice.

"Here you go." She handed the first glass to Reuben.

"Ah! Beautiful." He accepted the lemonade and promptly gulped down half the glass. "Mmm. Delicious. Thank you."

"Thank *you* for all your help today."

Reuben dipped his chin. "My pleasure."

"Oh, and to answer your question, you'll have at least six months to rest up before we order the new oven." Abby grinned at him. "We need about sixty dollars more to have sufficient funds to cover the purchase and shipping of the industrial oven. I'm hoping that with this addition," she said with a nod toward the new cookstove, "I'll be able to start putting money aside again. We'll have to see how things go, but I hope to have the Taste of Heaven back to peak performance by the new year."

"That's great." Sincerity eclipsed Reuben's usual teasing charm for a brief moment. But then he grinned and pressed a hand against his lower back. "Guess I better get home to rest up, then." He finished off his lemonade in one long drink, then handed the glass back into her keeping. "I'm off, Zach," he announced with a little salute. "Gonna see if Audrey needs some rest too. She works hard, you know. Could probably use a nap."

Zach looked down from where he'd been attaching the pipe to the vent in the wall and caught Abigail's eye. "I might need one myself after this."

Those pesky flutters started up in her belly again, like they always did when he looked at her like that. He was simply incorrigible. And she loved it.

As Reuben opened the door to leave, Rosalind and Ida Mae arrived on the step. He moved aside to allow them to enter, then gave a final wave and set off for home.

"Have you seen the paper?" Rosalind asked as she held up a copy of the *Honey Grove Signal*.

Abigail set Nate's glass of lemonade on the worktable along

with Reuben's empty one, then crossed to meet her sister. "What does it say?"

"Mayor Longfellow has resigned."

"What?" Abby took the paper from Rosalind and scanned the headline article: *Longfellow Stepping Down. Former Mayor J. H. Smith to Fill Vacancy.*

"The official story is that he decided to move to Clarksville to oversee his father's bank," Rosalind reported, "but the rumor mill has it that he's moving to get his wife away from all the memories tied to Honey Grove."

Memories of Benedict Crowley.

"Well, I wondered what Sophia meant yesterday when she accosted me in Patteson Dry Goods and accused me of ruining her life a second time," Abigail mused. "I guess this explains it."

"You didn't tell me she accosted you," Rosalind said, concern in her eyes.

Abigail shook her head. "Sorry. *Accosted* is too strong a word. Our paths merely crossed in the fabric section, and she hissed at me a bit. Said she hoped I was happy, now that I'd ruined her life a second time." She shrugged. "I ignored her and moved to a different section of the store, not wanting to engage in another of her verbal skirmishes, but now I wish I had said something. Tried to encourage her in some way. It breaks my heart to see her so bitter and miserable."

"Her heart's so hard, I doubt anything you could have said would have penetrated." Rosalind laid a comforting hand on Abigail's arm.

"Maybe not, but I'll say an extra prayer for her tonight. Chester too. Perhaps with God's help, Sophia can finally stop grieving over what she's lost and appreciate what she has."

Rosalind tipped her head. "Perhaps." A distracted look passed over her face, one that clearly indicated she had something more than the mayor and his wife on her mind.

Abigail smiled at Ida Mae, who was still lingering near Rosalind's side, no doubt eavesdropping on the conversation about Sophia. Given her own history with the mayor's wife, her interest was certainly understandable. Nevertheless, Abigail sensed Rosie wouldn't share the rest of what was on her mind until they had sufficient privacy.

Abigail pointed to the counter where the third glass of lemonade stood. "Ida Mae, will you take that last glass of lemonade over to Mr. Hamilton, please?"

The girl looked from one sister to the other, then nodded and hurried off to do what she'd been asked.

Abigail turned back to Rosalind. "There's more, isn't there?"

Rosalind bit her lower lip, then drew Abby aside. "Yes." She reclaimed the paper and flipped the pages to a section near the end. She pointed to an ad in the right column. "Here."

Abigail took the paper back and read the words.

Wanted: Young women, 18 to 30 years of age, of good character, attractive and intelligent, as waitresses in Harvey Houses in the West. Good wages, with room and meals furnished.

"I don't understand," Abigail said as she looked up from the paper. "What does this have to do with us?"

Rosalind took the paper back and crinkled the pages with the force of her grip. "I'll be eighteen in a couple months."

Her meaning clicked in Abigail's mind, sending a boulder of dread sinking in her belly. "You want to apply."

Rosalind nodded. "I do."

"Why?" Abigail forced her voice to remain calm even as panic built in her breast. What would she do without Rosie? They had depended on each other their entire lives. Her sister couldn't leave.

"Maybe I need to get away from the memories too." Rosalind's voice echoed softly in a room that suddenly seemed too quiet. Work on the oven had ceased.

Zach appeared at Abigail's side, his palm resting against her lower back, his attention fixed on Rosalind even as he braced Abigail. She glanced around, not wanting the kids to overhear this discussion, but they were nowhere to be found.

"Gave Nate a nickel and sent them to the store for some candy," Zach said. "They'll be gone for a bit."

How had he known? Had he been watching her that closely? He must have been, for here he stood, being exactly what she needed him to be—her anchor in a storm she hadn't seen coming.

Rosalind set the paper aside and widened her stance as if preparing for a battle. "I want a fresh start, Abby. A chance to leave the girl in those photo cards behind for good. Working for Fred Harvey will give me a chance to get out of Texas, to see new places and meet new people. I already know how to run a food service, thanks to you, so I know I can do the work."

She licked her lips, glanced from Zach back to Abby, then continued her plea. "You have Nate now to help you with the shop. He's picking things up so fast. He'll know the price list better than I do in another week. And you have Zach."

Was that what Rosalind wanted? A husband? If so, couldn't she find one here? Why did she have to travel to some far-off city?

No, it wasn't a husband she sought. Not really. She sought peace. Abigail had finally put her past to rest with God's help and Zach's understanding. Rosalind wanted to do the same.

So, setting aside the sorrow of losing her sister and dearest friend, the fear of all the things that could possibly go wrong, and the selfish desire to hold on tight and never let go, Abigail offered the one thing her sister had always offered her—support.

"All right."

Her agreement startled Rosalind. She blinked several times before she managed to speak. "You'll let me go?"

Abigail smiled. "You're a grown woman, Rosie. You don't need my permission. All I ask is that you pray about it before you apply. Make sure you are following God's leading and not simply trying to escape."

"I—I will."

"Then I will support your choice."

"Thank you!" Rosalind lurched forward and wrapped Abigail in a rib-crunching embrace.

Abigail hugged her back just as tightly, wishing she could hold on forever but knowing that wouldn't be right for either of them.

"You better write to me," she said, taking refuge in the bossy big sister role before she completely lost her composure and started bawling like a baby. "Often."

◈————◈

Later that night, Abigail sat with her husband on the sofa in the parlor. Nate and Ida Mae were back at their apartment, and Rosalind was washing her hair. Abby leaned her head on Zach's chest, letting the thump of his heart soothe her spirit.

"I'm proud of you," he murmured. "It's hard to let them set their own path."

He would know. He'd done it himself. Twice. It still amazed her to realize how well-matched they were, how similar their pasts. She might have come up with the crazy scheme to marry in order to protect her bakery, but only God could have given her a husband who fit her so perfectly.

Zach bent toward her and pressed a tender kiss on her forehead. "I love you, Abby-mine."

Her heart thrilled at the words. He didn't gift her with them often, but when he did, they shone like well-polished silver.

"I love you too. For always and forever."

He gave a little grunt and squeezed her close. Abby grinned. He'd just promised to love her forever too.

Author Note

Writing historical fiction is a challenge when setting a story in a real place. There is so much research that needs to be done to provide authenticity to the setting, and many times reliable records are few and far between. That is why I want to give special praise to the Honey Grove Preservation League. Their online historical resources are some of the best I have ever come across. Historical photos, newspaper articles, government records—it was like stepping through a time portal every time I visited.

It brought me so much joy to mention real people and places in this novel. Places like the Commercial Hotel; the home of James Gilmer that was built during this time period; Wilkins, Wood & Patteson Dry Goods; and Dora Galbraith Patteson's millinery shop on the east side of the town square. While Reuben Sinclair and Zacharias Hamilton are completely fictitious characters, there really was a lumberyard located on the corner of Sixth Street and Rail Road. And the tale of Davy Crockett carving the town name in a tree while on his way to the Alamo is well-documented in early Honey Grove accounts.

As fiction authors are wont to do, I have taken a few liberties with Honey Grove's history. To my knowledge, there was never any city ordinance banning women from owning businesses in town. In addition, Mayor Chester Longfellow was a complete invention of my imagination. The true mayor of Honey Grove during this time period was J. H. Smith, a man who served in that capacity from 1888–1897. He must have been a well-loved city official to hold office for nearly a decade. I paid brief homage to him by having him step back into office when my fictitious mayor resigned.

I hope you have enjoyed stepping back in time with me to Honey Grove, Texas. Zach and Abigail might not have lived there in truth, but I like to believe their tale is a representation of the many amazing love stories that have taken place in that sweet little town through the years.

Christy Award finalist and winner of the ACFW Carol Award, HOLT Medallion, and Inspirational Reader's Choice Award, bestselling author **Karen Witemeyer** writes historical romances because she believes the world needs more happily-ever-afters. She is an avid cross-stitcher and shower singer, and she bakes a mean apple cobbler. Karen makes her home in Abilene, Texas, with her husband and three children.

To learn more about Karen and her books and to sign up for her free newsletter featuring special giveaways and behind-the-scenes information, please visit www.karenwitemeyer.com.

Sign Up for Karen's Newsletter!

Keep up to date with news on Karen's upcoming book releases and events by signing up for her email list at karenwitemeyer.com.

More from Karen Witemeyer

Seeking justice against the man who destroyed his family, Logan Fowler arrives in Pecan Gap, Texas, to confront the person responsible. But his quest is derailed when, instead of a hardened criminal, he finds an ordinary man with a sister named Evangeline—an unusual beauty with mismatched eyes and a sweet spirit that he finds utterly captivating.

More Than Meets the Eye

You May Also Like . . .

After facing desperate heartache and loss, Mercy agrees to escape a bleak future in London and join a bride ship. Wealthy and titled, Joseph leaves home and takes to the sea as the ship's surgeon to escape the pain of losing his family. He has no intention of settling down, but when Mercy becomes his assistant, they must fight against a forbidden love.

A Reluctant Bride by Jody Hedlund
THE BRIDE SHIPS #1
jodyhedlund.com

In the midst of the Great War, Margot spends her days deciphering intercepted messages. But after a sudden loss, her world is turned upside down. Drake returns wounded from the field, followed by a destructive enemy. Immediately smitten with Margot, how can Drake convince a girl who lives entirely in her mind that sometimes life's answers lie in the heart?

The Number of Love by Roseanna M. White
THE CODEBREAKERS #1
roseannamwhite.com

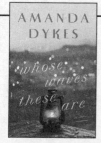

In the wake of WWII, a grieving fisherman submits a poem to a local newspaper asking readers to send rocks in honor of loved ones to create something life-giving—but the building halts when tragedy strikes. Decades later, Annie returns to the coastal Maine town where stone ruins spark her curiosity and her search for answers faces a battle against time.

Whose Waves These Are by Amanda Dykes
amandadykes.com

⬧ BETHANYHOUSE